DATE DUE

NOV 2 6 2003	
FEB 2 0 2007 APR 1 0 2007	
2 5 SEP 2009	

D0961251

THE MAGICKERS

EMILY DRAKE

FIC
DRA

DAW BOOKS, INC.

DONALD A. WOLLHEIM, FOUNDER

375 Hudson Street, New York, NY 10014

ELIZABETH R. WOLLHEIM
SHEILA E. GILBERT
PUBLISHERS

http://www.dawbooks.com

First printing, June 2001
1 2 3 4 5 6 7 8 9

Dedicated to Michael Gilbert:
Remembered for his artistic talent, dry wit,
and keen sensibilities, and missed by many friends.
He won the battle, but lost the war. . . .

Contents

1

Once Upon a Midnight

THE moon hung like a silver lantern in the midnight sky; white sand below his feet made a soft shushing sound as he moved. His sneakers sank with every step, and he pulled his T-shirt closer around him as the sea mist fell like a cold, cold rain. The sea looked like black glass, except where the tide broke on the shore in glowing foam and hissed into silence.

The castle stood before him on broken stone, as though the sea had pulled most of the shore from under it, wearing away the land. It looked more like a ruin than a castle; the dark jagged tears into the walls and towers were like shadowy breaches of despair. Jason stood for a moment, staring at it. A cold wind pressed around him. He'd gotten this far before. . . .

He walked widdershins three times around the castle, a long walk for his eleven-year-old stride although he stretched his legs as far as he could. Then, and only then, did he approach it. He could feel the stone sense him, awakening.

Putting his hand out to the great gate surrounding the castle, unlike a moat or drawbridge, he passed his palm over the immense brass door knocker and the lock sculpted as a dragon's head and tail. He snatched his hand back from the metal, knowing what would happen, and even then he almost wasn't in time! Flames sprouted from the opening jaws and flared nostrils. The air smelled hot and brassy.

"Sssssssson of wizardssssss passssss . . ." the door knocker hissed.

The gate creaked open with a howling screech.

Jason dashed through the opening gate before the knocker could do anything else. He tripped on rubble immediately and fell to his knees with a cry, his yelp echoing harshly back at him. He rose quickly, dusting himself off, and cast a look around. A broken roof overhead still blocked out most of the sky, but moonlight came through in razor rays, looking sharp enough to cut. As it illuminated the area, he saw where he stood. A fallen tombstone lay in front of him, half in moonlight, half in shadow, with another one tilted not too far ahead of him. Jason whirled around.

Out of the shadow, something grabbed at him. He spun to face it . . . a cold marble angel with her hand outstretched, a pleading look on her face, and her wings folded at her back. He took a deep breath and stepped away. This was no castle . . . it was an immense tomb. Stone walls built around a decaying burial ground. He took a deep breath to steady himself. Although he knew what he sought, he'd never been this far before.

"Don't stop me now," he beseeched quietly. His voice echoed back in a mutter he could not understand. Jason edged around a chunk of granite. As he passed by, the moonlight struck the letters R I P, engraved in a Gothic type.

The gate clattered and shuddered behind him as the wind shivered through harder and faster. He could feel it cutting through his clothes as though it came out of the dead of winter. Moonlight skipped across row after row of headstones and beyond them, a shadow-dark doorway into the castle wall . . . if indeed it was a castle at all. Perhaps a crypt! At the far side of the graveyard, a blackened stick of a tree twisted out of the ground, its gnarled branches and twigs like grasping arms with contorted hands reaching out to him.

He had to get to that doorway—had to. What he needed to know, what he had to find must lie beyond there. Jason steadied himself as he walked between the rows of headstones, many blank, some with their carvings worn away except for a letter here and there, others fallen to unreadable rubble. The wind tugged at the dead tree's branches and its stiff twigs pounded at a tombstone like skeletal fingers. Tap . . . tap . . . tap.

A yellow-eyed crow sat on the top branches, watching him. The immense bird seemed to soak up all the shadows of the graveyard and grow larger with every movement it made. It ruffled its wings.

Jason hurried past, his sneakers sending up puffs of ashy dust. He pinched his nose to stifle a sneeze, not wanting to wake whatever might sleep here . . . if anything did. The shuffle of his steps and the tap-tap of the tree branch was more than enough noise for him! Not everything here was dead, he thought . . . he hoped! And he had to hurry to find out if he was right.

A single splinter of moonlight pointed a way through the door. He stepped through it.

Inside, moonlight danced almost as if it were sunlight coming through a window. He stood in . . . a room. It was nearly bare, but there was a rocking chair and a window and a small writing desk up against the wall, and Jason thought his heart would stop because he *knew* this place! Oh, it wasn't the same, but he knew it and he hurried farther inside, because someone sat in the rocking chair. Could it be the person he'd hoped to find? The someone he could barely remember no matter how hard he tried?

"Mom?" called Jason softly as he drew near. Warped wooden floorboards creaked ominously under his weight. His heart thudded in his chest like a great drum beating. His hand went out to the shadowy woman's shoulder. He could just see the back of her head, her body as she sat resting in the chair. Only in a dream could he get this close—

Ker-ACK! He plunged downward as the floor gave way, tumbling him into total darkness. When he hit, it was on cold stone, and he lay for a moment, breathing hard, his pulse skipping erratically. The moonlight had followed him down, pooling around him like a puddle of spilled milk, sour spilled milk, and he stood up slowly.

Cold, icy stone was all around him, pressing close. At the other end of the narrow passageway, he could see a solid, long, yet tablelike object. He rubbed his eyes and took a cautious step forward, no longer sure what was solid and what was not. As he moved toward the object, he could see what it was. A stone sarcophagus, a coffin, like the ancient Egyptians had used. He turned around to go back, but the passage had narrowed to a mere slit behind him, and he had nowhere to go!

"I'm all right," he said to himself. "I'm fine." Like a chant, he repeated it over and over as he was forced toward the coffin step by step. He'd gone as far as he wanted to. Enough was enough; memory or dream, he didn't care, he did not want to go any closer.

But he had no choice as the passage continued to narrow behind him, nudging him forward. The stone coffin became clearer, a man lying on its top, arms crossed over his chest, himself granite or as still as stone. Etched into the side were two words: Jarred Adrian.

His father's name.

Jason could feel every inch of him raise in goose bumps. No! This wasn't what he wanted. He wanted to see them both alive! Alive and warm, and his. . . . He stopped in his tracks. He wanted out! Out or . . . he put his head back, looking to where the moonlight rayed through from above . . . out or up! He could hear the tap-tap of the dead tree in the cemetery overhead. Looking into the shadows, he could see black roots, twisting down, splitting the stone. There had to be a way out. Up! Yes . . . up! He jumped, grabbing the roots, and began to pull himself up hand over hand. The tree felt slimy and slippery, bark and stubs catching at him, snagging, but he shinnied up stubbornly as the tree tried to wrap itself about him. The roots surged around him like giant wings, trying to hug him and hold him. He swore he could see yellow crow's eyes in the winged darkness pecking and grasping at him. He fought back. Up! Up!

"Wake up!"

Jason bolted upright in his bed, blankets twisted around him, gasping. "Wake . . . up."

He took a deep breath. Sharp moonlight sprayed across his bed, as white as the bright sun, striking his face. He shook, then drew in another deep breath.

He rarely slept through an entire night. Jason sat there for a moment, forcing himself to calm down. He turned his head, trying to read his clock despite the dark, shifting shadows that filtered through his room in the still of the night. Rays of light like silvery swords guided his glance. There in the corner was a wooden rocking chair, the only thing he had left of his mother. His soccer gear sat neatly folded on the seat, his backpack hanging from its arm. Bookshelves stretched across one entire wall. He could read some of the titles: *The Sword in the Stone, The Dragonriders of Pern, The Last Unicorn, The Dragonbone Chair,* and others. Too many to actually see, but he knew them all well.

They were braced in their places on the shelf by stuffed animals here and there. Three teddy bears, a fat stuffed cat, and two bunnies. In the sunlight, all would look rather well loved and with a bare spot here and there. On the top shelf lay a squadron of toys from *X-Men* and *Star Wars,* squared off to contest one another. There was a small CD player on the nightstand next to him with a collection . . . well, a stack, of CDs, two of which needed to be returned to Alicia. A book lay folded back on the nightstand, too, its chapter heading reading: DRAGONS BARRED THE WAY to the kingdom of the dead.

So that's where he got that nightmare from this time. He should know better.

Everything was familiar. Jason felt a little better and prepared to scrunch back down in bed.

Then . . .

Tap. Tap. Tap.

He froze in place. From the north end of the house came the

light, fluttering snore of his stepmother. Punctuating it like a big kettledrum came the booming snore of his stepfather. The McIntires slept in what Jason referred to as the Heavy Metal part of the house. Of different blood, he apparently didn't have the snore gene. Or, at least, if he did . . . he slept through it.

Ker-rack! At the window again. Jason peered down the length of his attic bedroom, gloomy in the deep night. No trees reached this high. Something was at the porthole window, the only one in the odd-shaped attic that had no screen. It wasn't really meant to be opened and shut, although he could . . . and did.

He slept in the attic, undeniably the best room in the house, with its porthole window that faced the dimly seen ocean, and its second bay window facing the foothills. The door to his room was in the floor, not the wall. Jason rather liked the idea that he could pull up his ladder and lock himself away from the world. He didn't really belong here, not really. He was here by default.

Not that he could get away with hiding for long. William "Dozer" McIntire would stand in the hallway and bellow until the ladder was lowered.

"Boy," he'd roar. "Come down here and join your family!" Then Jason would risk having his teeth shaken out of his jaws by one of his stepfather's enormous bear hugs.

William "Bulldozer" McIntire stood tall enough that his thinning brown hair threatened to scrape the ceiling that led to the attic. His great tough hands felt like catchers' mitts on Jason's shoulders and he looked like he could carry a building on his back. Jason's stepfather was in construction. He tore things down, so he could rebuild them twice as big and four times as expensive.

Then there was Jason's stepmother Joanna. Dainty, petite, with wide blue eyes and a seemingly innocent stare. She could wrap the Dozer around any of her slender fingers. Daughter Alicia took after her mother, with quick, small hands and eyes that looked at you while she made secret plans.

Yet once he'd had two parents like everyone else. It was so

long ago, he didn't remember his mother dying. He remembered being alone with his dad, the two of them together. After a while, his father had married Joanna, giving him a stepmother and a stepsister. Then his father had died, and Joanna had married William McIntire. She liked to look fondly at her third husband and declare, "Third time's the charm!" Which, although it seemed okay to say, always made Jason feel funny deep down. It wasn't his father's fault that the second husband hadn't lasted. Jarred Adrian would have lived if he could have!

McIntire had thrown open his home, his heart, and swept all of them inside without even asking if it was what they wanted. But how could they not want it? McIntire enjoyed life. Hale and hearty, loud and laughing. Even Alicia seemed happy. At any rate, she was the darling of both now, and he was . . . what was he? A leftover? If he was loved, it was rather like a stray cat, he thought. And if he sometimes thought that Joanna had married awfully quickly after losing his father, he never said anything. It would not, he knew, have made a difference. Everyone else was happy. What did it matter if there were great, yawning gaps in his own feelings? What did it matter if he remembered, although dimly, far happier times?

Ker-ack!

It sounded as though the window itself had split! Jason rolled out of bed, his sandy blond hair sticking out all over. His pajamas were rumpled from the restless night. His feet stuck out like great clumsy things, and he stared at them and his bony ankles in dismay. He'd grown again?

A weed, Jason Adrian, he told himself. *That's what you are. A stray weed that wandered into the McIntire garden. . . .*

Jason dragged his desk chair over to the window and knelt on it, pulling aside the shutters. Silver light shot through, practically stunning him with brightness. It flared up from the brilliant moon outside and . . . he leaned on his knees. Someone was down below. Someone with a mirrorlike flash in her hands, gazing back up at him.

He rubbed his eyes to clear them. It looked like . . . Mrs. Cowling . . . his English teacher. Jason squinted down at the neighborhood street and the woman, whoever it was, disappeared, briskly walking down the sidewalk, behind trees and out of his view. One last bright flash illuminated his window. What the heck? Jason leaned his chin on the brass sill, nose almost to the glass.

Ker-ACK! Yellow-eyed blackness swooped at him! Crow! His heart jumped in his chest. Was it? How could it be?

Black wings fluttered; shadow filled the window, then disappeared. He pushed his face back to the window again.

Silently, it came at the glass and swerved away at the last moment before smashing into it. Frowning, Jason unscrewed the great brass clips that held the window firmly in place, and swung the glass out. He leaned out, looking. Warm spring air washed across his face as though the yellow moon hanging low in the sky exhaled at him. He wasn't still dreaming . . . was he?

Pain slashed through his scalp. "Ker-aw!"

"Yeow!" Jason swatted wildly. His hand jabbed at the air, then connected heavily. Feathers flew, followed by a dull thump on the roof.

Now what had he done? Killed it? If it wasn't dead, just hurt . . . well, he couldn't leave it there. With a grunt, Jason levered himself out the porthole and onto the rooftop. Crouched barefooted on the shingles, he swept his gaze about and saw nothing.

Streetlights glowed a soft yellow, muting the nearly colorless colors into drab beige. Nighttime cloaked the entire neighborhood. The walking woman could not be seen anywhere. His head stung. He was almost a hundred percent positive he was awake, yet . . .

He leaned away from the porthole window a bit more. His pajama sleeve caught on the framing and, as he yanked his arm to free it, the window swung shut. With a hollow sound, it fell into place.

Jason groaned. Locked out, and on the roof! What mischief he'd get blamed for, he wasn't quite sure, but he was definitely in trouble.

The brass frame to the porthole window rattled coldly under

his hand, refusing to budge. Jason stifled a groan. He'd have to get in through the front door somehow. He'd done this in reverse once before, up the back of the house, inching up on a rain gutter which was scarcely used in Southern California, and swinging across the roof gable. And where was the bird anyway? Nowhere. It had probably flown off, cackling at waking him from a deep sleep and making him fall out of his nest of a bed.

Jason took a deep breath and began to scramble sideways until he reached the gutter. As the metal took his weight, it creaked and swayed in protest. It threatened to bend away from the house entirely and send him crashing down.

Jason bit his lip, looking down. Was a jump out of the question? The faraway ground suggested that was the case. Maybe a mild thud into the flower bed of creeping charlies planted in this shadowed side of the house? He might even be able to do it without waking everyone. He might make it back to bed and sleep without getting a stern lecture and Joanna watching him sorrowfully as though she had somehow failed in her duties. He might even do it without hurting himself so badly he'd miss soccer tryouts, providing he hadn't been grounded. He hung his head over, considering the options.

No, at this point, at least a climb partway down seemed best.

The roughened metal of the rain gutter scratched his bare feet as he climbed, scraping his toes raw. The warm night hung over the neighborhood, and the sinking yellow moon could now barely be seen over the rooftops. Something black and swift darted at his head!

"Ow!" Jason twisted his head around. Back again! He glanced up. Scalp smarting, he shinnied down the gutter a little more carefully. Where the eaves jutted out and the second story began, he had to stop. Bare feet and ankles wrapped tightly around the coarse, pitted metal, he lifted both hands to pull himself over.

Then it came at him again, as intent as if protecting a nest of eggs or fledglings.

It sailed back, yellow eyes shining and talons outstretched.

Jason ducked, smothering his yelp of alarm. His whole body swung wildly away from the house. The gutter moved with him, creaking horribly. With a *skkkkrink* and a *skkkronk,* it tore lose. For a moment, he swayed wildly as though on a single giant stilt. It swayed toward the house. He scratched at the siding, trying to catch hold. It swayed away. His heart pounded. Back. Forth.

The rain gutter shuddered like a wild beast and then tossed him. He soared downward through the air, arms and elbows flying, and crashed into the hedge surrounding the yard with an *oooof!*

Good news. The hedge stopped his fall. Bad news. It prickled through his pajamas with a hundred nasty little thorns and forced the air right out of his solar plexus. The wind fled his lungs for a moment or two. He lay faceup, looking at the night sky and the golden eye of the huge moon and gulped for air like a beached guppy. After long moments, he finally inhaled deeply. Once he could breathe, he lay still, both his heart and his head pounding, and worried whether the crash had been heard.

With no dog or cat in the house, there was nothing to sound an alarm but the sharp ears of the McIntires themselves, yet the only sounds reaching him were a thunderous snore chased by a faint one.

He sighed. The gutter wobbled in the night air, waving at him, but it looked as if it would stay partially attached, now that his weight was gone. However, there was no chance he could shinny up it again.

Jason was done for, as far as sneaking back in the house. The moon hung over him, and as plain as could be, a shadow glided across the face of it. Glistening blackly with spread wings, it turned and came for him.

Jason sat up abruptly, gathering his feet under him.

The creature dove right past his eyes, stalled in mid-flight, and landed. It folded its wings about its body, an immense crow, as yellow-eyed as if it had absorbed the moon. The bird cocked his head, then hopped forward. It blinked and studied him. Took another crow-hop nearer.

Jason tensed.

With a gleam in its yellow eyes, the bird darted forward, pecked the back of his hand, and launched itself into the air with a great "Ker-aww!" Feathers and something white were shed as it soared skyward.

He snatched his hand back, but the bird's peck hardly amounted to anything compared to the stinging assault of the hedge's prickles. His hand was a mass of scratches already and his skin crawled with itching. Stupid hedge.

Strange crow.

He stood cautiously, eyeing the night sky to see if the shadow had come back. Nothing.

He bent over to see what the crow had dropped into the dewy grass. A scrap of paper. Jason retrieved it. The moon seemed to sit on his shoulder, illuminating spidery writing:

You May Have Already Won . . .

Jason scratched his head, the only part of him which did not itch abominably. He muttered quietly, "I've never won anything. And I am locked out with a thousand bloody scratches all over me, thanks to you . . . stupid bird."

He squinted. It must have been ripped off some junk mail contest entry, thrown in someone's trash, gilt edges attracting the bird's eyes. He shoved it in the pocket of his pajamas. He had no luck. His present predicament proved that.

Jason stared at the rain gutter again. Well, there was no sense putting it off any longer. He would have to ring the doorbell and awaken someone to get back in. With any luck, it might be Alicia. She could be bribed.

Jason limped to the corner of the house. A slow, dark cloud moved over the face of the golden moon, plunging the whole neighborhood into immense, purple shadows. He stumbled into the hedge (Ow!, again) and it exploded with a splitting hiss. He sprang back as leaves flew in all directions. A great ginger tomcat burst out, green eyes gleaming and bounded off, his crooked tail flipping in disgust with every leap. The cat stopped, turned, flashed a defiant flag of his tail, and dodged into a hole under the fencing.

With a deep breath of resignation, Jason sidled around the corner of the house. The front door opened as soon as he touched it, and Alicia stood on the threshold, looking at him, framed in glaring light.

"Oh," she said with a smile. "Are you going to owe me."

2

Rut-Roh

"ALICIA crossed her arms and said, 'This had better be good.'"

Sam danced in the early morning light as he hiked his backpack up on his shoulder. "She said that? Really?" His best friend stood, alert, awake, and listening.

Sam had been patiently waiting at the corner just before school. He'd dropped his battered backpack and was playing with a Hacky Sack, bouncing it up and down between his hands and his feet. He snatched it out of midair as Jason joined him. Sam was small, wiry, and brown all over—brown hair, brown eyes, and a dark brown tan. He made up for it by wearing bright yellows and reds.

"Oh, she said that and more."

They stood in a river of students making their way toward Jefferson Middle School. The sun, which had seemed incredibly bright earlier, now hid behind a clump of hazy, smoggy clouds. Leaves skittered and scattered away from his shoes as if worried they might be crunched underneath. Skaters boarded past, their wiry bodies poised in sleek balance over their skateboards, despite their baggy shorts and often untied sneakers. Jason watched them soar past, surfing the concrete walkways. He'd been trying to learn on his own, difficult to impossible without a decent skateboard. Anything with wheels could be guaranteed to draw a concerned look from Joanna. Even headgear and elbow pads would not appease her.

"Really," Jason answered. He paused and shouldered his books as a skateboarder whizzed by, nearly careening into both of them. By the time he struggled back into balance, the skater was long gone, around the corner, snaking in and out between other walking students. Voices rose in laughter. A group of girls passed, bursting out in giggles as they swung by, and he wondered if it was aimed at him or not. He watched them. A pack of girls? A gaggle of giggles?

"You're road kill." His best friend tugged at his pack again, the lumps and bumps and weight of his folded-up scooter bulging from inside.

"Well, not exactly." Jason had recounted the same story to Sam that he'd blurted out to Alicia. The difference had been that Sam had listened, believing, while Jason's stepsister had watched him with a mocking light in her eyes.

"A bird at the window, a big crow or something. It kept pecking at the glass. It wouldn't stop! I opened the window to get a look at it . . . and I fell out."

"You fell from the attic window?" Her eyes had widened, then narrowed.

"Right into the hedge," he had answered, limping forward.

"Right." Her eyebrow had raised slightly. "Two stories?"

"I tried to shin down the rain gutter." She still had not let him past and his body itched, his hands moving everywhere scratching. "Give me a break, Alicia, okay?"

She'd moved over then, letting him in, saying, "You owe me, big time."

Sam sighed as he pocketed his Hacky Sack. "That's bad."

Jason nodded. They started forward again. A small shadow darted overhead. He looked up. The crow winged its way into a neighboring tree, then vanished after giving him a yellow-eyed stare for a moment. A shiver went down his spine.

"What are you going to do?" asked Sam.

"With any luck, Joanna will make brownies this week. If I fork over my share, I should be off the hook."

"Man. And I thought *my* sister was a monster." He grinned. "What about your parents?"

"Nothing much." Jason shrugged stiffly. Everything hurt, but not as much as it had when he first woke to morning light clobbering his eyelids, streaming in through the window like a flashlight aimed directly at his eyes. He had rolled over in his creaking bed. There was nothing in his body that did *not* hurt. And the tryouts for soccer camp were today! It was bad enough he didn't play on the local teams yet, like most of the guys, or that he had chicken legs in PE shorts, but now he was going to have scratched chicken legs!

Jason had punched his pillow before getting out of bed, wishing he didn't have to face this day at all! With a sore grunt, he had grabbed a pair of jeans and started to dress. He wasn't very good at telling lies. He didn't believe in it, and he wasn't quick enough to think of good ones. Honesty served him best, even if it could be painful.

Sam's face scrunched up. "You're kidding? You came downstairs looking like you lost a cat fight and no one said anything?"

"Well . . . Joanna didn't have her contacts in. And the Dozer . . . he sat behind his paper and read her the sales ads and then . . . he looked at me." Jason stopped on the sidewalk. His breakfast did a flip-flop in his stomach as it had then, William McIntire looking at him over the top edge of the newspaper, and then his stepmother considering him vaguely.

"Jason, I have told you time and time again. If you have good manners, you can sit and eat with anyone in the world. Even the Queen of England. How can you come to breakfast without combing your hair and washing your face?"

Jason's teeth clicked as he closed his mouth.

The Dozer let out a low rumble that could have been in

agreement or just clearing his throat as he looked, really looked, at Jason. He felt his scratches grow hot and itchy.

"Son," vibrated William slowly. He leaned over. His brown eyes squinted as he stared into Jason's face. "If you think you need to shave, come and see me. Dull razors hurt. I know this is the sort of thing a father should show you, but I'll stand in as well as I can."

"Oh, my." Joanna glanced at her husband.

"Don't worry." The Dozer squeezed her hand tighter. "I've got it handled." He nodded at Jason. "You might want to splash some of my aftershave on your mug. It'll sting, but you'll heal faster."

Jason exhaled.

Sam exhaled, too. "Man, you're only eleven. And he thinks you were trying to *shave?*"

"At least he didn't ask me what happened."

"So you're still going to tryouts for soccer camp?"

"You bet."

Sam heaved a sigh of relief. "Partners, right?"

Jason slapped his hand. "Definitely!"

The fact he'd been okayed to try out for soccer camp had faintly surprised him. Evidently his stepmother thought that shin guards would protect him, although she had questioned him a few days ago about the difference between rugby and soccer, as if to reassure herself she'd made the right decision. She'd looked at him, her sunglasses tilted back on her forehead like a hair ornament, repeating his words now and then, faintly ending up, "And no tackling?"

"No, ma'am. No tackling. This is soccer." He pressed his mouth shut firmly on what was not exactly a lie.

"Well." She put her reading glasses on as she pulled out her organizer. "Work hard and make the team! You know we approve of summer camps. They build character."

Early bell sounded through the air as the stucco buildings of the school loomed in view. The flow of students had slowed to nearly a trickle, Jason's tale delaying them. The bell's echoes faded as two snickers came from behind.

"Partners, huh? Well . . . partner this!"

Movement too swift to duck grabbed him up, pulling his sweatshirt jacket over his head, blinding him. As he kicked and fought to get free, his feet and body suddenly left the ground. For a moment he was flying blind, hands on his arms tossing him through the air. He hit with a fragrant thump, Sam letting out a grunt beside him as he landed also, and then a thunderous clang as the dumpster lid slammed shut over them. Darkness fell even as Jason clawed his sweatshirt off his head.

"Oh, man," said Sam. "I'm going to stink all day."

They both struggled to stand on the heaps of garbage under them, and push up on the heavy metal lid overhead. It wouldn't budge. The noise of students moving past had stopped as everyone now was probably inside the classrooms, or at least the school gates.

Something tapped at the metal lid. Tap, tap.

Sam tilted his head. "Hello? Get us out!" He knocked and rattled loudly. There was silence. Then something walked across the lid: tick, tick, tick.

Jason listened. What on Earth . . . ?

They held their breath, listening. Someone was teasing them, toying with them.

Tap. Tap. Tap.

Then, "Kerr-awww." And a rattling "CAW!"

A crow! He'd had it with crows!

Jason made a fist and punched at the dumpster lid. There came an explosion of wings and caws as the crow took startled flight off the top. It came back with a heavy thud, CAW-ing even more loudly.

Both Jason and Sam put their hands up and rattled the dumpster lid, yelling at the top of their lungs.

Bright sunlight flooded in as the lid suddenly opened. Mrs. Cowling, Jason's English teacher, stared in, her big, fluffy brown hair in a sunny halo about her round face. "Goodness," she said. "What are you two doing in here?"

She helped Sam out and then Jason. The stench of the dumpster floated about them like a cloud, and then slowly faded. Jason looked back in the trash bin. They were in luck, it seemed, most of the rubbish seemed to be old boxes and dry stuff. The reek must be a permanent odor stuck inside. He shook himself, pulling his backpack and sweatshirt jacket down.

"We got thrown in," Sam answered sulkily. His dark hair stood out in wild thatches.

"Do you know who?"

"Didn't see a thing."

Jason traded looks with Sam. He had a wild guess who it might have been, but it wouldn't do any good to say anything. He shrugged. Mrs. Cowling nodded. "Well, off with you, then. Tardy bell is about to ring." The two sprinted off to the school gates and their first period classes.

Overhead, a crow rattled another raucous "CAW!"

SPRING, nearly summer, sang hotly through the late afternoon air, muted by the schoolroom window. The cries of boys already suited up for soccer team tryouts and running around the green field could barely be heard. He could see Sam's blazing red jersey and more than once, the faraway figure had turned and looked toward his building. He had to be wondering where Jason was.

Jason's fingers cramped around his pencil. If he looked at the wall clock one more time, Mrs. Cowling would spot him. Outside of cheaters, there was nothing she hated more than clock watchers. It would hurt her feelings that he wasn't paying attention, especially after her rescue of the morning.

His eyes watered with the effort of not looking. He needed to be out on the field warming up. Would class never end?

Mrs. Cowling returned to the front of the class and stood, her fluffy brown head tilted to one side. Thankfully, the school clock was just behind her, above the chalkboard. She smiled and said cheerfully, "To repeat, this final essay must be five hundred words long, in ink, and due by Friday. I want to see your best effort! This is your final grade of the year, and I am hoping to hear that many of you qualify for Honors English next fall!" She glanced toward Jason and smiled slightly. They'd talked about that after class. He liked writing, and she liked what he wrote.

Immediately, Martin Brinkford's hand shot up. Someone at the back groaned even as Jason bit his lip. Brinkford could talk for hours, endlessly, about nothing, and Mrs. Cowling had to let him. It had something to do with Brinkford's father being a generous donor to the school's many needs and charities.

"Yes, Martin?"

Tall, with cold blue eyes, and surfer-blond hair, Brinkford sat at the back with the big square boy called George Canby. "Will a computer printout be accepted?"

Mrs. Cowling smiled brightly. "Although a typed paper would be easier on my eyes, no. I want to see the essays done in your very own words, thoughts, and handwriting. I know you all have it in you to be very interesting and original."

Brinkford sank down into his chair. "I don't get my papers off the Internet," the blond-haired boy said, his mouth twisted sulkily.

"No, of course, you don't," Mrs. Cowling said. "But others may be tempted, so I've decided this is a fitting way to handle it. I want only your best thoughts!"

Jason resisted the notion to out-and-out stare at Martin. He was all but certain it was Brinkford and Canby who'd trash-canned him and Sam. Brinkford gave him a mocking look back.

The buzzer went off, as if punctuating her words. "See you tomorrow," Mrs. Cowling ended. "Oh," she added. "Tommy and Jason, please stay after a moment."

Jason, poised to leap from his desk chair as if shot from a cannon, deflated and fell back onto the seat, staring at her. If she was going to ask about the dumpster again, he still couldn't say anything.

"Silence is golden," Canby said as he passed by. He made his sneakers fart on the linoleum floor as he headed to the classroom door.

Jason rolled his eyes and slumped farther down in his desk.

The other students left in a blur of motion and a thunder of noise, until the classroom stood empty but for the three of them. "Jason, I'll be just a moment with Tommy," Mrs. Cowling said, and drew the thin, lanky student aside at her desk.

Jason got to his feet, slowly. The sun and grass called from outside. The soccer tryouts fairly screamed. Sam passed by again, jogging around the end of the field. He looked out the window with a longing so intense it hurt somewhere inside of him. Average, ordinary Jason—but out there he could show them what he was made of. Tough, long legs for speed and cornering. Quick eyes. The ability to angle downfield and wait for a pass. A kick at the goal. A noun is the object of the sentence. . . .

Jason blinked, as Mrs. Cowling's soft answer to Tommy penetrated his thoughts. A whole year of this and Tom "No Neck" Spears whose head was shaped like the football helmet he wore nearly year round had no idea what Mrs. Cowling was repeating to him. Jason stifled another groan. He'd be here all afternoon if she wanted him to wait until Tommy understood grammar. The asphalt just outside the windows rippled in the afternoon heat looking like a slick black sea. Beyond it, the green grass of the athletic fields lay like paradise. He sighed.

She gave him a look past Tommy's ears and put her hand on the boy's thick shoulder. "Just a moment, Tommy. Jason, I'll be right with you. Take a look on my desk and see what you think?"

He shifted.

"Well . . . okay. Sam's waiting for me. Soccer tryouts and everything." He thought of distracting her. All he could think of was the soccer sign-up table, dressing, warm-ups, stretches.

"I suppose you have your heart set on that camp," she repeated, her eyes behind her spectacles big and owlish. Her fluffy brown hair puffed out slightly on its own.

"I'm going with Sam. If we make it. Which we will."

"I'll be right with you, then." She turned her back on him, not seeing his disappointed fidget as he drifted to her desk.

She was not the English teacher they'd started with at the beginning of the year. That had been Mrs. Ervin, but she was going to have a baby and had left in February. He'd gotten along all right with her, but Mrs. Cowling was another matter. They'd gotten along *great*. She was fun in the classroom and shared a lot of neat things she brought in for them all to look at and, even better, she liked to read almost as much as he did.

He leaned on her desk, impeccably clean, as always. He'd never seen a teacher without piles everywhere. If there was something on her desk, it was always a neat something to touch, examine, ponder about. Once she'd brought in a miniature sarcophagus with a fake mummy inside and everything.

Today, a crystal ball sat on the battered wood top. He reached for it without thinking, and turned its coolness over and over in his hands. He looked into its clear, colorless depths. Could he see his fortune in it? Could anyone? He turned it again. A wave of color rippled through it and he looked around to see if he had sent a prism of rainbow light on the walls anywhere. Nothing.

The crystal ball warmed to his touch. He cradled it. *Give me luck,* he thought. For soccer! He stared into it and saw a warped image of himself. Scratches across the nose, lopsided mouth, eyes peering curiously.

Jason held the ball closer. How could it reflect like a mirror? He narrowed his eyes to examine the crystal ball better. A dark shape welled up inside. Grasping, a five-fingered hand seemed poised over his reflection, about to snatch him up. He blinked.

His hands trembled slightly. The dark hand shifted, turned, sailed about and became an immense black-winged bird that soared through the inner Jason, and then everything went clear—

"Jason?"

He jumped. Mrs. Cowling caught the crystal ball as it sprang from his hand. "Did you see anything?"

"I . . . I . . . I'm not sure." He shut his mouth firmly.

Her mouth twitched. "This is what I had for you."

She picked up a bound notebook from the desk. It had been resting under the ball. He flushed as he realized that, and she handed it to him.

"It's your story, the one I entered into the state Imagination Celebration. I thought it was something you should keep, always."

"Wow." He held the notebook. The cover was embossed with a dragon breathing flames. "Thank you."

"Thank you for letting me read it, and enter it. I hope—" She paused. "This isn't a good time to talk about it, is it?"

He shook his head.

"Run to tryouts, then."

Backpack in hand, Jason bolted for the classroom door. He skidded through the polished hallways and out the door. Waves of heat hit him as he emerged, blinking. He turned the corner of the building and slowed, trotting to the locker rooms to change. The sound of cleats on asphalt clattered behind him and he turned to see a wave of boys engulf and swerve around him. They were gone in a moment, jogging back to the field and its edge, a cloud of sweat following them.

Jason spotted the temporary tables dragged under the breezeway for sign-ups and darted over. Two men sat behind it, smiling at him, one of them a big square man who looked as though he had never run a step in his life, and the other a crew-cut, thin man who was wearing a faded soccer shirt and running shorts. "Little late."

"Sorry, teacher wouldn't let me go. I signed up at the pre-sign-up," Jason said, words tumbling out.

"Did you? We should have you on our list, then."

The big man eyed him. "Got to have good grades. Can't have poor students on the teams. Rules."

"It wasn't for that." Jason craned his neck, trying to read the lists upside down. He stabbed his finger at his name. "There. That's me." His name was squiggled next to Sam's.

"Is it?" The skinny man squinted at the list. "You don't look like you're headed for middle school."

Jason shifted under his backpack. "Well, I am. That's me."

"Ever played team soccer before? Get coaching?" The big man scratched his eyebrow vigorously.

"Just at school last year before I moved here. But I'm fast."

"Takes hard work, not magic, to make a team."

"Yes, sir, I know."

The skinny man cleared his throat. "Well. You'd better change clothes and get out and warm up. They're already running sprint trials. Take this, clip it on, and see Benny . . . he's in the dark blue Rovers suit, all right?"

"All right!" Jason grinned and took off for the locker rooms.

Once on the field, his small regular school locker jam-packed with his clothes and backpack, he felt better. Sam cornered him outside the lockers.

"Where have you been?"

"Mrs. Cowling kept me after. She had my story put into a book, it's really cool." He tugged his soccer shirt into position. "Help me find Benny."

"That's him." Sam pointed downfield. He spotted a harried-looking guy with frazzled red hair and a stopwatch in one hand and a clipboard in the other. Benny looked at him as they jogged up. "What do you need?"

"I was late getting on the field. Where do I go?"

"Right here. What age group in the fall?"

"Starting middle school."

Under Benny's frazzled red hair, shocking blue eyes stared at him. "Middle school?"

Jason nodded.

"All right. I run you two at a time. Brinkford! Got your running partner." Benny waved a hand. "Stretch, warm up, and wait. It'll be a few minutes. If you see someone walking around dressed like a soccer ball, that's our mascot. Get a rules handout from him."

"Okay." Jason turned away from Benny, his heart sinking as tall, weedy Brinkford stared at him over the tops of the others' heads. Sam nudged him.

"Brinkford's such a slime."

"Suppose he makes the camp, too?"

Sam shrugged. "You, me, we'll bunk together. Brinkford can go ooze somewhere else."

Jason bent over to stretch. Blood pounded in his ears as Brinkford sauntered up.

His classmate lifted the corner of his lip. "Running against me? You wish." He turned his back and said something to his shadow, and laughter echoed. George Canby glanced at him and made a remark back, and both boys bent over in glee.

Jason felt his ears pound. He trotted over to the edge of the grass, circled by a running path, Sam in his wake. "I've gotta make camp. Otherwise, it's a summer with Grandma McIntire. I won't even be able to see you!"

"You'll make it. Just remember, you don't have to beat Marty. You're running against the stopwatch time. He's the fastest kid here. Even being second to him, you'll probably beat a lot of other guys' times. Okay?"

"Okay!" He nodded at Sam.

Martin Brinkford stood a good head taller than Jason, with longer legs. He might not be able to stay even, but that wouldn't matter. It didn't matter if he won. It mattered only if he ran faster than a lot of the others. Even if all he saw were Martin Brinkford's heels, it was the stopwatch he had to worry about. But the laughter stung.

Jason hung at the back of the group, watching boys split off two by two and grunt and thunder their way across the field to where another soccer coach stood with a stopwatch in each hand. Old, weathered wooden bleachers framed the imaginary finish line. From time to time, girls sat there watching, or finished runners sprawled there, waiting for their turn to take the passing tests which involved dribbling a ball through a cone obstacle course using only their feet to keep the soccer ball in line, to an odd adult or two who just seemed to be there to cheer on their son. Just such a person perched there now and although Jason watched him, he could not quite clearly see who sat there, although the agility with which he leaped to the very top row of the bleachers almost certainly knocked him out of the parent category.

A sharp whistle split the air.

"Okay, to the line . . . Brinkford and Adrian. Let's go, hustle, hustle!"

Jason moved over to the coach's side. Brinkford looked him over slowly, grinned, and moved into position.

Jason almost closed his eyes. *It didn't matter who won. What mattered was the time on the stopwatches.* He took a deep breath and shook his hands loose. Martin Brinkford made a noise almost like a cat snarling. Jason rolled his neck and shoulders, trying to calm a suddenly jittery stomach.

"On your mark."

He fixed his gaze on Sam standing across the field.

"Get set."

Jason inhaled.

"Go!"

Martin Brinkford took off like a shot, Jason barely half a step behind. He dropped his chin, concentrating on pumping his legs faster, driving him after Brinkford. The gap between them widened, then closed.

His feet pounded the grass and ground. He narrowed his eyes. Martin grunted slightly and began to draw away again, but they were close, so close to the coach already! Breathing hard, Jason focused on the goal line.

Sam began jumping up and down and waved his arms. Urging him on. Jason dug in. His lungs were on fire. Brinkford sprinted barely ahead of him. He was catching up!

Something blurred in the corner of his eye.

WHAM! Hit and hit hard, Jason tumbled. He felt a sickening crunch in his ankle that did not stop until his body screeched to a halt on the grass. He sprawled, heart pounding and leg screaming in pain. Sam bent over him. "Oh, man!"

Jason writhed on the ground. The hot, heavy smell of another body hit him.

"Little body check," Canby noted. "Didn't you see me coming?" The chunky boy stood up, smirking. Divots of grass and dirt fell from his body.

All Jason could do was grab his leg and try not to cry.

"Canby!" yelled the coach. "You're not supposed to tackle the runners!"

"Oh, yeah?" Canby looked down at Jason, who tried to sit up and then lay flat with a groan. "He wasn't in the drill?"

"You know he wasn't!" Sam stood nose-to-nose—well, nose-to-chest—with Canby.

Canby looked at Sam. "Prove it." He backed off as the coach reached Jason.

"Come on, son, get up! Walk it off. Let's go."

Jason rolled to his side. He tried to get up. He put all he had into it. "I can't!"

His ankle shot lightning bolts of pain through him, and all he could manage was to kneel there, holding onto his right ankle, hot tears at the corner of his eyes. He shook his head, gasping for words.

The coach bent over him. "Sit back and let's have a look, then." He probed Jason's ankle thoroughly, each examination bringing gasps and grunts of pain from Jason. The coach squeezed Jason's shoulder. "That's a pretty bad sprain. I'd say soccer season is over. Might have some ligament damage. Anyone at home who can come pick you up?"

"Shoot," Sam muttered. "There goes everything."

A shadow fell over Jason as he began to recite his stepmother's cell phone number. Martin Brinkford looked down and smiled thinly, his slender face hardly even heated from the run. "I had you beat anyway."

The coach looked up sharply. Brinkford pulled his face into a concerned expression. "We'll have to match up again. There'll be tryouts for winter league. I'd like to beat your butt fairly."

"Brinkford!" the coach snapped. Brinkford shrugged.

"Yeah. I'll see you then." Jason stared into the other's face, the sheer pain of the ankle gone for a moment. Brinkford and Canby drifted away as the coach got an answer on the cellular phone and even Jason, sitting on the ground, could hear Joanna's brisk and excited responses. He was not to be moved. She'd be right there to pick him up.

"Oh, man," repeated Sam, his face wrinkled with worry and upset. "Tough luck."

Tough luck. Crystal ball or not. . . . Was there any other kind?

You May Have Already Won . . .

JOANNA frowned, then quickly relaxed her face as though worried she might create a line there. "I thought you said no tackling?"

"Well, it wasn't a tackle, exactly."

She put a glass of milk on the kitchen table and stood to watch as Jason fooled a bit more with his air splints. "Then what was it?"

"Not like a football full-body tackle. It was a sliding tackle. Like . . . hmm . . . when a runner in baseball slides into base and takes out the second baseman? They can knock you off your feet, and that's what he did to me." He could only be thankful they hadn't gone through this dialogue at the Emergency Room.

"But this is soccer, dear."

"I know, but . . ."

She looked at him, one eyebrow perfectly arched.

Jason inhaled. "You're right. But this is a soccer move, only I wasn't in the drill with him and never saw him coming. I was in a running trial. Sam waved at me. I thought he was trying to get me to run faster." He sighed.

"That sprain can be worse than a break." Joanna set a plate

in front of him, heaped with potato chips and a freshly made tuna salad sandwich on fluffy white bread. "You're going to have to wear that splint for a few weeks. You're going to need care and watching." She sighed.

"I'll be careful."

"Once it heals, you can think about soccer in the fall."

"You'll let me try out again?" He remembered to shut his mouth before she asked him to. His jaws ached with the surprise, though.

Joanna smiled. "Well, if they have to carry you out on a stretcher a second time, I think we're going to have to find a new sport. But, yes, William and I think sports build character. However, this leaves us with a quandary."

He filled his hand with the enormous sandwich. Someone at one of her many club meetings must have told her about growing appetites. He tried not to wolf it down while he thought of worrisome things.

Alicia had been remarkably quiet. She assembled some carrot sticks on her plate into what looked like a Chinese symbol. Carefully, she picked all around it till, suddenly aware that she was being watched, she looked up, blinked, then smiled.

"Mom?"

"Yes, dear?" Joanna answered as she sat down with a bowl heaped with salad greens and a sprinkling of dressing. Dozer was evidently off at one of his late meetings. She straightened the country gingham place mat, smiling brightly at her daughter.

"Did Jason screw everything up?"

Jason looked from one to the other. Why did he suddenly feel guilty? "I didn't mean to." His ankle throbbed in agreement. He crunched some chips to avoid saying anything else. His mouth filled with a burst of salt and potato flavor.

"I know, dear, and I know you're going to miss Sam all summer. Anyway, Mrs. Cowling phoned. She asked to come over."

"She did? What for?"

"She heard about your leg. She has something to discuss with us." And Joanna made a slight face which meant the subject was closed for the moment. Curious, he devoured the last half of his sandwich, under which he found a haystack of carrot sticks as well. Munching, he sat back in his chair, his foot propped up on the spare chair. His air-filled soft splints were nothing less than radical looking, and in a day or two he could wear shoes again. In the meantime, he got to wear sandals a week before anyone else at school, until classes let out for the summer. It was poor compensation for having his summer ruined, though.

"Mo-om," prompted Alicia. "Am I still going or not?"

Joanna jumped up and went to her daughter, hugging her. "Of course you're going!" She squeezed Alicia tightly. "The summer in Colorado at film camp! You're going to have such fun and learn so many things!"

Jason watched them. A mixture of feelings went through him. He sat silently for a moment, thinking. Camp had sounded neat. It really had. Playing soccer every day, doing camp stuff with Sam. Belonging in a certain place, day in and day out, without wondering if he was only there 'cause the others were just so darned polite!

He shifted in his chair. Something crinkled in his jeans pocket and he drew it out. *You may have already won . . .* He looked at the scrap of paper. How had that gotten there? It seemed to migrate through his clothing without any help from him! He buried it before Alicia could notice.

"And, of course, William and I have plans." Joanna frowned slightly. "That is, Jason, if we can find a place for you. Mrs. Canby offered, you know, to make amends by watching you for the summer. Now, her husband is a big supplier for William, but I don't trust that boy. He has always had a kind of mean look. Squinty eyes. So, I thanked her and said no. You don't mind, do you?"

Jason snorted. He almost inhaled his milk. Neither Canby nor Brinkford had made the team because of "bad sportsmanship" in the tackle on Jason, which the two had evidently planned. Alicia watched him as he put a napkin to his face and coughed. When his nose and throat seemed to have settled down, he said, "No, that's fine. So now what? What do I do?"

"I know you don't want to go to Grandma's, but most camps are already filled. We haven't much of a choice." Joanna's voice trailed off, and she looked at him thoughtfully.

It was torture. Like having your toenails pulled off one at a time, watching Joanna ponder. Were they going to send him to geekville or retirement city? Because it was obvious he was getting sent off *somewhere*.

Both looked at him now. Alicia seemed to have finished building whatever it was she was building with her food instead of eating it.

Jason stared at his plate as if Mrs. Cowling's crystal ball rested there and could give him a hint of what was going on. He waited hopefully. His eyes blurred and for a moment, the barest moment, he thought he could see the gleaming eye of that midnight crow looking up at him. He blinked and stared hard at the shiny porcelain plate, littered with bread crust crumbs and a broken potato chip. The image, if it had been there at all, was gone.

"There is an alternative to staying with Grandma McIntire, but it's last minute and you'll be on your own, not going with Sam. I don't think you'd like it, but I'm open to what Mrs. Cowling has to suggest."

He waited to hear more, his curiosity roused. What had Mrs. Cowling said?

Alicia wrinkled her nose. "C'mom, Mom." She squirmed impatiently.

Joanna tapped her butter knife on the table. "Did Jason make fun of your camp?"

Alicia's mouth snapped shut, and she sank back in her chair. Her bottom lip pouted out silently.

He shifted in his chair. "I don't want to stay with Grandma."

"It would kill two birds with one stone. She always gets terribly lonely when her nurse takes her vacation, and it would be nice to have someone there. And you have to have someplace to go. I don't want to cancel our plans, this is . . . well, it's our honeymoon. We delayed it, but now it's all planned and paid for." Joanna blushed faintly as she put her napkin to her lips.

"But Grandma . . . She's . . . she's dotty!"

"Eccentric," corrected Joanna. Behind her mother, Alicia rolled her eyes and mouthed, "D'oh." He pretended he hadn't seen her.

"She won't take cable television because she's afraid they're spying on her. The only thing she can still cook is jello and I'm sick and tired of that. I have to mow and trim the lawn twice a week—"

"She has fast-growing grass. And that's only a tiny area around her little home." Joanna patted his hand. "I know she has strange ideas, but she's very fond of you. You need to try, Jason, to think of all of us as your family. Sometimes, I don't think you do."

He stared at the table. Sometimes, he didn't. Sometimes, he didn't think they thought of him as anything other than a guest. A guest they were now trying to pawn off, very politely.

"There is a swimming pool there," Joanna said helpfully.

"I have to have a special pass to use it. They don't like kids there. Right, Alicia?"

"It's a retirement park. They have lots of rules." Alicia shrugged. "You've got to go somewhere. Maybe you could make money mowing the other lawns."

"Nearly everyone else has gravel." He stared at her. She was being no help at all. What did she care? She had *her* wish for the summer. He could feel the corner of his mouth turn into a surly curve as he opened it to protest again when the doorbell rang.

Joanna got up quickly. "That must be Mrs. Cowling now. Come into the living room with us. Alicia, clear the table."

He wrinkled his nose at her as he trailed his stepmother from the room. At least he didn't have kitchen duty.

His English teacher came into the house in a flourish of peacock-blue fabric. She hugged both of them and took up residence on the edge of the couch, a wide smile shining from ear to ear. "How's the ankle?" She watched as he sat down and propped his foot on the coffee table. Joanna smiled at Mrs. Cowling.

Jason looked around, found the ottoman and used that instead. "It hurts," he admitted. "I have to take some Tylenol every couple of hours. It'll be better tomorrow."

"Broken? That is a splint?"

"Bad sprain. That's really to keep some pressure on it and to keep me from twisting it more. I even have to wear it at night." Jason looked at it proudly.

"Good idea." Mrs. Cowling settled her long, sweeping blouse about her. "I am sorry you were hurt."

He shrugged. "It's all right."

"All may not be lost." She took a deep breath and spoke to his stepmother. "As you know, the school participates in the statewide Imagination Celebration. I like to assign essays. Other classes do skits, artwork, and so on. It all goes on display at the mall. But, of course, you know that. You were there for the ribbons and things." She gave Jason a proud glance.

Jason fought off a blush and sat straighter in his chair. Mrs. Cowling had been ten times prouder of him than either Joanna or the Dozer. Alicia had had a dance recital for that same celebration. She had a gold trophy sitting somewhere in her bedroom.

"Jason, a gentleman by the name of Gavan Rainwater wrote the school. He was very impressed by your essay, it appears, and he's sent in an offer of a scholarship to his camp. I confirmed it yesterday as soon as I heard about your accident. I have brochures—information—all right here. I looked into it. They are new, but they have references. I mentioned it to your mother when I called to come over, and she said it was your decision." Mrs. Cowling dipped into her rather large purse and produced a handful of colorful papers.

"Camp Ravenwyng?" noted Joanna thoughtfully. She spread a brochure open. "They don't mind taking him with that ankle?"

"Oh, no. This is a creativity and leadership camp, although there're activities of all kinds." Mrs. Cowling watched Jason.

"I'm not going to be crippled *all* summer. Maybe I can still go to soccer camp in a few weeks?"

"We already asked, hon. It's full. They can only take so many boys." Joanna looked back down at her brochure, then added, "I'm so proud of you, but I honestly don't think that you feel you've done anything." A soft smile flickered at the corners of his stepmother's mouth. "Your father was just like that. Quiet and modest, even when he'd done something great."

She rarely talked about his father, which made her words even more important. Jason stared, suddenly hungry for something that was not a sandwich or potato chip or waiting cookie.

"He would do these remarkable things yet seem so humble about it. . . ." Her voice trailed off and she bit her lip. She sighed and looked down at the brochure. "Well, I see there's a deadline here. Midnight tonight to accept. That doesn't give us much time to think about it. I'm not happy about this, letting him go when he's hurt and all. My husband's mother has offered to take him."

"From what I heard, it's a grand opportunity." Mrs. Cowling smiled brightly at them. "The references are good, and the program seems very interesting."

"You've checked it thoroughly?"

Mrs. Cowling smiled so brightly her cheeks glowed like polished apples. "I think Ravenwyng would be just perfect for Jason."

"A camp for geeks?" His voice squeaked and he shut his mouth.

Mrs. Cowling studied him. "A camp for bright, interesting people."

He ducked his head, slightly embarrassed.

"Unless, of course, Jason, you'd rather not consider it. It's up to you. Grandma or . . . geek camp." Joanna watched him.

Put that way, he didn't have much of a choice.

Camp. Be careful what you wish for . . .

4

Straight on Till Morning

"**G**OT everything?" Joanna asked for the tenth time that morning.

"I think so. Clothes, extra shoes, sleeping bag . . ." Jason paused, tugging on a fastening strap. In addition, the staff at Ravenwyng had sent her a list, and she'd promptly taken Jason in hand and gone off to find the several rather odd items at the bottom. *A Field Guide to Herbs,* a book on Celtic mythology (any book, the list had stated), a jeweler's loupe, and a handful of star charts.

Ever resourceful, his stepmother had had no trouble in finding any of the items. She'd been unfazed by the oddity, as well, even when the shop selling the star charts had also tried to sell her a deck of tarot cards. Jason rather regretted that she hadn't given in and bought those as well. The colorful designs and intrigue of the deck caught his attention with a delightful curiosity.

"Fortune-telling?" the shopkeeper had commented, with a shake of her dangling coin bracelet and a wink at Jason. He hovered over the card with a magician brightly painted on it until Joanna clucked her tongue and dragged him out of the shop.

"It's not scientific," she'd explained briskly, before hauling him down to the Wal-Mart to buy new shorts and socks.

Lots of things were not scientific, Jason thought, as he piled the sleeping bag and duffel near the front door and checked his watch. What was it that kept you hanging around the kitchen for a few minutes, without knowing why, until the phone rang? Or just knowing you were gonna be it the second before your name was called? He hadn't argued with her then, and he wouldn't now. Instead, he wondered how neat it would be if the laundry ink pen they'd used to mark his clothing could be invisible ink that wouldn't show at all till wet. Then it could read: Jason Adrian . . . someone remarkable.

"You're sure you have everything? Flashlight?"

"I have everything," he said firmly. In fact, he had one or two things beyond everything, having sneaked back to that store and bought the deck of tarot cards which was still in its wrapper, unopened, only that front card on the box which held it visible, the rest of its wonders to be savored later.

Alicia leaned against the doorjamb. "I hope there won't be this much fuss when I go," she remarked.

"That will be different, dear. We'll have to drive to the airport and put you on the plane." Joanna sighed slightly. "You'll only have two carry-on bags, and your camcorder and violin. Dear, dear, we'll have to do some more planning on that. Perhaps a trunk would be better, insured, of course. Going by plane is much more complicated than going by van." She moved away from the door and Jason's bags, as she frowned and took out her folio to start making some notes. She drifted off in thought.

He took a deep breath, grateful for the recess.

Alicia took a step to follow her mother off, then stopped, considering him. "I didn't say this before." She tucked a blonde strand of hair behind her ear. "I think it's neat, actually. You winning and everything. I mean, we're all astonished you could do something like that. I hope you have fun."

"Thanks. Me, too. I mean, I hope you have fun."

"Oh, I will." Alicia smiled and she sounded as if she had no doubt whatsoever in the world. She bounced a quick step down the foyer and after her mother's disappearing form. "Mom! I think I need new shoes, too. . . ."

McIntire had already crushed Jason's hand in good-bye before going off to his latest construction site.

So he sat alone in the small foyer, looking out the arched doorway, waiting to leave. The bus would be parked at the school grounds for precisely one half hour to gather students. He still didn't know exactly where he was going. The brochure had promised "clean air, cool water, newly renovated campsite in the Sierra Nevadas with all the amenities but phone usage and television prohibited to promote creativity among the campers." Cellular phones would not work because of the remote location and mountainous surroundings. That was something he could not imagine here. A faint haze of dirt and smog shimmered over the horizon as far as he could see, and even the foothills had towers to transmit signals. You'd think Northern California was like faraway Tibet or something.

How far away could it be?

How far did he want it to be?

A crow winged past, with a raucous caw.

Startled, Jason jumped to his feet, wincing as his ankle pulled. He blinked and leaned out the doorway. As quickly as it had flown over, the dark shadow was gone. The hairs at the back of his neck prickled. His eyes stung, and he looked at his watch. He'd gone to sleep sitting in the doorway! He grabbed his duffel while yelling toward the back of the house, "Mom! We've gotta go."

He hefted his sleeping bag and was out to the curb, loading the family van without waiting for an answer. Alicia and Joanna came out in a few moments to find him perched and ready.

The high school parking lot had filled. There were three camp buses—two, long, yellow, and shiny, each with a name stenciled boldly down the side. Sam had already left for soccer camp, so there was no sense looking for him there. Campers and parents circled around these buses, the luggage bays open, and sleeping bags and suitcases and duffels being tossed in by tall, tan camp counselors in white shirts, khaki shorts, and well-laced hiking boots. He took in the sight of a campus that awed him a bit, and the milling crowds of kids, counselors, and parents with cameras. It was definitely camper day, and this was definitely the launch point for any number of camps in the area.

Joanna drove past very slowly, searching. "That's not it," she said, peering at a bus.

"Nor that one." Alicia rubbed her nose thoughtfully.

Jason stared across the school. At the end of the lot, a battered, short bus sat with its sides painted white, a large coal-black wing outstretched in flight adorning it. "There!"

"Are you sure?"

"It has to be," Alicia said loftily. "Ravenwyng. How obvious. Bet you're glad it's not called Crow's Toes." Jason snorted at the teasing.

Joanna parked a few slots away, a tiny frown line between her eyes. "Not many here."

Alicia wrinkled her nose. "Old bus."

His stepmother did not look much happier as she stepped out of the van. "Do you think it's safe? It doesn't look very . . . very . . ."

Jason got out quickly before Joanna could mention Grandma McIntire again or think those second thoughts he could see settling in like wispy clouds. He grabbed his bags. "It's fine! New tires and everything, Mom. Look." He kicked one as he passed, headed to the curb where he'd spotted a pile of backpacks and bags. A tall, older boy smiled faintly as he approached, and pointed at the stack.

"Throw it anywhere for Ravenwyng." He watched as Jason did so, then turned his attention back to the Gameboy in his hands.

The man at the fore of the bus came around to meet them, smiling.

He stood and watched as the driver swept a baseball cap off his waving, dark brown hair and bowed.

"Gavan Rainwater, at your service." He looked at Jason then, his vivid blue eyes shining with laughter. "Said your good-byes?

Have all your gear?" He wore a tie-dyed shirt that brought out the brightness of his eyes, and faded jeans, and his hair curled down to his shoulders. He leaned on a cane, the carved silver wolf's head cupped in the palm of his free hand although he did not look the least bit crippled. The wolf's jaws held a large crystal in its teeth.

Jason stared, a little uncertain.

"I am speaking to Jason Adrian?"

"Ah. Yes, sir."

"Ready to go?" Gavan tapped the side of the bus gently, knocking the wolf's snout against the raven wing. "Hello and well met!" He beamed at Alicia and her mom as they came around the side of the bus. He bowed with a flourish. "Your sisters drove you?" He smiled past Jason at Joanna, and he could hear his stepmother make a flustered noise as they shook hands and Joanna explained that, no, she was his mother.

Rainwater answered, "No? Really?" as he shook hands all around. Joanna's face pinked, and Alicia rolled her eyes while Jason looked over the other campers. Barely a handful waited. The tall boy was quite clearly the oldest, by several years. A long-haired Asian girl, her face intent on a paperback book held in her hands as she sat cross-legged against the school grounds fence seemed to be waiting by the Ravenwyng gear; he wasn't sure. He could not catch the title of her book, but the cover looked like it was a fantasy of some kind, a flowing white horse and a minstrel or someone leaning against it. She looked up, smiled faintly, then went back to reading.

Two boys his age or a bit older sat on their sleeping bags, bolstered by the chain-link fencing, steadfastly ignoring everyone around them. They were playing cards, attention riveted on the colorful squares in their hands, looking up once and then back to their game as though nothing else were more interesting. One had flaming red hair and the other looked as wide as he was tall, but in a muscular way, and grunted every now and then over a card.

A car chugged in next to the bus. With a battered fender and dings all around, it smelled hot, and before it was fully parked, the girl inside had the door open. "Wait for me! Wait!" she cried out, all arms and legs, and dark golden-brown hair bobbing in a ponytail. Her hair caught the late afternoon sun in streaks of platinum. Her camping gear left the car in an avalanche, her body caught in the middle. Breathlessly, she kissed her mom good-bye. "I'll write! I promise! Lots and lots."

Her mother seemed an older version of the girl—heart-shaped face, no freckles, though, her own golden-brown hair pulled back at the nape of her neck. She laughed. "Slow down, Bailey, they're not even loading yet!" She laughed again as Gavan Rainwater took her hand. "I really recommend you keep her away from caffeine for a day or two," she said to the counselor.

He smiled. "Madam, your daughter is enchanting."

"That's one word for it." She tugged on Bailey's ponytail in a fond way. "I talked with an Eleanora. Isn't she here?"

Gavan Rainwater gave a slight bow. "She is most definitely here. She left in search of drinking water, I expect her back any moment now." He produced a small slip of paper out of no-where. "Well. One lad still expected, one Henry Squibb, and then we're off!"

Jason bent to help Bailey. She bent over at the same time, knocking their heads with an audible clunk. He staggered back a step. Bailey's face turned red as she stammered an apology and they both reached for the same bag, her hand grabbing his wrist instead. She jumped back as if burned, and practically fell over the young woman who had appeared by the front of the bus.

"Good heavens." She caught Bailey by the shoulders and steadied her, dusting her off. "Everyone here yet?"

Gavan bowed. "Even as promised, the incredibly talented Eleanora Andarielle."

The young woman flushed slightly and gave the group a lit-tle curtsy. She wore black from head to toe, although her skirt had small white flowers sprinkled on it, and the gauzy material looked thin and light. She wore a barely seeable white under-blouse, a billowing long-sleeved black blouse over it. "Not incredible, just a bit thirsty." She wore a very large and apparently heavy music case over one shoulder. She put a slender hand out to Bailey's mother and then to Joanna. "So pleased to meet everyone."

Bailey leaned close and whispered, "What did we get for counselors? Rejects from a Grateful Dead concert? He's in tie-dyes and she's a Victorian Goth."

He glanced at the counselors. Indeed, they seemed a world away from the khaki- and sandal-dressed adults standing at the other end of the parking lot, clipboards in their hands and whistles round their necks, tanned legs showing under their shorts.

The noise of one of the sleek buses firing up and preparing to pull out at the other end of the lot almost drowned out her soft voice. As it passed them, Jason could hear voices already raised in a chanting song, punctuated by cheers and laughter.

"Not everyone has to look alike!" he shot back at Bailey.

"True." She nodded sagely. "You don't look like anyone I've ever seen before."

As if overhearing, Eleanora apologized. "Forgive my attire. I was giving a dulcimer concert earlier." She tapped her music case.

"Oh, dulcimers!" Joanna clapped her hands together. "What a beautiful instrument to master."

"I'm afraid I've far from mastered it, but the tea seemed to go well. I may not look ready to be a camper, but I'm sure we're all eager to hit the road. Thank you for trusting us with your children."

Gavan knocked on the side of the short bus and threw open the luggage bay. "It's getting late, ladies and gentlemen. Let's start loading while we're waiting." He stood by while those sitting got to their feet, stretched, and began to toss their bags into the bays.

Bobbing for sleeping bags and duffels, both Jason and Bailey went to work, while he watched her out of the corner of his eye to avoid another skull rapping.

His stepmother loomed over him, her eyes glistening. He paused, holding his breath, and straightened. She actually looked sad to see him off. He wondered at that. Would she really miss him? More than just politely?

Joanna tried to smile. "Have a good time, then! We'll write you from the islands. If there're any problems, Grandma McIntire will come and get you."

If he had to eat gruel, he would not come home to Grandma McIntire. Whatever other doubts he might have, he was firm on that one. "I'll be fine," he said confidently.

Alicia waved smugly. He waved back. His stepmother pressed some bills into his hand before giving him a hug and walking away quickly, Alicia in her wake. He hardly dared breathe till the McIntire van disappeared in the distance. Then he let out a whoop, and ducked his head when Gavan turned, raised an eyebrow, then grinned.

"Dibs on the back seat," the two cardplayers said. The one with yellow-red hair and blue eyes squinted against the sun, adding, "Anyone have a problem with that?" The other, square, muscular, with dark eyes and dark hair buzzed around the ears, looked around for a challenge. He didn't get one.

Bailey hugged her mother good-bye fiercely. "Be safe driving home."

"I will." Her mother hugged her back, not letting her go for many moments. Then she got in her car and drove away quickly, without looking back at her daughter standing in the school parking lot. The car let out a small cloud of smoke as it turned the corner, disappearing.

Bailey rubbed her nose. "She's got a long drive. I hope she'll be okay."

Eleanora Andarielle moved to the girl's side in short, gliding steps, and put her hand on her shoulder. "I'm sure she'll be fine."

Without a word, like a shadow, the other girl passed by them, got on the bus, chose a window seat, and curled up, book in hand.

Rainwater tugged on a long silver chain, pulling a pocket watch out of his jeans. He clicked it open. It chimed softly as he read the watch face. He looked at Eleanora. "We can't wait much longer for young Master Squibb."

"Of course." She ushered Bailey on. With a solemn nod back, she gathered her skirts and got into the bus in the front passenger seat, setting the dulcimer case near the dashboard.

Jason started toward the bus door, but the two players brushed past him, one of them accidentally kicking his splint. He stopped, wincing. They clambered aboard without a look back. The small bus shook as the bigger boy mounted the steps and disappeared inside.

The tall older boy passed by as well, turned, and put his hand out to Jason. "Don't mind them," he said. His dark hair gleamed like the blue-black paint on the Ravenwyng.

"Oh, I don't." Jason got up the steps. Who could be worse than Brinkford and Canby?

He stood in the aisle and watched as the older boy picked a seat by himself, settling down his backpack.

Someone tugged on his sleeve. "There's room here. Come on! Misery loves company."

Jason looked down into Bailey's freckle-dusted face. He didn't think she meant quite what she said, but she did have a faintly unhappy look on her face, as she glanced out the window. He slid into place next to her as she pointed out the ends of the seat belt.

Gavan pulled his baseball cap into place. It had *Wizards* embroidered across the front in rainbow thread. Jason tried to remember which team that was, and couldn't.

"I'm Bailey Landau." She stuck out her slender hand.

He rubbed his forehead gently. "I think we've met. Jason Adrian."

She looked around and then said conspiratorially, "Are you nearly a winner?"

It took him aback for a moment. Then he grinned. "Yeah. You?"

"You bet!"

She seemed normal enough. He didn't quite know what to expect. Alicia had regaled him with stories of past camps she'd attended. Short sheeting, snipe hunts, shoes tied together and filled with unspeakable swamp goo. Maybe Bailey was already setting him up, in a good-natured way, for a prank.

"What happened there? Scooter?"

"Here?" Jason pointed at his splint, and shook his head. "Soccer."

Her eyes widened. "How?"

"Sliding tackle. At tryouts." Jason looked out the window.

"Who won?"

Jason grinned at Bailey. "Neither of us made the team. I was too injured, and he was too mean." He looked at his leg. "Only a sprain. I get to take these off in a week or so."

"Cool beans." Bailey leaned over, looking at the air splint. "If you have to wear something, those are radical. IMac bandages." She sat back with a giggle. She took a Gameboy out of the knapsack. "Want to play Monopoly?"

"Sure."

In a few moments, Bailey had them set with electronic tokens going round and round on a miniature electronic Monopoly board. She was beating him soundly when they both looked up and saw that the Ravenwyng bus was the only one left.

The empty parking lot suddenly came ablaze with headlights and a honking horn. The headlights blinked frantically in the late afternoon sun as they pierced the gathering shadows.

Doors opened. A jumble of family members popped out like bees swarming out of a hive, depositing their charge at the bus steps, he red of face and panting. He seemed to be Jason's and Bailey's age. His short, spiked brown hair, glasses, and round face gave him a slightly bewildered owllike expression.

"You're late," Eleanora said quietly from her corner of the front seat.

"But not very!" Gavan countered cheerfully. "And, look, it's almost the cool of the evening." He opened the passenger door to the front seat. "Need a hand?"

The camper huffed and puffed on board, trailing bag after bag, slung from his hands, around his shoulders, waist, and neck. The owlish lad plopped down next to the older boy although the bus was still half-empty. "I'm Henry," he said cheerfully and stuck his hand out. "Henry Squibb."

The other smiled faintly. "Jonnard Albrite," he said, and shook Henry's hand. "Call me, Jon. You just barely made it."

"Got that right. Dad wouldn't stop for instructions!" Henry let out a rolling laugh, and Jason instantly liked him. Bailey grinned, too. He waved cheerfully at the reading girl. "Ting!"

She looked up, her mouth curved, and she waved back.

"That's Ting Chuu," Henry announced cheerfully. "Ting is Chinese for graceful. I met her at the Imagination Festival." He tugged his windbreaker around his chunky form, getting comfortable on the seat as the bus engine started with a roar and began chugging. "Is everyone a winner?"

A snicker came from the back of the bus. "I see a bunch of losers."

Before anyone could protest, Gavan called out, "We're off!"

With a lurch and a hum of tires, the vehicle shot forward, and Jason saw the beige blur of his hometown slide past. The vehicle surged along the highway as the sky darkened in a blaze of pink-lemonade clouds and a layer of blues, deepening where it touched the foothills.

Eventually tired of Monopoly, both Jason and Bailey put their heads back and must have dozed. He woke and stared, disturbed. The countryside seemed to be flying past, but a look over Gavan Rainwater's shoulder showed the speedometer well within the speed limit. The crystal in his wolfhead cane caught the slant of the late afternoon sun and sent prism light dazzling into Jason's eyes. He sat back and rubbed his right one a little.

They could not possibly be headed the right way. Nor did any other car or truck seem to be on this highway. And that was truly incredible. Roads in Southern California simply were not empty. Not unless they headed off across the bleak desertlands or something but that would be headed east, not north to the mountains. And, by his calculations, they wouldn't arrive till the middle of the night or later.

Bailey had a small denim knapsack and hugged it to her, before loosening the flap. "Hungry?"

He shook his head. She pulled out a granola bar, unwrapped it, and began to pick at it delicately. While crinkling the bright foil, she bent her head and said, so only he could hear, "This trip has a time of its own."

He looked at her. "That's impossible."

"Cross my heart, hope to barf." Bailey finished half her bar, rewrapped it, and neatly put it away. "We're going nowhere fast."

Bailey saw the worry on Jason's face and looked out the window, too. She frowned and whispered, "Told ya." He didn't like the fact she'd been reading his mind.

Bodies to the rear shifted uneasily as well. "Hey, man, we're in the middle of nowhere."

A small green sign appeared, coming into view. Roadrunner Way off-ramp, it notified, ¾ miles. There was no way of determining if the sign was correct or not, as the highway itself was turning in and around small golden hills, browned by the sun and summer heat. As he peered toward them, he thought he saw a small, dun-colored dog trotting down the road. It swerved and dashed away as the car roared past. No homes out here, it could not have been anyone's pet. Coyote? His glimpse was too fleeting to tell.

As they turned down a gradual slope, the off-ramp of a much smaller road forking off came into sight, along with a faded and battered sign proclaiming: Gas Food Lodging. Someone had X'd out Food and Lodging.

Eleanora frowned. "We're lost," she said softly to Gavan. Jason could barely hear her.

"Nonsense. There's nothing out here to get lost on."

Her head came around sharply and she whispered something that sounded like Dark Hand that made Gavan look thoughtful. But Jason was almost sure she couldn't have said that, because it made no sense.

It immediately became very quiet. Jason found himself nearly asleep again, his chin jerking as he almost tumbled into a dream. His eyes did not want to stay awake. He pinched his kneecap and, though it smarted, the pain flung his eyes wide open. He found himself staring into a great dark mountain and the road ending abruptly at its foot.

Gavan murmured something to Eleanora. She answered back softly and leaned out of her seat to put her hand on the wolfhead cane. The car shuddered as if on rough road. Gavan struggled with the steering wheel. They bumped from side to side. The vehicle's lights beamed yellow rays into inky shadows. Jason found himself holding his breath.

Bailey jerked at Jason's elbow. Her eyes opened wide. "We're gonna die!" She covered her face with her hands and let out a squeaky shriek.

Eleanora looked around at them. "It's just a tunnel." But her voice seemed strained as if she could barely find the strength to say another word. Her hand quivered, and the wolf-head cane trembled in her hold. The bus danced and swerved on the dusky road.

Jason stared into the night. He could see no tunnel's edge in the massive rock ahead. Only pitch-black mountain dead in front of them. He took a deep breath.

They plunged into a cold darkness.

Camp Ravenwyng

THE tunnel swallowed them whole. The car bucked and tossed in the coldness. Jason scrubbed his eyes against the nothingness. It flowed past him, slimy and cold. Bailey shivered against his shoulder. He inhaled.

"Come on, Eleanora. Forget about your shoes and give me all you've got," Gavan muttered. Eleanora gave him an annoyed look, then frowned. The crystal in the wolfhead cane seemed to be the only light left. The silvery head seemed to glow with warmth, and the crystal flared. It let out a tiny flash and then, suddenly as if ejected, they shot forward and out of the tunnel.

Bailey hiccuped. Henry Squibb let out a shaky laugh as pale light flooded in through the windows. Someone whooped from the back of the bus.

Not only was it not total darkness . . . it was no longer evening, though close to dusk. Gavan slowed, dirt and gravel crunching under the tires, as he turned down a lane edged by wilderness. Thick with evergreens and other trees, and a jagged ridge of true mountains off to the east. A very blue sky with lowering purple clouds. A cardinal winged past in a streak of scarlet.

Bailey said, "Go tell Alice we're not in Kansas anymore." Her head swiveled about, taking in a forested area that obviously got far more rain than any forest in Southern California.

Jason was beginning to understand what she meant. He sat on the edge of the bus seat.

Eleanora settled back with a sigh, dropping the wolfhead cane. Gavan called out cheerfully, "We'll be just in time for the first campfire!" He drove in under a swinging white sign over a sagging metal gate, white paint flaking and edged with rust. Faded dark letters read CAMP RAVENWYNG, with another version of a bright-eyed soaring raven. The gate didn't look as if, even closed, it could hold fast. The terrain itself sloped gently as the road wound uphill. He could spot large cabins, roofs peaking through small clusters of trees and shrubs, the buildings grouped by twos and threes. The road broke into a very big clearing with three very large buildings, and Gavan pulled to a stop next to several other battered but evidently reliable old buses, their sides white with dark-winged logos.

They piled out, as Bailey would say later, like rats off a stinking ship. The redhead punched his friend in the shoulder and said, "Hey, Stef. This is a dump."

"You're a dump, Rich." Stefan thumbed his nose. He stretched his chunky body. "At least we're finally someplace." He ran his hand through his spiky brown hair. "Maybe we can pan for gold or something." He snickered.

He ignored the small crowd of campers and adults standing outside what appeared to be a large barn, the buildings old and weathered. "Although I gotta admit it doesn't look like much."

Gavan swept his hat off as he helped Eleanora down the bus steps. "Ladies and gentlemen, welcome to Ravenwyng. Dinner will be ready in a bit. After dinner, we will be meeting in the Lake Wannameecha Gathering Hall to go over cabin assignments, and tomorrow we'll start our first full day of camp! Gather up your things and put them in the Hall for now. In the meantime . . . toilets are in that building there. One side is for the ladies, one for the gents. Ladies' cottages are around the curve of the lake. Most, if not all, will be explained on the morrow!"

Eleanora dusted herself off before heading away to the distant building, moving with a graceful, gliding step, her shoes hidden by the sweeping hem of her long skirt.

"Platforms," muttered Bailey.

"Hmmm?"

"Platform shoes," she added. "She walks funny, huh?"

"Oh." Jason nodded.

Bailey rubbed her nose. "Sounds like a good idea!" She dashed off after Eleanora and caught up with her, headed to the restrooms.

Jason reached for his stuff and Bailey's, nearly locking elbows with someone—again. As he pulled loose, the other grabbed his arm. The boy looked up, revealing a thin face, darkly intense blue eyes and curly hair that fell over one eyebrow. He smiled, and it lit up his dark eyes.

"Heya," the other said. "I'm Trent."

"Jason."

"Glad you guys finally got here. We've been holding dinner." Trent gave a lopsided grin.

"You look like you can't afford to miss a meal."

"Got that right!" He hefted Bailey's bag over his shoulder with a grunt. "This yours?"

"Nah. My friend Bailey's. She went to the bathroom."

"Figures. Girls pack a ton. I had to throw out half the stuff my mom used to put in . . . when she was alive to pack." Trent strode with him toward the Gathering Hall. He looked down at Jason's leg, noticing the limp, then back up. "Broken leg, huh?"

"Sprain. Almost healed."

"Neat splits. Those plastic?"

"Sorta. You pump air into 'em. They're lighter, softer."

"Cool. Kinda geeky looking, but all right."

Jason looked up at the Hall door as they passed through. Someone had nailed a piece of wood, shaped rather like a lopsided and sideways figure eight, to it and painted it blue.

Trent tapped the object. "That's Lake Wannameecha."

"Seen it?"

"Not yet. So you came in with the big kahuna, huh?" Without waiting for Jason to nod, he added, "I drove in with Crowfeather. He's way cool, this Native American guide. Knows all sorts of stuff about wildlife." He dropped his voice. "Camp's not quite what they expected, seems. They just bought it. Bathroom's in good shape, though."

"What's wrong with it?"

"Supposed to have been remodeled and updated. Only about half the work was done, I guess."

Inside, electric lights burned, but low and weak, with a wavery yellow light. Trent dropped his bundles near a neat stack. "This's my stuff. Just park your stuff here, too."

Henry came chugging in, struggling with his things. Rich and Stefan were on his heels. Stefan smirked and said, "Let me help you with that, Squibb."

He reached out and tugged on the strap holding the bloated sleeping bag together. With a sharp yank, it came undone, exploding like a giant air bag. It all but swallowed Henry from sight. Suddenly blinded, Henry tripped and fell, skidding across the Hall's floor. He came to a stop looking somewhat like a sausage stuffed into a fluffy brown roll. The two boys strolled off, shoulders shaking with laughter.

Henry sighed and rolled out of his sleeping bag. Trent leaned over and gave him a hand up. He looked thoughtfully at the massively fluffy sleeping gear.

"Big . . . ummm . . . bag," he said.

"Down. Best kind, but once those feathers get air in 'em and get all poofed up . . ." Henry sighed again, and pushed his glasses back into place on the bridge of his nose. He leaned over and began to squeeze his bag down to size. Jason got on his knees and helped him gather the straps.

"Next time, pick on somebody your own size," Trent said to Stefan's back.

The two turned slowly. The square kid looked across the end of the Hall at Henry Squibb. "He is my size."

Trent grinned. "I meant intellect." He let out a hearty laugh before grabbing one strap and helping Henry and Jason pull the bag tight. "What is this thing, anyway? An air bag for a humvee?"

The three of them couldn't help smirking, Henry's round face going red in both humor and embarrassment. "My mom..." he sputtered finally.

"My mom," Trent said, "would have put a pillow on a skateboard, if she could have figured out a way. And I think she taught my dad how." He wrinkled his face up ruefully.

Henry fell over laughing. Bailey trotted up, watched them all silently for a moment, and then joined them. Jason pointed at her. "Trent, this is Bailey, Bailey, this's Trent."

She nodded even as she looked about the cavernous and well-worn Hall. "Thank goodness the bathrooms are modern."

"See the lake from there?"

"Wannameecha? Oh, yes. Looks nice. There's racks of canoes and kayaks stacked behind the mess hall."

"Speaking of mess hall!" Trent took a deep breath and beamed. "Smells like dinner!"

Jason could smell a savory scent as well.

"Wait'll you meet the cook. FireAnn. She has this big cloud of red hair and this cool Irish accent. We all had to go pound on pots and pans in the mess hall. She's got a crew coming in, but they're late."

"Why pounding?"

"We had to chase the raccoons outta the kitchen." Trent grinned again, merriment flashing in his dark blue eyes. "She was yelling at them that the slowest one out would be pot pie tomorrow!"

Jason laughed.

FireAnn did indeed have fiery red hair, held back by a dark blue bandanna that seemed as if it might burst open. She stood at the back of the mess hall while they sat and ate, and her green eyes flashed with satisfaction as the campers scarfed up every bite and a few came back for seconds.

"Tonight's free night," Trent said, as he wiped up the last of his gravy.

"How so?"

"Tomorrow they assign kitchen duty, toilet duty, camp duty. And they'll have us scheduled for classes till the cows come home." Trent's thin face considered him. "Never been to camp, huh?"

"First time."

"For every action there is a reaction and chore," Bailey said. She dropped her fork with a clink.

"Something like that," Trent agreed. He glanced at Jason. "She always like this?"

"Sometimes," Jason said. "Only more so."

By the time they left the mess hall, darkness had fallen once again. Little moon stayed out, a thin shivery sliver in the sky. The sound of music carried to them, and they set out in search of it. The smell of woodsmoke filled their nostrils, and a thin, gray funnel could be seen wafting up to the night sky. The melody grew brisker and brisker until they nearly ran to catch up to it.

The three found themselves in a clearing. Gavan Rainwater stood, surrounded by the orange sparks coming off an immense bonfire, fiddling away, a short black cape hanging from his shoulders, his body in motion as he danced and strode to the music he bowed. With his dark hair curling about his face, and the fiddle alive in his hands, he looked rather like a Gypsy.

Other campers and the counselors began to gather. Eleanora came in last, silently, and took a seat on a stump, looking up at Gavan as he reeled off the last of the air, and stood for a moment, inhaling deeply, becoming still. He bowed solemnly. "Time to meet some remarkable teachers."

He pointed with his bow. "Tomaz Crowfeather."

A short, thin man stood, his face weathered, his eyes dark, his hair parted in the middle and pulled back into a twist anchored by a shining feather. He wore a vest over a faded denim shirt and jeans that looked as if they had indeed been beaten into worn softness by rocks. Beaten silver disks set off by turquoise nuggets in his braided leather belt and bracelet flashed in the firelight. He gave a half bow of acknowledgment.

"Anita Patel." The shadows yielded a slight, graceful woman who wore a sari and pants, and as she turned and waved at all of them, tiny bells on one anklet pealed.

"I will show you how to breathe and move," she said softly, but everyone seemed to hear her. A crimson dot accented her forehead between dark brows.

"Adam Sousa!" Gavan pivoted on one heel and pointed his bow at an intense young man sitting on a log at the fire ring's far end. Sousa jumped up. His long, slender fingers tapped a rhythm on the silver cornet hanging from his belt as he flashed a grin. "Mathematics and Music," Gavan said and bowed to Sousa.

Trent and Bailey and Jason all looked at one another. "Do you think . . . ?"

They shrugged. "But I bet he plays Reveille in the morning."

"Eleanora Andarielle. Literature and Mythology."

Eleanora raised her hand and waved.

"Elliott Hightower and Lucas Jefferson, Sports and Crafts."

Across the bonfire from them, Jason could do little more than spot the two men by their gestures.

"Cook FireAnn! An enchantress with herbs and food." Fire-Ann danced into the gleaming bonfire light, her hair freed, and did a turn of an Irish jig around Gavan before bowing and dropping back into the shadows.

They all cheered FireAnn.

"Plus, we have one or two guest lecturers who may drop in from time to time! Now, I am done talking. Sit. We have marshmallows to roast and names to exchange and bedtime coming all too quickly."

So they sat, and Tomaz Crowfeather passed out green sticks he'd whittled for roasting spits and FireAnn passed out marshmallows and they sang camp songs and cheered until the flames grew smaller . . . and smaller . . . and smaller.

In the Gathering Hall, the campers assembled at their gear, faces weary, voices now quiet. Bedtime seemed a good idea. "I want to sit on something soft," Henry declared. He tugged his bag over toward the seating area.

Henry Squibb tugged and tugged, seemingly unable to get the bag open now. Jonnard went over and the two wrestled with it for a moment before it suddenly burst open, flattening both of them. While Henry turned red and apologized a thousand times to Jonnard, Jason looked his gear over.

Trent frowned. He leaned over to Jason. "Someone's been in my stuff."

"What? How can you tell?"

"Special knot my dad taught me. It's tied different."

"Anything missing?"

"I can't tell yet."

Jason looked at his things. He opened his duffel. Things that he knew had been packed first now lay on top, as though someone had neatly turned his bag inside out. He looked up, saw Trent watching him in the dim light. He nodded.

Gavan and Eleanora came to the front of the Hall, and the tired campers fell silent, watching.

"Ladies and gentlemen," he said. "It's late and we're all ready to turn in. But in what cabin, in what bed? What companions shall share your adventures with you in the coming weeks?" Gavan shook his head and tapped his cane on the floor. "Too difficult a problem for a mere mortal to solve. So we have called upon the Wishing Well, and a ritual older than any of us here! You'll be led out, and given words to speak. Remember them! Repeat them precisely! Your very future depends on it!"

He pointed his cane at Jonnard and then Stefan. "Crowfeather, Sousa, take your first victims!"

"Eleanora and Anita, take those two hostage!" He pointed at Ting and Bailey. Bailey went with a giggle, but Ting's eyes were very big as they were led out the door.

Gavan rapped on the floor. "Hightower, Jefferson—those two!" And the wolfhead cane pointed at Trent and Jason.

Outside, the lights seemed very thin against the darkness of the evening. The others shuffled through the grass and dirt to an old structure he had not noticed before. It seemed to be a genuine stone wishing well, complete with a great wooden crossbeam that had a bucket hanging from it. The roof was littered with pine needles. He could hear whispering voices ahead of him, but nothing clearly. Bailey suddenly bounced in excitement and started to bolt back to the Gathering Hall. She slid to a stop beside Jason.

"Kittencurl! I'm at Kittencurl Cottage!" Almost before she had stopped, she was off again.

Trent shook his head. "Better her than me," he muttered.

Jason laughed.

Hightower curled his strong coach's hand about Jason's arm. He bent down. "Now listen to what I say very carefully when you get to the well's edge. You'll be repeating after me."

"Mmmm . . . okay." Jason felt a little foolish. Ting passed them without a word, but her mouth curved in a secret smile.

The stone-walled well looked very old. A small sign, firmly fastened to its roofing said **Water Not Potable.** Trent hissed in his ear, "Means you can't actually drink from it."

Jason nodded. He put his hands on the rim of the well, the cold stone clean and firm to his touch. Dark water lapped below and reflected back the thin gleam of the moon.

"Now repeat after me," Hightower said quietly, and gave Jason the lines one at a time. He took a quick breath and blurted them out to the well. His voice echoed very faintly.

> *"Brick and Mortar, Stone and Stick,*
> *Which roof and walls*
> *For the summer call?*
> *Wishing well,*
> *It's time to tell!*
> *Which cabin shall I pick?"*

The last echo dropped away and for a moment, there was total silence. Then, breathily, in a voice that was neither male nor female but very odd, it answered:

> *"No matter where you roam*
> *Your heart holds your home.*

In my waters, the answer true
Of the cabin meant for you."

Jason sucked in his breath at the eerieness. Maybe someone was hiding in the trees behind them talking, maybe someone wasn't. He looked down into the well. The waters seemed to stir, and then the voice sighed a word he was not sure he caught.

He looked up. "S–starwind?"

"Good choice, lad! Nice cabin." Hightower thumped him on his shoulder. "Go get your gear, I'll be taking you and the others going that way in a bit."

Halfway back, Trent bumped into him. "What was that, d'you think? Throwing their voices?"

"I dunno. I'm just glad to get a place to sleep. Where are you going?"

"Someplace named Starwind. You?"

The chill of the cold from the Wishing Well warmed instantly. "Me, too!"

Trent pushed him slightly. "Now I know it's a put-up deal." But he grinned broadly.

Henry rushed past to roll up his sleeping bag in a hurry. They called after him, "Where're you going, Squibb?"

"I got Cabin Skybolt, with Jonnard!" He let out a chuckle before ducking off and tackling the mountain of gear he'd brought with him.

Jon, a tall shadow against the darker night, waited silently outside the hall for Henry to join him before heading down the pine-edged pathway toward the boys' cabins.

Their cabin, when they reached it, crested a small hill. From its front porch, Lake Wannameecha could be easily seen. Carved into the front porch eave was a large shooting star, with an immense comet tail, STARWIND etched under it.

"Too cool," Trent said. He lifted the latch and went in, Jason holding the flashlight behind him. It was deserted, dusty, with leaves littering the floor despite the shuttered windows, but no varmints lurked there as far as they could tell. They threw their bags on bunks.

"In the morning," Trent muttered, "I'm going to find out who was going through the stuff."

"Right." Jason slipped his shoes off. The two of them shook out the sheets, blankets, and towels they had rolled in their sleeping bags and tried to pull their cots into some kind of order. He threw his bag down like a comforter over the top and slipped in. He smelled faintly of woodsmoke as he drifted into sleep. The campfire Parting song had been neat, all the counselors chiming in and wishing them safe till morning. The morning would bring a shower, breakfast . . . and a mystery.

The cabin had grown very quiet when Jason woke. He lay there uncomfortable with the knowledge he should have hit the restrooms before he went to sleep. He tried ignoring it, but there was no way he was going to get back to sleep if he didn't hike down to the bathroom. And there was no way he was going to wake Trent or anybody else to go with him, despite the counselors' instructions to be careful at night.

Jason crawled out on hands and knees. His eyes adjusted quickly to the darkness and he found the doors easily, slipping outside, flashlight in hand. He twisted it on. Nothing happened. He shook it. Batteries rattled dully inside. He twisted it on and off a few times. Nothing. His body ached, and he decided to forge into the night anyway!

Down through the path of evergreens, the halo of lights surrounding the Gathering Hall and facilities drew him. He paused as he heard the soft murmur of adult voices head his way.

"It's not what I expected."

"It'll be fine. It's worn out, but there's magic in it. There is no doubt there's an Iron Gate about. If we can find that, can a Haven be far behind?"

"That's the good news, and the bad news. The Dark Hand will be as attracted as we were. We've time, but not much."

"We've done more with less."

"True . . ." the voices moved off.

Jason rubbed at one eye. Nothing they said made any sense. He waited three long heartbeats until his bladder told him he could wait no longer, and then he walked quickly, desperately across the grounds. The facilities were dark and chill, and he danced about a bit trying to stay warm, finishing as quickly as he could. Coming out, he breathed a sigh of relief that he had not been detected.

Halfway across, Jason stopped as he heard something nearby. He turned and saw a glint of moon reflected in green eyes. A large form moved through the shrubbery, leaves crackling. Something large and hot and wild growled. He froze.

He could see it slink past the wall of the mess hall, pause, and then trot his way.

Furred. It snarled, and Jason caught a flash of white teeth. Coyote? No. He stared at it and it stared back as it slunk closer. It crept forward a step at a time on clawed paws, eyes fixed on him, glowing green in the night. It looked like an immense jackal, ivory fangs dripping. His yell of disbelief stuck in his throat. He tried to force it out. Help! He needed help! He could smell the creature's hot breath as it growled menacingly.

Then it sprang. Jason fell back, the thing covered him, and he felt a sharp pain in his hand. Its weight forced him down into the soft dirt, and he did two things instinctively. He kicked hard at the underbelly. His hand, caught in the beast's jaws, tore open as he shoved it, punching deep into the mouth.

The beast gave a strangled, surprised snarl as Jason forced his hand deeper into its throat. It let go abruptly, leaping aside, and Jason struggled to his feet. He could feel the hot spit sting as it rolled down his torn hand. With a growl it circled, and Jason knew it would leap again.

White light floated across the ground. FireAnn stood in the mess hall doorway, a broom in her hands. "Who goes there?" she called out, her red hair a mass of flames licking about her head.

The creature sank back on its haunches in the shadows. Its green eyes flickered as it turned away. It paused. With a low growl, it said, "You're mine!" and then disappeared into the deep shadows by the lakeside.

Jason stood stock-still in shock. He shuddered after a moment. "It . . . it's just me."

FireAnn stood in the glowing doorway. His teeth clattered. "I . . . I . . . it bit me!"

"What?" She came out and bent over him. "What happened?"

His hand stung, and he could feel the blood dripping off it. He didn't think he could stay on his feet. "Something . . . big . . . it bit me. . . ."

She shook his hand gently, cradling it. Blood dripped into her palm. "Take a deep breath now. You're going to be all right. What happened?"

Bush prickles stuck all over his pajamas, and he felt their dull stings. "Am I gonna get rabies?"

"Did you fall in the bush? Coming out of the bathroom?"

He nodded. "It jumped me and I fell, and it went for my hand and . . ." He could hardly talk, his teeth chattering.

She smoothed his hand out in hers, eyes narrowed, looking closely at it in the golden rays of light falling from the kitchen doorway. "It doesn't look like a bite. Are you sure?"

"I . . . it . . . it said . . ."

"It said?" Her eyes looked into his.

He clamped his jaw shut tight. She didn't believe him. Or if she did, she'd think he was crazy. He shivered.

"Go wash it, and come into the kitchen, and I'll have a better look. I've some ointment, too."

He could feel her eyes on him as he scuttled back to the restrooms.

Water felt good on the bite. He scrubbed it with soap for long minutes, wondering what to do, leaning heavily against the sink. The beast had spoken. Could he tell anyone? Would they even believe him?

He patted paper towels over the back of his left hand a few times. Jason took a deep breath, trying to push away the sick feeling in his guts.

On the way back, FireAnn waved him in. He stepped into the warmth, still shivering, still scared. She took his hand again, saying quietly, "Ever been camping before, Jason? Out in the wilderness?" Her voice had a slight Irish lilt to it.

He shook his head. She smoothed her fingertips over the wound. He stared at it in disbelief. The ragged tear had already settled into place, sealing, looking more like an angry red welt. "This is no animal bite," she said. "I think maybe one of my kitchen varmints frightened you. The bush tore into you when you fell. Bites look entirely different, you see. You should not worry yourself." She smiled in reassurance and spread some salve on it. Instantly, the fiery hurt faded. "You'll be fine. But you should see Dr. Patel, all right?"

"But—but . . . rabies . . . ?"

"Bushes canna carry rabies, but believe me, if they did, my ointment would kill it." FireAnn gave him a reassuring pat. "Now, off to bed with you." He stood, feeling wobbly, and headed back to Starwind. He turned once and looked back to the mess hall. Beyond, in the bright kitchen, he could see a great, deep shiny steel cauldron and FireAnn over it, stirring. The smell of fruit and sugar being cooked wafted toward him. Then, as he passed Lake Wannameecha Gathering Hall, she closed the door.

He crossed the darkness quickly, every hair at the back of his neck standing up. Was it following him? Did it trail him? Would he make the cabin in time?

Finally, hardly able to breathe, he tore up the steps of waiting Starwind and threw himself inside. Trent stirred, mumbled something, and rolled over. Jason took a deep breath, then latched the cabin door and lay down on his bunk. How could the wound seal up so quickly? Why the strange crescent? It had bitten him, hadn't it? Hadn't it?

His hand on his chest, sore and throbbing slightly, he fell into a deep, troubled sleep.

Lanyard Ho!

"**G**ET out! Get out! GET OUT!"
Lids clanged like gongs. Pans thundered like drums. Shrill cries of fury pierced the morning.

With a yelp, Jason sat bolt upright in his sleeping bag. Images of feral eyes glowing in the dark still danced in his mind as he ran out the cabin door. Were they under attack? Across the way, Henry Squibb had not only gotten to his feet, still wrapped in his immense sleeping bag, he ran around trapped inside it, wailing. Others milled around.

But it was not Henry's loud cries that shook the camp.

"Out, I say! Out, out, OUT! And stay gone!" the loudspeakers bellowed.

"Something's wrong with breakfast!" Trent cried. He lit out for the mess hall, Jason at his heels. Doors to the building flung open, campers shooting off in every direction.

As they peered at the commotion, FireAnn appeared in the mess hall kitchen. She brandished her broom, laying about her with every cry. Her hair lashed around her as she danced in anger. A small herd of chipmunks bolted from the kitchen. In a wave of chitters and chatters, they dodged across the open ground and into the grasses and tall trees down by the lake's beach. A raccoon lumbered out of the kitchen, a pot lid caught on a hind paw that it kicked aside, and then it broke into a gallop just ahead of FireAnn and her broom. Its bandit face mask looked squinched up unhappily.

Trent rolled against Jason, laughing so hard he could barely stand. Behind them, other campers pushed forward to see what was going on.

"Excuse me."

Jason turned as he heard Eleanora Andarielle's soft voice at his ear. She passed by as he moved aside and he blinked in confusion. She was taller than he was, wasn't she? He seemed to have remembered that from yesterday. But today the top of her softly curled hair would have brushed under his chin. Before he could think any more about it, she had joined FireAnn, just as two more raccoons left the mess hall kitchens in a lumbering hurry, grumbling unhappily at being woken up. Eleanora bent over to collect pot lids, and joined FireAnn clashing them. "Well done! I'd say the enemy is in retreat!"

The cook gave a last triumphant wave of her broom in the air before disappearing into the kitchen. Her voice then wailed in dismay, "What a mess!"

Eleanora turned, her skirt swirling in a dark cloud about her ankles. "I'll need five campers this morning to help FireAnn clean up, so breakfast can be made." She pointed quickly, catching a sleepy-faced but already dressed Bailey with the sweep of her hand.

Bailey looked at the two of them, shrugged, and trotted down to the kitchens, her sneakers swinging from her hand. She dodged a last chipmunk barreling through the doors, little tail flipping with every leap and bound.

"The rest of you get changed and report to the crafts area down by the lake. I've buckets, mops, and brooms to give out. It's cabin cleaning time! You'll shower before lunch because you've got some real dirt pushing to do." Hightower shooed them toward the bathrooms. Jason stared at him a moment. The counselor was incredibly tall and lean, a shock of thin black hair standing almost straight up. He had a long, thin nose with a crooked bent to it. "Let's get a move on!" He picked up the whistle hanging around his neck and shrilled a note. Everyone raced off to get ready.

Jason winced as someone pushed past, hitting his hand. He ought to find a nurse or something, just in case. He waited till everyone went by on their way toward the lake before looking at it in the full morning sunlight. Lifting his left hand, he stared in surprise at a thin, purple line, like that of a crescent moon. Healed yet sore.

He traced a fingertip over it. Very sore. Yet seemingly nearly healed. But how . . . ? Would the camp doctor even believe him?

A sharp whistle jerked Jason's head up, as Hightower beckoned for the latecomers. He'd think about it later. Right now, he was awake, dressed, and hungry with no breakfast till some work got done.

Trent pushed a mop at him and swung his own over his shoulders with a bucket hanging from either end. "Look at it this way," he said, as they hit the winding pathways leading to the clusters of cabins. "At least we're cleaning up our *own* mess."

They trotted through the evergreens to the chatter of blue jays. The cabins seemed to come in twos. The first two were more like lodges, one roofed with dark green shingles, the other with dark blue. The second pair were rustic, actual log cabins, the windows storm-shuttered and with screens leaning up against the porch, covered with leaves and pine needles. Starwind and Skybolt. A jagged white lightning bolt marked the other cabin, where Jonnard was patiently peeling Henry out of his humongous sleeping bag.

"What did we miss? What was the racket all about?"

"FireAnn chasing raccoons and chipmunks out of the kitchen."

"Ah," said Jonnard. He smiled. "I bet it'll take a few days for them to decide to stay out. They've probably got comfortable nests in there."

"I think Cook lit a fire under 'em," cracked Trent. He swung his own mop. "Cabin cleaning time," said Jason, in case the other two didn't catch the drift. Trent took the steps in a leaping bound, more dried leaves flying away from his shoes.

"Can I see your place?" Squibb asked. He had turned red in the face, and a tiny trickle of sweat ran down his neck, which he wiped at uncomfortably. Jonnard nonchalantly threw the sleeping bag back inside the domain of Skybolt.

"Sure. Come on."

The rusty latch lifted with a small complaint. He was not sure what he had expected as light from the front door streamed in, not having seen it in anything but wavering light from his old, dim flashlight. Henry came puffing in behind them, muttering, "Better not be any spiders. I hate spiders." He stood in the middle of the cabin, looking around, pushing his glasses back up his nose from time to time. "Yeow!" He jumped as Trent sneaked up from behind and tickled his ear with a broom straw. He whirled around, then sputtered, "I guess I asked for that."

Jason laughed. "Never tell the enemy your weakness!"

Jonnard said mildly, "I keep telling you, Henry, spiders are good. They'll web the mosquitoes and gnats for us."

"I don't care. Don't like 'em! They give me the creeps." Henry shuddered all over. "This is sorta like our place and sorta not."

"What's different?"

"Well, you've got four bunks, like we do. But we don't have a window seat with a cabinet or bins—" he pointed across the room.

"We have," Jonnard said quietly, "a built-in writing desk. The top comes down. Rather primitive but nice. And a closet."

Henry said, "And you've got windows on three sides. We've got 'em on all four." He spun around. "But yours is a cool place, too."

Trying to work around the two with his broom, Trent muttered, "Hightower said no breakfast till your cabin was cleaned."

Henry jumped. "We'd better get going!"

Jonnard laughed as Henry turned and hustled out the cabin door. He waved and followed.

Working quickly, the two got the storm windows open, and cleaned screens in place, letting sunlight flood in so they could mop down the floor. By the time a cornet call floated through the air, they were done, dusty, and starving. Hightower and Jefferson met them at the boys' side of the bathrooms with towels and soap.

Soon, they were scrubbed and dressed and still starving, lined up at the mess hall doorway. Jason's stomach rumbled, as he smelled delicious aromas of breakfast ahead of them. Jostling to get trays, plates, and utensils, Jason could see a line of eager campers ahead of them. The hall was only a third filled, though, built to hold far more campers than their numbers.

Finally, they made it to the front of the line. The wait was worth it. There were piles of fresh, fluffy biscuits. Bowls of butter and homemade fruit jams to go with them. A dish of hot, steaming sausage gravy to pour over the biscuit, if you'd rather have it that way. Jason couldn't decide, so he split his in two and had one half with jam and the other with gravy. Down the line were scrambled eggs and crisp bacon. Nectarines and grapes and melon. Milk and individual boxes of cold cereal. Jason trailed after Trent and watched as the wiry boy heaped helping after helping onto his plate. By the time they headed to the tables, Trent carried a small mountain of food in front of him. Even Henry Squibb and Jonnard dropped their jaws in astonishment as he passed by.

"My theory is," Trent said, "you never know when you're eating next."

"This, however, is camp food," remarked Jonnard. He sat, his back straight, his dark hair neatly combed back, his plate consisting of two pieces of toast, a neatly dissected poached egg and several pieces of melon.

Trent paused with a forkful of fried potatoes halfway to his mouth. "And your point is . . ."

Jonnard quirked an eyebrow. "Never mind," he said. With two precise cuts of knife and fork, he skinned the rind from both slices of melon and proceeded to cut them into bite size pieces.

Actually, Jason was beginning to wish he had taken two whole biscuits as Trent had. The hearty flavor burst in his mouth as he gobbled his down. The bacon was crispy with a slight smoky flavor and the eggs creamy and fresh tasting. He polished off a just right, juicy nectarine, and looked for a paper napkin to wipe his chin. Jonnard passed him one.

Henry and Trent finished eating at about the same time. By then, Hightower and Jefferson had moved to the front of the mess hall.

"All right, ladies and gentlemen. I hear almost all the cabins are in tiptop shape! Well done to the dirt crews. This morning, you ate wherever you felt like it, but starting tonight, you'll be eating at the table that matches your cabin. And showering and so forth on your schedules. So keep in mind that your cabin mates will be with you a lot.

"Headmaster Rainwater and Jefferson and I will be looking you over throughout the day, seeing what you're made of and throwing together regular schedules according to your ages and abilities. We've campers here from ten to fifteen, so we want to make sure everyone's having fun. Okay, now. The day's schedule will be posted at the front of the mess hall. The schedule for tomorrow will be posted after evening meal. It's your job to read it and know what's going on, and show up for activities."

Hightower rubbed his bony hands together. "Any questions?"

Trent's hand shot up.

Elliott Hightower looked at him.

"Did you play basketball in school?"

Hightower's eyes widened in surprise and then he let out a chuckle. "A little. All right, then, turn in your trays. Be sure to scrape and clean your plates and sort out the recyclables. Be kind to the kitchen crew, your turn is next week!"

As they carried their plates to the cleanup area, they spied Bailey sitting on a stool in the kitchen, wearing an oversized white apron and a poofy white hat on her head. She was eating and, catching a glimpse of them from the corner of her eyes, she waved cheerily. Then she turned away, watching something across the kitchen intently. Jason edged up to the counter to see what it was.

He could hear someone's edgy voice. "I tell you, I have allergies. I need to know what's in some of these things or I can't eat them. It could kill me!"

FireAnn stood, a great frown making sharp lines between her vivid green eyes, her arms folded across her chest. "And I am answerin' you, lad. We are all aware of allergies and there is nothing in my recipes that will bother you. But my recipes are mine and likely to stay that way!"

The two redheads stood, nose to nose. "I could get deathly ill!"

"Not iffen your mum filled out your papers correctly. Think I'm daft, lad?" She raised her wooden spoon in emphasis. "There isn't enough tea in china or gold in Fort Knox to pay me for teaching a lad with poor manners. I am here because I wish to be, not because I am paid to be! Now, run along with you before I assign you kitchen duty for the next two weeks and you discover my cooking from the pot scrubbing up!" FireAnn brandished the wooden spoon.

Rich sputtered as he took a step backward. "We'll see about this."

"Indeed we will."

He turned, his face redder than his yellow-red hair, and stomped his way past Trent and Jason, headed outside.

The cook shook her head. "Temper, temper. He should try peppermint and chamomile tea."

Jason could not help but shoot FireAnn a big grin before leaving as well. Trent right behind him, they found the posted schedules and jostled their way to the front to read them. "Canoes!"

Jason scanned down the rest of the schedule. He tapped a class after lunch. "Lanyards?"

"Sure. Crafts, you know."

"What . . . ?"

"You've seen those braided key chains?"

Jason scratched his head. "Yeah, I think."

"Those are lanyards. Like roasted marshmallows, you gotta do lanyards at camp, man." Trent nudged him. "You'll like it. Sounds lame but it's fun."

"You wouldn't be kidding me, would you?" The blue edge of the lake looked far more inviting. The sound of waves lapping against the rocky shore and soft silt beach carried through the scattered trees.

"No, seriously, it's fun. Once you know what you're doing, you go on to leather crafts. I had a friend make this cool braided belt once. Of course, it kept stretching out and his pants would fall down. . . ."

Jason laughed as they trotted down to the beach, and the cooling breeze off Lake Wannameecha hit him. Crowfeather was already there, squatting next to the racks of canoes, running his hands over them in inspection. There was a weathered, wooden bin with its lid open. He waved at the bin. "Life vests. Grab one. Buckles and straps are pretty easy to figure out. Help each other if needed." A man of few words, he turned back to his examination of the boats and paddles.

"Know anything about canoeing?" Trent looked at Jason.

"Not a thing. They do float, right?"

"They're supposed to."

Crowfeather straightened with a slight grunt. "In fairly good shape. I'm sure you guys will give them a bang or two."

Dust rose in the landing as the rest of the group shuffled in. Crowfeather watched them silently, his arms crossed over his chest, till they all fell silent as well.

"Line up however you wish."

Trent muttered, "Uh-oh," as they bumped shoulders getting into some semblance of order. He grabbed Henry Squibb who came up, panting and red-faced, and thrust him between them. Jason looked at Trent, bewildered, then just shrugged. As soon as the last straggler fell in, Crowfeather went down and counted off, pointing at them. "One, two, one, two," until he'd ticked off the last boy. "Two-man teams, ones with ones, twos with twos."

Trent punched Jason lightly in the shoulder. Both, of course, had been counted off as twos. Henry pushed his glasses up, frowning until another boy headed for him, tanned hand stuck out in a grabbing handshake. "Alfaro," the other said. "Daniel, but everyone calls me Danno." Relieved, Henry pumped his hand.

"Henry Squibb . . . and everyone calls me Henry." He beamed in welcome. Clad in a bright orange life vest, he looked rather like a rotund orange. Jason snagged some faded yellow vests for himself and Trent, which was an improvement, even if slight. They looked more like lemons.

Lake Wannameecha lapped serenely at the beach. Crowfeather turned as though following Jason's gaze. "Let the wind come up," he said, "and that lake will be as rough as the Atlantic in a storm. Or it will seem that way."

He pivoted on one bootheel, the silver-and-turquoise linked belt around his waist chiming slightly. "All right. This session is short. Remember your partners, remember what I am going to show you about paddling. Then you'll be dismissed to write a letter home and let your folks know you got here in one piece. After lunch, at the swimming classes, we'll get an idea of your skills in and on the water. Tomorrow, we'll launch these canoes." He smiled slightly. "Be prepared to get wet."

He spaced them apart, handed them paddles, and ran them through what he called dry land exercises, all the while drilling safety rules into their heads. Jason liked the feel of the oar in his hands, but felt a little silly paddling at dry air. Until, when told to switch sides, he and Trent clapped their oars together with a loud smack. He staggered back just in time to see Danno hit the dirt, avoiding Henry's long swing.

Danno lay there laughing, even though his coffee-brown eyes grew large as Henry's oar swished back over his head a second time as Henry bent over, saying, "I'm sorry! Oh, no . . . I'm sorry again!"

By the time the session ended, they were all sore in the

shoulders but switching from side to side without threat of be-
heading their partners.

They retreated to their cabin gladly, wrote their letters, and
no sooner turned them in at the Gathering Hall office to Gavan
Rainwater than Adam Sousa swooped down on them.

"Orientation hike!" he announced, with a flourish of his silver cornet. "Three in line, marching formation!"

Bailey skidded into place between Trent and Jason, her
freckled face rosy. "Hey, guys! How's it going?"

"Canoeing looks awesome."

"Yeah? How's your cabin?" Without waiting for an answer,
she prattled on about her cottage, Kittencurl, until most of the
campers had fallen into formation and Sousa blew a blast on
his cornet, quieting everyone. Bailey switched breathlessly into
a whisper. "But there's this cabin on your side that no one ever
camps in—Dead Man's Cabin. It's . . . haunted."

"Well, d'oh," Trent returned. "If it had a dead man in it!"

They all fell silent as Adam Sousa signaled for the marchers
to follow him. He counted off their brisk strides before breaking
into song:

> "Well, I don't know, but I've been told
> Ravenwyng Campers are awful bold!
> Sound off, One, two
> Sound off, Three, four
> Sound off . . . One, two,
> Three, Four!"

With grins on their faces and the sun beating down, they
made up verses that grew sillier and sillier as the marchers
snaked their way through the grounds of Camp Ravenwyng and
ended up in front of the mess hall just as FireAnn sounded the
lunch bell.

As they fell out to wash their hands and faces, Bailey
grabbed their arms.

"Did you see it?" she asked.

"That blackwood cabin with the shuttered windows and the
great black slash over the doorway?"

She nodded solemnly.

"Nope."

She shoved at Trent. "You two! Beat you to lunch!"

As it turned out, she did. The Kittencurl Cottage table butted up end to end with the Starwind table, so she scooted her tray over as they sat down and they talked excitedly about their different mornings. Full of food and a little sleepy, they finally headed to lanyards.

Trent nudged him in the ribs. "See? It'll be nice to sit down and do something with our hands."

Jason picked at a splinter in his thumb. He stifled a yawn as they sat down at the craft tables, trays of colorful plastic strands in front of them, and silvery metal pieces like key chain loops and hooks in plastic bins next to them. Gavan Rainwater sat on the end of the head picnic table, watching as fifteen or so campers stumbled in, faces sunburned, and took their seats.

"Nice quiet afternoon on the lake," Gavan said. He smiled at them. "Now, as you take up the strands you choose and braid them in some of the patterns I'm going to be showing you, I want you to think behind the simplicity of the object. Beyond square knots and braids. I want you to think of the flow of the color, the energy that you are moving, back and forth, over and under." He leaned on his cane. "Just let your thoughts go."

Jason combed his fingers through the long plastic strands, finally settling on a cobalt blue, dark and mysterious, offset by a lighter blue that had a touch of redness in its tone. Gavan had gotten off his table and was strolling by. He stopped. "Only two strands, Jason?"

He pondered. He looked at the instruction sheets weighted down by the supply trays and then nodded. "To start with."

"Not stretching your limitations?" Gavan watched him, watched his hands.

Jason was careful to leave his left hand mostly palm up, for the moment. The crescent scar on the back of his hand ached and throbbed briefly, then subsided. "Not yet," he answered.

"Very well, then." Gavan nodded curtly and moved along.

Trent had five colors he wove skillfully in and out, while Jason struggled to braid his two which did not seem to want to cooperate. When he finally had his lanyard completed, he tied it off with a sigh of relief. He looked up to see that Gavan had made a design as well, a complicated, great knot of color.

Everyone got up to go and look at it.

"Anyone tell me what this is?" Rainwater asked, sitting back, a sparkle in his blazingly blue eyes.

No one answered. Finally Trent shrugged. "A Gordian knot?"

Rainwater's attention snapped to Trent. "A Gordian knot? Why would you say that?"

"Looks like one. I mean . . . a great, complicated knot."

Rainwater tilted his head, gaze sweeping across all of them. "Anyone else? Anyone know what a Gordian knot is?"

Jason shifted. He'd heard of it before, but couldn't quite remember.

Gavan pointed the wolfhead at Trent. "Tell us all what kind of knot that is."

Trent stared at the ground gathering his thoughts, then took a breath. "Well, this is the short version. It was a very complicated knot tied in ancient Greece. Whoever could untie or unravel it, would be worthy of conquering those lands. When Alexander the Great began his career, a bunch of wise men figured to stop him. They brought him to the knot. His advisers couldn't figure it out either. Alexander had no intention of being stopped. He took his sword out and sliced the knot in two. His solution was quicker, more direct, and much more forceful. He did pretty well what he set out to."

"And this knot? Would you slice it in two?" Gavan tapped the lanyard woven display.

"I'd have to be pretty sure I was ready for whatever the reaction would be," Trent said. He gave a lopsided grin.

"An excellent point." Gavan bowed to Trent. "Ladies and gentlemen. Now that your bodies have rested and the afternoon has grown to its hottest . . . I think swimming is in order."

They made their way to their cabins to change clothes. Jason said to Trent, "That was cool. You knowing that and all."

"I know a lot of stuff like that," Trent answered. "Mythology is my life." He grinned. "Last one to the lake gets turned into a frog!"

Red Jello

DINNER found Jason famished. He hit the line in front of Trent, just barely, and this time he took everything that looked good plus seconds. But as they moved to the end, where the desserts were set out, he shied away from the great sparkling heap of red jello squares. If he had wanted to be buried in gelatin, he'd have stayed with Grandma McIntire. In fact, he was willing to swear that was the main staple of her diet. Alicia told him once that wasn't true, it was just that she thought kids really liked jello. Well, he had . . . once. Now . . . Jason shuddered.

"Don't tell me you're not going to get any?"

"Nope."

"You're kidding? Well, get some for me, then."

Jason rolled his eyes. Dutifully he reached out and scooped up a dessert dish of the shivery cubes and set it on his tray. He opted for a cup of chilled fruit cocktail as well. FireAnn smiled at him as he carried his tray off to their table. "A hearty eatin' lad! More power to you."

Henry had already finished his dinner, and was sitting crosswise on the nearby bench, discussing the merits of chess with

Jonnard who looked extremely interested, as opposed to his normal look of polite faint interest. Bailey scooted over immediately, a frown darkening her face.

"Hey, what's wrong?"

"Someone," and she lowered her voice so no one else could hear, "has been stealing things from our cottage."

"What? Who? What kind of things?"

"We don't know. Everyone is missing something. My favorite set of barrettes is gone, and one of my hair scrunchies. Ting is missing her best purse comb. Even Jennifer says she is missing something." Bailey sat up straight as Jennifer approached them and went to sit at the far end of the table next to the wall. Pale and blonde and lovely, Jennifer hadn't said a word to Jason in the two days their tables had been joined. She sat down carefully, and tossed her long hair back over her shoulder. She was clearly older and the type of girl Alicia would refer to as "high maintenance." He wasn't sure what that meant exactly, but if she was at all like Alicia, she spent a lot of time in the bathroom getting presentable.

He leaned over to Bailey. "You think it's Jennifer?"

She shrugged. But her actions spoke differently as she viciously stabbed her fork at some grapes rolling around in her dessert cup.

Jason considered. Then he said quietly, "It may not be. Someone went through my things before we even got our cabins."

Bailey looked at him. Then she nodded. A slow smile returned to her as Trent sat down. Then she asked brightly, "How'd everyone do in swimming?"

Henry broke off talking to Jon and swung about completely, positively glowing. "I passed! I made intermediate swimmer. Never swam in a lake before."

Nor had Jason. The sensation of the silt beach bottom under his feet and the rockiness of the lake bottom had been different. But he was a good swimmer, or so he liked to think, and had enjoyed the afternoon session. Warmer, then cool waters as the lake deepened, felt great against the heat. Emerging had made his skin tingle in the breeze. "I did all right," he said.

"All right?" Trent sat down and ate half his meatloaf before expounding. "Boy's a fish in the water."

"C'mon." Jason stared at his dinner tray, too embarrassed to look elsewhere.

"I kid you not. He's a dolphin." With a swoop of his fork, his thin friend devoured the rest of the meatloaf.

"Dolphins are sea mammals. Saltwater."

Trent shook his head vigorously. "There's freshwater ones in China. Endangered, too. Ugly things, for dolphins." He pointed at Jason, grinning. "And he swims like one!"

"Eat your jello!" Jason got the extra dish off his tray and pushed it over to muffle Trent. That seemed to work. Trent looked rather like a chipmunk for a few moments.

Bailey giggled. She jumped to her feet. "I'll see everyone later at the campfire!" Passing Trent and Jason, she whispered, "I'm setting out a trap tonight." Then she was gone with a smell of vanilla as well as dinner. He looked after her.

Henry and Jonnard returned to their discussion on chess. Ting and Jennifer watched one another while they both ate alarmingly small portions of their dinner and said nothing. Jason thought guiltily of Sam and how he had hardly missed his best friend with Trent and Bailey around. 'Course, it had only been a few days.

"Sure you don't want any?" His buddy circled the last bowl of dessert.

Jason had to admit the cherry gelatin did look pretty, crowned by fluffy clouds of whipped topping. But even the sight of it brought back stifling memories of Grandma McIntire and his narrow escape for the summer. He shook his head.

"Your loss," Trent commented cheerfully, before diving in and polishing off the dessert.

By the time they left the mess hall, dusk had started to fall. Bailey caught up with them as she had promised. "Let's think of a ghost story to tell tonight," she said excitedly.

"Oh, I'm not any good at that." He didn't have a tale he

could make up, though the beast that had tackled him would scare anyone.

"I am," Trent offered. "I mean, I've read a lot of 'em." They sat down at the fire ring with nobody else in sight. As Bailey and Trent put their heads together, deciding to tell a spooky legend about Dead Man's Cabin, Jason caught a hint of movement. Almost as if his thought had summoned it, something moved in the growing twilight.

He turned his head slowly.

Something a little darker than the shadows made a gliding movement, then disappeared. He gathered himself, ready to leap to his feet, then told himself it was nothing. He heard nothing.

Then, again. In the deep trees ringing this end of the lake, something very dark, low to the ground, moved.

He fastened his gaze on the copse of trees and shrubs that hid whatever it was. The back of his hand throbbed slightly. Green glowing eyes flashed at him from the twilight. His breath froze in his lungs.

By the time he could move again, the narrowed eyes had retreated into the shadows. He had seen something . . . or had he?

"Trent."

"Hmmmm?" His friend looked up. He'd been laughing at something Bailey said.

"See anything out there? I mean." Jason cleared his throat. "Ever wonder if there is anything to see. Deer and stuff."

Trent gazed across the clearing toward the lake end. "Too early, isn't it? I mean, they come out at sunset." He turned his attention back to Bailey.

Jason watched the forest, half listening to them, half nervously searching for that which he could not quite see. Was it out there? Or did he imagine it?

A branch snapped. His friends didn't notice it, but he jumped to his feet. From the shadows of the trees, a figure stepped out.

"Well, well. Bailey. Trent, isn't it? And Jason. Already waiting?" Eleanora smiled. Despite the heat of the summer evening, she wore a long soft dress, and a filmy, floating cloak draped from her shoulders. She had a basket hanging from her wrist. "A little early for the bonfire, isn't it? How about I save your places if you'll run these raspberries down to FireAnn for me?" Smiling wider, Eleanora held out the basket, brimming with fresh picked raspberries.

Jason took the basket, amazed that his heart hadn't stopped in his chest from fright. He walked nervously back to the mess hall while Bailey and Trent chattered away at his heels.

He knew that whatever he had seen in the darkness, it hadn't been Eleanora.

FireAnn beamed in delight as they handed her the full basket. "Berries! Just what I needed, darlin's."

"I don't think they've been washed," Bailey offered. "Eleanora just picked them."

"Oh, aye, I'll clean them and cull them before I put them in the big pot." Behind her, in the kitchen that was already spanking clean even though dinner had hardly been finished, the singular huge pot simmered away. It smelled more than ever like jam. The pot seemed more like a cauldron to Jason, from what he knew of pots, which admittedly was little. Still . . . he eyed it curiously.

"Eleanora is a grand lass to think of me! Just wait till you take your Poetry and Chants class from her. A lively one, that girl is."

FireAnn dumped the basket into a bright, brass collander and put it in the sink. "Better run, you three, or you'll not get a good seat." Still smiling, she tucked her red hair under her bandanna and began to wash the berries for cooking.

Dismissed, the three of them strolled back through the camp as the tall lamppost lights came on, and the thin strings of flickering outdoor lights that graced some of the buildings. Jason was wondering what a poetry and chants class could be, when Bailey sighed.

"It's rather like Christmas," Bailey said wistfully. Her breath seemed to catch for a moment.

Jason looked at her. "Homesick?"

"Nope!" She kicked a pebble across the dirt and grass pathway. "Well, maybe a little. It's usually Mom and me. But, as Grandma always said, home is where you hang your clothes!" She skipped down ahead of them to where Eleanora did indeed hold their places amid a growing crowd of campers.

"That actually made sense," Trent remarked.

"Strange, huh?"

They sang "Captain Jenks of the Horse Marines" with Sousa leading the lively chorus. They listened to Trent's and Bailey's ghost story with avid attention, laughing and gasping in most of the right spots. Tomaz Crowfeather told them one of his many tales (or so, he said) of the Trickster Coyote. That one had the hair standing on the back of Jason's neck. But it wasn't a coyote that had attacked him. That, he knew. What it actually was, he didn't know.

"Almost time to head for your cabins," Gavan said, with a look at his pocket watch in the fire's glow. He took the poker and stirred the logs apart to settle their ashes down for cooling. One of the logs broke apart into bright red coals, then immediately cooled to feathery gray ashes. Out of its depths crawled a small lizard, hissing, tongue tasting the air.

Jennifer gasped. "It'll burn up in there!" She flailed her arms about in distress. Her pale face grew whiter in anguish.

The lizard, hardly visible in the darkness but for the faint glow of the dying flames, crawled over another log, tail slithering behind it, and disappeared.

"It'll be all right," Trent said. "That was a fire salamander. Flames can't hurt them."

"Do you think, Master Trent?" Gavan said brightly. "The stuff of legends, after all."

He shrugged. "Some legends are born from facts, although misunderstood ones. Chances are he's really just moving too fast for the coals to hurt him."

Gavan rubbed the wolfhead on his cane and nodded. "Naturally." He lifted his voice. "Lights out in twenty minutes, ladies and gentlemen!" Without further ado, he broke into the song known only as Parting, and his deep voice swirled around them.

> *"As Parting we take from one another,*
> *Let Life and Luck surround you*
> *Keeping you from harm and hopelessness*
> *Till once again our eyes meet in greeting . . .*
> *Hand in hand and heart in hope,*
> *We stand as friends always*
> *Wherever the road takes you*
> *Take strength in our Parting*
> *Till once again our eyes meet in greeting."*

Eleanora stilled her dulcimer as the last notes faded.

Most of the campers got to their feet and began to make their way down the path to the cabins and cottages. Jason didn't join the crush because resting across the top of his sneaker, coiled the lizard. It hadn't disappeared at all. Its warm red underside glowed against his shoe and he could feel its heat, just like that of the fire ring. The creature seemed quite content to rest there. Jason took a deep breath and started to tuck his feet under him as others crowded past. The lizard lifted its head, gold eyes seemingly examining his face, before it skittered off and slid into a hole under the log they sat on.

Jason got up, dusting himself off. Some things were strange. And others, stranger.

The lights were off and they had settled in their bunks when a frenzied shout from across the way brought them to their doorway. Henry Squibb danced about on the porch, white foam flying with every step. Squealing and howling, he finally came to a stop and bellowed, "I'll get you for this! Whoever you are!"

He stooped over to pull off his socks and flung them over the porch railing where shaving foam continued to drizzle off them.

Jason saw two hunched-over forms sneaking away, but the light was not so dim he could not recognize Rich and Stefan.

Henry danced one last shivery jig before going back inside Skybolt, slamming the door shut behind him.

Jason grinned in spite of himself as he latched their door shut. Trent was already back in his bunk and breathing deeply as he settled in.

An hour later, Jason was wide awake, sitting up in his bunk, breathing hard, and rubbing his eyes. His heartbeat drummed in his ears.

A nightmare of nightmares still danced behind his eyelids and he blinked hard, to fling it away. A dead man, lying on a stone platform, waiting for him. Beckoning with one whiter-than-death hand. Stretching his hand out to Jason. Silent pleas drawing him closer. The castle, the boneyard of his worst nightmares faded slowly.

His hand had writhed with pain. He had stared at it, his left hand, and the wound from the attack had opened up again, and streamed blood. It was the only color in the whole, awful place.

Stone had imprisoned him. He took no steps and yet moved closer though everything in his body fought it! The fingers curled . . . reached out for him— The last thing he wanted was for that dead man to touch him!

He'd awakened, his throat aching with a scream he couldn't force out. Now he fell back, shaking.

Jason gulped breath after breath. He couldn't close his eyes without the nightmare wavering before him. He had to think of something different! It seemed to take forever to conjure up something pleasant and sleep was far away. He had almost drifted off when he heard soft footsteps by the cabin. Voices murmured.

"Everyone sleeps?"

"Like charmed. And you?"

"Restless. I had the dream again, decided to walk it off. Do you think they're dreaming, too?"

"I hope not. If I can get them to sleep through the witching hour, they should be fine. Better they don't know yet. . . ."

"Tomaz says the storm may be gathering strength. He seems worried."

"So I heard. I can't catch a glimpse of it myself."

"You think he's wrong?"

"It's possible. He is not, after all, of our generation."

The voices blurred, moved away, and his sleepy mind could not follow the almost sense of what they had said anyway. Jason tumbled into a deep, dark, dreamless night.

Tomes and Tombs

H E rolled out of bed, hit his hand, and stifled a groan. For a moment, he thought it had all been some kind of dream, but no . . . there it was . . . plain as the gash on his hand, which looked angrier than before, puffy and red. It could be infected. He had no choice but to see the camp doctor.

The sky was still gray and no one else seemed awake as he washed and then went to the office inside the Gathering Hall which belonged to Dr. Patel. Her door, however, was cracked open and as he peeked inside, she looked up from her desk, saw him, and smiled.

"Come in, come in! You're up early. Not sick, I hope?"

He shook his head.

She gestured a slender dark hand at a chair next to her. "Sit and tell me, then." Her eyes smiled on him as well, dark as chestnuts, but lively.

"Well, it doesn't look too bad today . . . it happened the first night, but I got to thinking. Well . . . I don't want an infection or anything." How could he tell her it was an animal bite? Dare he?

"You are hurting yourself? Let me see." Her words immediately became a little brisker.

Shyly, he put his hand out and she took it in hers. She probed him quickly about the healing wound, feeling him wince as she touched the tender spots. "How did this happen?"

"I fell. I tripped over something by the bathrooms and my hand went sliding into the bushes and just got ripped open. Is it infected? Am I all right?"

"Night before last, you said?"

He nodded. She frowned slightly. "And who am I talking to?"

"Jason. Jason Adrian."

She smiled. "I was going to see you today anyway, to ask about your ankle. How's it coming?"

"Oh . . . fine."

"Still a bit sore?"

"Not really. I mean, a little now and then."

"Excellent." She pulled out a pair of glasses that looked more like miners' headgear and looked at the back of his hand again. "This seems to be healing cleanly, but I'll give you a bit of salve to put on it. Your shots are up to date, correct?"

He nodded. "I can't get lockjaw then, or . . . or anything?"

"Highly unlikely." She slipped her glasses back on her forehead. "You look a little worried."

"Well, you know. Rabies, that sort of thing."

Dr. Patel looked at him, her Indian face smoothed in a careful nonexpression. "Is there something you're not telling me?"

He fought back a squirm. "No. It's just that, well, you know. It was awful sharp when I fell. And I couldn't see. I thought maybe . . ." He felt his face grow hot. "I thought maybe I'd stuck my hand into something that was sleeping and it bit me."

She slid her glasses back down, great grotesque-looking things that covered half her face, and peered at him intently, the lenses making her eyes blurred and buglike. "Nnnnno," she said finally. "This is a slice, although there is a small puncture mark at the top, here," she tapped his hand lightly and he tried not to jump because it *hurt.* "Looks like a thorn grabbed you and then sliced around as you fell into it." She pushed the goggles back up and blinked as she refocused. Dr. Patel added, "Unless there's something you haven't told me."

"Oh, no. No."

She smiled then. "Only thing you'd have to worry about around here would be a wild animal, like a raccoon or possum, but they're pretty healthy. Spoiled, in fact, from the looks of them being chased out of the kitchen! And there hasn't been a recorded case of rabies in this area for over thirty years." She pulled a log out of the desk. "Just use that ointment and let me know if it doesn't keep healing."

He pocketed the medication in relief and stood. The loud-speaker sounded with the announcement for breakfast, and the doctor said, without looking up as she recorded something, "Don't miss breakfast."

Dismissed, he hurried out of the office, suddenly famished. Quick as he was, there was a line snaking ahead of him, and tables were filling as he got his tray and sat down.

"Catch anything with your trap?"

Bailey stabbed her spoon at a bowl full of cornflakes. "No." Droplets of milk splattered onto the tabletop and she wiped them up with her white paper napkin before crushing it. Next to her, Ting hardly missed reading a page while eating a dish of cottage cheese and fresh fruit.

"Better luck next time. Want us to help in setting it up?" Jason chased the last of his eggs around with a corner of toast.

She considered that, wrinkling her nose slightly. The dusting of freckles over her heart-shaped face crinkled. "Maybe. I'll have to find out about the guest rules."

"Guest rules?"

"Yeah. You know. Boys on this side of the lake, girls on that side of the lake." Bailey twirled her spoon. "Guest rules."

"Ah." Jason felt faintly foolish. "Probably best."

Henry leaned over from his near empty table. "Hey guys, guess what?"

Trent shot a look at him. "Your sleeping bag is full of shaving cream?"

"Ha. Not anymore. But that's not it! Jonnard got pulled aside for a special conference."

"What for?"

Henry tugged his glasses back into position, his owl-round face bewildered. "Don't know. Nobody would tell me. They just came and got him."

Jason and Trent and Bailey all looked at each other. Bailey said slowly, "Jennifer didn't come to breakfast this morning."

They glanced down the table. Ting sat, book in hand, but Jennifer's corner was indeed empty with no signs of the tall blonde girl ever having been there.

"I didn't even notice," said Jason.

Bailey beamed at him. She was still glowing when she left the table a few minutes later to go straighten her cabin and go to her first session.

"What did I say?"

Trent shrugged at Jason. "Something right, evidently. Who knows?"

Neither of them did. They finished off their trays and then trotted back to Starwind to straighten up. They spotted Jonnard hurrying in to the mess hall before it closed, a look of mild amusement on his face. He smoothed his dark hair back just before entering and ducked inside the doorway just in time to miss Trent's faint snicker.

"If I get like that in a few years, just shoot me."

"You mean, I'm tall and sure the girls will like me, like that?"

"Yup."

"I promise." Jason took Trent's hand and shook it firmly. He turned back to the day's agenda tacked to the bulletin board. "Tomes and Tombs with Eleanora?"

"No kidding? When's that?"

"Right after mail call." Jason shifted weight uneasily, thinking of his nightmare. "What is a tome?"

"That's an old word for book. Makes it sound . . . I dunno . . . more important."

Jason looked at the location, in the Gathering Hall. Sounded like the class was being held with all the campers at once. He shrugged. "We'll find out, I guess."

Indeed, they would.

* * *

But they almost didn't. Eleanora stood at the front of the lecture room, listening to the restless shuffle of desks, looking over the sea of campers alertly. "A minute or two longer," she said briskly. "While the stragglers trail in." She pulled at the light laced cuffs of her jacket and took a step or two to the side of the blackboard. Even in the heat of summer and at camp, she still dressed as she had that first day, coming from tea and a musical recital. She moved with a gliding grace that made him think of dancing, somehow. Once again, even though Jason was sitting now, she looked taller than he was. He blinked in thought.

The lecture room door burst open and Bailey came bolting in. She stopped just inside the threshold, as everyone turned to look, and her face turned red.

"Nice of you to join us, Miss Landau," Eleanora noted.

"I—I'm sorry." Bailey moved sideways, her gaze finding Jason and Trent. She found the empty desk chair next to Jason and sidled into it. Her golden-brown hair stuck every which way out of unmatched braids.

Under his breath, Jason whispered. "What happened?"

"They stole my brush and comb while I was at breakfast! You can't imagine. I turned the cottage upside down looking." Bailey tugged at one braid unhappily.

Eleanora cleared her throat. "All right, ladies and gentlemen, shall we begin? I want you to take notes, but I want them to be mental ones. I don't expect you to carry around scraps of paper with you your whole life to remember this class." She smiled.

"Most of you were asked to attend Camp Ravenwyng because of your writing skills. You showed creativity and imagination and a certain talent that caught the judges' eyes, whether you thought you had or not." Eleanora drew up a tall stool. "I am not here to turn you into English geeks, but I am here to teach you to appreciate the ability to know and use verbal and written language. There is power, you see, in naming things. A rose is a rose is a rose by any other name . . . but is it?"

"A tome is a dusty, musty old book and a tomb is a dusty

musty old burial plot, but both are very different. We are empowered by knowing the difference and the names that separate them. Anyone have any other examples they can think of?"

Bailey's hand shot into the air. "A lion who mews into the night is not the same as the lion who roars."

"Ah, but both are lions . . . or are they?" Eleanora smiled in response. She perched on her stool, bracing her feet on the crossbar. Her long skirt fell in graceful ripples about her legs. "A lion named a lion has no other voice but a roar, wouldn't you say? Just as a kitten must mew because that is what a kitten does."

She tapped the blackboard. "More power in names. An emperor, a king, and a president. Each rules in quite a different way, wouldn't you say? Each evokes a different response: the time, place and the manner in which they ruled, even though all are indisputably rulers."

From behind him somewhere, Stefan snickered lowly. "*X-Men* rule."

Eleanora lifted her gaze as if she had heard it, but she did not remark on it. Instead she turned around, picking up a piece of chalk, and moving off the stool. "Now. If a name has power, then a spoken name has even more. You can think Rose to yourself all you want, but until you name it aloud, its only power resides with yourself. Are you following?"

Trent put his hand up. "What if you're wrong? I mean . . . you can't call a wren a Phoenix. It doesn't work that way. One's a small bird, the other a legendary creature who is reborn through fire. The wren's in trouble if you think it's a Phoenix."

Laughter ran through the room. Eleanora smiled. "That's Crowfeather's class! Hopefully, he'll have taught you the difference. In this day and age there aren't many things which have not already been recognized and named by someone, unless you're into computer sciences. But you're right, Trent. The talent lies in recognition of the object's qualities and abilities. You have an obligation to think about it before you Name something." She paused. "I want you all to think on that. You'll realize its importance shortly."

"For now though, I am going to talk a bit about poetry. Why poetry? Because it celebrates the power of naming things for what they really are, and what they can mean to you."

Eleanora turned back around and for the next long time, she wrote about meter and beat and rhyming on the blackboard. They decided that nothing rhymed with orange, and that limericks were silly but fun, and that some poets were absolute geniuses. They made up more verses for Sousa's camp marching song and the hour fled as if it had wings.

Stefan showed, much to everyone's surprise, a talent at songwriting poetry. He still pushed his way out of the hall belligerently after giving Henry a wedgie, redheaded Rich tailing behind him muttering something about lunch and FireAnn's cooking.

"Hey!" Henry danced around for a moment or two, tugging his shorts and underwear back into the comfort zone. He sputtered one or two more times getting out the door.

Trent clapped him on the shoulder. "Just think, Henry. When you figure out what it is you're going to do to get even with Rich and Stefan, you get to Name it!"

"Hey," repeated Henry. He smiled slowly. "I will, won't I?" His smile spread as he left Lake Wannameecha Gathering Hall.

Outside, the brilliantly blue sky had become dotted with white-and-gray clouds. Jason could almost smell the incoming storm. Bailey tugged at one of her frazzled braids. "That was my grandmother's brush and comb set," she said. It looked as though a storm cloud had settled on her brow.

"How are you going to get it back?"

She shook her head bleakly. "With no idea who's been taking them, I can't complain or accuse or anything."

"Trap didn't work at all, huh?"

Bailey sighed.

"Tell you what. After Lights Out, Trent and I will come over and help set up a trap. You don't have time to wait on Guest Rules. Something else will be missing by dawn."

"You will? Really?"

Jason nodded. Trent looked away and he got the sense his friend disapproved. "You'll have to get rid of Jennifer somehow."

"Oh, she's got a counselor-in-training meeting, that's why she didn't make breakfast. Lights Out are an hour later for her."

"Great! We'll be there then."

A small smile replaced the unhappiness on Bailey's face. She waved.

Trent bumped shoulders with Jason as they trudged along the campground pathway. "That," he said quietly, "was dumb."

"Why?"

"It's after Lights Out."

"Well . . . it seemed the best time."

Trent rubbed his hand through his hair. "I know, I know."

"Don't you want to find out what's going on?"

"Yeah, but . . ." He shut his mouth.

"What?"

Trent shook his head. Something else was bothering him, but he said not another word, just pressed his lips together tightly. When Jason punched him lightly, saying, "You've got to help me think of something," he merely nodded.

After dinner, though, Trent seemed to loosen up. He dragged Jason with him into the kitchen and waited patiently for Fire-Ann to give her staff and the student assistants instructions on cleanup and preparation for the next day. She turned around, wiping her hands on her apron. The smell from the always-bubbling tall pot was next to heavenly. "Well, well. Waiting patiently. What can I do for you, gents?"

"We were wondering if you had some empty jars. Like . . . pickle jars or mayonnaise jars."

"Me? Lord love a duck. We've not been here long enough t' empty jars." She wrinkled her nose for a moment. "Tell you what. Have a look-see in the pantry, see if there's any under the bottom shelf." She pointed toward the storage area of the kitchen, an immense area nearly as big as the kitchen itself. As they entered it, Jason was awed by the size of the sugar and flour sacks, and containers of this, that, and the other.

"We must eat a lot."

"Are you kidding? Of course we do!"

They got down on their hands and knees, brushing aside empty battered old pots that had been stored there by FireAnn's staff when they brought in all her bright, new cooking pans. Behind them stood a row of dusty jars, with lids. Trent beamed. "Just what the doctor ordered!" He took three out, blowing the dust off.

Jason sneezed. Rubbing his nose, he asked, "Now what is this for, really?"

"Tonight. Later." Trent stood, carrying a jar in each hand. "You'll see."

Passing through the kitchen, he enthusiastically hefted his trophies for FireAnn to see. She smiled, tucking her wild hair back under her bandanna, and waved back.

Whatever it was, Jason hoped it wasn't supposed to be a surprise.

9

Glow in the Dark

"I T'S going to rain tomorrow."

"Feels like it." Jason looked at the sky, though it was dark. But clouds hid the stars and fleetingly covered the moon from time to time. The wind had come in, and the trees rustling around them sounded like high tide in the ocean. It was a noise both soothing and restless. He contemplated the velvet darkness. It rarely rained in the summers he was used to, and he wondered just where it was they were. In the low mountains, but not so low that the high wasn't just a bit thinner, and not so high that there weren't much higher mountains ringing the horizon. The crickets were singing loudly and quickly from the day's heat, but their noise began to slow as the evening cooled.

Trent gave him a jar. "We'll go down by the lake. I know where a patch of lightning bugs are."

Jason examined the jar lid. Trent had carefully poked a number of small airholes into it. "We're going to catch them?"

"Sure. Keep 'em for a day or two, and then let 'em go. They'll be fun to look at tomorrow. 'Sides. They're our alibi." He winked at Jason. "Come on, Bailey is probably chewing the end of her braid off!"

Quietly, they left Starwind. The cabin door forgot to squeak at all as they eased through it and left the porch from the side, rather than down the steps. He had already mapped out the way in his head, off the beaten path, and headed toward the far end of the lake where the girls' cottages were located. Like the boys' more rustic cabins, they were built in groups of twos and threes, resting among the curving paths that toured the lake. Thick forests shrouded the other side of the lake, and Crowfeather had promised them a kayak tour in a day or two, saying that the rest of the lakeshore was fairly rugged.

Trent trotted at Jason's heels as evergreen branches tugged on their sleeves. Lights from cabins along the way went out, one after another, leaving only the campground overheads on, and those by the lodges and the hall. The wispy white zigzag pattern of the flying lightning bugs could be seen more clearly in the dark. Like tiny stars hanging by the small coves and eddies of the lake, the bugs swung back and forth. Jason stopped to point out a gathering spot where the bugs seemed to move in hazy clouds. Trent stopped and watched, then nodded.

Jason heard a panting behind them. He turned on his heel and looked quickly . . . to see nothing. The camp lay in black shadows around them, except for faint patches of light that seemed far away. Yet he could almost smell the hot breath hanging on the air. He turned completely around, searching the night.

"What is it?"

"Do you hear something? Feel something?"

Trent paused, then shook his head. "Something wrong?"

Jason felt the back of his hand twitch. He swallowed tightly before managing, "Guess not." He hugged his jar to his rib cage.

There was a noise, which he did not recognize, and then he looked aside to see Trent unscrewing the jar lids on the two he held. "Let's get our jars filled before we get to Bailey's."

He nodded, and let Trent lead the way down to the backwash cove where the bugs seemed to have gathered. The hair at the back of his neck prickled as he felt, rather than heard, something trailing him through the darkness. He rubbed hard at his hand and felt the tenderness lying under the skin like a bruise. Only a thin welted line remained, but the pain underneath was like a warning to take the injury seriously, healed though it seemed to be.

They scooped the bugs out of the air on the fly. It was harder than it looked, but eventually they had four or five buzzing in each of their jars, soft flashes of light, captured. Trent kept his two jars after examining them, his hands filled with their glow through the glass walls. He stifled a yawn as he stowed his jars inside his windbreaker.

Jason watched the bugs crawl around inside their small prison. Up close, the faint green cast to their flashing was stronger. Watching them was like watching tiny fairies flitting back and forth. No wonder people believed in them once. "This won't hurt them, will it?"

"Nah. They'll be fine till we let them go tomorrow." Trent looked around. "Which way from here?"

Jason pointed. He backed away from the cove bank carefully, shoes slipping a little. Trent clambered after, branches bending from their passage through. They emerged on a side path, scratched and breathless, bugs humming noisily inside their jars. Stealthily, they approached Bailey's cottage. Built a little larger, with a porch that wrapped around, and a sloping roof, the cutout of a stretched-out cat, with its paws hanging down and curled about the door's threshold, was nailed overhead.

At their footfalls on the porch's edge, the door yanked open. Bailey peered out. "Jason? Trent?"

"That's us."

"Get in here!" She reached out, grabbing Jason's wrist and pulling him inside. Trent tumbled after. "It's almost Lights Out!"

"We won't take long," Jason said as Trent pushed a jar of lightning bugs at her.

"Hold this and don't drop it."

"Bugs?"

"Fireflies. Our alibis. So don't shake it, drop it, or put it down." Trent grinned and waved at Ting, who sat cross-legged on her bunk, reading yet another book. She smiled briefly and waved back.

Trent rubbed his hands together. "What do we have for bait?"

"Not much." Bailey sighed. "I've got a CD. Not that I want anyone to take it, it's my favorite. But my name is etched into it on the blank part." She opened the plastic case and showed them the faint spidery lettering. "It'll be easy to identify."

"All right, then. This is what we're going to do. . . ." Trent took the CD from her and told her about the trap as he and Jason quickly assembled it.

Bailey admired it when they were done. "Simple."

"Ought to make enough noise to catch anyone, if you're nearby. If you're not, they'll still be marked." The two boys stood and admired their little trap.

Bailey checked her watch. "It's past Lights Out!" She signaled Ting who made a face of disappointment as she set her book aside, and Bailey led them back to the cottage door. The cottage had two small nooks, and closets and a window seat. There were also two big chairs done in rose-hued, patterned upholstery to curl up in. Around the top of the walls just below the ceiling, was a bright wallpaper strip of cats and kittens, parading, sitting, curling, cleaning, and tumbling. She scooted them outside. "I'll let you know at breakfast what happened!"

Yawning, she closed the screen door on their heels and the cottage lights snapped off. Jason nearly slipped off the last porch step, his shoes still slick with lakeside mud and silt. Trent caught him as his ankle turned slightly. He bent to straighten his air splints and as he did, he caught the glint, the flash, of a green eye in the bushes behind the second cottage across the way, watching.

"We need to get back," he said tightly. He turned and fled across the campground.

Thunder rumbled across the dark sky. It was far away yet, like a low growling, and the lightning that had set it off was hidden behind the clouds and mountains. Trent leaped and ran after him, branches whipping around their bodies as the wind picked up. He did not stop to breathe till they were in front of their own cabin door, and then he doubled over, lungs aching. The fireflies in his jar rattled a bit angrily. He set them down on the rough wood of the porch. One of them glowed, and another answered.

Trent turned his jar around in his hands. "Makes you wonder, sometimes, how they came about doing it."

"Doing what?"

"Making light. I mean . . . did dinosaurs see fireflies, do you think? Or was it later . . . like woolly mammoths?" Trent leaned over and set his jar next to Jason's. The glass walls clicked against each other.

"Gentlemen," a voice said quietly from the porch's edge. "A little late for you, isn't it?"

Trent jumped in mid-yawn. Jason looked through the shifting shadows to see Gavan Rainwater leaning against the porch posts. He moved forward a little, to catch what moonlight managed to sneak out from behind the clouds.

"We're just going to bed now, sir," Jason answered.

Gavan glanced at their jars. "Out collecting?"

"I thought it would be fun," Trent said. "They don't have fireflies where he's from." He jerked a thumb toward Jason.

"No? This is a good area to study all kinds of wildlife and phenomena," the camp leader continued. He tapped his cane on the steps. "I suggest, however, that you hit the hay now. Plenty of time tomorrow to take on studies."

Jason listened to Trent drift off into regular deep breathing, almost a snore, as thunder rumbled dully from far away again. Too restless to sleep, he turned on his side. He didn't want to sleep, even if it was the only way he hoped to catch a glimpse, a memory of his father. All too often it was the cold tomb, and he couldn't bear that again, he couldn't.

After long, long moments, he thought he could hear steps outside, and the brush of a tree branch. He caught Tomaz Crowfeather's words from somewhere nearby, "You're right, Gavan, these are tracks here . . . circling. Fresh, too."

"Any idea what it is?"

"What I think it is, you don't want to know." There was a long pause during which Jason felt himself sink that much closer to sleep. "Not that I haven't seen them in a long while, but I was hoping it would be a longer time before I spotted any. Wolfjackal. Has to be."

A hiss of breath. "No. . . ."

"Gavan, I have not yet found a way to secure the entire campgrounds. A warding of that type takes more manpower than I have."

"Dark Hand . . ." Gavan muttered something before adding, "Do what you can. I won't have anyone at risk."

"I can put a few charm bags down, maybe throw it off the scent. I can't give you more than another day or two, even at that." A pause in Crowfeather's voice. Then, "You need to take care of matters. This is an undertaking greater than the handful we have here."

"I know. Believe me I know." Gavan sighed. "I'm up against a lot, Tomaz. The Council thinks we're too brash, this is too soon, and they won't throw their support in yet. They want to see what happens before they take a risk."

"Well, then. We'll just have to show them the potential, won't we?"

"Yes. Yes, we will."

He held his breath, waiting to hear if there were other words, but nothing came. Either they had moved away or lowered their voices so much he could not hear them any longer.

Wolfjackals. Jason's eyelids fluttered. He held his right hand over his left, palm down over the scar. *Gavan and Crowfeather knew what it was that had attacked him.*

The thought somehow comforted him. The danger was real. He had not been imagining things. He would not have to fight ghosts. In the morning, he would think of a way to deal with it. Maybe he could say something now.

10

Lightning in a Bottle

"THE Rain in Spain is Mainly a Pain . . ." Bailey recited. "But it does make mud," she added, as she turned away from the window.

"What's that got to do with anything?" Jon peered at her from his corner of the arts and crafts table, elbows resting on the newspapers spread from one end to the other. Big plastic bags of clay were thumped down in the center of every table in the great hall, and their voices seemed muffled. Every camper was here, swimming and boating lessons having been canceled, and although the rain had been interesting the first day or two, it wasn't at all now, nor did it cool the weather off. Each raindrop had been as hot as if there were teakettles in the clouds spitting them out.

"We'll be working with mud." She tossed her head, golden-brown ponytail flipping vigorously.

"Ceramics clay is not mud. Well, it is . . . but it's not."

"Indeed it isn't!" a brisk voice rang throughout the hall, and campers all over looked up from reading the cartoons which seemed to be the only thing printed on the many newspapers. A plump, apple-cheeked older woman swept into the hall, her silvery hair in many, many curls, wearing a paint-stained smock over an interminable set of clothes. Her dark eyes fairly sparked as she looked about and pulled a stool over to perch on, its wooden legs screeching against the floor. Jason blinked. She almost looked familiar, yet he hadn't met her . . . had he? He stared in fascination.

"This clay," and she thumped a heavy gray plastic bag with the back of her hand, "is much different. It's called Steve's white and it's . . ." she let out a mirthful chuckle, "highly sanitized and refined mud!" She, too, glanced out the windows at the drizzling sky. "You will find, if you study the histories of the world, that long ago empires rose and fell on the quality of their mud." She smiled. "It takes the finest mud in the world to make quality porcelain, for instance! Today is an excellent day to find out what you're made of . . . I mean, what you can make of clay." She smiled sweetly.

Stefan thumped on the bag of clay left on his table. He also smiled . . . slowly. "We're gonna get dirty."

"Only if you smear it all over yourselves." The woman added cheerfully, "My name is Freyah Goldbloom, Aunt Freyah to all of you. Not that I'm your aunt, but . . . well, it seems to suit me."

Jennifer put her slender hand up. At her nod, she asked, "Will we be throwing or just modeling? And will they be glazed and fired?"

"Aha! Someone who's done more than make mudpies. Believe it or not, there is a wheel and a kiln, but I haven't had a chance to inspect them to see what kind of shape they're in. No, I think this is a just dig in and do it session." Freyah's apple cheeks reddened even more. "Today, I think we'll stay with pinch pots and basic figurines, whatever you feel like doing." To demonstrate, she troweled out a handful of clay, rolling it between her palms until she had a thin snake, then coiled it into a pot. "Of course, if you come up with anything outstanding and want to have it fired, I will be happy to set it aside for you." Her hands manipulated, pulled and pinched until she finished forming her pot.

But not just any pot. As Jason watched, she gave it ears for handles and then sculpted a cow's head and muzzle for a pouring spout. "A creamer," she said, as she finally finished.

Ting, Bailey, and Jennifer applauded. Jon considered the item in faint bemusement as she then proceeded around the tables, troweling out clay and dropping it in lumps on the papers in front of them. Jason dug in. Cool, pasty, hardly wet. He worked it through his fingers to get a feel for it and an idea of what he wanted to do. Now the battered mugs and old jars partially filled with water also made sense, as he dipped a hand into one and got his clay a little moister, easier to work with. It squished wonderfully.

Trent immediately went to work, humming and drumming his fingers as he paused now and then to rework his artistry.

Aunt Freyah stopped by Jason's elbow. She watched as he worked a bit more water through the clay. "What are you working on, lad?"

"Nothing yet. Just trying to get a feel for it."

"It needs to be a bit dry, you know, to hold its shape . . . whatever shape that may be."

"Okay, no more water. I just wanted to . . . you know . . . feel it. All the way through. Not just shape the outside."

"Interesting," Freyah said, with a shake of her many silvery curls, and a pursing of her lips, and a blaze of her dark eyes. "Very interesting. I'll check back in later to see what you've come up with."

He nodded without looking as she moved away, his attention on the material in his hands. He wasn't quite sure what he was going to make as he hadn't had any idea, brilliant or stupid, pop into his head yet.

Across from him, Bailey already had a cunning mouse resting on the newspaper and she was busy adding a coiling tail.

Trent had made a reclining dragon of sorts. He looked up. "Hey, Bailey. Can my dragon devour your mouse as soon as I make his jaws bigger?"

Bailey made a snuffing noise. "I think not!" She turned her

newspaper about, pulling her creation closer to her, out of his reach.

All around him, campers worked busily. Stefan and Rich worked on a common project which looked to be some kind of low, sleek car, which even then he wouldn't have recognized, but Aunt Freyah had crooned, "Oooh, an automobile," as she'd passed them.

Henry worked on what looked to be a squat owl, with spectacles on its beak, although Jason wasn't really quite sure . . . it could be a bust of himself.

Ting made a teacup, with a clever handle.

And all over the room were a number of pinch pots, in various stages of being and uprightness (the clay seemed to have a tendency to sag).

He looked down at his clay, which seemed to be waiting patiently for him to decide what to make of it. From his observation of the sagging, and knowing how much water he'd added, he knew a stand-up piece was impossible. He flattened the clay in front of him, and after long moments, had a great seal or plate with the sculpture of a spread winged raven upon it, thinking of the creature which had awakened him one night, seemingly long ago.

"Know him, do you?" Freyah smiled at his elbow.

"It seems like it, but . . ." Jason shook his head. "It's a wild creature. How could I?"

"Perhaps that's why you made him flat. You know the one dimension."

Jason looked down, then into her apple-cheeked face. "Maybe," he agreed. He thought a moment. "Do I know you?"

She smiled. "I don't know . . . do you? Perhaps you know just the one dimension of me."

He shook his head, his face warming slightly. "I mean, I know I don't know you, but I feel like I should."

"Take a good look." Aunt Freyah watched him, her expression light, and he tried not to feel uncomfortable as he took a good look at her. Take away the faint wrinkles about the eyes and mouth. Make the eyes lighter. The hair with a soft and fluffy mind of its own . . . he blinked.

"Mrs. Cowling?"

"Why, of course! How could you miss it?" She clapped her hands together softly. "You must be one of the students my niece recommended! Sarah has quite an eye for a bright mind. How wonderful to meet you." She grasped Jason's hand warmly, her skin firm yet slightly gritty with clay not quite washed off.

"Then you are an Aunt Freyah." How could he have missed the apple-bright cheeks, the cheery smile? The more he stared now, the more obvious the resemblance was.

She beamed. "Well, of course, I am."

"Are you a teacher, too?"

"A developer of talent, we call it. Indeed. Sometime it skips a generation or two, but in my family, what's left of it, we appreciate discerning minds. I was very pleased when Sarah decided to follow in my footsteps." Chairs behind them scraped impatiently across the floor, and he became aware others were waiting.

Freyah clapped her hands. "Finish up, everyone. We can leave everything out for a few days to dry. It will be in what we call the greenware stage. Then, if the kiln is working, we'll get them glazed and fired, those of you who want to save your efforts." She laughed gently.

The sight of the clock caught his attention. He stared, his jaw dropping open. Two hours had gone by with hardly a notice. Outside, rain continued down, and now he heard it, pounding the rooftop continuously, and the sound of the dripping from the drainpipes of the building. Everyone filed out, heading to clean up and then to their cabins for letter writing, with the sky darkening over them.

He had gotten three postcards. Two from Joanna and the Dozer, from two different ports (the Dozer's card showed building cranes and skyscrapers in a faraway city) and a scribbled message of two or three lines each, and a third one from Colorado of the camp Alicia was in. It looked nice, although he thought Ravenwyng was probably prettier and much less crowded. He read them each, carefully, three times, in case he might have missed part of a message. They might have been sent to anyone, nothing particularly personal on any of them. Sam hadn't written yet, and Jason wondered how he liked soccer camp. If it were any more . . . normal . . . than this one. With a sigh, Jason tucked them inside his folder and backpack and dutifully sat down to write his grandmother who would pass on his words to his stepparents when they called, and a second letter to Alicia who at least had an address.

He wore his backpack to dinner so that he could drop the letters off at the office. Jennifer bumped into his shoulder as she was leaving, and his backpack shifted, letters and something else tumbling out. She bent to get it, blonde hair swinging about her shoulders and handed everything back but the pack which had fallen out, still in its colorful box.

"Tarot cards! Are they yours, Jason?"

He shrugged. "I guess."

She sat back down with her tray and pushed it aside. "Do you know how to use them?"

Bailey stared, hard, over Jennifer's shoulder. Dumbstruck, Jason just shook his head.

"Ah." She smiled slowly. "Mind if I open them? I'll read your fortune for you. There is the cutest little store in my mall, the New Cave, where they sell these. One of the ladies who works there taught me how to read them."

"No, ummm, go ahead." Jason shifted uncomfortably. Realizing how much Aunt Freyah reminded him of Mrs. Cowling also made him realize how much Jennifer reminded him of Alicia, tall and cool and always seeming to judge him a little.

Bailey rolled her eyes and then stubbornly stared back down at her dinner. Ting leaned forward on her elbows. She said quietly, "I use I-Ching sticks."

"Do you?" Jennifer shuffled the deck of oversized, colorful cards carefully. "You'll have to read for us sometime. Okay, Jason. Cut the cards and think of what it is you want to know." She selected a card and laid it on the table faceup. "This represents you. The cards I'll place around it will be the answers to your question."

He looked at the deck as she put it in a single stack, face-down, in front of him. He wanted to know . . . what he was doing here . . . what was going to happen to him. Did he have a family or not . . . what was he supposed to do about anything. Questions whirled through his mind.

Trent chewed in his ear. "Going to finish your potatoes?"

Without turning, he answered, "No, but that apple crisp is mine. Touch it—and you die."

Trent snorted.

Jason put his hands on the card, looking into Jennifer's pretty face. She smiled slightly. He cut the deck into three por-tions, and she gathered them up and prepared to deal the cards around in a pattern, the charm bracelet on her wrist giving a gentle chime as her hands moved. The first card . . . he gulped . . . as she snapped it over and said, "This covers you."

She frowned at the picture card of the High Priestess. "Se-crets," she said. "Mystery yet to be revealed."

She flipped another card over, placing it crosswise. "This covers you."

Trent sucked in his breath, choked, and coughed for a min-ute. Henry was so busy thumping Trent's back that Jason could study the card alone for a few moments. "The Nine of Swords." It showed a terrified man sitting up in his bed as if awakened by a nightmare or disaster, nine sharp swords hanging over his head.

"You know," said Jennifer, reaching for it, "we can do this some other time."

"No." Jason took a deep breath. "Go on."

"Of course go on," Jon put in smoothly. "The reading can't be done till all the cards are on the table. That may not be as bad as it looks."

"True." Her bracelet tinkled. "This crowns you." The Ace of Swords, a triumphant card, went down. Jennifer's face bright-ened. She quickly laid out the rest of the pattern and looked over it, frowning. In the position designated to reflect himself again, showed the Seven of Wands, a young man on a hilltop with a quarterstaff in his hand, fighting off others. She tapped it. "A fight for what you want, and it may seem the odds are against you, but you have the advantage."

"This is the most important card of the near future," she added, and turned the final one.

Jason's heart skipped a beat.

The Four of Swords.

"Cheerful card," cracked Trent. But he put his hand on Jason's shoulder and squeezed it.

Jason looked at a still figure lying atop a tomb. Three swords hung above him, one decorated the side of the coffin below. A stained-glass window in a corner of the card gave the scene a feeling of being in a church or mausoleum. He breathed in and out slowly, forcing nightmares from his mind. It was only a card. Only a card.

Henry squeaked out, "Jason's gonna die."

"No, no. This is not the Death card. Although . . ." Jennifer's voice trailed off. "Difficulties," she added.

Jonnard leaned over her shoulder then. "An interesting life of mystery and trial. And deception, perhaps. But this card," and he tapped the High Priestess again, almost at the beginning of the whole pattern. He looked at Jason, his own expression calm and quiet. "This card tells us that all that follows may be untrue, if She does not wish to reveal your future to you."

Jason managed to exhale, and Jennifer gave him a weak smile. "True. Very, very true." She picked up the cards and handed them back. "I think the cards decided to have a bit of fun with us."

Unconvinced, he put them back in their newly opened box and turned around to eat his apple crisp as everyone trailed off but Trent.

Trent watched him as he took a bite. "Just some paper and paint," he said.

"I know." Jason shrugged, still feeling eerie. "But weird."

"No kidding. Maybe you should check the deck later, see

if there's any good cards in it. Maybe you bought a defective deck."

Jason laughed in spite of himself. "I can always hope."

"Sure you can!"

Trent brightened up even more as Jason pushed the apple crisp his way, saying, "I don't feel like eating any more anyway." He watched his friend a few moments, thinking that the cards had shown him everything he knew—and nothing he didn't know, and nothing he understood. Jason sighed.

After dinner, he sneaked back into the Hall's crafts room, just to look at his raven again, wondering if he'd done as good a job as he remembered doing. He felt like he had to touch it, hold it in his hands. Firing, Freyah had explained to them, sometimes cracked a clay piece beyond repair or use. Golden light gleamed from the door, and he knew the room was not empty. He froze in the hallway, ready to head back in the other direction, not wanting to be found. He could see shadows of people moving about the room, hear voices.

"Take this one. Animal spirit. Bailey went right to it, without hesitation. She's got nimble fingers, that one, to go with her brashness. And this one? The teacup? Not only indicative of her cultural background, but of her understanding of herself as a kind of cup, waiting to be filled by life. Very Zen, don't you think?" Aunt Freyah's crisp, mirthful voice spilled over, as golden as the light filling the corridor.

Jason sidled a step or two sideways and froze when the floor creaked a bit.

"Any indication of what we really need? A Gatekeeper?" He knew that voice: Gavan Rainwater.

"Alas, not yet, but that talent is rare, as you know. And it doesn't always manifest itself early or easily."

Gavan sighed.

"Now, now!" exclaimed Freyah's chipper voice. "You can't give up, and you haven't even found the Iron Gate yet, so don't be putting the cart before the horse! Things will fall into place."

Gavan answered quietly, his voice sounding far away as if he had moved to the other end of the room. "We are short on time. There may be a mana storm headed this way. If it is mild, we can use it to aid us. If not. . . ." His words trailed off altogether.

"What about this one? A copy?" Eleanora sounded keenly interested in something.

"Oh, no, no. No, that is not a copy of the camp logo, at all. And, it's fairly well done. But even more interesting is how he went about it . . ." Freyah's voice dropped for a moment. He could not hear the rest of what she said, although he could hear it punctured by a questioning sound from someone who sounded like Dr. Patel as well. His ears burned as they talked about his work, his art, and his hand ached.

The hair went up on the back of his neck. What were they doing looking at the clay work like that? He felt as though he'd just been put under a microscope! It was too late to make something different from the clay, but he felt as if he had somehow shown his most secrets thoughts by what he'd made.

He crept away cautiously, his throat tight, until he made it to the rainy outside and stood in it for a moment, clearing his thoughts.

Bailey sat down and slumped over her tray, eyes weary and puffed. Without a word, she looked at them, and then shook her head. She trimmed the leather scrap she worked on, shaping it into a merit badge which could be embossed later to show Swimming or Archery or Herbs or any of the other classes they were attending. Trent looked very disappointed as he laid out some hide strips to weave a belt. The thief was still on the loose in the camp. Breakfast had been dreary and dull, the rain without letup.

Outside, it drummed on the ground and against the mess hall roof. It ran in gray rivulets down the windowpanes. Far off, thunder could still be heard, but that part of the storm never seemed to move any closer. They had run throughout yesterday dodging a downpour, and now it looked as though the drizzle would never end, although the rain itself was a summer rain and far from cool. Jason trimmed off the badge he had made and stamped, running his fingers over the raised emblem of a canoe. Rain or not, it was a neat idea to have them make their own merit badges.

Jennifer sat at the table, her long light blonde hair neatly combed and pinned back, with a notebook by the side of her crafts tray, pen clipped to it, and looked ready to take notes. She wouldn't quite meet Jason's smile. Ting also had a notebook by her tray, but it looked as though she had been writing a letter in it. In the upper right hand corner, she had sketched a bird from the look of it, although Jason tried not to stare. Letters were private, after all.

Maybe there would be some more coming in tomorrow. He'd just sent his second letter off to Sam.

Danno Alfaro came over from his table to sit next to Henry Squibb. Henry looked pale, the leather cutting shears dwarfing his plump, dimpled hand. Danno thumped him on the back. "Hey, no canoeing again. Wonder how they're going to keep us busy today."

Henry let out a groan. "I just want to go back to bed."

"That bad, huh?"

"Bad? I hardly slept." Henry lowered his voice slightly. "Waiting for the next prank." He said not another word but began picking pieces of leather as if trying to decide what to make. He had his choice of a pouch, a belt, or badges, but the mess in front of him hardly resembled any of them. His shoulders hunched as if waiting for Danno to make fun of him.

"Hey, at least you know who's after you and it's real. In my dreams, it's like the Dia de la Muerta . . . Day of the Dead." Danno shook his head slowly.

Jason shot him a glance. "What are you talking about?"

"Nothing." Danno shut his lips firmly. He glanced around as Gavan Rainwater, passing quietly between the tables, a coffee mug in his hand, slowed slightly and then went on by.

Then Danno only said quietly, "This place has secrets."

Jason felt his jaw drop and then carefully closed his mouth. Did Danno have nightmares like he did?

"What kind of secrets?" Ting asked.

Danno shrugged. "All kinds, you know?" They all looked at each other.

Henry, however, brightened a bit. He said softly, "If only there was something I could think of to get even."

"We'll get 'em. Don't you worry."

Trent shifted on the table bench next to Jason. He brought out his jar and set it on the table. The fireflies moved around the jar, glowing and dimming like lights being turned on and off. He grinned at Jason. "I think I'll make a bug badge." Outside, the skies got very dark.

"Lightning in a bottle," Jonnard said from behind them. He gestured at the glass jar, and they made a buzzing sound, like hornets. His voice seemed to echo.

The room darkened. The lights went off and came back on, fitfully, sputtering. Lightning struck outside, its light blazing off the lake surface, and thunder boom-CRACKED right overhead, the whole mess hall shaking. The lights went off to a flurry of screams. The fireflies made short, darting flights in their glass prison, their white-green spots the only illumination for a moment.

Gavan and Eleanora got to the front of the hall at the same time. "Everyone sit and stay quiet,"he said calmly. "We'll have power in just a moment." He glanced at Eleanora. "I think it's time." She took a deep breath and then nodded.

He tapped his wolfhead cane once, as if to steady himself. Then Gavan bowed his head, and lifted one hand slowly. As he raised his hand, the lights came up.

Trent leaned back. "Woah," he said softly, echoing the sounds of awe.

Gavan leaned back on his cane. "We have everyone here this morning?" His gaze swept the hall. "Because we believe the time has come to make an explanation. Because you're who you are, a number of you have noticed some odd occurrences around camp. And because you're who you are, there will be more. We had hoped to have more time for evaluations, but this has never been an exact science." He laughed then, and smiled.

"Ladies and gentlemen. You were all chosen to attend camp

because you showed us a certain talent, an aptitude. Like calls to like. We hope we recognized what we were shown."

The lights flickered again, and he frowned. This time he spat out a word, and if anyone doubted he was doing something to restore the power, all doubt fled. At his word, the lights blazed.

"How did you do that?" a shy voice asked from the second row of tables on the other side.

"Because I have the Will and Talent to do so."

Gavan rubbed the wolfhead on his cane in thought a moment, before looking up into the silence.

"What was once thought Lost forever is now known to merely have been Sleeping. This camp is intended to show you how to use your talent and develop it. To respect what you are and will become. Magick is alive in the world again, and you are its heirs. You can create it. Wield it. Welcome, ladies and gentlemen, to the world of Magickers."

Bailey's eyes went saucer big. Into a room of quiet, she dropped, "Wow. That is letting the cat out of the hat!"

Things that Go Bump
in the Night

ELEANORA drew herself straight, her gaze raking the mess hall. FireAnn had come out from the kitchen, and crossed her arms, wooden spoon still in her hand. Even though breakfast was long gone, and they were buried in leather crafts, she was busy getting ready for lunch. Gavan indicated them.

"All of us here are Magickers, in one way or another."

Eleanora added gently, but in a voice that carried to the far back corners of the room, "And because we once came from your world, we understand what you must be thinking now."

Stefan let out a rude sound, echoed by Rich.

She nodded in their direction. "Of course. I'd do the same in your place." She tugged at her flowing skirt, lifting the hem a bit. As the bottom of the skirt rose to expose her ankles, it also revealed another sight. Eleanora floated a good five inches above the floor, her shoes resting solidly on . . . nothing. As if to emphasize that, Gavan swung his cane under her.

Her face glowed faintly pink. "I don't like being short," she added softly.

Gavan snorted. "Waste of energy."

"It's my energy," Eleanora returned loftily. She looked back at them. "Even if you don't believe me now . . . you will." She stepped back with her usual grace, her shoes moving silently above the floor. She let her skirt fall back around her ankles. "Don't think we're going to hand you a magic wand and teach you to wave it. Magick doesn't come from a wand. Nothing is as simple as that."

"The first thing we need to teach you," Gavan said solemnly, "is how to stay alive. That may take a great deal of doing, seeing as how the enemy already knows we are here."

"Enemy?" echoed Jonnard.

"Of course," muttered Trent. "The balance. Where there is Light, there is Dark. Always." He leaned on his elbows, his fascinated attention on Rainwater and the others.

Gavan nodded toward Trent. "There is most definitely Dark. Although we didn't know it at first, and that is where our story begins." Gavan pulled up a kitchen stool and sat on it. Outside, the rain stopped, as though finally worn out. "Nearly three hundred years ago, Gregory the Gray met Antoine Brennard in combat over a disagreement on the basis of Magick. Because of that, all Magick was ripped out of the universe. It was not, then, a war of Good against Evil, although events afterward changed all of us. The shock of that incident killed many Magickers. Stunned others.

"Some of us were lucky to fall into a deep, deep sleep. Sheltered somewhere and miraculously left alone till we could awaken and find ourselves in a new world, a new century. Struggle to find ourselves at all." Gavan cleared his throat.

"Most of us who would awaken began to sometime in the last century. Because we are what we are, we found each other. Realized what had happened. Realized what we had won, and what we had lost. Decided on a course of action that, eventually, brought us to this day.

"Each and every one of you have exhibited enough Talent for us to decide you could use training and our help. We ask nothing for it. Most of us have spent the last decade or two finding other Magickers and working toward a day like today. The Circle increases; that is our only reward. Some of you here today, will fail to learn. It is not a failure to be someone of worth. Magick is fickle. In some of us, it can come and go unless we learn how to steady it and use it well.

"So. In the meantime, we ask that you spend your days here with an open mind, and a closed mouth. What we do must be secret. I've no desire to find myself in a lab somewhere being dissected to see what makes me tick or why Eleanora is on invisible stilts.

"Everyone take the hand of someone standing next to you. I want everyone in this room joined." His gaze swept across them, and Jason moved to take Bailey's hand on one side and Trent's on the other. Their hands felt as his did, a little dry and rather nervous. After a moment of stirring and commotion, they all fell quiet again.

"Repeat after me," Gavan commanded. His voice started quietly, and as they echoed his words, rose to a thunder on the last.

> *"By hand, by touch, by sight, by mind*
> *By heart, by soul, this vow does bind.*
> *Of this circle and magical ways*
> *Locked in my body, the secret stays.*
> *I so swear!"*

He smiled. "Now. There will be some of you tempted to test this binding. I recommend you don't. The disease tetanus was famous for its symptom of locked jaws, but in my time, not all those who had locked jaws had caught that dread disease. Some were merely oath-breakers."

Trent's hand shot up. Eleanora nodded to him.

"What about our parents? They're not part of the Circle."

"No, they're not." She brushed a long dark curl from her forehead as she frowned. "We need your silence this summer, while we can train you to know yourself and learn how to protect and deal with your families. They did send you here, knowing that this is a camp for the talented. How extraordinary . . ." She paused, with a slight smile. "It might be a real shock for them."

Gavan added, "Now, while we set up classes for tomorrow in the Gathering Hall, there is an afternoon movie, a mudbowl tug-of-war, and an early night so you can catch up on your sleep. Tomorrow our setup for phone conferences will be working and everyone has a call home coming. Also, we will be having a Talent Show that we are going to videotape and send to all the parents, since we are not having visits. Look for that on the schedule, so you can start practicing. As far as being a Magicker, you'll have lots of questions to ask, and we'll have some answers. But not all. Many answers are for you to find on your own."

The mudbowl tug-of-war was as messy as promised. But no one minded, for at the end of the free-for-all, the sky opened up again and drenched them all so thoroughly there was little mud left for the indoor showers to take care of. Bailey preened at being on the winning side, declaring she was "happy as a pig in mud."

Trent scratched his head. "I think she got that one right on the nose." He watched as Rich and Stefan thudded past, grumbling at poor calls and weak wrists. "Nothing like sore losers," he commented when they'd disappeared. He bent over to help coil up the immense rope with Jason.

"Going to the movie? I hear it's optional."

"I didn't catch the title, did you?"

Trent's eyes shone in glee. "It's one of Jim Carrey's, should be a scream."

Jason considered the idea of some gross-out slapstick comedy, then nodded. It stopped raining as they made their way to the long line at the showers.

"I think it's a still," Bailey said quietly, as she joined the two waiting for her at the back of the mess hall after dinner.

"What's a still?

"That bubbling pot FireAnn is always fussing over. And they're going to make magical elixirs from it. We couldn't possibly have known that before, but now we do."

"We do?" echoed Trent.

"A still?" Jason stared at her.

"Did you get mud in your ears? Both of you?" She put her finger to her lips as they ducked through the flaps and went outside. The moist air of the summer night hit them, and a firefly floated lazily past, a brief white zigzag lighting their way.

"A still," she said confidentially, "is a contraption people use to make their own liquor with."

"I've seen those. That's a cauldron. It doesn't look anything like a still. They've got tubes and distillers and all sorts of things wired together." Trent sounded openly doubtful.

Bailey shot them a look. "She's gotta start somewhere," she retorted. "Now that we know she's using Magick."

"Well . . . yeah . . . maybe. I still think she's making jam."

"For days? And days and days?" Bailey made a huffy noise.

Jason shrugged. When Joanna wanted good jam, she went to the gourmet food market. What did he know about making your own? Still, he did know that the back of the kitchen around the great stewpot smelled of berries and sugar. Spelled fruit something or other to him. He said as much.

"Don't be silly. Cook is up to something. She kept shooing me away. You don't fuss like that over some jelly."

"Did you try to get a spoon to taste or something?"

Bailey looked forward. "I did." She looked around.

"What happened?"

She made a funny face. "The spoon melted."

They spoke in unison. "It what?"

"Went all wobbly and then . . . nothing! Just flat disappeared in my hand. Started at the bottom and worked all the way up till I dropped it!" She waved her empty hand in the air and then frowned. "Maybe that's why Cook always uses wooden spoons."

"I," said Trent firmly, "don't want to eat anything that dissolves spoons."

Jason thought. "Maybe it's vanishing cream."

They stared at him a moment. Then Bailey grinned. "Cool! I'll have to check it out when she's done cooking it!"

From the great shadowy hills which loomed pitch-black in the summer night, something howled. It echoed down the mountaintops, cold and stark. All three of them stopped in their tracks.

Trent frowned, then rubbed his nose. "I've heard that before. Usually in the middle of night though."

Floating notes shivered through the air.

"It's a wolf."

He shook his head at Bailey. "They don't have wolves in this part of the States. It's just a coyote, like Tomaz Crowfeather talked about. Lonely, though . . . you should hear others. There should be a pack, you know?"

Jason had goose bumps on his arms. He swung them vigorously. "I'd just as soon not hear a pack all night. It's hard enough to sleep around here with all the noise."

Bailey stopped in her tracks and tilted her head to look at him. Trent bumped into her and caught himself, hanging off her shoulder. Both of them stared at him.

"I don't hear anything."

Trent muttered, "I sleep like a log."

Jason scratched his eyebrow. "But there's people coming and going all night. I mean . . . they try to be quiet, but—"

"They? You went out and checked it out, right?"

"Ummm . . . no."

"Jason!" Bailey stared in disbelief. "Maybe it's that thief who goes through our cabins."

He shifted his weight. He didn't want to admit he intended to, but not with them. "I know, I know. With curfew and all, I don't want to get in trouble. But I will."

"When? I want my stuff back."

"When I have a little bit better idea of what's going on here. I mean . . . Magickers and all . . ." He paused. "There's a lot to learn. It's all pretty amazing stuff."

"You can bet," Trent offered, "that we've only seen the tip of the iceberg. I bet there's all sorts of stuff they're hiding from us."

"Has to be. We're just not ready for most of it yet."

"But how much do they have to teach? Has to be tons, Jason."

Trent said softly, "You could probably spend your whole life learning to be a Magicker."

"Exactly. Now's the time to learn it. Once we go home . . . we're back in a world of mundanes. I don't know about you two, but I want to learn everything I can while I can!" Bailey looked from Jason's face to Trent's.

"You don't want to make any enemies, Bailey."

"Enemies schmenemies. Aren't you curious?"

Jason cleared his throat. "Very. But I don't want to get sent home either. Tell you what. I'll see what's happening tonight. And then we'll have a meeting and decide what to do."

"Sounds good to me," Trent said. He put his hand out. "Buddy shake."

They all piled their hands on his and gave a team shake with a grunting "Huh!"

More fireflies were gathering as they escorted Bailey to her cottage and then sprinted to their own as another lone howl drifted out of the northeastern mountains. On the way, Trent explained seriously to him about the increase of coyotes even in city areas. "Very smart," he finished, as they trotted inside. "Sometimes they trot through your block, and you don't even recognize them as coyotes."

The air reeked of fresh popped popcorn from Skybolt. Trent pointed and said, "Charge!" They took the porch by storm and as soon as they entered, Danno and Henry began pelting them with hot fluffy kernels. Trent dodged, laughing, but Jason stood and caught them, and stuffed the salty-buttery kernels into his mouth. He grinned. Jonnard sat at the chessboard, looking tall and calm, but his eyes were fixed on the game.

He sat on the bunk and grabbed Henry's back-scratcher. Gingerly and yet with a noise of utter contentment, he slid it inside his air splint and scratched away.

"When do you get rid of that, anyway?" Henry slid his bishop across the board, eliciting a howl from Jonnard, and looked back across the room.

Jon sputtered. "How did you—how could you—what—" He ran out of air. He glared down at the board.

"Next week, I hope," Jason answered Henry. "Feels pretty good, actually, even if I do itch. Sprain. Only been about three weeks."

"It's the heat," Danno commented. "Makes you itch." He scratched his torso as if in sympathy, his unruly thatch of dark brown head hair practically standing on end. He frowned at the chessboard and muttered. "Henry, you got him again."

"I know," said Henry. He grabbed a handful of popcorn and munched it confidently. "Give up?" He watched Jonnard.

Jonnard grunted, before adding, "Not yet."

"Never give up!" Trent said, throwing himself on Jonnard's bunk and digging out a stack of comic books from his backpack.

"Easy for you to say. He's only beaten me like a zillion times. It's my turn!"

"Everybody," Jon said quietly, "has to be good at something." No one else said anything. How could they argue with that? Jason watched Henry rub at his eyes. The sun had gone down, finally, it was late and they were all yawning by the time Jonnard heaved a sigh and pushed the chessboard back at Henry. "I give." Danno swept the fallen popcorn out with him as he sprinted to his own cabin down the lane.

Henry beamed sleepily as he gathered up his pieces into his felt-lined, folding chessboard case, packing everything away neatly before crawling into his bottom bunk in the corner. Jonnard raised an eyebrow and said, finally, "Well done."

Trent and Jason wandered back to Starwind.

Everyone but Jason was nearly sound asleep by then.

He lay down on his cot. Something skittered across the cabin rooftop, pausing now and then. Probably a squirrel, raccoons were heavier. Pine branches rustled as the wind picked up a little. He looked at the gnarled beam, not that far overhead from the top bunk, reminding him of his attic bedroom. Moonlight snaked in through each and every crack in the boards, just a dot here and there, light fanning across the wooden floor.

He took a deep breath, rolling onto his side. He should sleep.

If he could. But he wasn't sleepy. Everyone else already seemed deep in their dreams.

Something tapped on the roof. Jason sat up. Tap, tap. A crow? Then a branch cracked loudly as something or someone stepped on it. A muffled "oof," and then a smothered protest, then quick footsteps headed down the slope.

He swung his legs out and slid carefully out of the bunk, still clothed in shirt and long pants. He quickly shoved his feet into his sneakers before slipping out the cabin door. Jason clung to the shadows, letting his eyes get used to the night again. A sliver of moon hung over the sharp, jagged peaks to the northeast. With little moon out, the night was very dark with an immense field of stars, stars whose light was usually drowned out by city lights.

Then something bumped into him, yeowched faintly, and grabbed at him to keep from falling over. She clutched once she caught hold, and swayed. Jason squinted into Bailey's face.

"What are you doing out here?"

"Investigating." She yawned and wobbled in her tracks.

"You'll get us both caught!" He grabbed her elbow, steering her away from the cabin.

"I didn't think you'd do anything." Bailey rubbed at her freckled nose. "After all, it wasn't your stuff that got taken."

"You didn't think I had the guts."

"Well." She shrugged. "Guess I didn't." She yawned again, and he nearly joined her. "Aren't you the least bit sleepy?"

"No. Well, I wasn't." He pointed down the slope. "That's where they went."

"Who?"

"People. Unless raccoons giggle."

Bailey blinked at him. "I . . . don't think they do," she said slowly. She swayed in her tracks. Carefully she massaged her eyelids.

"Why don't you go back to bed?"

"And miss the fun?" She took a deep breath. " 'Sides, if we get caught, we can say you were escorting me to the bathrooms."

"You're around the end of the lake!"

Bailey rolled her eyes. "Come on! I'll be right behind you."

If only he'd realized that would be half the trouble.

Jason spotted the empty cabin down the hill, hidden in a small grove of evergreen, one window glowing yellow against the night. He started down, carefully picking his way in the dark.

A few pebbles rolled his way as Bailey stumbled and caught herself. He put his hand back to steady her. She bumped heavily into him. "Sorry," she said in his ear, then giggled.

He pointed at the window. "Someone's in there," he said. "If we can get close enough, maybe we can hear who."

"Good idea," Bailey whispered back. Her breath smelled faintly of peppermint toothpaste, sweet and clean.

Moving carefully, for the hill was steeper than it looked—or could be seen, in the nighttime—Jason led the way down. Pine needles went slick under his shoe soles. He slid a ways before catching himself. He could hear the soft murmur of voices.

"Is she almost done?" A man's voice, faintly familiar.

"I think so. We know it takes time." This one, soft, barely above a whisper. Jason could hardly hear it.

"We haven't much more time. We need to start weeding them out."

Jason swallowed hard at that. One of the answers they would find out on their own? Not everyone would make it through camp?

"Patience," said Eleanora quietly.

"I've no time for patience! The Council was happy finding Magickers one by one. They are not happy we're trying to train a camp full of them. You know that. The only reason we have their backing is the faint evidence that a Gate might be close." Gavan made an impatient sound. "Any findings in here? I don't like having a cold room like this, without reason."

"It's haunted," answered Eleanora faintly.

Someone snorted in derision.

Almost to the abandoned cabin now, he straightened and

prepared to take a step leading to the cabin's window. What were they looking for? What did they mean by a cold room?

A loud yawn rumbled behind him. Then a stumble. Then Bailey barreled into him like a huge snowball rolling down a mountain, sweeping him off his feet and crashing them both into the cabin.

Lights went on everywhere. Jason lay on his back, staring upward at white flashes.

"Well, well. Mr. Adrian. Miss Landau." Gavan leaned angrily over them. "Have you anything to say for yourselves?"

12

Thin Air

"AN explanation would be nice." Eleanora bent in as well. The bright light behind her head shone a little like a halo, but it would have to have been one for an avenging angel. She looked rather irate.

"Or even necessary," echoed Tomaz Crowfeather. The normally silent man leaned one shoulder against the edge of the cabin as Jason sat up. His blue-black hair glinted darker in the shadows, pulled back and tied at the back of his neck. He held a circle of turquoise beads in his hands and they went click-click-click as he fingered them. The silver disks on his watch glinted.

Jason cleared his throat. "We . . . ah . . . were . . . well, she had to get to the bathrooms."

Eleanora turned the flashlight in her hand toward Bailey. Bailey lay peacefully on the ground, softly snoring, eyes closed. "She appears to have forgotten that."

Jason stared. "She's . . . asleep!"

"Apparently."

"But . . . but . . ." He stood up, raining pine needles and dirt. Bailey stayed sprawled, blissfully dreaming. He pointed. "She wasn't asleep when—" His mouth snapped shut.

Eleanora looked at him, her eyes softening somewhat. "Everyone in camp is asleep, Jason, except for you."

He stared at the three of them. He did not drop his gaze until Gavan shifted. "And the three of us, too, it seems. Well. I cannot prove you a hero, nor can I prove you a fool." He gestured, and Tomaz knelt down and carefully picked up Bailey. "Follow Eleanora back to her cabin, and she'll tuck Bailey in. She won't be pleased in the morning to hear about another week's assignment on mess hall duty, but at least she'll have her friends with her."

Jason sighed, and nodded.

The two moved away as Rainwater stared down at him. "I can say this." Gavan moved next to Jason and looked into his eyes. "If you were meant to know, you'd have been invited to the meeting."

Jason's face went hot, even in the cool night air. He struggled back up the slope alone, his ankle a bit tender but not terribly sore, combing pine needles out of his hair with his fingers. By the time he got to the top of the slope and crawled into his own bunk, he was as sleepy as anyone in camp . . . and he probably snored louder.

Bailey dropped her breakfast tray next to Trent's and Jason's. "How did you sleep last night? I slept like a sack of bricks and woke up with my hair looking like a squirrel tried to nest in it!" She grinned as she grabbed a spoon and prepared to dig into her cold cereal.

Trent and Jason swapped looks. Her hair looked okay now, sleek and wet from the showers, and braided back neatly.

"I slept, uh, fine," Jason answered.

Trent took a moment to roll a pancake up and swallow it whole. "Never heard a thing." He speared another pancake to duplicate the feat.

"So when are you going to investigate?"

Jason's fork dropped with a clatter. He slapped his hand palm down, trapping it on the tabletop. He grabbed it up as snickers floated toward him, and Stefan could be heard saying something. Not what, but he didn't want to know. He could feel Stefan's cold eyes on the back of his neck.

Bailey elbowed him. "How'd you get yourself on duty with me? That's too cool. Now we can find out what Cook is doing in that stewpot for sure."

His jaw dropped. She didn't remember a thing about last night. And not only didn't she remember a thing, she didn't care about getting stuck with another week of mess duty.

"Not telling, huh? Some day, Jason Adrian, you're going to be too clever for your own good." She crunched down happily on raisin bran. "Trent, why don't you take next week, too? Cook likes volunteers, and it's not so bad, really."

Trent scratched his head. "Actually," he considered. "It could be fun."

"Great! I'll tell Cook. Now all we have to do is vote and see who gets to vanish first." Bailey grinned and dug seriously into her breakfast.

He could have used disappearing cream last night. The only question was—whom would he have used it on first?

Trent drummed his fingers on the tabletop as he demolished his stack of pancakes and began to work on a pile of crispy bacon strips. He dipped his chin now and then as if bobbing his head in time to a tune no one could hear. He looked up to see Jason watching him with a sideways look, and grinned. "I hate it when the voices in my head get louder than the music."

Jason laughed. He pulled his plate of what seemed to be nicely scrambled eggs with chopped bits of ham and French toast closer and dug in. Bailey finished her breakfast, took the tray off to the cleanup counter and came back with a glass of juice. "What's up today?"

"Arts and Crafts at ten. Lanyards again."

Trent cracked his knuckles. "Hey, don't knock lanyards. That's weaving. Probably for dexterity or something."

"Dexterity? Are you crazy?"

He shook his head at Bailey. "Think about it. Finger agility. Who knows what we need to cast spells and such? They didn't pass out any magic wands, you know."

"Cabin," Jason got out, still chewing and swallowing.

"Cabin?" Bailey arched her brow, staring at him.

"Cabin cleaning is first."

"Oh, yeah. Right."

All three of them sighed.

"It's not so bad," Bailey said finally. "I mean everyone pitches in."

"Maybe you'll find your stuff."

She considered that a moment then shook her head. "I didn't lose it. It just disappeared." She stood and finished her juice. "See you guys later. I might as well go get started."

Trent got a second stack of pancakes and sat down, rolling them and eating them like breadsticks, syrup and strawberry jam tucked inside.

"Where do you fit it?"

Trent laughed. "That's why I roll 'em up. Easier to stack 'em inside!" He licked at a dribble of jam. At last he pushed his tray away. "Ready?"

"Sort of. I want to look at Deadman's Cabin first."

Trent wiped his hands on a paper napkin, aimed, and made a basket into the trash can as they walked out the mess hall door. "How come?" he asked when they were outside and headed down the gravel path.

"Bailey and I went down to see it last night."

"You did?" Trent scrubbed one hand through his hair, spiking it up. "She didn't say a word. Keeps a good secret."

"I don't think she remembers."

"How could she not remember?"

"She fell asleep," Jason replied simply. He paused at the bottom of the path, which curved around through evergreens and snaked its way toward the empty cabin. Last night they'd come from above, and he swore he could see slide marks down through the carpet of old pine needles and leaves.

Trent kept a lookout while they approached the cabin and watched it for a moment or two, to see if any noise or movement came from inside. Then both boys dashed inside. For a moment, the total darkness blinded them, and then the thin ray coming in from the door was enough to see by.

Dusty, empty, not even a chair. Jason squinted.

"Nothing," said Trent.

"Not a thing," Jason agreed. "Except . . ." He took a deep breath. A faint aroma lingered on the air. It smelled faintly familiar.

Trent inhaled. "Cook's stewpot," he said.

"That's it! But why . . . ?" Jason took a step or two deeper into the cabin. His sneaker kicked something, and it clattered into the corner. A half-eaten spoon rocked in the corner, its silvery, jagged edges catching the light rays. He stared at the evidence.

Trent jerked. "I hear something outside."

He didn't want to be caught again. He'd have to think about this later. "Let's go!"

Later, hiking through the camp behind Sousa, picking up strays as they went, Bailey joined them, her face pink with frustration, muttering to Ting who also looked very unhappy. Their explanation, however, could not be heard over Sousa's spirited marching music.

The two boys could only wonder what had happened. They watched curiously, though, unable to figure out what the problem seemed to be. Sousa marched down the winding pathway, cornet in hand, trotting them across the grounds, then leading the campers out in a parade behind him as they wound through Ravenwyng's acres. Bailey bumped shoulders with them finally, still frowning, and muttered under Sousa's happy tooting, "Someone took my candy money this time."

"Your candy money?"

"A shoe full of quarters, in case we ever find civilization again. I had it in my old, stinky, swamp waders. Someone had to be desperate." She wrinkled her nose.

"No kidding!"

Trent dodged her elbow.

"How much did they get?"

"Close to three dollars. Not a fortune, but enough for a

handful of candy bars." She sighed. "I'm going to set a trap!" The cornet peeled again, and they trotted after the paraders. After working their way across a meadow of summer flowers, even Bailey seemed cheered, all of them following Sousa as if he were the Pied Piper. Trent fished around in his pocket and came up with a kazoo. He started a lively tune that had Bailey in red-faced giggles by the time they got to the craft tables by the small lake.

Although it was midmorning, the sun reflected hotly off the lake and the small breeze felt good as they scattered to their various tables. Gavan and Eleanora stood to one side, quietly talking. It looked as if a thousand diamonds had been scattered over the tabletops but there was an immense banner hanging from the old oak's branch. DO NOT TOUCH.

Trent glanced at Jason. "Looks like they mean business." He slipped his kazoo into a pocket and sat down.

Jason considered the crystals and quartzes shimmering in front of them. Bailey sat down across from them, uttering a small word of awe. Her dusting of freckles paled on her face. She put a finger out and a tiny arc of lightning zapped forth, snapping.

"Ow!" She yanked her hand back, pinking.

Eleanora's gaze swept the campers. "No touching," she said quietly.

No one else dared. Bailey sat for a moment with her finger in her mouth, as if burned, before sheepishly leaning back. Her eyes, though, stayed on the glittering objects.

Sousa gave a trumpeting flourish on his cornet, saluted Gavan, and marched off, his tailed coat swinging as he walked.

Gavan moved to the center of the craft area and waited. In just a moment, there was an absolute hush. "Ladies and gentlemen," he said. "Welcome to your first lesson as a Magicker."

Jason sat straight. A chill ran down the back of his spine.

"You've had fun these past few days as campers, but you all know now why you are here and I'm sure you're more than ready to learn. Today Eleanora and I will introduce to you what will become your closest friend and ally, your closest bond as a

Magicker . . . your crystal. The crystal you choose will probably not stay with you more than a few years as you grow, but most Magickers never entirely put theirs aside. It remains as a talisman to those first, exciting, hazardous years learning your crafts."

"We will lose some of you over the years as Magickers," he added solemnly. "There can be accidents in this world as in any other. I want you to take your time this afternoon, as we work with you. If your life does not depend on your crystal today . . . it *will*."

Eleanora began to walk between the tables. Not too far from them, Jonnard ran his fingers through his hair and commented, "No crystal is alike, just like fingerprints."

She looked sharply at him. "That is correct. So today, what we will do is something as simple and complex as picking out your crystal. Needless to say if, after study and observation, the crystal you reach for shocks you . . ."

Rich snickered, and Bailey blushed again.

Eleanora patted her on the shoulder. "It is not meant for you." She leaned down and whispered to Bailey, but not so quietly that Jason could not hear her say, "Don't worry, dear. Someone had to make the mistake of touching them. It just turned out to be you. I did the very same thing, way back when."

Bailey smiled gratefully as Eleanora floated down the aisle. She took a place just behind Jonnard although even standing she could scarcely be seen behind the tall, seated youth.

Gavan nodded at Eleanora. "All right, then. As you look at the crystals, I want you to consider each one. I suggest not making a choice unless it is clear to you that there is no other crystal that appeals as much to you. Stand up, Magickers, and begin your first lesson."

Trent rolled his eyes as he clambered to his feet. "Just what I need," he muttered to Jason. "Belted by a piece of rock."

"Hmmm?" Jason answered. He leaned over the table, intrigued by the walnut-sized gems. They all seemed to want his touch. How could he choose? And there wasn't just this table

. . . there were seven other tables. How could only one become his?

With a snort, Stefan scooped a rock off the ground and tossed it onto the table in front of him. "This one's for you, Jason." He looked at Rich, and their shoulders rocked in mirth, which they smothered as Gavan looked over at them, and said, "I suggest you find your own matches."

Still chortling, the redhead shrugged and reached for a pale yellow quartz across the table from him. There was a crackle, a pop, and a yell, followed by a dust cloud as Rich sat down abruptly. He shook his head, eyes round and blinking.

Gavan cleared his throat. "I also suggest you all take this a bit more seriously."

Trent slowly put his palm out over a pale blue stone. There was a rustling rather like the crackle of static electricity, and he pulled his hand back quickly. His brow knit in a expression of concentration.

Jason decided to look at all the tables before even thinking about a stone. Most looked as if they had just been chiseled out of their quarry or vein, not polished or even cleaned, but they were still beautiful. The edges were sharp or brittle. As he leaned over, he could see the shadowy hint of the planes inside, the facets that made them the kind of stones they were.

Bailey had evidently followed him. Her freckled arm darted past him, as he paused, and without hesitation she plucked a large amethyst from the table and cradled it triumphantly in the palm of her hand. He smiled at her as she threw him a wide, beaming grin.

"Well done," Eleanora murmured as she passed them by.

Bailey retreated to their table in the shadow and stood, turning the crystal over and over in her fingers. "Jason, look at this," she breathed in a voice full of soft wonder.

"I'm trying to find my own," he answered. He drifted farther away.

"But I can see inside . . ."

He found himself drawn to a rough quartz of nearly flawless clear beauty except for a rough vein of gold and dark blue chips.

He started to do as Trent had done, hold his hand over it to see if the warding energy inside would react to him. Inside, a cooling warmth drifted up.

Gavan was behind him. "Not," he began to say, but he was too late, as Jason picked up the quartz and a welcoming thrill went through his entire body. "That one," Gavan finished. Jason twisted around to look at him.

"Why?"

Gavan instead looked at Eleanora. "I thought we decided not to put that one out."

She looked back, a defiant expression on her face. "I agreed to no such thing."

Gavan met Jason's curious stare. "You may pick another if you wish. I will Unbond that."

"No." He shook his head quickly. "I like it."

"Yes, but . . ." Gavan paused. "I'll discuss it with you later."

"Come look at mine, Jason," called out Bailey persistently.

"Hold your horses." He took a moment to look at his crystal closely, turning it over and over on his palm. It was both a fine and rough object, beautiful and ugly.

Jason heard a muffled shriek. He turned back to Bailey impatiently, only to see thin air where she had stood. Thin air and a crystal hanging in it. Then it quivered and plunged to the ground. His jaw dropped, and he blurted, "Bailey's gone!"

Now You Tell Me

"THE absolute first rule of Magicking is never drop your crystal." Gavan sheathed his cane inside his short cape and then added briskly, "No one move."

Too late. Jason had already jumped the bench and scooped up the amethyst before the words left Rainwater's lips. The purple gem felt warm in his hand as its rich facets twinkled up at him. No wonder Bailey had picked it, he thought, cupping the crystal. As to what had happened to Bailey . . . he looked up as Gavan reached him and gently took the crystal from his hand.

With a shake of his head and a knotting of his brow, Rainwater rolled the object between his palms. The camp leader seemed to blink in and out of focus for a moment. Jason rubbed the corner of his eye and tried to fix Gavan firmly in his sight as Rainwater glanced toward Eleanora and shook his head, once. She paled.

"As you may note," Gavan said dryly. "The crystals can help you unlock any number of abilities. It is important, mortally important, not to attempt to do anything with them until you've been instructed how to handle them. Bailey is fine, that much I know. That is not always the case."

"What do you mean mortally important?" Rich leaned on his elbows, tossing his crystal up and down, up and down. A faint sneer curled one corner of his mouth. He seemed very unconcerned about what had happened. Jason felt a glower creeping over him.

"He means," Eleanora said, frowning, "your lives will depend on it." She moved quickly, sweeping the unchosen crystals into trays and setting them aside, covered. Although every move was briskly efficient, her usually bright eyes seemed shadowed with an expression of worry.

"It didn't zap me," Jason murmured, as he realized something. His hands itched vaguely in memory of holding Bailey's crystal.

"No, it wouldn't. It's been attuned to Bailey." Gavan turned the crystal over and over. Afternoon sunlight gleamed throughout the purple walls tumbling through his fingers. "It's imperative we find her as soon as possible."

"But . . . what happened?" asked Ting faintly.

"Miss Landau is gone," Eleanora said.

"D'oh," commented Rich. He nudged Stefan's thick shoulder.

"Once you have learned a bit," she returned smartly, "you will realize there is a world of possibilities that could have happened. This is the most dangerous time in any Magicker's life, the beginning, when you first learn how to handle yourself. It's when you make the most mistakes, of course . . . and when you are first hunted."

At her last words a hush fell over the campers. Jason looked at her pale face. He should put his own crystal in a pocket, he knew, or some place safer, but he felt better with it in his hand where he could grip it, feel it. Ridged edges pressed sharply into his fingers as he curled his fist tightly about the object.

"Hunted?" echoed Jon.

She nodded to him. "By those who can't understand or are jealous. And by those on the Dark side, whose nature it is . . . to hunt." She glanced at Gavan who stood very still, cupping the amethyst, and who looked back with a faint frown, and shook his head, again, very slightly. He pocketed the amethyst.

Ting stared with wide, dark eyes. She held her faintly pink crystal at her throat, and stared at the blank space where Bailey had vanished. A cold shiver ran through her slender figure.

Jason put one hand over the other, covering his mark, his own crystal still in his fingers. Who were the hunters? Of what and why? And was he now marked forever as prey? Was he hunted? He tried to hide a shudder, echoing Ting.

Jennifer moved over next to Ting and rested her hand on the girl's shoulder. "They'll find Bailey."

"Of course we will!" Eleanora nodded emphatically and added, "Because Gavan and I will be busy, I'm going to dismiss the class today, with homework. All of you were asked to bring a jeweler's glass or loupe to camp. I want you to take a look at your crystal with it and see if you can draw what you discover under the lens. There will be facets, angles, and chambers. Let's see what you can translate to paper, if you can, those of you who have studied geometry. Even more importantly, I want you to note the colors in your crystals and see if they have a feeling for you. Color is the result of light energy, and energy is what we Magickers draw on." Eleanora clapped her hands lightly.

"And most importantly, do not look too deeply into your crystals or try to enter them . . . or we will lose you as well. There will come a time for that, with training," Rainwater added tautly. Eleanora's slight form dipped for a moment as if she lost altitude suddenly, and she put a hand out to Gavan to steady herself. They exchanged a low word or two that Jason could not catch. She then inhaled very slowly. "This is not as serious as it looks. We'll have Bailey back by dinner."

Stefan snorted. "The question is . . . in how many pieces?"

Gavan shot the boy a hard look. Stefan and Rich backed into each other, suddenly silent, and milled around as if both were trying to leave quickly.

Trent shook Jason's shoulder as they trudged back to the cabin. "Bailey will be all right."

"You can't be sure of that. They aren't." He rubbed his hand again. "I wonder what happened. Do you think something took her?"

"I think they have some idea, but they're not going to tell us, at least not yet. They don't need anybody else disappearing. That thing still bothering you?"

"Yeah. It's sore, like a stone bruise or something." Jason rubbed his hand again.

"Just let me know whenever you decide to brush your teeth, so I know when you're foaming at the mouth for real."

"Great. Thanks."

His buddy grinned. "You're welcome." Trent tossed his crystal up and caught it. Jason had a glimpse of the opaque, frosted gem. The thought of losing touch with his own, at the moment, made him slightly queasy. He frowned and fidgeted.

"Aren't you afraid of dropping yours?"

"And vanishing like Bailey?" Trent scratched the corner of his eyebrow. "Nope. At least not yet. I can hardly wait to get a closer look at it though. My dad had fits trying to find one of those jeweler's glasses. What about you?"

"My stepmom is very organized. If she doesn't know anything about something, she knows how to find someone who does. She bought me a very nice one."

"Wait a minute. You've got a stepfather . . . and a stepmother?"

"Yup."

"Okay, I don't get it."

Jason brushed his hair from his eyes. "It's complicated. First . . . my mom died. A long time ago, I don't really remember her. For a while it was just my dad and me. My aunt helped, then she married and moved away, and my dad got married to Joanna. Then he—" Jason's throat tightened, and he looked away, across the twisting trails of the camp and to the brief, blue glimpse of the lake. "Then he died. So I just had Joanna." He took a breath. "Then she married William McIntire, or the Dozer, as a lot of people call him."

"Wow," said Trent. His friend looked at him. "Here I am bunking with you, and I had no idea how twisted you are.

You've got a lot of potential to be really screwed up. You could get away with a lot."

That made Jason laugh in spite of himself. As they pushed inside their cabin and threw open the shutters to let the light flood in, and the fresh afternoon air stirred through the pools of heat inside, he said, "What do you think happened to Bailey? Seriously."

"No way of knowing."

"*They* know."

"Well." Trent pulled his chair up. "They probably have some ideas, but if they absolutely knew . . . they'd have gotten her back already. They're probably figuring out how to track her." He opened his backpack, rifling through it, before getting out pencil and paper and his small, closed-up magnifying glass made especially for gems.

"Track her? I don't like it. Anything could have happened to her. Stuck in her crystal like a genie in a bottle?"

"Sure. Don't you think Magick leaves some kind of trail? Maybe an aura. Something. I bet they're in conference right now, mulling it over."

"Maybe." Feeling a little better, Jason stared out the screen door. He tried to imagine a comet tail of sparkling motes left behind Bailey as she vanished. What convoluted saying of astonishment would be trailing after her? Across the way, Danno and Henry tumbled into Skybolt, with Jon trudging up the steps after them, in his older, more dignified way. A moment later he came bolting down the steps, pillows flying through the air after him. He laughed once, then straightened and shook his fist at the cabin. "Don't you have any place to go!" Fits of giggles welcomed him as he gathered up the pillows with the dignity of being older, and went back inside.

Jason's air splints felt hot and heavy on his leg. Reaching down, he let the air out and then unfastened them, putting them aside on the tabletop while he laid his crystal down on a piece of crisp, white paper. His own jeweler's loupe was folded up in a neat, black leather case. It was almost like opening up a Swiss army knife, bringing out the tear-drop shaped lenses. He set his crystal down and looked at it with his own eye first. It was a stone of flawed beauty, but the flaws themselves were intriguing and beautiful. The bands divided a third of the stone into a chamber which had a quartz texture all its own. The most serious flaw, though, was cold and hard granite, nearly shearing the stone in two. It wasn't supposed to have been out on the table, yet it had called him. What did that mean?

Across from him, Trent hummed as he looked his frosted stone over, tumbling it between his fingertips. Again, for a slight moment, Jason felt horribly queasy at the movement, then looked away and gripped his pencil. What did Trent feel trying to look into the foggy depths of the rock he'd chosen? What had Bailey felt? What *had* happened to Bailey? He frowned at his crystal. The sooner he had some understanding of it, the sooner he might have a hint. He wished he had not let Gavan take the amethyst . . . surely there was something there which could tell him what she had done, or had had done to her. This was going to take some time. The cabin creaked slightly, wood against wood, as the afternoon wind began to pick up.

Something tickled the back of his ear, and he scrubbed at it, scratching the itch. After a moment or two, the other ear tingled, and he brushed at it. Trent looked up as the table wobbled.

"Problem?"

"I'm worried about Bailey. And there's a gnat or something in here."

"I'm worried, too. As soon as it gets dark, I figure we need to find her crystal and look at it. I mean, they're not telling us everything, and we might know more than they do anyway."

Jason grinned at Trent, pleased to have found a coconspirator. "Great. We'll plan later."

Trent's face split in a lopsided smile. "I'm always scheming." With a laugh, he brought his jeweler's loupe back up to his eye and peered through the magnifying lenses at his quartz. "Pretty rocks, you know? Easier to carry about than a crystal ball."

Jason ran his finger over the bands. "Gavan didn't want me to get this one, did you notice?"

"I saw that." Trent stood up and came over, peering over Jason's shoulder. "That almost looks like a crystal melted into an agate or something, the way it's banded. I like it. It's neat looking."

"My dad used to say that it was a person's flaws that made them interesting." Jason shifted in his chair. "How do you suppose these are used . . . and for what?"

"I imagine they're just a focal point, for discipline or meditation or such. So you can concentrate on whatever and learn to harness it." Trent sat back down after twisting his chair around so he could face Jason.

"Why do you say that?"

He shrugged. "Well. Rocks in themselves can't be magical, or anybody could just pick one up and use it. I doubt they're batteries or channels. I mean, don't you think that what makes you a Magicker is inside you—not the crystal?"

"I haven't had much chance to think about it. It all hit so quick." Jason sat back in his chair. "It's like . . ." He paused to scratch at his ear tickle again. "It's like someone said to me, okay, you're everything you ever wanted to be, now—what are you going to do first? And there's so much to do; you can't decide what to do first . . . only there's a catch. You have to know how to do it." He hung his arm over the chair back. " 'Sides, I'm worried about Bailey right now. What about you?"

"Bailey worries me, too."

A slight breeze caught at Jason's sketch paper and began to waft it off the table. He grabbed at it, anchoring it down with his left forearm as he began sketching again. "No, what I mean is, what do you think?"

Trent didn't say anything for a long time. Jason looked up to see his friend sitting quietly, eyebrows knotted together. He put his pencil down. "You don't believe them."

"It's not that. Although, you've got to admit, it's a hard one to swallow. They could all be conning us. What better way to make a kid think he's special than to tell him he's Magick? Hey, you! Ever wanna be one of the X-Men? Darn right I do! But . . . do I want it to be real? Yeah. Every book I've ever read, every computer game I play . . . is something like this." He let out a soft sigh. "But is it real? I don't know yet, and I don't feel different."

"But you want it."

"Of course. Don't you?"

Jason looked at the back of his hand. The crescent there had healed into a thin, pale ridge. It still hurt if touched or bumped accidentally, and he thought of the snarling, green-eyed beast which had left it. "I'm not sure," he answered slowly. "I think there's a lot more to this than any of us can guess."

The bug that had been tickling decided to bite, in a quick, hot pinch. "Ow!" Jason leaped to his feet, swatting at the curve of his ear. He whirled around and saw nothing, but the hot sting of his ear told him *something* had definitely just taken a bite of him!

"Quit rocking the table!" Trent threw a colored pencil at him. Jason threw one of his splints back. In moments, the fight had carried out onto the pathway between the cottages with Henry and Danno joining in until Jon came out and threw a bucket of water on all of the participants, grumbling about a nap. Trent looked at Jason who looked at Henry who looked at Danno who promptly tackled Jonnard into the muddy puddle and in a few more moments, no one could tell anyone apart except for his height and general eye color in a mass of mud. Bailey would have loved the mock fight, providing them with teasing remarks and laughing at them.

There was no Bailey at dinnertime either. Nor at the camp-fire. Ting sat miserably, a handkerchief twisted in her fingers. She leaned close to Jason. "I miss her," the slender girl said quietly. "And to top it off, someone took my favorite watch."

"Trap didn't work?"

She shook her head at Trent, her long dark hair falling forward over her shoulder. "I can feel her. Can't you? I'm scared she's lost somewhere and can't get back."

Trent just shrugged. Jason held Ting's wrist for a moment, her skin soft but slightly cool to his touch. "We'll find her, and that's a promise." A log split open with a loud pop, sending a shower of orange sparks up into the night. When the Magickers gathered everyone and held hands to sing the Parting song, Jason was already planning what he wanted to do about his missing friend.

"You're sure," Trent said into his ear, "it's the red jello."

"No, I'm not sure . . . but you're still awake, right?" Jason paused in the darkened corridor of the Lake Wannameecha Gathering Hall, and he could all but feel Trent's hot breath down the back of his neck.

"Yeah."

Jason inched forward. This back way smelled of dust and old wax, and musty still air that hadn't stirred in a long time. It felt like the mummy wing of the great museum he'd loved when he was younger, when he still had a father who would take him, and still lived in a great city that had a huge, stuffy museum. The air tickled at his nose, and the fine hairs on his arms.

"This," remarked Trent quietly, "is dead."

Jason nodded. It did, indeed, feel lifeless, as though they had stepped into a huge mausoleum or tomb, though it was far different from the tomb that haunted his dreams. He inhaled. Their very presence ought to be enough to wake the Dead. He gritted his teeth. Something nudged at him, an insistent thought. Nothing could be this quiet . . . unless it were a trap. It could be Magick . . . it *had* to be Magick. He stopped in his tracks. "Don't breathe, Trent. Don't think. Be as . . . lifeless . . . as the Hall is."

Trent sucked in his breath. "Of course!" he answered in a low voice, as if Jason had discovered something basic, something primal. And so, quietly, scarcely breathing or thinking, they inched toward the doors to Gavan Rainwater's office. A tiny band of light fell upon them, and they froze in their tracks. Trent slipped to his knees as Jason leaned over Trent's shoulder, looking in, and he peered in as well.

Eleanora sat on the edge of a great, cluttered desk carved of dark gleaming oak. Her shoed feet dangled a long way from the floor. Gavan sat back in an immense leather chair, his face

creased, one hand rubbing his brow. The bright purple amethyst
filled his other hand.

"At least we know she is alive," Gavan said. He passed his
open hand over the crystal.

"It's almost as if she doesn't want to be found."

The two stared at each other. "Sometimes they forget . . ."
Gavan said slowly.

"Oh, no. No! Don't say that."

"Eleanora, she could wander lost until it's too late, you
know that. Once she's forgotten, we've little chance of getting
to her."

"Is she trapped . . . inside?"

"I can't tell. Damn me, but I can't tell!"

Eleanora leaned over and put her hand on Rainwater's knee.
"It's not your fault."

"It is. I should have warned them first. But the moment is
so wonderful . . . that first bonding, that first crystal . . . I didn't
want to cloud it for them."

"You didn't know."

He shook his head. "And I should have known! Gregory
would have known. . . ." Still clutching the crystal, he leaned
back heavily in the chair. "They'll begin to panic if we can't
rescue her soon. We'll lose some of them, they'll call home, we'll
have to let them go."

"FireAnn is ready with the Draft."

He shook his head, an expression of profound loss settling
on his features. "What a waste. What a dreadful, horrible
waste."

"We do what we can. Look at all the lives we've touched
here. Nearly fifty, Gavan! Fifty with the strength to be a Magicker in them. . . ."

He looked at her. "Not enough," he commented. "Not
enough for what needs to be done, not enough for what we all
face."

"You always were impatient," Eleanora said softly. "It's a
beginning. The toddler does not begin to walk without a first
step."

"Yes, well . . . we've had to fight for this step. If we stumble, the Council won't fund us for another session. We'll have to return to training one by one . . . and watching the Talented slip through our fingers or be lost to the Dark Hand. She must be frightened, and she's hiding. Hiding so well we can't find a trace of her. In the crystal or out." He sighed and rubbed his forehead, then paused as if listening. Gavan turned his head, staring toward the door. "Do you feel something?"

"Me? Yes, but my nerves have been jangled since we came through the pass!" She twisted around on the desk. "Who's there?" she called out sharply.

Gavan stood up quickly.

But Jason had already pulled back, retreating, hauling Trent behind him. He did not dare even breathe until they were in the normal areas of the Hall. They both gasped for breath, dodged out the side door and into the shadows. Even at that, Jason thought he could hear something moving with them, breathing, and pacing their steps.

They moved slowly, so as not to frighten the crickets into silence or fall over a branch. Back at the cabin, lights having been long turned out all over the camp, they dropped their clothes on the floor and slipped into their bunks. Jason let out a sigh of relief that they had not been short sheeted . . . yet.

He could hear the rustle of Trent settling into his blankets. "What now?" he asked.

"Sleep. See what the morning brings."

If it did not bring Bailey, he would have to do something drastic. Wherever she was, she shouldn't be there. And with every passing moment, it got more dangerous for her. If the Magickers themselves were worried, she should be terrified.

To Catch a Thief

THE brassy sound of Reveille woke them. Jason stretched in his tangled blankets, blinking sleepily at the cabin roof. He could hear Trent grunt as he pounded his pillow and tried to settle back in, but it was hopeless. Gray morning seeped in as did FireAnn's morning yell and pot clanging at those who had invaded her kitchen during the night. He grinned in spite of himself. If not scared away permanently after days of this, the varmints must almost certainly be half deaf by now!

It was Trent who got up first, then smothered a curse as he bumped the table in the near dark of the cabin. "Very funny," he muttered, swiping at the papers which covered the tabletop. "Who moved the table? And lookit this." Jason, throwing the shutters open to let what little light there was into the cabin, turned.

"What?"

"Spelling out SOS with my drawing papers! Funny guy." With a half smile, Trent swept up the papers and shuffled them into a short stack.

"What?" Jason stared at his friend.

"SOS. At least, that's what it looked like." Trent looked

back, and then in realization, added slowly, "You didn't do it, did you?" He stared at the wooden tabletop. "Maybe I didn't see it the way it was."

"Maybe you did." Jason reached for his clothes uneasily.

Trent snorted. "And maybe if we stand around here all morning, we'll miss hot water and then breakfast!" He grabbed a stack of clean clothes and began shoving them on before dashing out the door a length ahead of Jason. The mess hall was half-empty by the time they sat down at the tables to eat, their hair still wet and slicked down around their ears.

A fog lay over the surface of the lake, and low clouds made the day sullen, but it looked as if the sun would win through shortly. Trent dove in, eating as if he were starved, as usual. Jason stared at his tray. Everything had looked good when he'd chosen it, but he wasn't really all that hungry. The table at the other end was horribly, terribly empty. Not to mention ominously quiet. Someone tapped him on the shoulder. He swung around on the bench to where Henry sat, scraping his fork around his plate.

"What?"

Squibb looked up. "What what?" He squirmed halfway about, and pushed his glasses into place on the bridge of his nose.

"Thought you wanted something."

Henry shook his head. They must have bumped shoulders accidentally. "You're sure?"

Henry ran his hand through his fuzzy black hair, then brightened a little. "Well, actually, yes. I was supposed to tell you Jennifer and Ting already had breakfast and left."

"Is Ting still upset?"

Henry nodded sadly. "Not only with Bailey gone. She says there's a ghost in their cabin."

"Besides the thief?"

"A thief and a ghost? Ting couldn't sleep all night, they said." Henry's eyes got rounder. "Woof." He stood up, tray in hand. "Catch you later," he got out before hurrying off.

"You think there's both?" Trent asked, snapping a crisp

piece of bacon in two and devouring it. "Or one making enough noise for two?"

"I don't know. First of all . . . the thief has been going through our things, too. But not stealing anything . . . so why just steal from Kittencurl? I don't get it. And as far as a ghost goes . . . well, I think it's just nerves, but I don't blame her. I mean, Bailey just vanished. Where did she go? What happened?"

Trent waved his fork around. "Beam me up, Scotty?"

Jason elbowed him. Someone a table or two down snickered, as though they'd heard that also. He lowered his voice. "We already know there's a lot they haven't told us yet, and probably a lot they can't tell us. Not yet. And what if we went home, bragging about camp and why we're so special? They can't risk that."

"So they're gonna keep us here forever? Camp Brigadoon? We only wake up every hundred years?"

"No. Of course not. But . . . something."

"We'd cook our own gooses by talking. Someone, somewhere, would want to dissect us for sure. Or burn us at a stake."

"That won't shut everyone up, and you and I know it. So we learn, but we're in danger. In danger from what?"

"Ourselves? Other Magickers?"

Jason thought of the whispered comments about the Dark Hand. Someone or something worried Eleanora. Was it a good thing or bad thing they had all been gathered into one place at one time? "Could be both, Trent. Why would only the good guys survive, you know?"

Jason sat in thought a moment, pushed his French toast around, had a bite or two, then pushed his tray away. "I've got an appointment with Dr. Patel before I start classes."

Mouth full and munching away, Trent managed a nod.

Jason felt a little odd going into the back office area of Lake Wannameecha Hall, unable to detect the quiet heaviness they'd felt last night. Of course, a lot of things seemed different at night, but he was fairly certain they'd run into a warding or something magical. He was relieved the eerie and menacing atmosphere was gone this morning.

Anita Patel looked up with a smile as he leaned in the doorway and knocked, her dark hair smoothed into quiet wings about her small face, her sari and jacket in soft blues, tiny mirrors sewn on them reflecting slightly as she shifted her weight. "Ah, Jason! Come in. Right on time. How is that ankle feeling?" She patted the cushion next to her as he sat down. He swung his leg up on it, and she unfastened the splints, pulling down the cuff of his sock.

He watched as she probed the mottled flesh with gentle fingertips. The color had gone from purplish to greenish and now was mostly yellowish, and the bruised area was shrinking quickly. It didn't hurt at all.

"You're healing very well."

"Can I take 'em off?"

"I'd say so. Wear them only if you're hiking with Sousa or Jefferson, or maybe canoeing . . . use them when you're doing something really strenuous where you might need the support. Otherwise, I'd say, do your flex exercises, and you should be fine." She smiled. "About time?"

He nodded. "Seems forever. Only four weeks though."

"You heal quickly," the doctor and yoga teacher said quietly. "It is a good thing, and equally lucky you didn't tear a ligament or tendon. Nasty to repair, those are." Her almond eyes considered him. "Now, your hand please."

"My . . . hand?"

"Yes. I'd like to see how that scratch is healing." She paused, waiting.

Reluctantly, he laid his hand on the desktop. She raised a hairline-thin eyebrow, then gathered up his hand. "Healed," she remarked in a very doctorly voice, looking the thin white crescent-shaped scar over carefully. She probed it gently and although he managed not to hiss his breath inward, she must have felt him tighten. "Or is it?" She felt again, gently, and he winced. "Strange. It is still tender, no?"

He nodded.

"I would not worry for another few days. Then, if it still hurts . . . you may have a thorn or splinter from the bushes under there. I will get out my special glasses and take a look, all right?"

"Special glasses?" Lenses with Magick, he wondered?

She pulled open a desk drawer and tapped her goggles headgear. He remembered them, then. She smiled. "Gives me bug eyes!"

He let out a quick laugh in spite of his worry. Would she be sitting there laughing with him if she thought he was seriously wounded or infected? He tried not to think about it anymore. "Dr. Patel . . ."

She closed her desk again, still smiling slightly, and tilted her head, indicating she was listening to him.

"Did you become a doctor before you found out you were a Magicker?"

"That is quite a story, and one you should hear, but I think I will save it till some evening at the campfire, now that you all know what we share." A white envelope shifted on the desk slightly, skittering close to her hand, and she said, "Oh! Jason . . . would you mind taking this down to Ting at Kittencurl Cottage? She has a bit of a headache, and these are some pills for her."

He took the crisp envelope, felt two oblong pills bulging inside it. The phone rang, and with a nod to him, she picked it up. After listening a moment, she said, "Poison oak? Oh, that can be nasty. I know there's a big patch of it around here somewhere, I should ferret it out and mark it. The kids keep getting into it. FireAnn has cooked up a nice little ointment for that, though, which should take care of it in a jiffy." She waved at Jason who got to his feet and began to edge sideways out the door.

While she gave instructions for applying FireAnn's ointment, he ducked his head and left, wondering if that was what had been cooking in the great pot in the mess hall kitchen for days. If so, it had to be the best smelling medicine he'd ever sniffed! The envelope rattled in his fingers as he began to trot down the path toward the girls' side of the lake. The clouds had lifted some, leaving the air heavy and damp. Swimming later would feel good. For that matter, so would canoeing, with a splash or two.

"Jason! Hey! Wait up!" Jonnard's deep voice rang after him, and as he paused, the tall boy loped up.

"Trouble?"

"No. I just have something to take over to the other side for one of the counselors." He shook his envelope.

Jonnard nodded. "Someone not well?"

"Ting's upset over Bailey. Dr. Patel sent her something."

Jonnard nodded. "Let me know if I can do anything."

"Sure thing." He watched as Jason trotted on down the path, and stood there for a long time. The back of Jason's shoulder blades prickled for a moment with the knowledge he was being watched. When he reached the far end of the lake and looked back, the other had finally gone.

Ting opened the door very slowly. "Oh, Jason!" She let out a long breath.

"Dr. Patel sent you these." He passed the envelope through the crack in the screen door. "Are you okay?"

She wrinkled her nose. "No, and I'm worried sick about Bailey and . . . something is here." She stepped outside onto the porch, her dark hair swinging about her shoulders, and shivered despite the summer heat. "Well . . . it's not here now. It comes and goes."

"Anything else get stolen?"

"No."

"Look, I'm sorry our trap didn't work."

"Oh—it did. But there was no one there when I got up to check it!" Ting waved a thin hand in puzzlement. "Not a sight of anything. No doors closing, steps, nothing. Just the trap and tin cans scattered everywhere."

Jason beamed. "It worked? Cool. Cookies still there?"

"Gone," Ting said dramatically. "Not a crumb."

Jason blinked. "Gone?" he echoed.

She nodded, and then had to push a wing of raven-dark hair

from one eye. Behind them, the screen door banged in the slight breeze, and the Kittencurl sign thudded gently against the cottage. The porch itself creaked as if the wind could walk over it. Ting shivered. She looked back over her shoulder nervously, and her fingers crumpled the envelope he'd given her. "I keep hearing . . . noises," she said hesitantly. "I think the cottage is haunted."

"Can't be. Only place we've heard about is Dead Man's Cabin. Listen, I can't stay, but if you need anything, we'll help all we can, all right?"

Ting nodded slowly. Then she said, "I know you must think I'm foolish. I can't help it. Ghosts are part of my ancestry." She sighed.

"You're not foolish. We'll figure out something to do!" He waved, leaving her standing alone on the porch, hugging one thin arm about herself.

What he was going to do, he had no idea.

Scheduling at the camp kept him so busy, he almost gave up the idea of thinking. That evening, he plunked down beside Trent at the campfire, tired and yawning. He waved away a charred marshmallow and picked up a stick to toast one for himself.

Trent sneered as he said, "I like mine browned, not burned."

Eleanora was playing her dulcimer as everyone settled in. Then, in the back, Lucy, a stocky girl with brown hair bunched in stubborn pigtails, asked, "Why did Gregory and Brennard fight, anyway? Why did they ruin everything?"

She stilled her strings with the palm of her hand. "No one is quite sure, actually. No one was there but the two of them. It happened something like this. . . .

"Once upon a time, hundreds of years ago, when civilization was still rather young, two wizards met in a discussion over their beliefs: an old fool, and a young fool."

"Teacher and student," Trent blurted out. Then he twisted his hand on the knee of his jeans.

Eleanora turned to him, the firelight making her face glow as it played over her skin. "Yes," she said, nodding. "That is often the way of it, isn't it?" She smoothed her skirt again. "The young fool claimed Magick was finite. To demonstrate his belief to the master, he held up a pitcher of water and emptied it. 'When it is gone, it is gone!' he claimed triumphantly. His teacher took the pitcher from him and looked into it. 'Of course it is gone,' he said. He took his student by the hand and took him down to the riverside. 'Here is where it is. A pitcher cannot make water, it only holds it. But the seas, the rivers . . . are of water themselves, and make water as well as hold it. Although there may be a day when all rivers and oceans dry up, I do not think it will happen for thousands of years, no matter how many times we may dip our pitcher into it to refill it.' And the teacher stepped back, feeling very wise indeed."

Eleanora took a soft breath. "But the student said, 'Then you are still a fool, for if Magick were like water, then any fool could have it and use it!' And he left in a fury. He did not hear the old teacher saying after him, 'But not any fool can see those rivers or fashion a pitcher to carry the element we call Magick.' " Her face creased in a faint wrinkle. "That was not the first of their arguments, nor was it to be their last, but it was perhaps the argument that defined both. It had become clear that Magickers disagreed over the source and care of their ability, and two camps formed. Now, you must understand that the two had been good friends as well as teacher and pupil so the old fool was very hurt by the sudden turn of the other. He had long preached that care must be taken of Magicking for its consequences were not always readily seeable. He worried about Brennard's view of Magick and what it might lead to, and in the years to follow, what he heard worried him even more. Brennard and his followers had found a way to leech the Magick out of a person, draining them dry forever. The shock of it left many near death. And why do it? Could Brennard not find the ley lines? Could he not sense the mana which lay about for his use? True, the pockets and troves of mana were not always easily findable, but they *were* there. No need to steal and harm another! Gregory grew deeply troubled. As teacher, and generally regarded leader of the Magickers, it was his duty to stop misdoings. So he challenged Brennard to a duel."

A murmur of surprise ran through the campers. Eleanora waited till they quieted before continuing. "They met in a remote area so as not to harm others by their actions but—" She paused, then shook her head. "No, that is getting ahead of myself. Just remember what I said about . . . consequences."

She inhaled, lacing her fingers together and sliding them over one knee. "A great duel commenced. It became clear that all Brennard had been accused of, and more, was true. He attacked Gregory vigorously, first trying to weaken him enough to drain his Magick and then, when that failed, launched an all-out attack to kill him.

"Dark deeds and disdain were bad enough, but murderous intents shook Gregory down to his core, and soon he knew he was in a fight for his life . . . and the lives of all Magickers who opposed Brennard. Gregory, it is supposed, decided that it was kill or be killed, though killing was beyond his beliefs."

Someone let out a tiny gasp. Eleanora paused but did not stop talking. "Because he would not murder another, he did something more . . . interesting. He bonded himself to Brennard, bonded himself so closely that whatever Brennard did to Gregory returned on himself, hoping he could stop his pupil that way.

"But Brennard would not be slowed. He had a mission, you see, to keep Magick from being burned out and becoming extinct forever. He would take the fight to the end!" Eleanora inhaled deeply again, her face pale, her eyes very bright. "Then Brennard lashed out with all of his strength to fell Gregory, once and for all! With that blow, he destroyed the Magickers as we knew them."

A hush fell over the gathering, disturbed only by the snap and pop of a pine cone or two amongst the bonfire logs.

"The shock of that attack slew Gregory and sent Brennard into a deep, deep coma. Magickers all over felt the final attack. Some died of the echoes of that blow. Most fell into a coma themselves from the shock, and many died from that, their families unknowing of where they were or how to protect them. Some were thrown across time, those that were closest to both of the wizards. Whatever happened to them then, one thing has become clear now. Magick was lost for centuries. Only now is it being reclaimed, and the same two factions still argue about its properties. We do know this . . . there are those on both sides who will stop at nothing to prove themselves right, and the others wrong."

She paused, as Tomaz Crowfeather stepped forward to scatter the coals of the burned-down campfire. "Nothing," she repeated.

White as a Ghost

JASON woke at midnight. Shivering despite the summer heat, the camp quiet except for crickets and katydids, his blankets were knotted and thrown aside as if he'd been wrestling with them. He took a deep breath, then sat up. His pulse roared in his ears like high surf at the beach. He could not remember the dream this time. Only that he had fought it. Across the room, Trent breathed hard and moved about restlessly, but did not awaken.

Jason watched him briefly in the dim light. It looked as though Trent might be having nightmares as well, dreaming just like he did, but not remembering the next day. Or perhaps not fully dreaming the terror. Was there something about the other campers that kept them safe from what he had just gone through?

He rubbed sleep from his eyes, not willing to lie back down just yet. He stood up and went to the door, and opened it, just leaving the screen door shut. The porch creaked slightly. He put his nose to the screen to see out. Nothing could be seen in the moonlight-streaked night . . . or at least, nothing but the porch with its heavily shadowed corners. He heard a grunt.

Jason squinted through the cross-grained screen. Two
hunched-over figures passed, not on the walkway, but through
the fringe of trees and shrubbery bordering it. He couldn't see
their faces clearly, but he recognized the heavy-shouldered one
by the way he walked. What were they even doing up? Where
were Stefan and Rich going this time of night? They'd already
bypassed Squibb, their favorite target. Stefan seemed to be carrying something heavy, pressed against his chest.

"You're sure that's what this is?"

Rich laughed low. "You can't tell? I can smell it through the
wrapping paper. Soon as we get there, we'll look it over, but I
can tell you . . . my cousin sent me what he said he would!"

"You're going to need to hide this."

"Everyone around here is too nosy. I've got an idea anyway."

"How much farther?" A yawn muffled the rest of Stefan's
words.

They disappeared into the brush, but the crackle and heavy
breathing told Jason which way they were headed. He hesitated, then grabbed a pair of hiking shorts and shoved his feet
into his tennis shoes. He wanted to know what they were carrying about. What could be smelled through its wrapper? Food?
Candy, perhaps? The thought made his mouth water. He slipped
into the night after them.

Like grasping hands, shrubs and branches seemed to grab at
him as he wiggled past, hoping for silence. A twig snapped
under his foot, and he froze, but from the heavy breathing and
grunting of Stefan to Rich, he did not think they'd heard him.

But something else had. He heard a movement behind him.
Quiet. A soft panting. It stopped when he did. Jason looked
back over his shoulder uneasily. He saw nothing but shadows
and brush, and yet. . . .

Stefan and Rich trundled off again, in another direction, this
time with a wavering yellow beam in front of them. It barely
cut through the thickness of the night, but he knew where they
were heading, the old boathouse down by the landing in the
shallow end of the lake. He set off after them, not wanting to
be discovered, but knowing that if he were being trailed in turn,

he dared not stand around alone in the dark. Feeling jumpy, the hairs standing up on his arms, he trotted after the two, not so quietly as quickly now. He thought he could hear something trailing him even as he slowly caught up to the other two.

With a last pulse of their fading flashlight, the boys disappeared into the weathered boathouse. Jason glanced up at the overhead string of tiny white lights, barely enough to outline the building. He crept to the door that hung permanently ajar, its wood warped by many summers and winters near the lake. The light inside was pale and rippled as though underwater. He scrubbed at his eyes to see more clearly. Rich was tearing off string and paper, exposing the long, deep cardboard box.

"Wait," he said, his copper hair gleaming in the half-light. "Wait until you see these babies!" Paper crackled about his ankles as he dropped the box and leaned over it.

Stefan let his breath out in a long hiss. "Oh, man," he breathed. He hunched his heavy shoulders as he squatted down, broad face split in a wide grin.

Jason squinted, unable to see into the box. What was it they had?

Rich rummaged around and then brought up a string of tiny cylinders hooked together. Jason blinked. Firecrackers?

Rich grinned. "I'd like to set these babies off now . . . right under Rainwater! Snap, crackle, bang!" He gave a low laugh.

"Bottle rockets, fountains . . . and—*sweet*, cherry bombs!" Stefan sounded as if he could hug the box. "You've got a treasure here."

"One we need to hide."

Jason watched the two as they continued to paw through their booty until even he could smell the faint aroma of sulfur from the fireworks. The two he watched drew closer together and their voices became muffled as they discussed their plans. He leaned a bit more. He could almost . . . but not quite . . . hear.

Something spidery brushed against him. Jason spun around! He sucked his breath in as he looked—and saw nothing.

But something had been there. Maybe for the barest of moments. He breathed in slowly. Could he smell it, if it had been animal? Nothing but the vaguely sweet smell of the night-blooming flowers, and the crushed scent of the needles and greenery about him. He inhaled again, and pressed himself back to the building. Suddenly the door swung open.

Jason dropped. Chin buried in the dust, fighting to keep from sneezing, he lay on the ground as the door banged wide open in front of him. All he could see of Stefan and Rich were their battered shoes.

"That's agreed, then?"

"Best place to hide something is under their noses," Rich said smugly. "And no getting into it early. Either one of us sets 'em off early, we'll get caught. I've plans," he cautioned. "Big plans."

Jason watched them shuffle past. So did he. He got to his feet when they were just out of earshot and followed quickly. Something snatched at the pockets of his shorts as he brushed past a gnarled tree and he dropped his hand to shake off the branch, only to find nothing there. With a frown, Jason hurried to catch up.

With the strung lights growing ever more dim as if the night itself were trying to snuff them out, the three boys made their way back to Lake Wannameecha Hall, Jason only a few steps behind and still in hiding. He caught his breath as he saw them enter the hall near the rear offices. Should he warn them? Should he follow them in, knowing the wards that stood on guard duty?

After a long second, Jason ducked inside warily. He heard the crisp sound of paper and headed in that direction, rounding a corner nearly skidding into them, but he caught himself in time. Scarcely breathing, he plastered himself to the wall. The brown, paper-wrapped package crinkled again, echoed by a grunt.

"There," Rich whispered loud enough for Jason to catch. "In the emergency supplies. Unless there's an emergency, no one would even think of looking there."

"Good enough." Another grunt, then the creak of a door being shut stealthily. "I can hardly wait!"

"Me neither. Let's get out of here. This place is giving me the creeps."

Jason slipped down the hall and around another bend, into the shadows. He waited until they had gone before creeping out. With a quick look around, and the dread of the wards on him, he found the supply closet marked "emergency" and opened it slowly. The plain brown package had been shoved all the way into the back, on the bottom shelf. He crawled in on hands and knees, opening it carefully. Four strings of firecrackers lay among the goods. He eased one out, tucked it inside his shirt, closed the box up again, and crept back out.

Low words caught his attention. He hesitated, knowing that he could be caught at any moment. He dipped his fingers in his pocket, to stroke the crystal that had already become like a friend to him, and found his pocket empty. He caught his breath, then remembered he'd left it out to switch it to clean clothing in the morning. Another word, louder, and one he knew: Bailey.

That gave him little choice. He *had* to know who was talking about the missing girl. Pressing close to the wall, he edged closer and closer to the speakers until he could distinguish the voices beyond just vibrating tones: Tomaz, Eleanora, and Gavan.

". . . time is now the enemy."

Jason peeked through the office window. The blind had been drawn, but there was a tiny slit of light showing through. He put one eye to it, seeing Tomaz's sleeve, and part of Eleanora's worried face, and the restless wolfhead of Gavan's cane, moving up and down and back and forth like his teacher might tap a pencil nervously.

"I'm open to suggestions." Gavan sounded weary though his cane stayed active.

"I haven't any." Eleanora rested her chin in her hands. It seemed to be her desk she sat at, the chair behind her was plum velvet and winged slightly. It fit her. "With every moment, we lose hope of tracing her through the amethyst."

Tomaz said, "What if she does not wish to be found?"

Eleanora's face tilted up. "Don't even say such a thing."

"I would explain why we can't."

She shook her head. "Yes and no. The crystals are complicated . . ."

Gavan interrupted, saying, "That's why I asked your help, Tomaz. Because we're awakened, we know a bit more about the crystals. But you've spent your whole life as a Magicker, and you know this world—" He tapped his cane, "—better than we ever could."

"I think she's gone home," said Eleanora. "But she's afraid to show herself because she knows she hasn't got a good explanation. Bailey is sharp and Talented. And she loves her mother dearly. It's just the two of them."

"So, then. I need to go and coax her out, it looks like."

Eleanora said faintly, "If I'm right."

"And if you're not?"

Eleanora had held something in her hand. She laid her hand on the desk and slowly uncurled her fingers. The amethyst lay on her palm. Its brilliant purple color had begun to dull. She tried to speak, choked, and could not.

"If she's trapped in the crystal itself, Ellie, I'll bring her back. You know that." Gavan leaned into the tiny frame of Jason's view. He hugged Eleanora.

"But will it be in time?"

He shook his head. "We can't know that. All we know is if I go in there looking for her and she is *not* trapped within, with my strength, I could pull her in and she'd be even more lost."

Tomaz said mildly, "Perhaps we should have introduced the crystals later in the summer."

"No. No, if Magickers are to grow and learn how to protect themselves, they must learn their crystals. It comes before anything else." Eleanora sighed. "And there are other matters. Two. One, there is a thief about the camp. A petty, annoying thief."

"What?" The wolfhead cane was tossed in the air and caught by a tight-knuckled hand. "Why wasn't I told earlier?"

"Because virtually nothing has been stolen; things have just been rifled through . . . disturbed. Except for the Kittencurl and Rosebriar Cottages, which are on my side of the lake, right next to each other. Small personal items of little consequence were taken from each. The only thing of any real value was Ting's wristwatch, and it's an inexpensive one from what I understand."

"Of no importance, then." Gavan sounded impatient. "Set up a charm or two, the thief will be deterred."

Tomaz shifted, and for a moment, his denim-clad back hid Eleanora from view. "I differ on that."

"Why? We've worse problems to deal with."

"Maybe, maybe not. Personal items can be used to make fetishes and such. That is a magic in the world I come from. It is like stealing a bit of yourself, to turn against you." Tomaz moved again, and this time Jason could see Gavan, looking in Tomaz's direction, then biting his lip in thought.

"Interesting."

Eleanora echoed, "Very."

"Well, then. We can't have that." Gavan rubbed the bridge of his nose. "Can it wait until after you look for Bailey?"

"As long as the thief doesn't leave camp, sure." Tomaz nodded, his ponytail bobbing like liquid black smoke upon his back.

"All right. We'll deal with that, then. What else, Eleanora?"

"We've a Ghost."

The cane thumped the floor like a gunshot. "Now that, I will not allow. Not here, not now. We're working hard enough to shield them from the nightmares, and their own stray abuses of Talent. I will not tolerate a noncorporeal presence here, leeching on them before they're strong enough to know what they're dealing with!" Gavan leaped to his feet. "That, you and I can deal with."

"A Ritual?"

"A Ritual indeed. There will be nothing left of that Ghost when I'm through with him!" He tucked his cane under his arm. "Tomaz, come with me to my office. I'll give you the particulars on Bailey, and the sooner you leave the better." He kissed

Eleanora on the forehead. "I'll see you in the morning, and we'll have the Ghost done for by midnight tomorrow." Gavan began to stride toward the door and Jason.

He sprinted for the exit door of the Hall, and gulped for breath once outside. Now he had a hiding place of his own to find.

Ducking his head, Jason hurried back to the cabin. He ran with the strength of old, his ankle barely tender, swift and sure through the darkness. It felt good to stretch out, as though he had been cramped and contained for a long time. His footsteps fell in a quiet rhythm and he imagined himself a ghost, running unseen through the cooling summer air.

Fingers pinched at his sleeve. Jason twisted his head, swerving. Nothing but air around him, and evergreens with heavy-needled branches. He swerved again, with a cold shiver snaking down his spine. What was it? Was Ting right? Did a ghost indeed haunt this camp? A ghost powerful enough to worry Gavan and the others? He spun around and saw nothing, not a thing. He gasped for breath and stood very still, shivering.

Then, off to his left, toward the lake, he spied the gleaming reflection of a green eye. Jason inhaled, turned, and ran for his life. He gained his porch in one leap. His ankle gave a slight tweak as he fumbled at the latch and then shut the cabin door heavily behind him. He thought he heard and felt a thump as a heavy body hit the door after him. Panting, he dropped the latch bolt into place and waited to see if anything else could be heard.

A shuffling, dragging sound came across the porch. It stopped. Started. Stopped again. Rather like Jason's heartbeat. He took a deep breath, went to the nearest shuttered window, and opened it.

It did not notice as he looked out, a gray-and-silver possum, with two tiny babies clinging to her underbelly. She had part of an orange clutched in her front paw, and her crabbed movement across the porch was hampered by her treasure. He heaved a sigh of relief as he fastened the shutter back into position.

Trent stirred in his bed. Jason quickly pulled the string of crackers from his shirt, and tucked them between the mattress and platform. Depending on what Gavan and Eleanora did, his theft might be useless. Or it could be just what the doctor ordered.

He fell onto his bed and slipped into a long, dreamless sleep.

In the morning, Jefferson took over the canoeing class. He waded into the lake, his skin shining darkly in contrast to his white shirt and shorts, and picked Henry Squibb up by the scruff of the neck at least twice, righting the canoe and putting him back in. Then, with a splash and a laugh, Danno and Henry finally managed to paddle away from shore without capsizing. Trent grinned and led Jason in a circle with their canoe, the two of them paddling gracefully in tandem in their craft, while Henry and Danno, laughing, flailed about in theirs. At the last, Henry discovered he could splash with his oar, if not guide the canoe well, and everyone ended up as drenched as if they'd capsized, too.

Jefferson stood on the beach, his muscular arms folded across his chest, and smiled.

Then they had another Crystal Class.

Eleanora paused at the front of the tables. "First," she said, "I would like to talk to you about the care of your crystals and quartzes. We had selected a wide variety for you to choose from. Most are rock crystal, which gives you a nice arrangement of planes and facets to focus through. Like anything you use constantly, they can get dirty, oiled from coatings on your hands, and so on. We recommend using only plain water to clean them. Occasionally, water with sea salt. Nothing stronger or different. Your crystals can react with certain other liquids in some cases, or even be dissolved by them. Understood? Plain water, a soft cloth." Eleanora smiled.

Rich's hand shot up, and she nodded at him. "Can we be allergic to our crystals?"

"Not in this state, I believe. Are you having any reactions?"

He shook his head slowly, looking dubious.

"No welts or itching?"

Rich shook his head again.

"Then you're fine. Any other questions?"

Rich's hand shot up again. Eleanora looked at him again.

"Can they make you do things? Like, you know, have strange cravings?"

"Like chocolate, for example?"

Jason grinned as the girls all giggled. Rich squirmed. "Not like that, but—"

"Like what?"

"I don't know, but . . . what's to keep us from disappearing like Bailey did?"

"Common sense, I hope. We'll have Miss Landau in hand very shortly. In the meantime, nothing should go amiss."

Trent muttered out of the side of his mouth. "Little late for that. We've already got a miss missing."

Jason bit the inside of his mouth to keep from snorting and drowning out Eleanora's talk.

"My suggestion is that you copy down all the strange things you're worried about and make an appointment to meet with me in my office later."

Rich paled and shut his mouth tightly. He squirmed as if he wished to say more. Eleanora watched him silently with one eyebrow arched. Evidently deciding not to take the dare, he kept quiet.

"Now, then." She smiled brightly. "Today we're going to learn one of the fundamental benefits of having a crystal, one of its nicest functions." She held hers up, smiled, spoke a word, and a soft golden light flared out, visible even in the sunlit day.

Ting leaned forward on her elbows. "Wow," she said softly.

"You wouldn't be afraid of the dark," Jennifer said to her. She patted Ting's shoulder.

"How do you *do* that?" Trent breathed at Jason's shoulder. He had his crystal out, but his gaze was fixed intently on Eleanora, and he was rolling his stone through his fingers without noticing it.

The light spilled through the Magicker's fingers like a waterfall of gold, cool to the touch, Jason guessed, but glowing as warm as firelight. He looked at his crystal, wondering how she did it.

"Focus," Eleanora said. She moved her hand over her crystal, and the light went out. "Focus into your crystal, find the plane you feel most comfortable on . . . the facet you can see easiest and you can handle . . . and I want you to build a flame there. Think it, imagine it." She passed along the tables as Jason got his out and palmed it. "That's it, Jason." She raised her voice. "Hold your crystal to Focus on it. It's bonded to you and attuned to you. Setting it on a table or desk and looking at it will not activate it."

There was a stir all around as the others got out their crystals, digging into pockets everywhere. Henry dropped his with a dismayed squeak, bent over to pick it up, let out a howl when Stefan gave him a wedgie, danced around a bit getting his underwear unknotted, and dropped his crystal a second time. Finally, he stood somewhat quietly, round face very red, hair sticking up all over, and eyes blinking behind the round lenses of his spectacles. He cupped his crystal fiercely, moving to put Danno and Jon between him and the rest of the class.

Ting and Jennifer bumped shoulders, trying hard not to giggle, as they held their crystals, hands wiggling as they suppressed their laughter with a muffled snort. Ting's rock crystal held a pleasant pink tinge to it. Jason could not help but notice the two girls, their noses wrinkling in concentration as they stared. Jennifer's blonde hair swung forward, like a fine golden curtain, covering part of her face as she ducked her chin and looked down at her hand.

A pang went through him for the missing Bailey. Trent's comment aside, he fretted over the fact that the Magickers seemed to have no idea what had happened except that they seemed somewhat unconcerned in front of everyone but sounded worried when they thought they were unobserved. Crystals and *poofing* Magickers did not seem to be entirely unexpected though. Wishing he knew what they did, he stared down into his crystal and tried to keep to the subject at hand. Or, in his hand, as it was. Having an object that could light up like a flashlight, with no batteries needed, would be great, he had to admit.

The cool depths of his crystal seemed an unlikely place to hold fire or light, though. He tried to project a spark onto its surface, only to lose the glint over and over. Like a snowflake melting, it would fade before he could build it into a larger glow, even as he frowned and stared until he could feel a dull, throbbing headache pain between his brows. Pressure descended till he felt like he had an elephant standing on his head.

Looking away, Jason rubbed his eyes. Across from him, Ting's crystal hummed in a rosy glow, her face rapt as she stared at it. Jennifer's pale rock also glowed, with a strong, silvery light that rayed brightly across her hand. Ting's almond eyes widened slightly. "It's . . . getting warm . . ." she said, alarmed. Her hand jerked as though she might toss it, but before she could, a ker-RACK! split the air, and her crystal shattered into pieces. She let out a startled squeak.

Jennifer immediately grabbed her wrist. "Oh, Ting!" she said in dismay. "Your crystal."

Eleanora hurried over, saying, "Don't worry, these things happen. We can find you another—" and she stopped, staring at the pieces in Ting's hand. "Well," she said finally. "I've seen that before but not often." She stirred through the fragments with a gentle fingertip. "Usually they darken, and go lifeless. However, yours, Ting, still hold the light." She smiled. "Keep them, they might be useful someday. In the meantime, we've got to get you a replacement! Jennifer, why don't you snuff your lantern and take her to Master Rainwater's office in the Gathering Hall, and he'll pick out another." She looked around. "Is anyone else having success in getting their lantern focused? Don't be discouraged. It takes time."

Jon held his palm up, where his green citrine cast an eerie light green light over the table. She nodded at him, unsurprised.

Jason rubbed his nose, hard, where an itch seemed to be succeeding far more than his concentration on his crystal. He scrubbed it again, to keep the itch from coming back, and stared down at his crystal. A little twinkle flared and flickered about, almost like a fairy light. Like a small spark in a heavy wind, it threatened to go out. He cupped his hands about the crystal, sheltering it, willing it to just *be. Stay . . . stay!*

Danno, at his back, let out a startled exclamation, "Madre de Dios!" and Henry Squibb gave an excited yelp.

Jason whirled around just in time to see Henry's crystal flare like a nova with light and then shoot into skyrocketing flames! He leaped onto one foot, howling, then dropped his crystal into the dust. The light immediately went out but it took all three of them—Jon, Danno, and Henry—to kick dust over the flames and put the crystal out.

Eleanora stood in puzzlement a moment, her face white. "Now that," she said, "is something I've never seen." She went to Henry and took his hands. "Are you burned?"

"I . . . I . . . don't think so." Henry shook all over, then straightened. "Well, maybe a little."

She nodded, looking over his reddened palm. "Not badly, but I still think you should see Dr. Patel. Off with you . . ." She paused as Henry trotted off a few steps. "Henry."

"Yes'm?" He turned around, blinking owlishly through his glasses.

"Your crystal, Henry."

He took a deep breath and came back to a dirty lump. "What if it . . . what if it . . . ?"

"You are its master, Henry, not the other way around."

He nodded, and picked it up, dusting it off. Not a singe on it. With a half-smile of relief, he pocketed it, then turned again to trot down to Dr. Patel's quarters.

She let them Focus for another ten or fifteen minutes before holding her hands up, saying, "I think that's enough for today, class. You may have some headaches and crossed eyes from the concentration, that's normal. A nice walk in the brisk air should take care of that! Good work, everyone."

Nobody else had gotten his or her crystal firmly glowing yet, although Jason felt he was very close. Eleanora paused by the end of their table. "How did you do, Trent?"

He shrugged. "Not very well. I mean, it got clearer on me, more transparent, but that's about it."

"Interesting. Actually, with that stone, it's quite a bit. It's . . ." she paused. "It's stubborn."

"Good! 'Cause I am, too."

She nodded, and then her gaze fell on Jason. "Jason, you look unhappy."

"It just kept slipping away." He flexed his hands, surprisingly tense and tight after cradling his crystal.

"It'll come. It shouldn't be easy, making cold fire, don't you think?" She smiled slightly, then glided past to the next group of students.

"Nothing," whispered Trent in Jason's ear as they hurried for break and to make it to FireAnne's herbal class, "is easy about this."

Jason nodded, matching strides with Trent's lope. The only great thing about the afternoon was knowing that Bailey, at least, hadn't disappeared in an eruption of flame!

At dinnertime, Ting came late, and slid into line between Jason and Trent, a worried look on her face.

"What's wrong?" Jason said softly.

"Something very strange," she whispered back. "Our thief left a note. Or, at least, I think he did."

"What?"

"Cookie crumbs. I stumbled over them, but . . . but I'd swear they spelled out 'Help me'."

Trent coughed. "A thief who asks for help?"

She nodded. "I know it sounds weird."

"Why not a pen and ink?"

Ting shrugged. "I don't know. I don't even know if . . . if the crumbs really spelled anything out. It just looked like it to me."

"Can you show us after dinner?"

With a faint blush, Ting shook her head. "Gone. Something ate them. It was while you guys were at canoeing, and I came to get you, but you were out on the lake. By the time I got back to Kittencurl, everything was gone."

Jason let out a sigh of regret.

Trent shuffled ahead in line and waited till they caught up before remarking. "There are people like that, you know. People who can't keep from stealing. Maybe it's someone like that."

"And that's why they asked for help?" Ting looked at him, doubt in her almond eyes.

"Won't know till we catch him, will we? But it's something to think about."

"Well . . . I set the trap again. I added a few more tin cans. We ought to catch *something*," Ting vowed. "Only I'd rather you guys were there when it happened."

"What about Jennifer?"

"She's got another counselor meeting tonight." Ting looked around then ducked her head, her voice getting even more quiet. "I took a look at her notes. She's getting advanced Magick training in those sessions, too."

"Oh, really?"

"That's what it looked like."

Trent looked almost as interested as Jason felt. The corner of his mouth went up. "I'll ask Henry about Jonnard. Squibb couldn't keep a secret if his life depended on it." As Jason and Ting laughed, Trent found himself at the head of the serving line and boldly went to pile up food on his plate.

Ting shook her head. "I don't know how he does it," she murmured to Jason. "He eats so much!"

"He's got one of those bodies that burns it up. He doesn't even lie still at night," he told her.

She nodded before stepping forward herself to get plate, utensils, and napkins.

Jason got some carrot and raisin salad and regular green salad before stopping in line and looking at a great tray of Mulligatawny. It looked like nothing he'd ever seen before, its aroma intriguing and spicy. He stared at the dinner selection in fascination while, ahead of him, Ting swerved past it to get some spaghetti which looked ordinary compared to the fragrant dish. Trent beckoned to him.

"Get some rice and spoon that over. It's like a . . . a spicy stew. Try some!"

Jason hesitated again. Then, he took Trent's advice, and added bread and fruit as well as dessert (no gelatin of any kind, thank you!) in case the Mulligatawny was awful. Once spooned over the rice, he could see chunks of meat and onion and some other vegetables in a rich, golden brown broth more clearly. It smelled intriguing. Behind him, he could hear equal discussions of fascination over the dish, including Rich who said, "God! She's trying to kill me."

Stefan snickered. "Then you don't hafta eat it, do you? Just get the chicken noodle soup or something. Jeez, what a wuss. Looks good to me."

"Stef, anything looks good to you. If it doesn't gobble you down first, you gobble it down." Rich grumbled another word or two before Jason left the crowd behind as he headed to their table.

Jennifer was just finishing and standing up. She leaned over to give Ting a half hug. "I've got sessions tonight, don't forget!"

"I know."

"Want me to send someone over to keep you company?" Jennifer asked, her well-glossed lips turned up in a hesitant smile.

"I'll just read for a while. I'm kind of tired, actually."

"Okay. I'll try to come in quietly, in case you fall asleep." Jennifer allowed herself to smile then, and was gone with a toss of her blonde head. Trent watched her leave before digging into his dinner.

"Interesting," was all he said.

Jason knew better. He knew what kinds of wheels were turning when Trent said something like that. "What is?"

"She's wearing her crystal like a pendant, around her neck. Didn't you see?"

Jason shook his head, but he felt a touch of envy for a moment. As Ting had noted, advanced lessons. Not that he wanted to wear his stone in a girlish necklace about his neck, but . . . what was she learning that they hadn't had a chance to yet? What wonders of Magick?

Caught up in his own thoughts, he scarcely noticed the first few rich bites of the Mulligatawny stew. Then, his mouth bursting with the flavor, spicy and rich, and the warmth of the tender meat and gravy, toned down by the rice, he noticed his dinner and dug in. The chilled salads cooled his tongue back down, but he decided he liked this markedly different food.

While they were all eating, Sousa appeared at the doorway, cornet in his hand. "No campfire tonight," he announced, much to the dismay of everyone who enjoyed the nightly meets. He put his hand up to quiet the protests. He looked about the mess hall. "It's important tonight that you be safely in your assigned housing so we know where you are. I promise you that tomorrow night, we'll have a tale of adventure to tell you and I think FireAnne promised fresh-baked chocolate chip cookies and brownies for all.

The campers cheered at that. Sousa tooted a cheery bar or two in return and left, while the murmurs of the curious rose again.

"What do you think that was all about?" Trent mopped up the last of his Mulligatawny with a slice of bread.

Jason thought he knew. The Ritual that Gavan had promised Eleanora . . . by midnight, and whatever that Ritual was, it must be dire, even dangerous. He couldn't say, "I don't know," so he just ducked his head and concentrated on finishing his carrot and raisin salad.

Ting chewed on a fingernail. "You two are still coming by, aren't you?"

Trent and Jason swapped looks. "Sure," Jason returned even as Trent said, "Better not."

They looked at each other again.

"But—" they said in unison.

Her face crumpled slightly in worry.

"All right," they said together.

Ting managed a smile.

Outside, after dinner, Jason punched Trent in the shoulder. "What was that about? I thought you were fearless."

Trent screwed up his face a bit and shrugged. "I've got my

reasons. This isn't just any camp, you know? This is one you can't afford to get thrown out of, if you want to know who you are and what you can do." He stopped in his tracks. "Listen, I'll see you later. I've got some laundry to do before bedtime." He headed off in the opposition direction, leaving Jason standing baffled and alone.

He was still alone when the time came for lights out, because Trent had come in and gone to bed without a word and now snored lightly. Jason fidgeted a moment, remembered what he had promised Ting, and withdrew the string of firecrackers from under his bunk, tucking them inside his windbreaker jacket. He took the box of matches from the window seat drawer, left there to light candles in an emergency. How long they'd been left there, he had no idea. He hoped they would still strike and light quickly.

Like a slim shadow, Ting waited for him in the corner of the porch, her back to the cottage outer wall. "Where's Trent?" she asked quietly, her eyes turning down a bit in disappointment.

"Fell asleep. I couldn't wake him."

"Oh."

"Hey. I'm here."

She smiled slightly. "Yes, you are!" She dropped her voice to an even lower whisper. "Sessions were cancelled tonight, Jennifer is reading. What do you think is going on?"

He shook his head. "All I know is . . . you need to go to bed, with Lights Out. Everyone needs to be quiet and seemingly asleep before he makes his move. I'll be out here. I've got something guaranteed to scare off your Ghost . . . and probably your thief, too!"

"What?" Her eyes widened.

"Don't worry about it. But I guarantee, you'll know it when it happens, and it's in the best Chinese tradition."

Eyes still wondering, Ting moved back inside the cottage and there was a faint click as she slid the bolt into place. Jason moved around to the rear of the cottage, where he sat down in a bush and tried not to think about the various things that crawled about, whether it was night or day, and waited. Even as he tried to ignore it, it felt like a dozen of them were crawling over his ankles or arms. He fought not to scratch. Instead, to keep his mind off the tiny creatures tickling across his skin, he began to think about the thief, the Ghost and the strange things that had been happening.

He heard the Magickers as they came up the back slope of the cottages, chanting. Jason bit his lip. They would catch him, for sure. He wasn't certain what they'd do for catching him a second time, but it couldn't be good. He hugged his arms around his legs and tried to feel invisible.

The words sang out and caught Jason, pulling at him. He could hear Gavan's pleasant tenor tones, and the lovely voices of Eleanora, and Dr. Patel, and the slightly off-key and deeper voice of FireAnn. They paused a moment, and then Eleanora said, pleased, "That wards the cottage. Nice harmony. The girls should sleep right through." They ringed the clearing nearest Kittencurl, and then the dark seemed to mask them from sight. He rubbed his eyes as they began to recite strange words again. Their chanting made him sleepy and he fought to listen, to keep his eyes open. When he finally understood their words, what he heard chilled his blood.

The Ritual was irresistible. It tugged at his own thoughts and soul, threatened to send him away—except he belonged here, *he did*, and Jason anchored himself to that while a cold, hard Banshee wailed about and plucked at him. Tugged at his collar and sleeve, promising, then threatening to take him away, or to banish him.

He blinked, hard, as they stood in a circle, candles in their hands, their voices growing louder and faster. He tried to breathe, and could not, unless it was in time to their chanting. He felt dizzy.

"Be gone!" commanded Gavan.

Jason's heart thumped hard in his chest. He put a hand out to the ground and dug his fingers in. He was no Ghost! Yet . . .

Eleanora began chanting again. He was able to take a breath. He curled his other hand about his crystal, and as its edges pressed roughly into his skin, he felt a bit better.

"Be gone!" commanded Gavan again.

Jason's whole body quivered, in spite of himself. And then, and then, out of the corner of his eye, he saw a pale scrap. A wavering glimpse of . . . something . . . being pulled out by the Ritual.

He stared as he saw it flicker.

"Come no more to this reality, this plane, this time, this earth!" recited Gavan. He took a deep breath. He was going to chant, "Be gone!" for the third and last time. Jason knew it. And that would be the last of the Ghost.

He blinked as it paused by him, stretched out an imploring hand. He knew that wisp, that scrap of existence!

His body felt like lead, fastened to the earth, anchored there so the Ritual could not sweep him away. He'd chained himself there. Jason took a breath, tried to stand, and couldn't.

"Wait!" He gulped for breath and yelled again. "No! Wait!"

Then, as the Magickers turned to look at him, and Gavan Rainwater frowned in a thunderous expression, he blurted out, "Stop! Bailey's the Ghost!"

16

Lions and Tigers and Bears, Oh, My!

"WHAT?" Eleanora turned on him, candlelight reflecting her pale, shocked face.

But nothing was as pale as the wispy being before him. He grabbed at it, feeling something spidery tingling across the skin but not Bailey's hand . . . if it was Bailey, and it had to be, he could think of no one else!

"Gavan! Quickly, the crystal! Before we drive her into the other plane and lose her entirely." The flame on her candle shook as Eleanora's hands trembled.

"Don't be taken in, Eleanora. Haunts can be very devious." Gavan frowned heavily.

Jason stood still, watching the ethereal mist gather round him. "Bailey?" he asked quietly. The wind sighed around him.

"If it be our lost lass," FireAnn said softly, "she might be forgettin' who she is. A Ghostly existence is not an easy one." She reached over and gently took Eleanora's candle from her, adding, "Before you spill wax all over or burn yourself."

Dr. Patel watched Jason with a slight frown. She wore her sari with a matching shawl covering her sleek head, its edge hemmed in silvery thread that sparkled in the moonlight. "Are you all right, Jason?"

"Yes. It—it just made me feel very weird for a moment or two."

"Understandable. This is not a Magick for the unprepared." She smiled slightly, and he felt a comfort emanating from her, cool and dry and efficient. "You'll let me know if you worsen?"

"I will." He thought a moment, then dug his hand into his windbreaker. A chocolate chip cookie came back out. Slightly stale, from dinner before last, he'd forgotten he'd put one aside for later. He held his hand out, palm flat. "Bailey, I know you've gotta be hungry."

"Jason—" Eleanora said in warning, then halted as Gavan unwrapped the amethyst crystal from his silk handkerchief. He took her hand and cupped it with his, their warm flesh enveloping the purple stone. She let out a soft sound of dismay.

Gavan shook his head as he looked into her face. "I can't tell if it's her, and we can't afford to be wrong. To stop the Ritual now means we may not be able to deal with the Ghost later, it will have grown too strong."

"But if it's Bailey, we can't banish her!"

The pale fog shimmering around Jason seemed to thicken, gathering, until the outline was about his height, and definitely that of a person. He bounced the cookie on his palm. "It's chocolate chip," he coaxed.

The night gave a soft moan.

The sound made the hairs on the back of his neck stand up straight, and he fought not to shiver.

"Poor dear," said Anita Patel, looking about with concern. She pushed her shawl from her head, dropping it around her shoulders. "I think the boy is right. I can sense her aura."

FireAnne held her two candles high. After a moment, disappointment rode her face. "I canna tell."

Gavan took a deep breath. He looked down into Eleanora's face as she wavered a bit, bobbing slightly up and down as if her strength were taxed. "I'll do it," he said. "But if it is not Bailey . . ."

"I'll do what I can for you," she said quietly.

He nodded. Then Gavan Rainwater closed his eyes, and

tightened his hands over hers and the crystal, and a look of intense concentration crossed his face. The tiny lines at the corners of his eyelids deepened, as did the ones near his mouth. His jaw tightened.

A wind picked up, off the lake, chill and brisk. The trees around them ruffled. Jason stood uncertainly, as the fog near him seemed to grow colder and colder as the night breeze whirled around it. It grew thicker, too, but instead of becoming more distinct so that he could see Bailey's face, it did not. It flapped its arms at him, and he felt an icicle touch on his face.

Gavan jerked suddenly, one hand flying off the grasp of the crystal. His eyes flew open in surprise and dismay. He reeled back almost as if he had been hit. Eleanora cried out, and Jason could see she tightened her grip on the amethyst crystal. He staggered back another step, his one remaining hand on the crystal shaking, his arm outstretched to its fullest length. He brought his other hand up, and, gritting his teeth, once again cupped his fingers about Eleanora's hand and the stone. "There is more at work here than we know," he managed to say, his voice tight in his throat. "I'm not sure I can . . ."

"Don't even think that, Gavan!" Eleanora tilted her face up to look into his eyes.

Jason shivered. The Ghost wavered again, and this time when it moaned, he could see the cloud of its head open, dark night shining through, as it wailed in eerie tones. Its eyes shone like two dark spots. The Ghost floated nearer. Its chill struck him to the bone, and his teeth began to chatter in spite of himself. Dr. Patel shrugged into her silk shawl while FireAnn chafed her hands. The temperature continued to drop until his nose went numb and frozen.

"Bailey . . . take the cookie?" His hand shook as his whole body seemed to dance with cold shivers. He thought the cookie would surely pop off. Something even icier touched his fingers and slid off his skin. The cookie lurched sideways suddenly and he pinched his hand shut to keep from dropping it.

"Keep trying, Jason! Don't let her think we've given up on her!" Eleanora called to him, even though her gaze remained locked on Gavan, who had grown paler even than the ghostly apparition before them.

He took a breath, expiration frosting on the air as though it were the deepest of winters, and held the cookie back out. Something slimy ran across his hand again, a wispy tendril, and he tried not to make a disgusted noise. He held steady and, instead said, "Come on, Bailey. You can do it!"

The wind died suddenly. The air all around them grew still and frosty. Gavan shuddered.

Through tight lips growing blue, he said, "Come to me, Bailey. You've got to find the way to do it. Come . . . NOW!"

A sound split the clearing, like that of a scream, yet almost too high to hear. Jolted, Jason felt his hand, his whole body jerk. The cookie flew into the air as he staggered back on his heels. Gavan dropped as though he had been pole axed and, unbalanced, Eleanora nearly toppled over on top of him. The candles FireAnn held snuffed out. With a cry, she dropped them in surprise.

Only Dr. Patel seemed unmoved. Her almond eyes fixed on the cloud of white as if she could see what moved there.

With a tremendous WHOOOSH the fog left.

Jason grabbed for the cookie, out of habit, and found . . . nothing.

"I've lost her," Gavan said, as he rolled over onto his back and took a few deep breaths. "Eleanora, she's gone." As soon as the color came back to his face, he stood, and steadied Eleanora.

"No." She shook her head. "Oh, no."

"I won't give up, but . . ." He paused, and leaned on his cane as if he actually needed it to bear his weight. His deep blue gaze swept over all of them. "We know that once lost like that, retrievals are . . . difficult, at best. If not impossible."

Dr. Patel said softly, "It *was* Bailey. I saw her clearly, though only for a moment."

Jason only half-listened, because he already felt sure he knew who the ghost was. What he didn't know was . . . where had the cookie gone? If he'd missed snatching it back, where was it on the ground? He shuffled his feet a bit in the night and saw . . . nothing.

Gavan nodded. "I won't give up easily."

Jason stood stock-still, as something brushed the back of his ear. The evening breeze had come back, and the trees stirred around him, but he heard something ever so faintly. He thought he heard someone say, "Saves mine . . ."

His blood went cold. Or was it . . . you're mine? As the creature had promised him.

FireAnn picked up her candles and said briskly, "Everyone should be in bed. If you can't sleep, I'll send a draft of chamomile by. Tomorrow, as they say, is another day, and now that we know it's our missing lass, we can take steps."

"Are you all right, Jason?" asked the doctor softly. Standing beside him, she was hardly taller than he was, and the faint smell of incense clung to her silken sari.

"Yeah." He shivered. He'd have to think about this later, when he was warmer, and the night wasn't pressing on him. The back of his hand twitched and as he covered it with his other, he winced at new tenderness. "We can't lose Bailey. She's . . . she's . . . special," he finished lamely, for want of a better word.

"You're all special," Gavan said. He bowed to FireAnn. "I think we should follow our own advice, and this time, young man, I won't ask why—"

A howl tore his words in half. Another one followed it, sharp and coming nearer. The noise swirled down on the clearing like a whirlwind, and he could almost hear the running of the pack, the gnashing of their teeth as the howlers bore down on them. The throbbing in his hand quickened as though keeping pace with their thundering strides. Jason wobbled, nearly overwhelmed by it.

"Wolfjackals!" Gavan swung about, his cane in his hands. "I should have known they'd sense the breach. FireAnn, get Eleanora and Anita back to the Hall, quickly!" He pulled at Jason. "You, stay with me." He seemed not to notice Jason's pain as he took the boy's elbow and tucked him in close.

FireAnn linked arms with Eleanora and Anita Patel. "Back to back," she said to Gavan Rainwater, and to the others, she added, "Here we go, duckies. One step at a time. They'll not take us all on at once!"

Gavan stepped in behind the women, turning, and they moved as one unit, FireAnn leading the others ahead and Gavan and Jason walking backward, on alert, watching the woods fringing the campground.

He would ask what wolfjackals were, but he already knew. Sweat beaded Jason's forehead.

"Got your crystal on you?"

"I—yes," Jason got out. His throat creaked as he tried to talk.

"Good. Take it out. Hold it tightly. And, mind you, don't drop it!"

"No, sir."

"I'm going to draw on you. If you get to feeling really faint, call out. Otherwise, just stay with me, stand firm, and I'll keep us all from harm, no matter what it looks like is going to happen. Understand?"

"Yes, sir," said Jason faintly. He already felt weak. How could he give any strength to Gavan? But if he said anything, if he showed him the mark, how much more trouble would he be in? He clamped his jaw shut and took a deep breath. The backs of his calves ached as they walked backward faster and faster to keep up with FireAnn leading a brisk retreat.

"Our energies are spent, but the wards on the cottages should hold. We're the only ones in danger for the moment," Gavan muttered to Eleanora as they trotted toward the main hall. His hand gripped Jason's shoulder tightly.

Then came the moment which he knew, if he lived beyond it, he would never forget. From the darkened sky itself, they seemed to come, running down out of the clouds and iron mountain peaks and alighting onto the common ground of the camp, their eyes shining green, their teeth like white, sharp slivers of the moon. With howls and growls, they emerged one by one and fanned out into a pack. Five of them descended onto the pathway and slowed to a stop, their tails wagging low and stiff from side to side, their jaws agape. The wolfjackals lowered their heads, and he had not a doubt they could rip his throat out whenever they wished.

A sharp tear went through the back of his hand. It felt damp, as though bitten, but he could not look at it. He could not do anything but stare at the hunting pack just as they stared down their prey.

"Away with you. You are denied," Gavan called out. His statement might have been more convincing were they not backing up quickly, to keep at the backs of the three more vulnerable women.

The pack trotted slowly to keep even. The air smelled of them, hot furred beast, coppery blood tang, musk, saliva, sharpened teeth, eagerness to run them down.

The leader's head twitched, jaws widening, crimson tongue lolling. His head jerked about again, as though birthing a voice with great difficulty. "This is open land. We hunt."

"No. No, this is our land, and you know it. Our mana seeps into the very earth joints here."

"I know nothing. We hunt here. If you would deny us, close the Gate."

Gavan muttered something under his breath. He cupped his left hand, clutching Jason's fist where he held his crystal tightly. He inhaled. "You are denied! Leave now!"

"Or . . ." The wolfjackals trotted closer yet. "Your threatssss seeeeem empty."

Gavan raised his cane. A searing blue beam shot from the end of it, blackening the ground. Dirt and crushed grasses sizzled. With a yelp, the beast jumped out of range. Gavan inhaled tightly, and a second bolt shot from the cane. It zapped one of the beasts. The wolfjackal rolled with a yelp, and the smell of burning fur filled the air.

The pack leader whirled about, snapping. Then he lowered his head, facing Gavan again. "For that, I will have bloodddddd," he grimaced and snarled out of ivory-toothed jaws.

Gavan jumped forward with a great stamp, and two of the

wolfjackals bolted away in sheer reaction. They circled and came back to the rear of the pack, heads down as if embarrassed. Their packmates snapped sharply at them for their cowardice.

Fiery pain crept up Jason's hand to his arm and into his neck. He concentrated on breathing, on Gavan's words. He felt as though he were leaking. As though everything inside of him faded away . . . They continued to walk backward, one slow steady step at a time. A soft glow behind told him they were close to the building.

But he had been close to the building when bitten. So they weren't afraid of the lights and such. They weren't entirely wild. They were . . . beyond his knowing. The one spoke. The others milled about with a savage intelligence. His heart thudded in his breast as though the only thing in a vast, hollow drum. It hurt to feel it pounding so hard.

Something pale and white flitted past them. Jason barely caught sight of it, but he felt it. The wolfjackals did as well. The pack wheeled about in sudden confusion, smelling new prey and yet not quite sighting it. "What is thissss?" the leader snarled, and snapped at empty air. Hot saliva dripped from his jaw in eagerness.

With a fear for more than himself, Jason thought he knew. They saw, sensed, what he could not. And alone, she was in even more danger than he was! He yelled, "Run, Bailey!" with all the air left in his lungs.

The wolfjackals scattered, leaping after the faint ghostly apparition. They howled in fierce joy at the new hunt. The white wisp darted away, out of reach. It bobbed back and forth, almost frantic seeming, just in front of the snapping wolfjackals. The beasts whirled and spun and lashed out again and again.

Gavan called out, "NOW!" He bodily picked up Jason by the waist and they all lunged for the Lake Wannameecha Gathering Hall.

Once inside, FireAnn bolted the door, and Eleanora let out a sharp, crisp curse before heading to her office. "I can't leave the Ghost to them!" She came back with a very large, clear crystal in her hands. "Now," she said firmly. "They'll be sorry." She took her place near Gavan who gently set Jason back on his sneakered feet.

Wobbly, Jason sat down.

Eleanora tossed her head and linked her arm with Gavan's. She threw the door back open and the two of them stepped into the golden courtyard as the five wolfjackals lunged into sight.

Jason saw only a brilliant flash of light. He heard the yelps and snarls and then—nothing. He didn't know if it was because they'd won . . . or he'd keeled over as he felt his mind go blank and his body slump down. The only feeling he had anywhere was in his hands . . . pain in the left one where the scar felt newly ripped open, and pain in the right one where he held his crystal so tightly it cut into his palm. Then the dark snarled around and enclosed him.

17

Scars and Scares

ICY cold. He woke up shivering, teeth chattering, as if he'd been dunked in a tub of ice water. Dr. Patel was gently unfolding his fingers from around his crystal, saying softly, "Just relax a bit, Jason." He tried to, but his body reacted on its own, jerking about like a puppet on loose strings. It took him a moment to realize he was staring at the ceiling of Lake Wannameecha Gathering Hall, and not the sky, or his own cabin, or even his very own attic room, so far away. She frowned at the bruising and tiny cuts around his crystal, but only said, "We'll have to wash the grit out of those. Your crystals aren't polished and cleaned yet."

Dr. Patel leaned over him, and so did FireAnn, a worried look knitting her cinnamon brows together. Her hair had come unbound again, and surrounded her face in a hazy, burnished cloud of red. "You're tough, laddie," she said quietly. "Just take a deep breath."

Jason nodded.

FireAnn shook his shoulder. "Dinna nod at me, laddie, breathe!"

He inhaled deeply. The warm air burned inside his lungs. He

knew he'd never be warm again. Why was he so cold? Dr. Patel laid her silken shawl over him and despite its lightness, it seemed to blanket him with soothing heat as she tucked it about him with a few words of a language he did not recognize, then added, "What happened?"

"Ah, well." FireAnn looked up briefly. "We're nay sure yet! It's a battle of wills out there."

"What happens if we lose?" Jason forced words out through teeth determined to chatter.

Anita Patel hissed, and then gently added, "We can't be losing. This is not the kind of battle we can afford to lose." She helped him sit up.

He dared a glance at his scarred hand, saw nothing and tucked it under him. He could have sworn the skin had broken anew, the blood freshly running down his hand and trickling off his fingers from a jagged gash. But he saw nothing in his quick glance.

Not too quick for Dr. Patel to catch, though. She grabbed his wrist firmly. "Let me see that hand, Jason."

He yielded to her because he had no choice. Fire began to creep through his body as the feeling came back, prickly heat pinching and poking numb places. He clenched his jaw tightly to keep his teeth from chattering. She spread his fingers to examine the scar carefully.

"I think it's time you told me the truth about this, Jason."

He couldn't meet her level gaze.

"What is it?" asked FireAnn.

"A bite or scratch. He wasn't quite sure when he came in at first. Scratch, we decided, and it looked like it, though deep but closing quickly. He had babbled a bit about a wild animal first, then let it go. Do you remember the night?"

The cook rubbed her head, fiery hair moving about her like smoke. "Without a crew to help with the kitchen, I was a mite distracted. Gavan was hounding me to get the Draft concocted. There was someone lost near the toilets . . . I canna say I remember that being you, though, Jason. Lad, we're a chain that's only as strong as the weakest link. If there's something we need to know, you should be telling us."

He squirmed. Dr. Patel smoothed her fingertips over the crescent scar. She already knew, he sensed. He sighed. She let go of his hand.

"I didn't know what it was then. It jumped me . . . you scared it off." He stared beseechingly at FireAnn.

FireAnn let out her breath in a gust. She smelled faintly of spearmint. "Oh, lad."

Dr. Patel frowned. "They've been here since the first night? That's not good, FireAnn. I had no idea, and I don't think anyone else did."

Cook laid a hand gently on his shoulder. "What happened?"

"It took hold of me. I . . . well, I couldn't pull loose, so I shoved my fist down its throat. It let go in surprise, I think. Then it heard a clatter from the kitchens, so it growled at me and left."

"Well. I was scarin' more varmints than I knew, eh?" FireAnn looked faintly pleased.

"I washed up. It hurt a lot but by morning, the gash had nearly healed up. Just looked like a bad scratch, but still, I was worried. I mean . . . rabies and stuff. I didn't know what to think, but you seemed very calm about it, and it didn't look that bad in your office. Maybe I had jabbed it into a branch when I fell."

She nodded solemnly.

He exhaled. The moment had come, he knew it. With all that he had been through, he would be sent home. "I'm sorry to have been so much trouble," he said.

FireAnn poked him gently. "The most Talented are often the most troublesome. Dinna you think Gavan Rainwater knows that? Why, as a lad himself—" She rolled her green eyes.

"Don't give him false hope. It's bad if he's been marked, very bad. You worried about infection, but I can tell you that you've no idea what a wolfjackal can sink into you." Dr. Patel sighed. "Regardless of what Gavan wants, he may not be able to help, this time." She stood, straightening her sari. "And he drew blood, don't forget that, FireAnn."

She sucked in her breath, and looked sadly at Jason. "A blood pact?"

"Not quite, but . . ." the doctor's voice trailed off.

Jason shivered. "You have to tell?"

"Do you think it wise to keep a thing like this hidden?"

After a long moment, he shook his head. The thought that he might be the weakness that would get Bailey or someone else hurt, or bring the wolfjackals back, knifed through him. "No," he said quietly. "I wouldn't wish this on anyone!"

"That's a good lad," returned FireAnn soothingly. She wiped her hands on her apron as she straightened. "Wonder if they need help out there."

"I imagine they could use a bracing cup of tea when they're done."

Cook nodded. "Fix a cuppa, I will, then." She hurried down the corridor to what must be a small kitchenette off the offices because shortly thereafter, he could hear some pans rattling, although a great deal quieter than the usual clatter and bang at the mess hall.

Dr. Patel leaned against the corridor. She studied her own hands a moment, before meeting Jason's gaze. "There is no way I could not tell."

He sighed. "I know." Finally, he felt warm again although it might be with shame. Standing up, he handed the shawl back to her, the silken fabric shimmering for a moment between his fingers. Magical? He would not doubt it, if she told him. "Sometimes, I ask myself, why me?" He rubbed his hand again. The slight tenderness that had almost gone was back, as painful as it had ever been.

"Perhaps, in that, we are all lucky. Another young Magicker might not have handled it. Do you think just anyone could have stood against the wolfjackals now, marked as you were?" Whatever else the doctor might have added was cut off by the sharp, piercing whistle of the teakettle and FireAnn's cheerful voice calling them back for tea.

Before either could head down the corridor, the door banged open and Gavan blew in, pulling Eleanora behind him. He kicked the door shut, grinning ear to ear, his hair mussed as though he'd been standing in a high wind. Eleanora cleared her throat, as she patted down her clothes, and tried to put some order back in her dark, tangled hair.

"Well," he said, in a deep, pleased tone. "I think we showed them what we can do." He looked at Jason then. "And it appears to be time for a talk with you, Jason. You know both more . . . and less . . . than you should."

Eleanora walked on her shoe soles, and she was so diminutive that she barely came to Jason's throat. She drew her shoulders up, but could not levitate, and it was then he knew the toll it had taken to stand off the wolfjackals. Magick demanded a price. She looked as pale as alabaster. The thought scared him. She put a hand up on Gavan's shoulder to steady herself.

Before Gavan could utter another word, however, Anita interrupted. "FireAnn," she said, "has tea ready. Shall we all have a bracer before we discuss anything?"

"Most excellent idea," breathed Eleanora. Gavan moved down the hall, pacing himself to her unsteady steps. He murmured something toward her ear that Jason couldn't catch, but it brought two bright dots of color to her cheeks.

FireAnn not only had a huge, steaming pot of tea ready, but she'd also set out a plate of cookies and a second plate of little jam tarts. Jason slid into his chair with a rumble from his stomach that said food would be very welcome. He helped himself to one tart and two big gingerbread cookies, their tops crackled from baking and sprinkled with sugar. No one said anything but, "Please pass the cookies," or, "Cream and sugar, anyone?" and "Thank you, I will have another," for several long minutes.

Then Gavan put his cup down, and as the doctor refilled it for him, he mopped cookie crumbs off his mouth and remarked, "We chased them off with their tails tucked between their legs."

FireAnn cheered. "Well done!"

He nodded. "It taxed us more than it should have. They were very strong. That lends credence to Tomaz's worry that a mana storm is approaching. They're drawing on it already. How, I've no idea. The Dark Hand has ways I'm not familiar with."

Anita stared at the tablecloth thoughtfully as FireAnn rocked back in her chair. Then the doctor looked up, gazing at Jason. "Before more is said," she remarked quietly, "there is something you should know."

"Yes?" Gavan arched an eyebrow.

Jason waited uncomfortably, then as the silence dragged on, he realized she would not say it, and she waited for him to. Tart halfway to his mouth, he put it down on his plate. "I was bitten," he told Rainwater and Eleanora, putting his left hand out, palm flat on the table, so that his crescent scar would be clearly seen on the back of his hand. The thin white scarline had gone purple and angry looking. That did not worry him so much; he knew it would be faded by morning.

"That's not from tonight." Eleanora looked at him, and the worry in her eyes made him feel awful.

"No. It happened the first night. I ran into this beast coming out of the restroom."

Gavan rubbed the side of his nose. "And no one knew? You told no one?" He threw his linen napkin on the table. "Damn it, how can we keep safe if we're too weak to even know when the Dark Hand is among us?"

Eleanora reached out and laid her hand over his. "Gavan," was all she said, a note of warning ringing in her voice.

He inhaled and looked to Jason. "Go on, Master Adrian. I sense there is more."

"It grabbed me. Its teeth . . . tore me. I pushed it away, and it heard FireAnn in the mess hall. It backed away and just disappeared, then."

"Said anything, did it?" Rainwater's clear blue gaze rested on him.

Unable to trust his voice, Jason shook his head. How much worse could it be? Would they deny him the chance to be one of them? Perhaps much, much worse if he repeated what the wolfjackal had said to him. *You're mine . . .*

Gavan also nodded in agreement. "Talking does not come

easy to them. They are not made for it. I imagine it causes them pain, but I doubt their maker cares. What did you do then?"

"I went back to the restroom. I washed, over and over. It hurt. It was this bloody gash."

Eleanora gave a muffled sound. He looked up to see her wringing her hands, musician's hands that it would be a crime to hurt or scar.

"I'm . . . I'm all right now," Jason told her. "When I got up in the morning, it was nearly all healed. I went to see Dr. Patel anyway. The pain went all deep inside, like a bad bruise or something. I was worried. Well . . . rabies and stuff, you know?"

"They are from beyond the veil," Gavan said. "They do not carry our diseases, nor are they vulnerable to them. They carry plagues of their own, however, and we do fall to them."

"He didn't tell me," the doctor interrupted softly, "that he had been bitten. I should have pressed him a bit. He was worried about infection, so I cleansed it and gave him some ointment for it."

FireAnn had only been listening, leaning on one elbow, and sipping her cup of tea. Now she commented, "Perhaps that is why Jason doesn't sleep like the others. One Magick outweighing the charm? He doesn't succumb to the Parting song and blessing."

They all stared at him. He shrugged. "I don't know why I don't sleep. I wake up at home, but I don't have trouble going back to sleep."

"Another mystery," Gavan sketched a fingernail on the tablecloth. "You have a nose for them," the camp leader said. "You keep showing up."

Jason flushed with embarrassment. "I don't mean to," he answered slowly.

"Nonsense!" FireAnn stood and freshened all their teacups. "Of course you do! You've a large curiosity bump, nothing wrong with that. Me mum and you would get along right well."

Eleanora smiled wistfully. "I haven't seen Beulah in years," she responded. "How is she?"

FireAnn nodded. "She's doing well enough. Now, lad. Keep talking." She settled back at the table.

"I don't know what else to say."

"Have you seen wolfjackals again, before tonight?"

"Once or twice, I thought . . . could have been something else, in the brush." His own voice sounded funny to his ears, and he stopped short of telling them he thought he'd been followed several times. They probably thought he was coward enough.

Gavan scratched at his chin. "Not good news, but then, not unexpected either. We knew they would come hunting, I had just hoped we'd have our defenses up first, our Iron Gate shut. Now we'll have to step up our efforts to locate it. We're going to start mapping the ley lines tomorrow."

"Lay lines?" Jason looked about in confusion. "And what do you mean about a Gate?"

"L E Y," furnished Eleanora. "Trust me, you will know far more about them than you want to know. A more boring task, I cannot imagine, but it has to be done. Ley lines are natural bands of Magick, or mana, the energy that Magick uses, rather like magnetic fields that occur in the earth naturally, and we're going to be identifying our network in the next few days. Think of them like power lines, cables, buried deep within the earth for us to discover."

"As for the Gate." Gavan rubbed his palm over the top of his cane. "Imagine that we can fence in this camp with magical wards. There are Havens that were fenced like that centuries ago, and Gated. The Gates move a bit, on ley lines, but we're fairly sure one is here. We can move that fencing to surround the camp and merge into a Haven, we believe. It won't be easy, but it can be done, and then we can have a safe place to learn and teach."

"It must not be easy to be a Magicker." Jason picked up his tart and began to nibble before his stomach could let out a rumble of hunger loud enough to be heard by everyone else. Smiling, FireAnn nudged the tart plate a little closer.

"Never has been, nor does it ever seem to be destined to be."

Gavan tapped his cane upon the floor. "I must ask you, Jason, to hold your tongue about what you've seen and heard. I can't explain everything to you now, and even if I could, you don't know quite enough to understand it. Be patient with me?"

"Can I ask you a question?"

"One, and let us pray it is not longer than what is left of our night, for me to answer."

"Do you know about the nightmares?"

He threw a look at Eleanora, then glanced back to Jason. "Yes," he said quietly. "We know a bit about the nightmares."

"Who is the man in the tomb?"

"We're not sure. Do you remember well enough to tell us?"

"He's very, very pale. Sometimes he has short, dark curly hair. He wants me to come to his side. He reaches out with his hand. I used to think—I used to think it was my father. I had dreams of him like that, before. Now I don't know anymore."

"Sometimes?" echoed Eleanora. Her teacup shook slightly in her hand.

Jason nodded. "Sometimes, I would swear, it's a different man. Long, silvery-gray hair. He seems . . . older. He doesn't reach for me, though, and he doesn't scare me so much."

FireAnn sucked in her breath and then coughed several times as though she'd inhaled a cookie crumb. She put her napkin to her face and turned away.

"Perhaps, Jason, on another night . . . you'd do a bit of dream exploring for us? Until then, I really haven't any answers I can give you." Gavan smiled lightly. "But those nightmares are why we try to give everyone a good night's sleep, even if they don't want it."

Jason nodded. "One more?"

"Only if it is exceedingly short."

"You're not going to throw me out?"

"No," said Gavan Rainwater thoughtfully. "At least, not yet." He rolled the silvery wolfhead sculpture on his cane between his palms. "Don't think that some of you won't be sent home, because some will. That's why FireAnn here has been cooking up a Draft of Forgetfulness for days. Not everyone is cut out to handle the Talents we've been given, and we cannot send them home remembering what has occurred."

"You just . . . take their memories?"

"The potion does."

"You'd mess with their minds like that? What about the oath we swore?"

"The Draft makes it easier to live. If you don't know you've lost something, you can't mourn for it or search to get it back. The Oath keeps them safe, even though they've forgotten. We have no choice, Jason. There is a vast world out there that would love to . . . mess with our minds . . . if we are ever found out. I don't know about you, but I'd not care to be on the Internet in an autopsy finding out what made me tick!" Gavan stood.

"All right then. New agenda, items of import. Mapping the ley lines so the Gate can be located and closed against the coming storm. Getting Bailey Landau back. General training must be speeded up a bit; we've a lot to teach them and the days are flying past."

"Bailey will be found," Eleanora reassured him.

"Master Rainwater," Jason got out as Gavan started to leave.

"Yes, Jason?"

"Do you think anyone could ever go back to ordinary after seeing a Magicker?"

"Like anything in life, sometimes you've got no choice." Gavan pivoted in a swirl of dark cloak and then was gone down the hallway, his footsteps echoing.

Dr. Patel stood smoothly. "I'll walk you back to your cabin, Jason."

He nodded, then could not help smiling as FireAnn put two great gingerbread cookies and two tarts in a napkin, folded the ends over and handed the package to him. "Roommates," she explained, "can sometimes get horribly grumpy if they find out you've been somewhere without them . . . and you've had good things to eat that they haven't."

Jason tucked the package inside his shirt gratefully as he thanked her. They all left the building a bit cautiously, but other than the fact that the night was later and darker, nothing seemed untoward.

The doctor hugged him about the shoulders before letting him go into his cabin. She waited outside in the shadows until he dropped the latch into place, and he stood, listening to Trent's soft, deep breathing.

He should fall into bed and sleep, but he didn't think he could. More than anything, he thought of the Ghost. What had he heard the second time . . . "saves mine" or "you're mine"? And how could he tell Gavan his fears that the enemy somehow had a hold on him he didn't know about and could do nothing about? And what was the Dark Hand, and why was it the enemy, and what had happened to all the other Magickers, once upon a time?

And how could he help Bailey before she was lost to them all forever or the wolfjackals got her? When he finally drifted off, it was into a tangle of half dreams and nightmares, none of which he could escape from or wake up from, until he remembered none of them at all. Even the ones which might have held clues.

A Stitch in Time

J ASON woke to the sound of crunching. He couldn't quite place the noise as he craned his head from his pillow and rubbed his eyes. The night, as Gavan Rainwater had predicted, had been much too short. He yawned.

The crunching grew louder and as he sat up, he saw Trent at the table, elbows propped up, happily consuming one of Fire-Ann's cookies.

"If you're going to sneak out," Trent stated, "at least you brought back goodies!" He imitated a contented purr.

Still muffled by sleep, Jason answered, "Glad you like 'em." He swung his legs out and stretched. If FireAnn had beaten her pots or Sousa blown the camp-rousing melody on his cornet, he'd slept right through it. "Everyone else up yet?"

"Nope. Thought I heard something at the door, so I woke."

"Something?"

"Yeah, the screen door was rattling and bumping. Must have been the wind."

Or . . . Jason concealed a shudder. He didn't want to think what else it could be. He padded over to the table and sat down. Trent had already eaten the little tarts, according to the pattern of crumbs on the table. He stifled another yawn. "So . . . wanna know what happened?"

Trent licked a finger. "I figure you'll tell me sooner or later." He hummed slightly.

"Maybe." Jason leaned back in his chair, stuck his foot on the table, and looked at his ankle. Despite last night's doings, it seemed to be even more healed, the colors fading. He decided not to wear his air splints again.

"Do you *mind?*" Trent pushed his foot off the table. "I'm eating here!"

"You," observed Jason, "are always eating somewhere."

"True. So, did you catch the thief?"

"No, I ended up Ghost hunting instead."

"Wow." Trent sat up. "No kidding? I missed that?"

Jason shrugged. "You didn't want to come," he pointed out. "Anyway, I caught the camp leader and Eleanora and Dr. Patel and FireAnn doing some kind of ritual, to send the Ghost away. Only, it hit me . . . and I don't know why we didn't think of this before . . . Bailey is the Ghost!"

Trent dropped his cookie. "Bailey is dead?"

"Oh, no. No, no no. But she's neither here nor there. She's been leaving clues or trying to." He frowned heavily, wondering what he was going to do to help her now.

"How can she be a Ghost? What did the crystal do to her anyway?" Trent left his cookie on the table and took out his own crystal. Cloudy, it looked more like a frosty snowflake than any of the other crystals Jason had seen. It could be looked into, Trent had shown Jason that, but it was like looking into a very dark, shadowy chamber.

"I don't know. They haven't told us much about them yet. I don't know how they figure she could have gone home either, unless . . ." Jason fished his out. "Unless . . ." He tumbled the crystal about in his fingers thoughtfully. His jeweler's loupe lay on the table, next to his sketches. He picked it up and held it over his gem, looking at it . . . into it . . . each facet of the quartz like a chamber or door, opening, leading. . . .

Jason stared deeper. He could, if he concentrated hard

enough, see something. A crack. No, not a crack, an edge of something opening, like a door. An image forming. His own home's doorway inside, wavering, growing more distinct the harder he looked. Home . . . The doorknob turned as if he reached for it, the door opening inward slowly and he leaned forward, eager suddenly to see if it was home, eager to be back—he could feel the cold brass of the knob between his fingers, turning, turning, the tumblers clicking as the door opened wider.

"Jason!" Trent knocked the crystal out of his cramped fingers. It shot across the cabin, and Jason sat back, dazed and blinking. The feeling of being home faded slowly. "Man!" Trent glared at him. "They said not to do that! What were you doing?"

"I'm . . . not sure." He stretched his fingers, got up, and retrieved his crystal, checking it over for nicks or fractures. Then, with a sigh of relief, he set it down on the tabletop, where it rested. It seemed a bit different, somehow, for all that. He poked at it. "What did you see?"

"You, staring like a geek, into that." Trent seemed unnerved. He paced about the cabin, back and forth, back and forth. "I thought it was going to suck you in."

"Suck me in?" Jason stared.

"Like a vacuum cleaner. I figured you were just going to get sucked in headfirst and disappear like Bailey."

"I think I could have gone there. . . ."

"Where?" Trent threw his hands up.

"Oh." Jason drew his crystal back and pocketed it. "Home. I thought I saw home for a second there. I could have walked through the front door. You know how there are planes inside? Just like doors."

His friend stopped short. He shot a glance at his own crystal. "Transportation? Or, more correctly, teleportation? No brooms or magic carpets? Just walk through a crystal door?"

"Maybe."

"Then what happened to Bailey?"

"She dropped the crystal? She hasn't been trained? The crystals don't really work that way? I would think that Gavan and

Eleanora tried that already." Jason got to his feet, and further words were cut off by the sound of brass bugling throughout the camp, Sousa's homage to morning. He snatched for the last half of a cookie, but Trent beat him to it. The sight of the disappearing cookie tickled his mind. He almost thought of something. Almost. Trent grabbed his bath towel and snapped him in the butt, before turning and running. Racing, they bolted toward the showers and breakfast.

Tomaz had returned. He stood in the hall posting the day's schedule, but looked up as Jason walked over, and their eyes met briefly. The man gave a silent nod, before returning to his chore. The turquoise and silver on his rings and heavy bracelet flashed in the light from the wide, mess hall windows.

"What was all that about?" Trent whispered.

"Darned if I know." Jason felt as though something important had happened that he had no inkling of. Behind him, Jonnard and Danno and Henry shuffled into line, Jon looking more than ever like a scoutmaster in charge of an unruly troop as they headed to the restrooms. He also looked quizzically at Jason, who could only shrug in reply.

Henry, however, fairly bounced in excitement. "I can't wait!" His rosy face glowed from the hot showers and the corners of his glasses steamed faintly. He took them off and wiped them dry. "I can hardly wait," he said for a second time, no one having responded immediately.

"What's happening, Squibb?"

"Best news ever. The computer room is opening later. Three brand new 'puters. No Internet, but some good software, I hear."

"Computer room?" Trent's face brightened. "You're kidding me."

"Absolutely not."

"That's great! I was beginning to have the shakes!" He put his hand up and high-fived Squibb who nearly dropped his towel and whose round face beamed in joy anyway. For the next few moments, going through the line, they swapped nearly incomprehensible statements about speed, memory, RAM, monitor sizes, and sundry other computer speak which Jason only understood vaguely and neither Danno nor Jon seemed to understand at all. In fact, Jason thought that Jonnard's eyes had glazed over slightly by the time Trent and Henry started discussing mouse types versus tracing balls and other devices.

By the time they got inside the building, the two were lost deep in the subject of computer gaming and the rest of the world might as well have disappeared.

Jon waited patiently for both of them to take a deep breath at the same time, then interjected mildly, "Yes, but why do they have computers *here?*"

Everyone stopped and looked at him. "I mean, you can't expect they have them so that the two of you can play games, can you?" He paused while Henry and Trent sputtered a moment. "I mean. Think about it. Three brand-new machines, so that you can play super Gameboy on them? I don't think so."

"This is technology supreme," Trent argued. "What would a Magicker be using them for? I can only guess. For taping and editing the Talent Show, if nothing else."

"Exactly," Jon said as if he'd made a point. "We can only guess, and I suppose we'll find out soon enough."

Somewhat disappointed, Trent and Henry quieted, but Jason for one was glad for the sudden silence. He had begun to drown in a sea of computerisms. Then a shadow fell over him.

Tomaz Crowfeather stood patiently, waiting to be noticed. The Magicker dropped his hand to Jason's shoulder with a firm pressure.

"I hear you have been busy," Tomaz said.

"Ummm . . . I'm afraid so."

Tomaz winked, his tanned face wrinkling about his eyes. "There is nothing wrong with a young Magicker casting a long shadow. Many of us here have been waiting years in hope for such signs of Talent. But you draw troubles as well. Wear this. It should help."

He dropped a small bag in Jason's hand, a carefully plaited

string of yarn to hold it. Blanket weave designs decorated the small, plump fabric bag.

Jason cradled it. It crunched slightly, and a fragrant but odd smell came out, as though the bag was full of herbs and leaves. He put it around his neck and dropped it inside his shirt. "What's that for?"

"That, young master, is for the wolfjackals."

"Oh." He looked around, afraid that the others might hear, but they did not seem to notice.

Tomaz stayed silently by his side, smiling slightly, and Jason realized that no one but the two of them could hear the words he spoke. "What's in it?"

"What you think is in it." Tomaz smiled slowly. "Dried things. Powders. Herbs. Magic of my own. Do not get it wet, but wear it otherwise. Will you do that for me, young master?"

Jason nodded. "Thank you," he said, and meant it. The touch of the little bag against the hollow of his throat helped lighten the worry about the crescent scar on his hand. He did not know how it did, but it did.

Tomaz nodded. "I will see you for canoeing," he reminded Jason before he left. "But not wearing that." He winked and strode away.

Jason touched the lump under his shirt.

Trent fidgeted as though waking up. He stared at Jason. "What's that?"

"Tomaz gave me something." True to his impression, Trent had apparently not heard a word that had been said.

"Oh, yeah? What?"

Jason hooked his finger about the cord, withdrawing the bag from beneath his shirt and taking it off so Trent could get a look at it. Then he dropped it into his pocket so it would stay with his clothes and safely dry while he showered.

"A fetish. Cool."

"A what?"

"Fetish. Like a . . . charm or talisman. Herbs, feathers, fur, made out of that sort of thing."

"Oh." Jason momentarily pulled it out of his pocket to look at it again. "It is cool."

Then the line moved again, and Trent rushed him into the finally open showers. "Come on, I want a look at the computers before we have to go to another activity."

Jason let the other's enthusiasm suck him in and draw him off after breakfast. True to Henry Squibb's word, there was a classroom lab open at the Gathering Hall. Inside it, computer desks, tables, and chairs reigned among the debris of many cardboard shipping boxes and a tangle of cords that looked quite complicated, leading from the various machines in stages of being unpacked. Trent walked among them, looking but not touching.

"They're going to be networked, apparently," he said. He looked up to see Jason watching him, and grinned. "Hooked together. So I can, like, type a file on my machine and you can access that file."

"Can't I do that anyway, if you send it to me?"

"Yeah, but that means I have to send it to someone outside like an agency or site which may or may not see it before he sends it to you. Or the cows may come home before traffic slows enough that he *can* send it. Networking is instantaneous. What's mine is yours, what's yours is mine. Straight from me to you." Trent tapped a computer connecting cable.

"Ah." Jason looked the units over. He used computers at school, but they didn't particularly fascinate him, although he did vaguely wonder, like Jon, what they were doing here at camp. Finally, fidgeting, he tugged at Trent, not wanting to be late to calisthenics. That would mean extra push-ups and hiking, and he had other things on his mind.

Lucas Jefferson met them with a big grin on his face and long iron rods with an end bent for a short handle. Trent and Jason fell in at the back. Ting turned around and waved at them, drawing Jennifer's attention who also turned and waved. They did a quick roll call, and then Jefferson tapped on a camp table, rattling a stack of clipboards.

"All right, ladies and gents, you are mine for the rest of the

morning. I want you to listen up, because Mistress Eleanora is
going to cover the book learning and lore of much of what it is
we're going to be doing today. This morning, we are going to do
the grunt work." He flashed a wide, ivory smile.

Stefan grunted, on cue. He lumbered up to a table and sat
down heavily, arms crossed. Rich thumped him on the back of
the head, a playful hit which Stefan scarcely seemed to register.

"As soon as I'm done explaining a bit, I'm going to have you
break into pairs. What we are going to do today is mapping. It's
not fun. It's hot. And it's boring. But it's essential because it has
to do with where a Magicker gets his Magick from."

"Ooooh," breathed Danno softly. Henry took his glasses off
and cleaned them solemnly.

"Magick is sunk into the earth itself. It can lie there, deep
and dormant, as though lost under a great ocean. Or it can surface, like a pretty shell we can easily pick up off the sand. It is
everywhere . . . and nowhere. It is a power that comes from the
land and its elements, and although it is everywhere, it tends to
run in deep streams and patterns. We call them ley lines. Know
where your ley lines and power nodes are and you can . . . if it's
your Talent . . . do quite a bit of Magick. You're going to hear
more about this from Miss Eleanora later. Now, you're going to
help me find the ley lines." Lucas hefted a fistful of metal rods.
They looked like straight rods, with a handle or grip bent at the
ends at right angles. Very simple. A long letter L in metal. "Anyone ever seen one of these before?"

Danno put his hand up. "I have."

"What's it called? What did you use it for?" Jefferson smiled
broadly at Danno.

"My grandfather calls 'em witching sticks. He used peeled
wood branches with a fork to hold. Those are metal, though,
and called dowsing rods. They're used to find water. He digs
wells where they tell him."

"Ever use one? Or just watch him?"

Danno looked uncomfortable. "I used 'em."

"Did they work?"

After a long moment, Danno ducked his head in a nod.

"Excellent! Because they can work, and do. I know contractors and builders, who even use them to find power lines, sometimes building studs."

Jason blinked. He'd seen a pair of those rods in the Dozer's big tool boxes. He knew they'd looked vaguely familiar!

Lucas separated a rod out and held it in front of him. "Now, with power lines, cables, and such, there are better tools. But for dowsing ley lines," he winked, "we have to do it the old-fashioned way. We use them in pairs." He pulled another rod free from a stack. One in each hand, he held them side by side, the short ends disappearing into his large hands. He held them easily in front of him, pointing straight out. "You hold them parallel, like this. You squeeze 'em kind of easy so they can't swing around as you walk, but you hold 'em gentle like. We'll be walking in rows, side by side, step by step. If the rods feel like swinging apart, you let 'em. Or the points dipping down. When they stop moving, you stop! You freeze, right there. Your partner, the one with the clipboard, is going to mark the spot, best as he can, on the topography maps we have printed out. The reason the rods move is they are sensitive to fields of energy we can't find easily otherwise. We'll be spread out, but you'll be able to see campers on your left and right. If your fellow campers are stopped as well, you wait till their rods are in position again and they're ready to walk again, before you move out. Any questions?"

Hands shot up and voices peppered the air, but Trent stepped to the stack of clipboards and grabbed one up. He pointed at Jason. "You're dowsing. I'm mapping."

Lucas patiently answered a number of questions before he said firmly, "Get your gear, and follow me, and we'll have a try at it. Then I think you'll understand it a bit better."

They hiked to the edge of the campground where wilderness pressed heavily and the fencing, if any, seemed broken down. Jason touched his charm bag against his neck uneasily, feeling chilled although the summer sun burned down hotly on them all. Jason held his metal rods, one in each hand as he'd been told. He stepped forward and felt nothing, absolutely nothing, with Trent trotting along behind him, humming and drumming his pencil against the clipboard until Jason wanted to yell. With each step dust puffed up from drying grass and pine needles. Suddenly, the rods in his hands slowly began to swing apart. He slowed, then stopped as they moved all the way to each side, his jaw dropped in astonishment.

Jefferson jogged up. He held a single rod in his hand and it swung wildly as he drew even with Trent and Jason. "Well, well. Looks like you've found a strong one. Let's see if the others can catch the stream."

Pleased, Jason stood very still. The sun beat down on his head. He could see Henry and Jonnard, of all people, mapping, off to the right. Way to the left, past several groups, Jennifer and Ting worked. Soon, all halted. It was an uneven wavering line of campers. Trent shaded his eyes, then began to sketch, quickly, on a second piece of paper.

"What are you doing?"

"Well. We've got our spot here." Trent tapped the pencil on the map he had. "And the whole line here." He flipped the first sheet up and tapped the second page. "Otherwise, someone's got to go through and coordinate everyone's spot, see?"

Jason didn't quite, but he nodded as if he had. Jefferson bellowed, from somewhere over a small hillock to Jason's left, "Move out!"

Jason righted his dowsing rods and began to stride forward again, slowly. They'd gone maybe the distance of the schoolyard at home, when his rods began to swing in his hands again. He stopped as they suddenly flung open to each side, making a wide vee, and quivered.

There was a shout or two next to him, and Trent once again began sketching quickly, his face furrowed in concentration.

As the morning wore on, the momentary excitement of having the rods actually move seemingly on their own wore off. Jefferson had the area laid out in grids and once they worked one direction, they came back and worked the other at right angles. When they finally turned in their clipboards and rods, he was hot, dusty, sweaty, and scratched. Jefferson thumped him on the shoulder. "No guts, no glory," he said, grinning.

Stefan looked as if he'd fallen headfirst into a hedge as the pair of them trudged up to turn in their gear. The heavy boy shuffled about as Rich piled his metal rods into Jefferson's stack.

"What happened?" Trent stared in fascination.

"Nothing." Stefan grunted and shrugged away. Rich, though, snickered. "Fell into a brier patch," he said.

"Didn't see it?" Jason thought that even Stefan must be smart enough to avoid a brier patch, if he knew it was there.

Stefan grumbled and scrubbed at his nose, where a long angry scratch ran across it. "Long story." He lumbered off, Rich in his wake.

Trent whispered in his ear, "Ever try to figure out what it is that makes those two Magickers?"

Jason nodded thoughtfully. At the cabin, he packed his fetish away as he got towels and trunks and they went to swimming class gratefully, letting the cooling waters of Lake Wannameecha wash away the dirt and grit and the heat of the sun. The promised lecture from Eleanora, however, did not materialize as that class was canceled and instead, Dr. Patel led them all in yoga and breathing exercises, which was okay, but had Jason wondering.

Where was the glory in being a Magicker? When was he going to see something wondrous done? What good was it if they couldn't even find Bailey?

After dinner, they sat at the fire ring. Jennifer was reading notes in her notebook by the last of the sun, her face hidden by a curtain of long blonde hair, her legs tucked under her. Trent lay flat on his back, watching the last of the daylight catching the clouds drifting overhead. Henry sat miserably, having failed at dowsing. Jonnard was off somewhere and Danno had kitchen duty. Ting sat on the log, needle in hand, expertly sewing back on a pocket that had been ripped free earlier.

And Jason leaned against Trent's knees, angry and unhappy

that Bailey was still gone. She had depended on *him,* and he'd failed her so far. All the clues meant nothing to him. She had vanished into thin air just like that cookie he'd tried to hand her. . . .

"Do you think we'll have Bailey back by the Fourth of July? We need her for the big game. Not to mention her mother will be frantic with no letters and no calls. How do you tell someone her daughter is a Ghost?"

Ting shivered. "At least I know it's a friendly Ghost."

"We could cover, I guess," said Trent thoughtfully. "But not for long."

"We shouldn't have to cover," said Jason firmly. "There must be a way to find her."

Ting pulled on her needle and thread quickly, and a small smile crossed her face. "There!" she said in satisfaction, and held her shorts up. "A stitch in time saves nine!"

Jason's head snapped around. "What was that?"

"Sewing," said Ting. She waved her needle and thread about. "Mending? You do know that things can be repaired?"

"No . . . no . . . what was that you said? I only half heard you."

"A stitch in time saves nine?" Ting looked at him through curious almond-shaped eyes.

"That's it! That's it!" Jason leaped to his feet and did a war dance around the fire ring, scattering chipmunks and sending blue jays winging off, and drawing stares all around. "A stitch in time saves mine," she'd whispered in his ear. It could only have been Bailey twisting that saying about. In time! "That's why they can't find her! Bailey's isn't some*where.* She's some-*when!*"

19

A Cheese to Catch a Cheese

JENNIFER flung her hair over her shoulder and peered at Jason. "Whatever are you talking about?"

Jason stopped dancing, slightly out of breath. "I know where Bailey is. She's right here. Only, she's out of time somehow, offtrack. Out of sync."

Ting put away her sewing things neatly, mulling over what he'd suggested, before saying, "I think he's right. He has to be. Too many things have happened."

Jennifer clipped her pen to her notebook. She stood. "What are we going to do about it?"

He stopped still. "I've no idea," he answered slowly. "I have to tell the Magickers, of course."

Jennifer snorted. "We are all concerned, but I think that's the wisest course."

"We're also on probation," Trent said. He dug the toe of his sneaker into the dirt around the fire ring.

"We don't even have a plan. Yet," Jason answered.

The sun lowered behind the mountains, dusk settling in, and the clouds Trent had been watching turned a fiery pink and gold in the sky. Its heat lingered behind, though, blanketing the whole camp, and another swim sounded great, but no one was allowed in the lake after late afternoon. That did not mean no one went swimming . . . they had all heard of swimming trips sneaked in, but Jason did not feel like venturing out tonight. Other campers filtered in, and whatever plans were being thought of, were quickly put aside.

Eleanora joined them. "Nice evening," she said quietly. She carried her dulcimer. "No bonfire tonight."

Sighs of protest greeted her, and she smiled faintly. "All is not lost. FireAnn and her staff have been cranking at ice cream, and I hear they're serving sundaes in the mess hall."

"Ice cream!" Henry Squibb jumped to his feet and trotted off without another word.

Cool, creamy ice cream sounded too good to miss for any reason, but Jason hung back till they were all alone. Eleanora smiled at him. Trent stayed in the background, almost close enough to overhear, but too far away to participate in the chat. "Not screaming for ice cream, Jason?"

"Oh, it sounds good, but . . . I think I know about Bailey."

Eleanora had let her hand fall upon the dulcimer, and its strings chimed very faintly. "Tell me," she said, after she stilled it.

"She's out of sync."

"Out of sync? Synchronization?" Eleanora watched his face.

"Exactly. She's out of time with us. Either a step or two ahead or behind. I don't know for sure which way and I don't think she knows either, other than she's almost but not quite here."

"And you figured this out for yourself?"

"Not exactly. She managed to tell me something. I only heard part of it, and it didn't make sense. Bailey gets things twisted around sometimes."

Eleanora laughed softly. "I have heard a saying or two she's put into knots."

Jason grinned. "This one was 'a stitch in time saves mine.' I only heard half of it and just realized a few minutes ago what she was saying, and what she meant."

"That does have a ring of truth about it." Eleanora sat down on a tree stump, gathering her skirts about her. "That would explain what we've done wrong trying to track her. Even why she dropped her crystal."

"Why?"

"Well, if she's fallen a step behind, she had not even chosen it yet." Eleanora made a slight face. "Time is very difficult to deal with. We don't, usually, unless there is an accident of this sort. It takes a lot of mana and discipline. And we can't alter Time. But Bailey is like . . . well, let me think of a way to put it. If Time were a stream, a river, Bailey would be a stone put into it . . . a stone that didn't belong there, then. We can retrieve her. We can't change the tide or flow of the river in any way whatsoever."

Trent edged closer. "Can't . . . or won't."

"Both." Eleanora considered him. "Sets off too many ripples, don't you think? And every one of us, for some reason or other, would want at least one small moment in our timelines changed. The final effect would be like, oh, a covered pan of popcorn kernels being heated up and popping more and more rapidly until the pan is one big explosion. No." She shook her head. "I don't think any of us wants that."

"Removing Bailey won't harm anything?"

"No. But the longer she stays, the more potential harm she can cause. She is not meant to be there, and not only will Time fight her, her own body will begin to fight her. The Bailey we know will cease to exist. We have to rescue her, and I fear we've only one or two more chances to try." She stood. "How about we head to the mess hall? I think I can persuade FireAnn to put some ice cream aside until later. With any luck, Bailey can join us."

Trent trotted a little behind them as they went down the gentle sloping trails toward the bright lights, muttering to himself. Jason cast him a puzzled glance over his shoulder, wondering where the "I'll try anything" Trent had gone to. Cheers and the happy clattering of spoons in dishes greeted them at the mess hall.

Three silvery and frosted kegs sat on the counter, with Fire-Ann's crew dipping out great spoonfuls of ice cream from them. There was vanilla, with flecks of the savory bean in the ivory cream; chocolate, deep and rich looking; and fresh berry ice cream in swirls of pink and purple fruit. Everyone licking his or her spoon looked extremely happy. Jason slowed down unhappily. Despite Eleanora's suggestion, it didn't seem that there would be any left for later! That chocolate looked as if it were meant for him. He sighed.

Eleanora looked about. "I don't see Gavan yet. I think perhaps ice cream now is in order," she said in sympathy.

Without further urging, Jason and Trent dashed to the small line still waiting for the frosty desserts. Up at the front, Stefan growled a bit, saying, "No chocolate. Just the berries. I want the berry ice cream."

Rich's jaw dropped. "But, Stefan, my man. You're crazy about chocolate."

"I said . . . berries. I want berries!"

"And that you shall have," FireAnn said joyfully. She towered his bowl and smiled as Stefan shuffled out of line, a blissful smile on his broad face, Rich trailing behind with a look of disbelief plastered all over his.

Jason was able to get his bowl heaped with a good helping of all three, FireAnn winking at him as she dolloped the last bite of vanilla on top. Behind him, Trent broke out into a happy hum, back to normal. Eleanora settled for fresh berries only, with just a bare spoonful of the fruited ice cream on top.

She looked at her dish with a wry smile. "Diets," she remarked, before joining them. "Although," she added, with a faint purr after the first taste, "this is quite a treat!"

Jason had just finished, and Trent had gone back to beg for seconds, when Gavan came in. He searched the hall before spotting Eleanora and heading over. She spooned up a last mouthful of fresh berries, offering them to him as he sat down.

"Yum." His blue eyes sparkled with appreciation. "Think I could get FireAnn to save me a bowl?"

"I'm sure you could."

He nodded, and then ran his hand through his hair. "Well, lads." He smiled at Trent and Jason. "The lot of you did some nice work earlier today. There are some good mappers about. You, in particular." He patted Trent's shoulder.

"Thank you," Trent mumbled around the bowl of his spoon, his words muffled and half-frozen.

"Another day or two of mapping like that, inputting into the computer, and we should have a good idea of what immediately surrounds the camp. We'll have to go farther afield, of course, to get the whole area done, but . . . well, it looks promising."

"Is it safer away from camp?"

Gavan looked down at his cane. "No, Eleanora, it won't be. This is a project I have to take, literally, step by step. They have us at a disadvantage, and they know it, and they'll harry us."

"Bad news with the good, then."

"Aye, it is." He took a deep breath, straightening his shoulders.

"I've some more good news, then. Jason here has solved the conundrum of Bailey's whereabouts."

"What?" The sparkle returned to his blue eyes as he looked upon Jason. "Spit it out!"

"Well." Jason set his dish aside. "She's not lost somewhere, but somewhen. She's a step or two out of time. I'd guess behind, but I'm not sure about that."

"In time. Of course, of course! I should have thought of that . . . she's parallel." He frowned. "We'll get her back, then, but it'll take a bit of planning. Someone with a definite link to her will have the best shot, someone who can go in, get in rhythm with her, and bring her back."

"That would be me," Jason said firmly.

"You?" Gavan arched his eyebrow. The wolfhead crystal seemed to glow at him.

"As Bailey would say, 'Send a cheese to catch a cheese.' I've heard her, once or twice. She's been able to leave a hint or two for me, and I'd have thought of where she was sooner if I'd been smarter." He took a deep breath and said, "I don't know what to do, but if you show me, I'll do it."

Gavan nodded solemnly. He said to Trent, "Sorry, lad, but I think Jason had better go this alone."

Trent nodded back, but Jason thought he saw an expression of relief cross his face quickly before he ducked his head and finished off the last of his dessert.

Something pinched his ear again, leaving a fleeting feeling behind of cold fingers, tweaking to get his attention. If only it *was* Bailey. Perhaps she already knew what they were going to try and do! If only things could be that easy. . . .

The three sat around Gavan's desk. He cleared it with a sweep of his cane, papers flying and Eleanora settling with a slight frown on her face as if she realized she might well be the one picking up the mess. He fetched Bailey's amethyst crystal out of his drawer, unwrapping it from the silk handkerchief and setting it in the center of the desktop. "Yours next to it, but comfortably within reach," he directed Jason.

"Yes, sir." Carefully he placed his crystal next to Bailey's. His was larger, he hadn't realized that, but either was small enough to cup in the palm of his hand.

"Cover both."

He stretched his arms out and began to do that, his left hand over her crystal, right hand over his, and his crescent moon scar gave a sudden throb. He jerked his hands back, wincing.

"What's wrong?"

"Nothing." Jason touched the fetish bag at his throat and put his hands out again. He switched the crystals first, then settled his left hand over his own. No lancing pain. He relaxed a bit and settled into position, Eleanora and Gavan trading glances over his head. He squirmed in his chair a bit and Eleanora hooked her foot over the chair rung, scooting him close to the desk. He shot her a grateful look as he rolled his shoulders and got more comfortable.

"Now," said Gavan firmly. "If anything goes wrong, you're to find us and return immediately. Close your eyes."

He did so. He felt a hand settle on each of his shoulders.

"This is where we shall be, Jason. Find us there."

A bit bewildered, he answered, "I can feel you."

"Not with your everyday senses. Find our Magick there, anchoring you."

He didn't know how! Jason clenched his eyes shut, till his lids crinkled together. How did they expect him to know something like that? He couldn't do this! He had no way of knowing; what had they shown him of Magick really? And yet . . . and yet . . . on his right shoulder, he could feel a steady warmth, like a banked fire. And on his left, well, it wasn't a feeling at all, it was a sound. He could hear the very faint chime of music rippling past his ear. Slowly he said, "Eleanora is music. And you are fire."

"Very good. Now, open your eyes. Focus on your crystal first and when you feel good about it, you're going to look into Bailey's. You're going to see if you can find that door she disappeared through, and follow her."

Jason nodded carefully. "Yes, sir." He looked at his crystal, seeing in his mind's eye the way the jeweler's glass showed it to him, magnified into all its various layers and angles. He loved the look of his stone. Even the flawed part of it. With reluctance, he shifted his attention to Bailey's amethyst and looked at it intently.

A spiky crystal, with many, many facets and sharp edges, like a dozen or so brilliant purple gems stacked up unevenly and fused together, it was still a beautiful cluster. He could see why Bailey had chosen it. It would have looked pretty in a setting for a necklace, he supposed, or some piece of jewelry. With a faint pang of homesickness, he thought of his stepmother and how she loved to shop for jewelry. She rarely bought any; her taste was expensive, but she used to talk to him and Alicia when they were along. He hadn't listened then and wished now he had. He looked sharply into the gem blanketed under his right hand.

He thought he saw a faint line, stretching and then opening, like a door slightly ajar. He knew that vision and plunged forward toward it eagerly. It was a door, it was Bailey's, and he had to catch it!

Honeycomb

HE dove through into a threshold of stunning cold, like plunging headfirst into an icy pool. He sputtered in surprise, shaking his head vigorously as it pounded with the sensation. Jason stood for a moment in purple shadow and looked about, then saw a fleeting glimpse just ahead of him. He ran after, calling, "Bailey! Wait!"

The wispy nothing turned about, then became solid. It was Bailey in all her freckled and golden-brown-haired glory. She spun around, her jaw dropping in surprise, and then she let out a cry of joy. "Jason!" She started to bound toward him.

He stopped short, as a loud grating noise came from in front of him. A deep black crack opened up as the crystal under his feet vibrated for a long moment, rather like an earthquake. He stared down into it. Was it breaking up around them? Time did not seem to be on his side. "Come on," he said urgently, and held his hand out.

"I can't." Her voice trailed off, and she came to the edge of the chasm and stood hesitantly. "I've tried and tried." She shivered and hugged her arms about her ribs. "I'm cold. I'm hungry. And I'm sleepy."

"Sleepy?"

"I don't dare nap. I doze off now and then, but . . ." She looked at him, her face pleading. "Please help me, Jason!"

He leaned forward across the darkness, stretching closer. "Bailey, you've got to meet me halfway."

"I can't."

"Bailey, you can't stay. You're going to . . . you're going to die in here." As he spoke, the chill settled around him like a cloak, until its numbness went right to his bones. His ears felt brittle, like icicles that might break off. The only part of him that stayed warm was a small spot on his right shoulder.

Gavan, he thought. He shrugged his shoulder high, putting his ear and cheek to the warm spot for a moment. It heated him right through, as though he'd spread his body near a fireplace, and he managed to shake off most of the cold.

She just stood and looked at him, her heart-shaped face pale and afraid behind her freckles, her hair tangled and disheveled. She lifted her hand to her face and nibbled on the corner of a nail. "I . . . can't."

" 'Course you can!" He stood on the brink, and stretched out both hands. "Come on! You can't get home from there."

She turned on one foot, pointing into the shadows behind her. "The camp is that way."

"The way back to our camp is this way." He jerked a thumb over his shoulder. "You're out of step, Bailey. Just a Ghost. You've got to come with me."

"No one saw me." Bailey frowned. "I'm so hungry! All I've had is that cookie. And I want to sleep in my warm bed and . . ." She took a step backward.

"Bailey!" Jason sharpened his voice. "Listen to me. I'm here. Take hold of my hand and come with me." Music played softly in his ear, as if Eleanora tried to remind him of something. Was she hurrying him? Encouraging? He couldn't tell; all he knew was that Bailey was balking and he couldn't lose her. "We don't have a lot of time anymore, Bailey." He couldn't understand why she hesitated, why she just looked at him. Why she seemed so pale. Then he realized that she was fading, gradually. She was not the Bailey he knew, not quite, not altogether. And it would only get worse. He *would* lose her. "Come on," he coaxed. "FireAnn made ice cream. More cookies than you can eat."

"I want a hamburger."

"Those, too. And your own bed at Kittencurl waiting for you. Ting has it all ready. Jennifer has letters from your mom. Everyone is this way." He half-turned, showing the way.

She stood on tiptoe. She looked down into the dark crack between them, then back up at him. "I'll have to jump."

He stifled a mutter. "I'll catch you!" He stretched his hands out again.

"I don't think I can do it. . . ."

"Bailey," he said firmly. "You can do anything." He wiggled his fingers. "You're just a long step away. Not far at all. And I won't let you fall in, I promise!" She looked into his eyes across the dark chasm. "Come on. We've got things to do. Canoe races. Helping Henry get even with Stefan and Rich. Learning our crystals. Catching that thief."

"That thief!" Bailey cracked a grin. "I've a plan."

"Trent and I will help, just . . . take my hand . . . and jump."

She took a deep breath. She looked back over her shoulder, to something only she could see in the purple shadows. "Maybe I should go home instead. Mom must be so worried. I think I can make it from here," she said wistfully.

A sinking feeling hit him. He was losing her. "Someday, Bailey. But not from here, and not without help."

She swung around. Without another word, she leaped.

It caught him off guard. She came at him, arms and legs akimbo, golden-brown hair streaming, hands grasping desperately for him. He waved frantically, trying to catch her flying hands. In an awful moment, as she hung in midair over the darkening gap, he knew she wouldn't make it.

"No!" Leaning farther forward than he dared, he locked wrists with her. She cried out and tore her right hand away from his left as though stung. Jason fell to his knees, off-balance, and gave a great pull, yanking her on top of him, and they both went tumbling.

But she was on his side of the awful gap. He got to his feet and pulled her up. Bailey leaned on him, and took a great gulping breath. "I can't see," she whispered. "It's all . . . dark and purple shadow."

"I can," he reassured her. He linked his right arm about her arm, tucking her close to his side. He turned and looked and saw only mirrorlike walls facing them, tinted with the inner glow of the crystal.

Jason pondered. "Ummm."

"Anything to eat?" Bailey's voice sounded wispy and weak.

"Not on me."

She giggled faintly. "Should have sent Trent. He's always got food on him, unless he's eaten it first."

"Hey!" said Jason, mock-insulted. Without trying to worry her, he examined the area around them, searching for the way out. There was none. Now they were both trapped. He stopped in his tracks. Bailey shivered next to him and he could feel how cold she was, how lifeless this crystal was becoming. She was running out of time.

He closed his eyes, thinking. The fire on his right shoulder seemed to flicker. The music in his left ear tinkled faintly. He couldn't lose them! Without them . . . Jason's eyes flew open. He looked ahead. As long as he had the two Magickers anchoring him, he was not lost. He couldn't be. The planes ahead of him might look solid, but they had not shut away Eleanora and Gavan. He hugged Bailey. "One step at a time," he told her confidently. He moved forward into the purple shadows, his friend leaning on him.

From behind, a howl sounded. It echoed and resounded off the crystal walls, rising and falling.

Bailey gasped and clutched at him. Jason fought the impulse to spin around. "There's a canyon between it and us," he said. He moved another step closer to the heat, the music.

"It followed me in when I tried to keep them from getting you. One of them tracked me. They can see me. Smell me. That's why I can't sleep, I've been running and running ever since. I ran in here to hide, and I've been trapped. I couldn't find a way out!" Bailey's voice trembled.

"I won't let them catch us. Just hang on to me!"

The wolfjackal howled again, louder, closer. He though he could hear triumph in its throat. He had no doubt it could jump the canyon. But he was almost home, and of that, he had little doubt as well.

He could hear the chimes, like a waterfall of notes, cascading about him. Heat washed up against them, banked warmth from an unseen source, but he knew who it was. On his heels, he could hear the noise as the running beast gathered itself, and jumped.

"This way, Bailey!" He grabbed her and pushed her ahead into . . . nothingness.

"Next time, I want pillows," she said. Contentedly, she licked off her spoon, leaning back in the great winged back chair in Eleanora's office, because Gavan's was undeniably still a mess . . . what with papers and objects from his desk toppled everywhere, not to mention overturned chairs from when Jason and Bailey had hit ground.

"Next time?" Both Gavan and Eleanora looked at Bailey.

She blushed. "Well. You know. If I ever have to fall out of a crystal again . . . once burned, twice careful."

Jason took a small tart from his plate and passed it to her, saying, "Still hungry?"

She snatched it up with a muffled "Thank you," crumbs dribbling from the corner of her mouth. Finally, she sat back, empty bowl on her lap, a cat-who-ate-the-canary pleased look on her face. Her eyelids drooped.

"I think," observed Eleanora, "that a good night's sleep is in order. And then, tomorrow, young lady, we will listen to your adventures and reacquaint you with your crystal . . . from the outside!"

Bailey nodded slowly as Eleanora reached forward to take the dirty dishes. Gavan leaned over the chair, then picked her up in his arms, as though she were a small child. "To Kittencurl and bed," he said.

Jason watched them go. Suddenly, Bailey peeked from around Gavan's arm.

"Thank you," she got out sleepily. He beamed.

Ting and Bailey sat chatting away, laughing and giggling, with an occasional smile and thrown-in laugh from Jennifer as Bailey devoured a breakfast fit for either Trent or Henry Squibb. She grinned at Jason and Trent as they slid into their seats. "I'm almost all caught up!" she announced, pointing at her tray.

"Good." He didn't like the image of a quiet, lackluster Bailey. She seemed to be back, in more ways than one. She sidled over and whispered, "Have I got things to tell you!"

"I don't know," he whispered back. "Have you?"

"I'm serious! You won't believe what I heard, ghosting about." She glanced around the mess hall. "For instance, Tomaz is looking for a skinwalker."

"A what?"

"I'll tell you later!" She giggled and put her elbow in his ribs. "Later!"

"Okay."

She slid back to Ting, and they exchanged some more words, quietly this time, except that Ting looked up, over Bailey's head, at the two of them, before ducking back down and the two girls burst into loud laughter. Was it something he'd said? Puzzled, Jason studied his breakfast.

"Girls," muttered Trent. "Can't live with 'em, and can't live with 'em."

That made Jason laugh. "Now," he said, "you're beginning to sound like Bailey." He started to eat his frosted flakes before they got soggy.

Back at their cabins, with some spare time to clean up the area because inspection would be tomorrow, they found Jonnard marching Henry about the small clearing and path, dowsing rods in his hand. Henry's round face looked more owlish than ever, huffed and puffed up with frustration.

"I can't do it! I just can't." Henry shoved his glasses back to rest properly on the bridge of his nose.

Jon looked down on him, saying mildly, "If you can't, that's perfectly all right. Magickers have all kinds of Talents. There are all sorts of perfectly capable people who can't dowse. But you *are* the one who asked for extra practice."

"I can't do anything!" Henry began to wail and then stopped short. He sighed instead. "I'm going to be drummed out, I just know it."

"You're here at camp. Meanwhile . . ." Jon glanced at the two of them standing there. "Anyone have a clean handkerchief or bandanna?"

"Bandanna in the cabin!" Trent shot off and came back with a bright red bandanna in his hands. He handed it to Jon.

John stretched it out between his fingers. "Okay, Henry, one last try before I let you give up on dowsing." He held out the bandanna as a blindfold. Henry fidgeted while he fastened it about his eyes. Stefan and Rich sauntered up, and stood, smirking, at the path's edge. Jon eyed them, then decided to ignore them as he bent over to retrieve a line of pennies he'd laid out on the ground. After a moment or two, he had them laid out in a new line.

"All right. In the same general area we were before, there's a line. Find it, Henry," Jon said quietly.

Henry's hands flexed around his dowsing rods. Before he could bring them into position and start, both Stefan and Rich darted to his side, saying, "That's too easy." Grabbing him, they began to spin him round and round in circles, till—when they halted and stepped back—his glasses had slipped all the way to the end of his nose and he wobbled in his shoes. "Now, try it!" They stepped back, chortling at their cleverness.

Jonnard shot the two of them a dirty look before saying, "It's all right, Henry. Let me know when you're ready."

"N . . . now," Henry quavered. He stumbled, then righted himself as he walked forward.

With Trent, Jason, and Jon all encouraging him, his path

snaked all over the small clearing dizzily. Even when he steadied, not once as he neared the line of coins did his metal rods even twitch. Rich and Stefan snickered and smirked till even they were tired of it and wandered off. Squibb finally halted with a sigh, tugged the blindfold down around his neck. "It's no use. I'm just an idiot."

Jon took the rods from him and patted him on the shoulder. "No, you're not. When's the last time anyone ever dug a well hoping to hit pennies? At any rate, you're a whiz on the computers, I hear."

"But that's not Magick."

"It is to someone like me." Jon smiled. "Come on, let's play chess a bit before class." Without another word, he turned and went into their cabin, his long legs taking him up two strides at a time over the steps and porch. With a sniffle, Henry took off the bandanna, tossed it to Trent, and followed. Trent watched them disappear thoughtfully.

Inside, Jason remembered something.

"Hey, Trent. You ever heard of a skinwalker?"

Trent stopped in the middle of making a basket with a pair of rolled-up dirty socks. "A what?"

"A skinwalker?"

He scratched his nose and shot the socks into the corner from across the room anyway. "I don't know if this is what you mean . . . but I think it's like a Native American term for a shapeshifter. A skin changer, like. Like . . . I dunno . . . a werewolf. Where'd you heard about one, anyway?"

"Bailey told me. She heard stuff while she was walking around, half here and half not. She says Tomaz is looking for one."

"Whoa. That's pretty heavy." Trent stood up. "Someone who sprouts hair and claws and stuff in the full moon." He bared his teeth and began to stagger across the cabin at Jason.

Jason wound up and thwapped him with a pillow, and Trent fell over, laughing. When he stopped, he asked, "What do you think?"

"I don't know. She said she had a lot to tell me. We'll see."
He shrugged.

"May you live in interesting, weird times," Trent said, as he
got to his feet and began to knot his socks up so he could pelt
them at Jason.

"Thank you!" Jason beamed at him.

21

Gimme Some Peanuts and Crackerjacks

"ARE you sure you're up to this?"

" 'Course, I'm sure!" Bailey yawned and stretched. "I'm almost all caught up!" She grinned, then hid her mouth. " 'Sides . . . this is get even day! And it's the Fourth! Who could miss a baseball game on the Fourth of July?"

Ting hugged her. Jason eyed Bailey. She still looked a bit pale behind her freckled nose, but all in all, much better. He crossed his arms as Rich and Stefan snickered.

"No way is she gonna be on my team," Rich said. Stefan lumbered across the baseball diamond, putting on his catcher's gear as he moved, strapping the protective padding across his chest and bulky thighs.

"No way I'd ever want to be," Bailey shot back. She pressed her lips shut thinly as Jefferson came round the corner of the backstop, clipboard in hand.

"All right, ladies and gentlemen. It's been a fine day. Are we ready to hold our vengeance match this late afternoon?" He smiled broadly as though he had been listening. "Let's get teams picked."

The warped wooden stands thundered dully as campers who

weren't playing settled themselves down with colorful paper sacks of fresh popcorn from the kitchens. The aroma wafted deliciously over the baseball diamond, and Jason almost opted to go sit and watch as well. Trent's stomach gave a faint rumble, but he put his hand on Jason's wrist, frowning.

"We can't let 'em get away with this," he whispered.

Jason nodded. He pushed the desire for popcorn to the back of his thoughts and squared his shoulders as Jefferson asked, "Do we have both captains here?"

"I'm here," said Rich, the corner of his mouth curling back unpleasantly. "Dunno what happened to Fred, though."

"He's still at the swimming relays. He should be here any second," Ting shot back.

"With dead arms, if he's swimming," said Stefan gleefully. He gave a grunt as Jefferson eyed him a moment. He shuffled around and found himself, somehow, standing behind Rich.

Bailey stood with her arms folded. Jennifer leaned over and whispered something in Bailey's ear.

"I don't think that was the least bit funny," said Bailey. "And you guys are going to lose."

Jennifer smiled. She pulled her hair back into a ponytail and tucked it up into her baseball cap, looking as if she meant business.

Fred came loping up, hair all slicked back from swimming, pulling a sweatshirt on over his clothes. He grinned and slapped Trent's upheld hand. "Okay, let's get this grudge match going!"

Jennifer sniffed, casting a glance Stefan's way, who despite being all bundled up in catcher's equipment, looked more rumpled and dustier than ever. "Grudge or grunge?"

Even Jefferson laughed while Stefan just scowled and rubbed his stubby nose. Jefferson tapped his clipboard again. "Okay, you two, let's pick teams."

In just a few moments, with bodies scrambling to keep up as the team captains chanted names off, two lines of players soon faced each other. Fred and Rich quickly did the hand over hand on the bat Jefferson held out to them, with Fred winning. He smiled. "We'll be the home team."

Rich's lip curled. "You'll need last ups," he warned. "We're gonna knock you outta the ballpark!"

Fred looked at Rich's players, and then up and down his line at Jason and the others. He smiled slowly. "You're going to need more than luck," he promised. "Okay, huddle up for field assignments!"

He looked Bailey in the eyes. "First base."

"M . . . me?" She stood on one foot and then the other.

"You. You're fast, you think fast. Ting, you're pitching." Fred rattled off everyone's assignments and they gathered gloves and trotted out to the field to enthusiastic cheers from the rest of the campers in the stands. After a rousing rendition of "The Star Spangled Banner" led by Sousa, the game was on!

Jason took his place in right field. Trent was shortstop, Jonnard center field, Jennifer second base, Henry was catching, Danno was at third base, and Fred in left field. Ting did some stretches, then narrowed her eyes and glared down at home plate, sizing up the first of Rich's batters. She wound up and threw, dead on, and Jefferson loudly called "Steeee-rike!"

She beamed.

Her second pitch sailed past the home plate, down and a little outside. George Anders swung his bat at it threateningly, but held up, and Jefferson called out, "Ball one!"

George hit the fifth pitch, popping it up, and Trent came in a little, catching it neatly. The stands wildly cheered the first out. The smell of popcorn had faded, or maybe Jason was too far out in the field to catch it, but the thought stayed at the back of his mind. Stefan came up to bat and with one swing, he sent the ball sailing over the weathered back fence of the field. Campers came to their feet screaming as it sailed into the bushes and Fred went trotting after to retrieve it. Ting sagged on the pitcher's mound.

Jason and Trent both came in. Trent thumped her on the back. "Good going!"

Bailey walked in, just in time to catch that. Her face went pinched. "What do you mean by that?"

"I mean . . . good going. Every pitcher is gonna lose a pitch like that. Ting got it out of her system early, no harm done!" Trent thumped Ting again, who staggered a little.

"Oh." Bailey looked back and forth. "Well . . . that's good, then!" She hugged Ting.

Ting let out a small sound. Fred showed up, ball in hand, cleaning off the dirt with his sweatshirt before dropping it into her hands. "Got that out of the way. Now let's play!" He grinned. She took a deep breath and nodded.

Ting struck out one and walked one, but the team came to her aid and made the other outs on good plays. By the time they took their ups at the plate and then returned to the field, Jon's line drive had sent Fred across for a score, and the game was tied 1–1.

As the day trudged into dusk, it was 7–7, clearly not a pitcher's duel. Tired, Ting went to sit on the bench, happily munching popcorn, and Fred took her place, drafting Christopher Bacon out of the stands to replace him in center field. And so the day went. Jason had two good hits, a strikeout, and two pop flies. Trent had solid hits but only got around the bases one more time, and as the sun went down in the sky and the mosquitoes began to gather, everyone came to a tired huddle before taking their at-bats.

Jefferson consulted his clipboard. "Listen up, everyone. Because this is the Fourth of July, and FireAnn has a special dinner cooking, and there's going to be a big bonfire after, with some special effects . . ." He winked at this. "Game will be called at the end of this inning."

Everyone cheered even more wildly. Hunger rattled around inside Jason's ribs. He looked longingly at the bench where Ting now sat with a cone of red, white, and blue cotton candy in her hands. She saw his look and waved back happily. His stomach growled.

Positions had been rotated and new players volunteered from the stands. Stefan was now pacing around heavily in center field, stopping occasionally to lean mockingly on the drooping fence. No one else had hit a home run.

Jason waved his bat, pointed it at the new pitcher, and took up a stance. Not that he thought he'd get a home run, but just to rattle him a little. Tran's face was, as always, closed and unreadable, but Jason thought he saw a flicker in his eyes. He moved on the pitcher's mound and Jason got ready.

He met the ball squarely with the bat. He could feel the impact and followed through on the swing, knowing it was a good one. He sprinted for first base, dropping the bat on the way, head down, digging in his heels, ankle twinging only the barest bit. The ball shot between first base and second base, but he had no time to make it to second and stayed at first on a good, solid hit.

Fred put his hands up over his head and applauded. Jason caught his breath and waited to be brought home. He slapped at a mosquito at the back of his neck, muttering. The sky had gotten very dark, and the hanging lights that festooned the campgrounds twinkled in golden winks, intermingled with lightning bugs imitating them, in slow lazy swarms by the lake's edge. He waited while Trent popped out and then Danno got hit by a pitched ball, so they both moved forward. Then Tran struck Fred out, and Bailey stepped up to bat.

She took her cap off, smoothed back her golden-brown hair, and then put her cap on backward, and settled down at the plate like she meant it. Rich was catching now and grunted something at her Jason didn't quite hear. Bailey's response was to kick a cloud of dirt over the plate, making Rich burst into sneezes and coughs. She tried to look apologetic as she dusted him off. Jason hid a smirk. He tagged up at second. Behind him, he could hear Stefan grumbling about something from his position in center field.

Bailey stepped back into the batter's box. Dusky shadows hid her face except for the determined expression on it as she waggled her bat and settled into a hitter's stance. A lightning bug whizzed by as she began to sing, "Take me out to the ball game, take me out to the crowd, buy me some peanuts and crackerjacks, I don't care if I ever get back . . ."

"C'mon, Tran, let's get this out before Bailey disappears on us again," Rich sneered.

Bailey wrinkled her nose and tightened her hands on the bat. Out in front of the stands, Henry orchestrated an animated cheer. For which team, Jason couldn't quite tell from the yelling, but it was spirited. The audience sensed a game about to end . . . which meant a dinner about to be served!

Tran pitched. Bailey hit. The ball—soared.

Jason stood and blinked for a moment, then touched the base as Danno ran his way, urging Jason. "Move, move, move!"

The ball seemed to whistle through the twilight air as it passed. Jason slowed his stride a bit as it arced overhead. Stefan gave a grunt as he began to run. He could see Bailey from the corner of his eye, pounding down the right field line, from home plate to first. It wouldn't . . . couldn't . . . be a home run. Jefferson had straightened from his umpire's stance, taken his mask off and stood, watching the hit ball.

If Stefan caught it, the game was over. If he dropped it, the game was over. Either way, Jason knew he could round the diamond and cross home plate. He dug in happily.

Behind him, there was an immense crash. Jason crossed, then turned around to see that the back field fence was . . . gone . . . and Stefan with it. Danno and then Bailey joined him. They stood, looking at center field. Bailey bounced. "Did he catch it? Did I hit a home run?"

"I dunno," Jason told her. Jefferson looked at her and shrugged, saying, "I don't know either."

Grunts and growls came from the thick, prickly bushes on the other side of the fence, as something heaved around in them. Then, slowly, Stefan stood and raised his glove in the air, the baseball nested firmly inside it. The crowd cheered madly and stampeded toward the mess hall.

Bailey rubbed her nose. Then, with a sigh, she turned away. Jason grabbed her wrist. "Hey! That was some hit anyway."

Jefferson waited till Stefan jogged slowly in from the brush, then he declared the winners.

Bailey cheered up at the bonfire when Lucas sang "Casey at the Bat," and then, with a startling boom and snap, fireworks began out on the lake. Jason could see the profile of Hightower on a flat raft, setting them off and standing back.

Flowers and sparks of color shot up and bloomed in the dark skies until their ears ached from the noise, their eyes were dazzled, and the smell of the smoke stung their nostrils.

Jason heard Rich as he leaned over and whispered to Stefan, "Not as good as ours are gonna be!"

Gavan Rainwater heard also. He turned his head, and leaned into the conference. "Actually . . . those *are* your fireworks. We cannot thank you boys enough for contributing to the holiday." He winked before walking off to join Eleanora and Dr. Patel.

Rich's jaw dropped and he blinked in disbelief as he stared at the lake. "Oh, man. . . ."

Stefan scratched at a welt and prickle and thumped his friend on the shoulder in sympathy, a tangle of brush still hanging from his shirt. "Hey, at least we got to see 'em. And we did win the game 'cause I jumped the fence an' caught that ball." He reached at the weed in distraction, scattering leaves and grass and dirt all over both of them.

The night ended in a great burst of fountains, big and little, and sky rockets zooming all over the lake. Ting let out a contented sigh as they said good night before heading off to their cottage.

In the morning, Rich and Stefan were first in line at Dr. Patel's door, scratching and broken out in blisters from head to toe. Bailey sailed past them with a wide ear-to-ear grin.

"I," she said triumphantly to Jason, "hit the ball that put him in the poison oak patch!"

Bailey caught up to the crystal class quickly. In the blink of an eye, she had a cold flame centered in her amethyst. Crystal in the palm of her hand, she smiled at the lantern light within as she showed Ting. Ting's crystal flickered with a heart-shaped pink glow while Bailey's had almost a cat's-eye gleam to it. Trent lit his quickly and snuffed it just as quickly, before even Jason could catch a glimpse of it.

Eleanora stood behind Jason as if she'd also been hoping to

see what Trent warmed inside his strange crystal, but she said quietly, "Some Magickers are not comfortable with Fire. Water is more their Element," before she moved away.

Henry pulled an oven mitt out of his backpack. Rich looked at it and let out a roaring laugh. Henry's face went pink. "What?" he said, waving his bemitted hand about. "FireAnn let me borrow it."

Rich tried to contain his chortles. "G . . . good thing," he managed, "it's already singed!"

Henry sighed. Danno gave him a slight shake of encouragement. "I'm ready," he said. He toed the bucket of water from under the picnic table.

Squibb didn't look all that confident. He pushed his glasses back onto the bridge of his nose and ran a hand through his bushy hair before taking a deep breath. Jon stood to the side, eyebrow arched in interest, his tall, slender body poised alertly as Henry fetched his crystal out and placed it in the center of the oven mitt's palm.

Frowning, he spoke a single word and the crystal flared up like a Roman candle. One single flame shot upward with a WHOOSH! Birds took wing with cries of startlement, filling the sky. Henry choked and the flame shot down into the crystal and extinguished. The oven mitt appeared none the worse for damage though the air stank of charred hair. When Henry turned to look at Jason, his face stricken, Jason could see why. The hair had been burned right off his forehead!

Gavan cleared his throat. "Better control this time, Henry. In no time at all, you'll have that tamed."

Stefan grunted. "It'll be like having a flamethrower in your pocket."

"Useful." Rich nodded.

"Stuff a sock in it, you two." Danno took the mitt off Henry's hand and put it back in his pack. "Another day or two and you'll have it." Henry stood blinking, looking a little stunned.

"Indeed," said Jonnard. "A bit more practice, is all. Fire is clearly your Element."

"It is?" Round-eyed, Henry looked around him.

"Well, of course it is. It's eager to answer you. A little too eager, that's all." Jonnard smiled slightly.

Gavan nodded at Jonnard. Jennifer tucked a strand of hair behind one graceful ear. "Perhaps," she said, a little shyly, "I could help them read their Elements."

Gavan looked at her thoughtfully. "That might be very helpful, Jennifer. Think you can do it?"

"I've been studying." She touched Henry on the shoulder as she came and stood by his side, and paused for a moment, her crystal pendant in hand. "Oh, definitely Fire." She smiled at Henry.

"Oh." Henry relaxed slightly, and a lopsided grin came to rest on his otherwise harried looking face. "I'll have to try harder, then."

"I think," Rainwater said smoothly, "the key is in trying a bit less." He winked and moved on between the students.

"Oh," said Henry. "Right. I can see that." He reached up, removed his glasses, wiping the steam from them before replacing them on his forehead. A dry, crinkled hair fell as he did so.

"Henry," suggested Eleanora. "I think you should retire for the day, and return that mitt to FireAnn as her staff will probably need it." She smiled encouragingly.

With another poke aimed at stabilizing his glasses on his sunburned nose, Henry nodded and trotted off in the direction of the main buildings.

Nothing else as interesting happened in any of the other classes although Bailey seemed to need little catching up. She watched and listened with intent interest, sitting or standing back with a faint already-knew-it expression on her face. During break, as they trotted to wash up for lunch, she repeated to Jason, "Have I got things to tell you!" Then she frowned slightly and rubbed her freckled nose. "If I can remember them all."

"I don't have any free time till after dinner," he said.

"That's fine. Come over and take a look at the trap. I have some changes to make."

"Did you see who it was as Ghost?"

"Not . . . quite. I have an idea, though." She winked and headed off for swimming, her ponytail bouncing behind her.

Jason watched her thoughtfully. The old Bailey was back. Nearly. Neither of them had spoken much about what she had felt when grabbing for his left hand, his marked hand. She had only said that "it hurt," and a small flicker of fear gleamed in her eyes before she changed the subject quickly. He sighed. The crescent twinged a little as it always did when he thought about it.

After dinner, the sun still hung brightly over the western hills, although the sky deepened to a dark, clear blue. It was a perfect summer evening and they all sat around on her porch waiting for it to get dark. Sousa had promised a singalong for later.

Bailey sat with her ponytail pulled over her shoulder, curling the end of it round and round her finger. "First of all, I saw things."

Trent let out a whoop, making her blush after she thumped him. "Not that kind of stuff! I stayed away from the showers!" She rolled her eyes. "If you're not going to listen, I won't tell."

He pulled his face into serious lines. "I'll listen. See? I'm looking like Jason."

"Hmmpf."

Ting tapped her pencil on Jason's knee. "Both of you stop it. I want to hear, even if you don't!" She balanced her notebook on her lap, poised to take notes. Bailey shot her a grateful look.

"Now . . . if there are no more interruptions?" She looked around. Feet shuffled restlessly, but no one made a sound as she settled herself on the steps of Kittencurl Cottage. "Good. First of all, I couldn't eat. Everything was half a step ahead of me. If I reached for it, it was gone. The only thing I managed to get was a cookie which Jason stubbornly kept out for me, and I barely got that."

Trent looked at Ting. "Make a note: take food."

Ting giggled, but her pencil wiggled as she jotted something down quickly. Jason peered over her shoulder. It read: Make sure Trent has food at all times. He covered his grinning face with a well-aimed scratch at an eyebrow.

"But I heard things, and could read things left out, and saw things, although I couldn't do anything about them till later. By then, it was usually too late." Bailey sighed. "First of all . . . not everybody is going to make it as a Magicker. Being here doesn't mean everyone has enough Talent or ability to make it. That stuff FireAnn has been brewing for days now is called the Draft of Forgetfulness." She looked about and lowered her voice a bit more. "And it works. Anyone leaving isn't going to remember much of anything. And . . . some of us have been working with Magickers for a year or so already, like Jennifer and Jon."

Jason let his breath out in a hiss. "Doesn't sound good."

Trent shrugged. "When you think about it, what choice do they have? They can't send someone home who will talk about it, if they remember. By the time we're ready to go home, we'll have a stake in being a Magicker. That means we'll keep it quiet. As far as Jennifer and Jon go . . . well, they've always been like counselors and stuff. I always got the feeling they knew a lot more than they let on."

"Some idiots will talk about anything." Ting shook her head, looking worried. "They'll ruin anything, just to get attention. The Draft is the only way to go."

Bailey nodded. "The Magickers have a plan for that."

Jason said, "What are you saying, Bailey? That we can't trust them?"

She looked solemnly at him. "There are Magickers in and out of here all the time we haven't even *seen,* let alone met. There's a whole Council that meets at night."

"There is?"

She nodded at Trent. "You'll never see them. They come in late at night and leave early."

Jason did not mention that he *had* seen them, or at least heard them.

"You get a look at them, Bailey?"

"Well . . . sorta. I was kind of seeing everybody a half step behind what they looked like." She sighed. "I know they meet to talk about us, and make plans, and there's a storm coming that has all of them awfully worried."

"Mana storm?"

"That's the one."

Ting stopped writing again. "What is that? Is it like a hurricane?"

"It's a storm of power, from what I hear," Jason told her. "It turns everything upside down. It's like Magick goes uncontrollably wild, I think."

Ting and Bailey shivered together. Trent said quietly, "If we don't know what it is, we can't jump to conclusions."

"Right. What else, Bailey?"

"The Dark Hand is thought to be behind those nightmares we have."

"How?"

She shook her head. "No idea. And Tomaz is looking for a shapechanger in camp. That sounds really bad. They don't know if he's from the Dark Hand or one of us. That's all I heard about that, I couldn't get into the rooms. Doors." She sighed. "I had to sneak into the toilets when I could. Not much sleep. I slept one night in the chair here, but Ting almost sat on me. I didn't want to scare you." She grinned at her friend. "No. I didn't see the thief. Almost, but, well, being out of step and all, not quite. Still, I know what time the thief comes by and I think we can catch it tonight, after Lights Out."

"You think so, Bailey? I want my watch back."

Bailey shrugged and added, "Won't know till we try!" She paused, as Stefan and Rich sauntered by, hiking around the lake, but also giving them the eye. Rich particularly looked them all over as if memorizing who was in what place. He snickered. "Double-dating?"

Trent muttered as they nearly passed out of earshot.

Jason's eyes narrowed as he watched them laugh and lumber past.

Ting ignored them totally. "Have a trap for the thief in mind?"

"Well. As my grandma always says, you can catch more bears with honey than vinegar—"

A noise came from the other side of the cottage before Bailey's emphatic words even faded. There was a crash as something heavy plowed through the underbrush near the cottage's edge, the side that fronted into a lot of the wilderness near the lake.

A big burly shape went by, with Rich trotting at his heels, red hair sticking out. "Oh, not again. One of you guys stop him!"

Trent glanced at the big bear cub headed deeper into the woods that fringed the cottages and answered, "And I should stop him . . . why?"

"Because he'll get in trouble, that's why!" Rich tried to tackle the bear, and it shook him off, bawling and snuffling. It kicked off what looked like tennis shoes before loping away on all fours. Ting's jaw dropped.

Rich threw his hands up. "Get back here!" he bellowed.

The bear seemed to whine "Hun-eeee" as Rich tried to catch up with him.

Jason stood up. "What's going on? That's a wild animal . . . isn't it?"

They all traded shrugs.

He said. "I guess we should help." He started in the general direction of Rich and the bear. After a few moments of hesitation, the others followed him.

They tromped to where they could hear a low, grunting voice, and Rich's higher one, pleading. They rounded an evergreen tree and then stopped in astonishment.

A brown bear wearing the shreds of Stefan's shirt and trousers sat on the ground, contentedly and repeatedly scratching his back against a stout tree trunk, over and over and over. They stared at the young bear and then at Rich. Rich looked at them. He sighed. "Well. Now you know. At least it's not another brier patch, and don't any of you dare mention the H word or I'll be chasing him around the lake."

At that, the bear stopped scratching and tossed his head a

bit, rolling his eyes. He gave a most Stefanish grunt and looked at them with beady brown eyes.

"Good grief. Is that . . . ?"

Rich glared at them. "Who do you think it is?"

Trent swung on Bailey. "There's your shapeshifter."

The bear let out a half-growl, and pawed at his nose.

Jason looked at the creature sitting in the remains of Stefan's gear. "No doubt about it."

Dust Bunnies

THEY all stared, fascinated, as Stefan-bear cradled something in its paws, eating and slurping. Bailey pointed up, overhead, at a beehive that was drizzling honey from one of its broken sides. "Good thing it's almost dark."

Rich signed again. He began picking up shreds of items and tucking them in his backpack. The sneakers appeared to be intact and he thumped Stefan-bear on the shoulder, saying, "Good boy! Atta boy, you remembered to kick your sneakers off!"

Ting backed away a step, glancing at the bear as he grunted and chewed at his honeycomb. "Is it *safe* to do that?"

"Well." Rich considered his hairy friend. "I'm not really sure. He knows me." He shrugged. "All I know is, I can't go where he goes. And sometimes he can't even go there." Ruefully, he picked brambles out of his sleeve.

"Brier patch," Jason said suddenly.

Rich looked at him mournfully, then nodded.

Trent squatted down, staring into the bear's face. "How does he turn back? How long does he stay a bear? He doesn't look full grown either, somewhere between a cub and an adult."

"Last couple of times, right away. Now . . ." Rich looked as Stefan happily continued to grunt, slurp, and munch. "Got me."

Bailey giggled. "At least not until he's done, I should imagine. He's really enjoying it."

The chubby cub tossed his head about, eyed her, grunted again, and shifted the honeycomb in his paws. He had a white diamond-sized patch on his russet-brown chest, and droplets of honey drizzled down into it.

"I'd say that was a yes."

Trent stood. "I'd say you're going to have to hose him down."

The bear made a bleating sound, pinning his ears back. His long pink tongue curled around an end of the honeycomb, scooping out more amber honey. His ears flicked forward again in sheer pleasure.

"Actually," Rich shifted from one foot to the other. "He likes bathing in the lake. Listen, you guys, you can't tell anyone."

Ting looked uneasily from Stefan-bear to Rich. She said slowly, "I don't see how you're going to hide it. I mean . . . he's pretty big . . . and noisy. And he smells like a bear."

The bear rolled his eyes about. He crunched down the last waxy bit of his honeycomb and tried to lick his chest off before getting to his feet. A last shred of T-shirt fell from his back as he did. He looked terribly odd with trousers still on, although they scarcely fit him as they hit his knees. He reminded Jason of a very old Smokey the Bear stuffed toy he used to have. Another thought occurred to him. There might be an advantage to having Stefan and Rich owing all of them for keeping a secret. "Tomaz is looking for a shapechanger," he mused.

"They'll kick us out, man." Rich's pale complexion went to pasty white. "He's a freak. We can't leave before he finds out how to . . . how to . . ." He seemed at a loss for words.

"How to deal with it?" Jason nodded. "Okay. We won't say anything. That doesn't mean you won't get found out, though. Eventually . . ."

Rich twisted his backpack in his hands. "All we need is a

little time. I hope." He grabbed an ear and tugged on it gently. "Come on, Stefan. You can be seen!"

With a low bleat and a grunt, the bear followed Rich deeper into the shrubbery. Trent shook his head as the two disappeared temporarily. "Tomaz is already on their trail."

"Maybe. Maybe not. Anyway, maybe we can get Squibb some peace and quiet."

Trent leaned on him. "A little blackmail? I see you've learned from me, grasshopper!"

But Ting only shivered as they walked back to Kittencurl.

"What's wrong?" Bailey asked.

"What if he's not the one Tomaz is looking for. What if Crowfeather is looking for something worse? Something dark and dangerous?"

"Then let's hope he finds out quickly. I haven't heard anything, though, have you? I mean, the wolfjackals are bad enough. . . ." Bailey kept chattering as they walked back.

Their voices trailed off as the sky turned night dark and they climbed their porch steps. Sousa's rendition of Lights Out sounded throughout the camp, oddly faint on this side of the lake. Trent and Jason could not follow, so they stood at the trail and waved as the girls disappeared inside. Trent waited for the screen door to bang shut, then said, "What if she's right?"

"Something dark prowling around?" He didn't want to think of it. He rubbed his hand. "Trust me, Trent. Wolfjackals are bad enough."

"I'm not saying they aren't. But sometimes your worst enemy is the one inside of you." Without waiting for an answer, he started toward their end of the lake.

With a funny feeling in the pit of his stomach, Jason trotted after Trent. He wanted to ask just what Trent meant by that, but he was afraid he knew. The thought of being imprisoned in a body that wanted to hunt, to hurt, was animal wild . . . without being able to change or control it . . . made his blood run cold. The nightmare memory of the chill, silent tomb and the being that wanted to draw him always closer rose unbidden. What did the being want to tell him? What would he do if he got his hands on Jason? Was that what made a skinwalker out of you? How much longer could he even resist?

A shiver ran down the back of his neck clear to his feet.

A faraway howl echoed down from high jagged peaks that the night almost hid. Coyote. Or wolfjackal? He spun around on the path, grateful that it seemed a long way off, yet wondering if that was a lie. He heard Trent's fading steps and turned around to hurry and catch up.

Something dark and big reared up in front of him. It reached out and caught his elbow. Jason let out a squeak and tried to dodge. His ankle turned, sending a ping of pain all the way to his nose.

"Yeowch!" Jason flapped his arms for balance.

"Hold on there," Tomaz Crowfeather said quietly. His hand tightened around Jason's arm, steadying him on the pathway. He waited till Jason caught his breath, then said mildly, "Out a little late?"

"We walked the girls back to their cabin. Ting is a little nervous, and Bailey is, well, Bailey," Jason finished lamely. He didn't like lying, and he was almost certain that Tomaz could see right through him. He shifted his weight uneasily.

Tomaz watched him. "I have not decided if trouble sniffs you out, or you sniff trouble out. You're safer back at the cabin."

Jason nodded as Tomaz released him and helpfully pointed him in the right direction. "Wolfjackals?"

"Many things travel the night," Tomaz said. "Some evil with their quarry in mind, others . . . more confused than anything. But a frightened animal is as dangerous as a mean one, remember that." He raised his hand and waved it in farewell.

Before Jason could take the hint and bolt for home, a scream split the night. Before the terrified wail stopped, both Tomaz and Jason were in motion. Jason led the way. "That's Ting," he said, vaulting up the steps at Kittencurl.

Tomaz reached for the screen door, interrupted by a horrible jangling and clanging of bells and cans. Jason slowed down. Their trap had just gone off! "The thief! That's Bailey's thief trap!" Squeals and yells filled their ears as they entered the cottage.

Ting, still dressed, her pajamas clutched to her chest, stood on a chair, dancing and yelling, "It's a rat! A rat!"

Bailey, on her hands and knees, dove into the strings of cans and bells, trying to catch something that was scampering about wildly. Both Tomaz and Jason watched in total bewilderment.

"Thief?" the Magicker said to Jason.

Jason nodded. "Someone's been taking things." His further explanation was cut short by Bailey's triumphant yell.

"Gotcha!" She stood in a jangle of sound and string, looking rather like an odd Christmas tree. There was something in her hands, a small ball of soft charcoal-and-white fur. Its long tail hung through Bailey's fingers, a little black tuft at the end, with a puff of dust and cobwebs dangling from it. Whiskers flicked back and forth desperately. Amber eyes stared at them, blinking rapidly as the creature searched for a way out of Bailey's clutches.

Ting stopped yelling. "It . . . it's a dust bunny." She stared at Bailey who smoothed a fingertip over the frightened animal's head.

"Some kind of mouse," said Bailey. She cooed to it. "Poor thing's scared to death."

"It's a rodent," corrected Tomaz. "Kangaroo rat, actually, although more related to the mouse part of the rodent family. This particular variety of kangaroo rat is often called a pack rat." He eyed the creature trembling in Bailey's palms. "Missing items, you said? Small things, often shiny?"

"Well . . . yes." Ting climbed off the chair.

With a smile, Tomaz began to walk about the cottage carefully, treading on each board. Everyone followed but Bailey who couldn't move in her tangle of traps. He listened to every moan of wood as he stepped carefully, until he stopped in a corner of the porch. Bailey and the pack rat were out of sight in the main cottage. There he knelt down and, with one hand, gently pried up a warped board.

Bailey called out, "What's going on? What's happening?"

"He's looking for something," Ting answered.

Jason peered over Tomaz's shoulder, then added, "And he's found it!"

They looked into a little nest of strawlike twigs and colorful lint. In it lay a silver-toned watch, a shiny barrette, a handful of quarters and one cat's-eye marble, and a dainty silver-handled brush and mirror. "I think," Tomaz announced, "we've found your thief." He quickly collected everything and stomped the board back into place.

Bailey waited with a most perturbed look on her face. Ting laughed and began to carefully untangle her. The pack rat had settled down in Bailey's hands. Tomaz looked at her thoughtfully. He spread the booty out on the table. "I think everything lost can be found in here. They like to take and store pretty things in their nests."

Bailey let out a sigh of relief as Ting unwound the last noisy string from her.

"That is a wild creature."

"A very frightened one." Bailey rubbed her thumb over the pack rat's head again. The creature relaxed her soft, folding mouselike ears and let out a soft chirr. "Can't I keep it till we can release her somewhere safer?"

"Safer?"

"Well." Bailey nibbled her lip. "She could get eaten out there." She stared out their screen door.

"Yes," agreed Tomaz. "It is a dangerous world out there. Perhaps you should keep her safe for a while. I suggest something hard plastic or rubber or metal. She'll chew her way out of anything else. Something soft for a nest, something shiny to keep her happy." He smiled slightly.

Bailey fairly beamed. "Thank you!"

"Do not thank me," the Indian shaman said quietly. "The animal has made her own choice, I think." He nodded to the creature who had settled comfortably on Bailey's palms and now groomed her whiskers carefully, much like a cat making herself at home. "Sleep well," he said, guiding Jason to the door. "And remember," he added, with a wink. "Unlike the rest of us, pack rats are nocturnal."

Jason took the hint and headed back to the cabin where Trent was already in his cot, reading a book by flashlight. He sat up. "I figured you stopped by the restroom."

Jason shook his head. "No, first I ran into Tomaz . . ."

"Really? What was he doing? Did he spot Stefan?"

"No, but I bet he was out scouting and patrolling. Anyway . . . the trap went off at Kittencurl! You should have heard the noise."

"No kidding? We caught the thief? Who was it?"

"Bailey caught it."

"It?"

"Yup. A wee little mousie thing, about this big. Tomaz said it was a packrat."

Trent rolled his eyes. "Pack rat? Don't they squirrel stuff away?"

"Anything and everything!" He described the nest while he stripped down for bed and tucked away his dirty clothes and laid out clean ones for the morning. As he lay down, they could hear muffled footsteps outside.

Rich's voice said, quietly and unhappily, "Next time I tell you to stay away from something, do it!"

Stefan let out a grunt. Then, miserably, "Bears like skunks, I guess."

The noise of the two of them shuffling past faded, with a bold distinct odor left behind. Stefan was obviously back in human form.

"Skunk!" repeated Trent, snickering.

The two of them sank into their cots with peals of laughter. The last thing Jason remembered hearing was Trent, every now and then, echoing, "Skunk!"

Crystal Clear

"THEY took my amethyst from me," Bailey whispered, as the group came together for Crystal Class.

Jason's hand went to his crystal in his pocket and he wrapped his fingers about it quickly before asking, "Why?"

She shook her head. Jennifer reached over and patted her hand. "I'm sure it's nothing. The sea salts and tubs are out. I bet we're just going to learn how to cleanse our crystals." She smiled. "Once we know how to do that, and know our auras, then I can start showing you how to make items from them." She touched her pendant, which consisted of her crystal wrapped in a spiral of silver wire and hung from a chain.

Bailey looked a bit happier. "Cool."

Trent leaned on his elbows. "Ever get everyone's aura read, Jen?"

Blonde hair swung as she shook her head slightly. "Not even close. With forty-nine campers here, I don't even know everyone yet. But I'm going to try!"

Jon had been showing Danno something, with Henry and Tran looking on. It appeared to be a diagram of chess moves. He looked up with a slight frown. "But what if you're wrong?"

She gave him her attention. "What if I'm wrong?"

"You can make mistakes. You're not that far into training."

"Anyone can make mistakes."

Jon looked at her steadily. "But what if someone depends on what you tell them. Say . . . Henry here. He needs to know what his Elemental nature is, as far as his Talents are concerned, and you tell him . . . Water. You can see how dangerous that would be."

The older girl smiled slightly. "Anyone can tell Henry is Fire."

Jason stirred, saying, "I can't. I mean, it seems reasonable, but I can't."

"It takes training, like anything else."

"Tell me what I am," Jon said quietly.

Jennifer paused, her face coloring slightly. "You know I can't. I've tried before. You've been working on Shielding."

He shrugged as he turned away. "It's dangerous to rely on anyone but yourself."

Jennifer bit her lip slightly but did not argue with him. She bent her attention to the small tubs on the tables in front of them, filled with clear water and little else. Campers milled around curiously as the heat of the day settled in and a splash here and there sprayed across the rocks. Crystals caught the sunlight and spiked it about in a rainbow of colors.

Stefan swiped his big paw of a hand across the surface of one tub, sending up a tidal wave of water right in the pathway just as Gavan walked into the clearing to start the class. Even as Ting gasped and Rich let out a cry of warning, he raised his cane, unconcerned, a brightness catching the water in midair, droplets splattering into a fine mist and raining down onto the dirt as though hitting an unseen barrier. Grinning, Gavan gave his cane a playful shake and growled before lowering it as he stepped to the front of the tables. He leaned on it, cape folded back on his shoulders, at ease in his light shirt tucked into faded blue jeans.

"Not that that wouldn't have felt good," he said, glancing up at the sun overhead. "All right. We've been handling the crystals for a while now, learning the one that is bonded to you, and everyone is generally doing quite well." His attention swept over his students, even Henry Squibb, who flinched as though he could duck behind Jonnard or somehow make himself invisible, and he drew something out of his pocket and laid it on the table. A great white quartz sparkled in the light, its many crystals shining almost completely clear. He tapped it. "This is an ordinary rock crystal, found quite commonly, although not always in this size or clarity. You've all been working with your bonded crystals, but a Magicker can use a master crystal such as this or bond with any number of crystals if his Talents are inclined that way. So, while we urge you never to drop your crystal," and his clear blue eyes fastened on Bailey a moment, "it is possible to find and use a master like this if you have real need."

"What's the catch?" asked Trent.

"Catch?"

"Why use a bonded one if any will do?"

"Ah." Gavan picked up the quartz. "The catch is the performance. Let me think if I can put it another way." He scratched the side of his crooked nose. "A bonded crystal would be like a race car, high energy and tuned to do one job, with one driver, quite well. A master crystal would be like a small subcompact economy model. It may get you where you're going, but much slower and without as much flash. Or it may be unable to get you where you really want to go but it will keep you safe while you figure out a plan if you're in trouble."

"How will you know if you're in trouble? Other than the obvious?" Gavan pulled Bailey's amethyst out of his pocket and held it forth on his palm. The once brilliant purple crystal sat, dulled and dark, a shadow of its former self. Bailey sighed.

"Oh, Bailey," breathed Ting. "I didn't know it had gotten so bad!"

"I didn't want anyone to know," Bailey answered, her voice miserable. She sat down at one end of her table and cupped her chin in her hands as she leaned forward on her elbows.

Jennifer eyed the object resting on Gavan's palm. "I don't know," she said slowly, "if cleansing will help that."

"Nor I," the Magicker responded. "I want everyone to take their crystals and get a feel for their aura. We've done this before," he added as he began to walk slowly among them, "so you already know what your crystal probably feels like to you, but I want you to refresh that knowledge. Take a few moments, and then we're going to cleanse our crystals and see if the aura feels stronger or different."

Trent grinned. "I hope Stefan's crystal is cleaner than his socks, or we'll be here all day cleaning." He ducked his head as Stefan let out a growling mutter and laughter rolled through the others. He rolled his own misty crystal through his hands, closing his eyes in concentration and trying to look innocent as Gaven passed him by.

Jason cupped his. Gavan paused, and put a finger out, stroking the band of granitelike material that divided the crystal. "Ever give you trouble?"

"I don't think so. What kind of trouble?"

"When you're Focusing on it, ever go cold or feel blocked?"

Jason shook his head. "Never."

Gavan looked searchingly into his face a moment, then commented, "Good," before moving away. Jason looked after him, wondering. None of the Magickers had ever explained why his crystal was not meant to have been bonded. He gripped his crystal tightly, feeling its energy wash over him. Never had he felt it divided. If the band were a barrier, it had always been open, not locked. Perhaps this was one of the things he was meant to discover for himself. Or perhaps not, if he found the right question to ask.

Trent bumped him. Jason peered at his friend. "What?"

"Something wrong?"

"Nah. Just thinking."

"You do that a lot." Trent nodded to himself as Bailey giggled faintly and Trent looked happy to have made her do so.

Gavan took a small bag of white rocks and filled his palm, then scattered it into the tub of water in front of him, and swirled his hand around, dissolving them. "Sea salt," he said. "About half a handful for each tub. Only one crystal at a time should soak and be washed in this, so take turns. I want you to swish the crystal about, then hold it in the water, and I want you to think it clean. Tell it to be pure and clean, if you will. Then let it sit for, oh . . . five minutes. Take it out and dry it with one of these rags laid out here, and then I want you to Focus on the aura. Let me know what you think." He pointed at Bailey. "Come here and let's do yours, but don't Focus first."

Trent dropped his crystal into the small tub, elbowing Jason into a short line behind him. Jason didn't mind as Henry and Danno tussled each other to fall in after Jason. After what seemed a very long time, he fished his up and moved aside, drying it off. Bailey was already holding her crystal and looking at it in dismay, the color still cloudy as she rubbed and rubbed at it.

"Hey," said Trent. "It works." He tossed his polishing cloth back on the table and turned his about, admiring the newly shining surfaces.

Jason swished his crystal in the cool water, smelling the very faint aroma of salt. His crystal seemed so much clearer and vibrant underwater. He waited five long minutes before fishing it out to dry.

Holding it, feeling the water-cooled mineral warm to his skin, he felt its aura build and run through him, a clean light tinted ever so faintly with a soft green. To his relief, the aura felt even stronger than before, and he pocketed it without realizing he had a big grin on his face until Jennifer smiled at him.

"It's always nice if it's done right," she said.

Slightly embarrassed, he mumbled "Yeah," before moving away from the table. Bailey caught his eye again. She sat in an unhappy heap at the table's end, watching Gavan closely.

As he drew near, all he could clearly hear her say was ". . . don't want another one. Can't we do something? What's wrong with it?"

Gavan put his hand on her shoulder. "Before I go on, I want to say this. We rarely stay with one crystal our whole life. They have different properties and we have different needs and abilities. We often outgrow the first and move on."

"I don't want to move on. I'm not ready to!" Bailey looked at the Magicker with her soft brown eyes. Lacey, the packrat, poked her head out of Bailey's shirt pocket to let out a nervous chitter before diving back in, her tufted tail hanging out and twitching now and then.

"Isn't there anything we can do?"

Gavan shrugged at Jason. "Not that I can think of. The crystal is attuned to Bailey, but once we got her back here, and her well-being was assured, it should have returned to normal. Instead, it's dying out. She's not going to be able to use it as a Focus."

Bailey rubbed at her nose.

Jason sat down next to her. "I'm sorry," he said to her. "After it kept you safe even with the wolfjackal that followed you in, and all."

She nodded, and looked even more miserable.

Gavan tilted his head. "What was that you said?"

"When I went in to get her, she had a wolfjackal who'd followed her in. We were only one step ahead of it when we came out. We told you . . ."

Gavan looked as if he could smack his forehead. "You did, that's right. At that moment, I didn't quite catch what you meant. I thought . . . we all thought . . . you were talking about the Ritual. That's it, then. The wolfjackal is still trapped inside, and it's poisoning the crystal."

"You can do something?"

"If that's it, yes. But Tomaz will be best to handle it. Shall we try, Bailey?"

She nodded rapidly.

"Good. If it works, I'll have it back to you by sundown!" Gavan tossed the crystal in the air and caught it, tucking it away in his cape. He considered her. "You shall have to tell me how you managed that. It could be a useful trick someday."

Bailey wrinkled her nose. "I didn't mean to, but if I remember, I'll let you know."

"Do that." Gavan straightened then, to give his attention to the others. "Anyone have any changes to report?"

Danno said nervously, "Mine went to orange."

"But that's excellent, Danno. An excellent aura color . . . it usually reflects joy, and an energy coming out of that." Gavan pointed at Stefan. "How about you?"

Stefan grunted. "Nothing changed, I guess. Is this class gonna run all afternoon, or can we get a break? I'm hungry." Even from across several tables, now, Jason could hear the boy's stomach rumble. Like Trent, he was always hungry, only Trent stayed wiry while Stefan just seemed to get broader and taller. "No change at all is better than losing the aura. Anyone else have any changes to report? Anything unusual happen?"

"I," said Henry quickly, "got zapped."

"Zapped?"

He nodded, his round owllike face reddened from the sun despite the bar of sunblock across his nose. "Zzzzapped."

"Hmmm. We may have had a double ward on it for the Choosing. If so, that could be half your problem." Gavan took out a small notebook and jotted something down. "Remind me to check it later?"

"Yes, sir." Henry sighed.

As it turned out, most of the crystals improved, and while Gavan was checking and looking at them, Tomaz appeared. One moment the wide dirt path to the craft area seemed empty, the next moment he was there, slapping the dust from his denim jacket, his turquoise-and-silver bracelet jangling softly. Gavan did not look at all surprised as he passed him the amethyst and they conferred, their voices not carrying to the campers. Tomaz nodded once, then patted Bailey on the shoulder before returning down the path, his blue-black hair gleaming in its pulled-back ponytail.

"Almost like Gavan had called for him."

Trent nudged Jason in the ribs. "What makes you think he didn't?"

"Hmmmm." Before he could say anything further, the loudspeakers rang out for break, and Stefan nearly plowed them over as he headed out.

After break, they had short sessions on using the master crystal, then FireAnn came to get them for Herb Class. Bailey didn't brighten until the late afternoon session of Frisbee pitch, where sailing the cheerful plastic disk across the marked field and trying to score points for longest toss, and highest toss, and most accurate toss gave way to the joy of simply leaping around the field and catching whatever Frisbee they could.

At the fire ring, long into the night, Tomaz appeared at Bailey's elbow while she was singing, took her hand, and put her crystal in it. The purple colors, even in the dim glow of the flame, shone with all their old brilliance. Bailey gasped.

"You did it!"

He nodded. "It taught me a valuable lesson, too, one which may be of help to us all someday. I need to strengthen it a bit, though. I had a difficult time." He chuckled then, dark eyes snapping with his laughter. "You are full of surprises, Miss Landau."

"I bet that wolfjackal was surprised when you caught up with it!"

He inclined his head, saying nothing else, before falling back into the shadows at the edge of the bonfire's casting, and Bailey clutched her crystal tightly, throwing one arm around Ting and the other around Jennifer before returning to sing.

Jason fished out his crystal and looked at it. Had he ever looked beyond or behind that band? Was it as open as he felt . . . or could something be locked away inside, and he not know it? He held his crystal thoughtfully for a very long time before putting it away, as the fire burned down to crackling embers.

24

Wanda

"TALENT Show!" breathed Ting. "They finally posted it! It's been days and days since they said watch for the announcement." Her hand eagerly tapped the camp calendar.

"Really? No kidding? When's it set for?" Bailey tried to push closer to see through the crowd of campers buzzing around the calendar.

"Saturday night. That gives us six days to finesse our rehearsing."

Jennifer, who had no trouble seeing over both Ting's and Bailey's heads, smiled faintly. "Just like karaoke."

Ting bounced. She tugged on Bailey's hand. "Are you ready!"

Bailey hung back a little. "Well . . . I dunno. The shower is one thing, up on stage is another. . . ."

"We'll be fine," Jennifer said coaxingly. She tucked a long strand of blonde hair behind her ear. "We might even scrounge up some matching costumes. I have things I haven't even worn yet."

"That would be too cool," pronounced Ting. "Let's do the Fifties."

"But I'm not ready!" With Bailey protesting faintly, her roommates towed her away, chattering eagerly. She cast a wild-eyed look at Jason like a skittish pony, and he grinned.

Trent scratched his nose as the girls left. "Think we could do something?"

Jason looked at him, shrugging. "Maybe. It's not like we've been practicing or anything, though, and I know a few who have."

"Yeah, but it's for the video. I want my dad to see it."

Henry eagerly began taking notes as he turned away from the calendar, talking Danno's ear off. "Looks like Squibb has something planned."

Trent snorted. As the two backed up to leave, they nearly bumped into Stefan and Rich. Trent eyed Stefan. "I bet you could have a puppet show," he said to Stefan. "Those dirty socks of yours probably walk and talk all on their own."

Stefan grunted. "Very funny."

"I thought so." Trent watched them boldly, relishing the knowledge they held over the two boys' heads. It had been days since they'd watched Stefan's incredible transformation, and yet they seemed to be the only ones who knew of it. Rich was getting worry lines as he desperately tried to keep the secret.

Rich stared. "We'll see who laughs last." He folded his arms and ignored Jason and Trent, his yellow-copper hair standing in stubborn thatches.

As they left, Jason said thoughtfully to Trent, "I don't think we've seen the last of trouble from those two, and I don't think you should be teasing them like that."

"You're no fun either." Trent lightly punched him in the shoulder. He sprinted off, leaving Jason sputtering.

"No, no, no," said Jefferson as he paced the beach. "It takes teamwork to move a canoe swiftly. Decide where you're going to go and then work with each other. Don't paddle against each other!" His voice echoed from his cupped hands as he waded through the shallow water. The canoes on Lake Wannameecha seemed determined to conduct a demolition derby, bouncing into and off of each other despite the frantic paddling of their occupants. They were all capable of canoeing with basic strokes, but Jefferson's attempt to teach them racing strategy had gone wrong . . . horribly wrong. Canoes thudded back and forth and paddles cracked against each other sharply, amidst the yells and laughter of the campers.

Water slapped and splashed everywhere as the campers squawked and warned each other and ducked, but everyone seemed to be dripping wet from head to toe and not really unhappy about it. A hot July sun blazed down. Even when a canoe tipped over, dumping everyone in it and drenching others, no one seemed unhappy. Heads bobbed up from the lake, grinning, as the unlucky canoers grabbed their boat in an attempt to push it back to shore and right it. As usual, Jason had left his fetish in the cabin for this class, knowing he'd end up soaking wet.

Jefferson waved his arms about. "What are you all doing?" he bellowed. His sunglasses hung on a cord about his neck, and he looked to be almost as wet as everyone else. He laughed.

Jason stopped, oar in midair, lake water sliding off his face, cooling him as it dripped. "Having fun?" His shirt clung to his body, and water squished in his tennis shoes, and he felt great.

The tall, dark instructor looked at all of them and finally shrugged. "Well . . . good. But try to learn to paddle while you're at it. This could be a skill you'll need one day! Swimming is later!" But he smiled widely as he yelled it out over the water. He then turned and ran for his life as a capsized canoe jumped out of the water, seemingly headed right at him. He covered the crystal on his wide bracelet and a flash dazzled the lake water a moment, catching the canoe in midair and settling it back onto the water calmly. The campers let out an ahhhhh of wonder. He grabbed an oar as it floated past.

Trent tossed a look back at Jason. "Shall we show them how it's done?"

Jason countered, "On the count of one-two?"

Trent nodded. "One," he called out, stroking strongly from the front of the canoe.

"Two," called Jason, paddling. And so they worked, one,

two, one, two, the canoe shooting away from the beach and the other canoers. It glided smoothly across the water, creating a breeze as it moved that ruffled their hair and cooled their skin. In moments they were beyond earshot of Jefferson, and even the gleeful shouts of the other campers seemed faint. Lake Wannameecha flowed under them like glass with scarcely a wave or ripple except for that trailing from the rear of the canoe. Jason felt the pull in his shoulders as he paddled behind Trent, but it felt good and in short order, they sailed into a part of the lake they'd never been, beyond the silvery beach coves of the campground. They kept paddling to where the water was deep blue and clear, and they were all alone.

Of a single mind, both of them put their paddles across their knees, and let the canoe skim to a halt. It bobbed gently on the tiny waves. Trent leaned out of the bow to point. "That's all wilderness," he said. "I don't think we've even hiked back in there."

Jason eyed the thick greenery and rugged coastline at this end of Lake Wannameecha. The wonder of open land, still relatively untouched, struck him. Anything could be in there. Perhaps even the Iron Gate that bothered the Magickers so much lay hidden in there, its whereabouts waiting to be discovered.

Something splashed behind them. Both turned to look at the deep-blue water, where circles of ripples spread out, then faded. "Fish," said Trent. "Jumping at a bug." Tiny lines spread across the lake. Trent dipped his hand into the water. "Don't you wish you could see underneath? Like with a waterproof camera? All the stuff happening down there we have no idea about?"

Jason carefully leaned his weight the other way to keep the canoe balanced. He eyed the lake. "Probably," he said slowly, "just a few fish. Grasses. Maybe a turtle or two? Water isn't clear enough to see through very deep. Not like a crystal or anything."

He looked up.

"Maybe." Trent nodded. He played his fingers through the

water. "I guess we'd better get back before Jefferson has a cow. We're not supposed to be out of sight of the beach."

Jason's hand ached. He lifted it to look for blisters from the paddle, but it was the back, the scar that burned. He dropped it back into the soothing water again. Something stirred below, and there was another splash, louder, from behind them.

"I wish I had my pole with me!" Trent turned around in the canoe, and squinted over the lake's surface, looking for the fish wistfully. "They sure are jumping."

Jason peered back, his arm up to his elbow in the water. Something cold and slimy tickled past his fingers. He jerked his hand out with a yelp and peered down.

"What's wrong?"

"Something . . ." Jason said. He looked at his fingers. They seemed fine. "Something touched me."

"Cool."

"And . . . icky."

"Just a fish. Or maybe some lakeweed." Trent picked up his paddle. "You city boys are wusses. You should have caught it with your bare hand! Tickled it close and snatched it up."

"Me? Are you calling me a wuss?"

"If it doesn't have concrete or plaster at the bottom, you don't want to swim in it!" teased Trent.

"Yeah, well, if it doesn't plug in and surf the Internet, neither do you!" He plunged his arm back into the water, leaning over. Tickle a fish into his hands! Who did Trent think he was, Henry Squibb? He wiggled his fingers in annoyance. From the corner of his eye, he caught a glimpse of a long, dark shadow moving under the canoe and then, something caught his arm and YANKED! Jason was pulled overboard.

He hit the water with a very loud splash and went straight down, his arm in the grip of two cold, wet hands. Water bubbled up around him. He tried to keep his eyes open and his mouth shut but neither seemed to work the way he wanted. Bubbles flew all about his face, and the dark lake water, as something towed him under, lifejacket and all, tugging hard before his jacket stubbornly refused to let him be dragged under any more.

He had a wild glimpse of the lake surface and canoe overhead, bubbles flowing upward from his nose and mouth, and something . . . someone . . . pulling at him.

Not a fish. He saw her—dark and shadowy, hair flowing about her like a storm adrift. Not human. Scales. Mermaid? No, she had legs, kicking to try to pull them both down to the lake bottom and failing. Slender, willowy form hardly taller than he was. He twisted his arm in her hands, but she was strong, far stronger than he. She let go suddenly, shoving him away and disappearing into the murky depths of the lake.

Like a cork, Jason bobbed to the top, sputtering and coughing. He rose to the surface like a breaching whale. Something slapped the water as he inhaled, coughed, spit, and inhaled again.

"Jeeez, doofus. I said to catch a fish with your hands, not your teeth!" Trent slapped the water with his paddle again. "Come on, grab it! Grab hold!"

Still choking, Jason thrashed over to the paddle and gripped it. Trent hauled him to the side of the canoe and braced his weight while Jason clung to the side and tried to breathe regularly. "Okay, that was not fun." He inhaled and only gargled a little bit that time.

"No kidding. Warn a guy next time? Good thing you had your jacket on."

"I saw . . . I saw . . ."

Trent looked down at him. "You saw what?"

"The underside of the canoe, for one." Jason wolfed down another gulp of air. He thought he felt a faint tug on his sneakers and did not dare look. He didn't want to capsize the canoe. She must be teasing him, because she was certainly—whoever and whatever she was—strong enough to yank him back under. And he had a feeling Trent would not believe him when he told what he'd seen.

"Breathing okay? Let's see if we can get you back in." Trent took up the proper position as taught them by Jefferson and braced himself.

Jason shook his head. "No way we can try that."

"Hang on, then. I'll head for the shore and pull you out there."

Despite the heat of the day, Jason felt chilled. He didn't want to stay in the water, but knew he had no choice. The canoe might capsize and they would both be overboard if he tried to climb back over the side.

Trent grabbed a paddle and began to propel the canoe. Jason hung on as tightly as he could, but as the cool water of the lake pulled at him, he thought he could feel fingers around his ankles. Trent looked behind and yelled, "Something is there!"

"I know!" panted Jason. He hit the water around him, splashing wildly in hopes of scaring whatever it was away.

Cold fingers tugged at his sneakers. Jason felt as if he were going to be pulled under again at any moment.

Trent slapped his canoe paddle on the water. The loud noise echoed like a gunshot around the lake. White foam shot everywhere. But the tugging on his sneakers got harder. Jason held on for all he was worth. He kicked, struggling. She bobbed up besides him, blue hair wild in the spray, giggling and blowing bubbles. She thought he was funny! She disappeared under the canoe again and he felt her cold, wet arms wrap around his knees.

She'd drown him. He had no doubt of that. She didn't understand, or without Tomaz's fetish about his neck, he'd drawn something Evil. . . .

"Almost there!"

"Hurry!" gasped Jason. She pulled at him. If she was from the Dark, taking his life would mean nothing to her. His insides went cold. He could barely hang on. His hands burned with the effort, his arms and body were being stretched too far. Did his hand throb or was it all part of his desperation? She was pulling him under. . . .

Trent grunted with effort. The canoe skewed about wildly as Jason's weight threw it off-balance. His hand slid over the molded rim. "I can't hold on!"

"Almost there." Trent panted, breathless.

Jason tried to kick, but she had a firm grip on his legs. One good yank and he would go under again—

Then he felt a tickling at the buckles on his life jacket. No . . . no . . . she was trying to free him from the jacket. One side suddenly slipped lose. "Hurry!"

Trent laid into it, paddle dipping strongly into the water. The canoe shot forward in spite of Jason's dragging pull on it. The water warmed slightly as it became shallower. Jason closed his eyes. His hands were slipping. His arms felt numb. She began to apply steady force. He was going to go under. . . .

The canoe bumped into the rocky shoreline. It rocked madly as Trent leaped to solid ground and then lay down on his stomach, grabbing Jason by the wrists. "Come on. Pull on me!"

He gave a twisting kick and then, suddenly, the hold on him broke away. The rocks on the shoreline met his feet and he scrambled up them, braced by Trent until he stood on dry land. Well, nearly dry land. Water streamed off him in an immense puddle. A huge strand of grass was tangled about his sneaker and ankle. Bending, it took him a few moments to unwrap it and shake it off. Was this what had gripped him? He turned and looked back at the canoe as he gulped to catch his breath. It waggled once, as if something struck or pushed at it, then it bobbed quietly in the deeper water near the rugged shore.

Just off the point where they stood, a big boulder poked out of the waters like an iceberg. It was split, and in that crack, a tall pine grew stubbornly. Water frothed about it suddenly.

"What was that?" asked Trent. He stared at the lake water.

"I don't know." Jason looked away. He did not feel like telling what he'd seen or felt. "Something."

Trent dusted himself off. "Wanda."

"What?"

"Loch Ness has Nessie. Lake Wannameecha has . . . Wanda." Trent grinned. "Any tentacle marks on you? Sea dragon bites?"

Jason shot him a look and Trent just punched his shoulder. "Wuss."

"Yeah, maybe." He took a shaky breath. He put his hand to his throat, where the fetish bag usually snuggled. He thought of finding a way to wrap it, keep it dry, so that he never had to take it off again.

"Ready to head back?"

"Give me a minute." Jason stood in the hot sun. Rattled, he hardly knew where on the lake they were. He began to dry out a bit. Something glinted in the woods a few paces away. "Where are we, anyway?"

"No idea. We could be inside or outside the campgrounds. I just know which way we need to go to get back." Trent shadowed his eyes. "I don't think we've been this way with Sousa, though."

"I'm turned around." Jason spun on one heel as if to prove his point. "I can't tell north from west here."

The sun, just about directly overhead, was no help that way although, soaked as he was, he felt grateful for its warmth. He looked at the almost spearlike glint shining through a patch of green. "I want to see what that is. You hold onto the canoe."

Trent stared at him blankly. "Like the canoe is going anywhere."

"If it drifts off, we've got a very long walk," Jason pointed out. *Or was pulled out to the lake's center.* She could very well drag it off out of disappointment or spite. Or by design. He wasn't anxious to climb back in right away, either, but knew he would have to.

Trent reached into the bow and got the mooring line. He wrapped it around one of the heavy rocks edging the shoreline and then dusted his hands off. "If you're going to look at something, I'm going with you," he said firmly.

"I can almost guarantee they don't have cookies." But Jason grinned as Trent caught up with him. They cut through the deep piney forest in search of whatever the sunlight was reflecting. Branches reached and grabbed at them. After a very short trek, they bulled their way through onto a . . . road. A sagging overhead signpost creaked in the slight breeze, and a rusting gateway sat open on the land. Jason blinked.

Trent laughed. "It's the front gate," he said.

Jason looked at the dark mountain range looming over

where the road disappeared. He doubted that the tunnel they had come through was in those mountains. He doubted that their bus ride had taken them anywhere near those mountains, but he did not doubt that wolfjackals ranged them. He shivered, as his still damp T-shirt cooled on his torso. "Can't be. Would have to be the back gate, if anything. Let's get out of here."

"Sure," Trent agreed. "I think we've found enough trouble for the day." As quickly as possible, they made their way back to the lake. Jason tugged his life jacket back into place, tightening the buckles. Trent waited till he was seated before casting off and jumping into the canoe. They brought it about quickly and started paddling toward the camp. Once, Jason looked back.

"Should we tell anyone about her?"

"Her who?"

"Wanda." Trent grinned at him over one shoulder. "We never saw her, but something was there. She'd make a good campfire story."

"You can tell it," Jason said firmly, "but *only* if you leave me out of it!"

"Deal! You get too much glory anyway."

Jason aimed a paddleful of water at Trent's back and managed to hit most of his target. Laughing, Trent said, "I'd get you back—but you're already all wet!"

"Just get me home. I'm probably grounded for the rest of camp." Jason stretched his shoulders, then began to paddle strongly in rhythm with Trent. The canoe shot ahead, gliding silently over dark blue waters . . . and he thought he could see a darker, small shadow pacing them till it tired and darted away. He put his hand to his neck again, his left hand, and felt a dull pain knife through the back of it. He frowned.

When they paddled into the cove, Jefferson was still wading among a few of the canoes, trying to straighten them out. Bailey and Ting flew by, waving their paddles. Jefferson checked his watch and frowned.

"Two days beached," he said, pointing at them. "And get

that cabin in shape, you've got inspection coming up as soon as I break classes for lunch."

Trent groaned. That meant no swimming or canoeing. In the heat of early July, that was cruel punishment. Jason was almost glad, though. He was not sure he wanted to go back into the water just yet!

They jostled shoulders heading back. They'd left the clean laundry lying every which way, and it looked as though it had rained socks. Other than that, it didn't take them long and they had just finished when they heard Stefan lumbering past outside, Rich at his heels, sneering something they couldn't quite hear. Trent went to the window. He motioned for Jason.

"They've got something." Trent eyed the pillowcases slung over their shoulders.

"What do you mean?"

"They're up to something. Somehow I don't think that's their laundry."

Jason watched the two disappear down the trail toward the main buildings. "He didn't say we were confined to the cabin, did he?"

"Nope." Trent slipped out the screen door. "Let's see what they're up to."

Staying just far enough behind, they stalked the two down to the restrooms. There, Rich handed his bulging pillowcase to Stefan and took up a casual watch at the corner of the building. He looked around, then motioned to Stefan who did a mad dash into the girls' side of the building.

"What—"

Trent shushed him. "This is going to be good," he said. "Whatever it is."

Jason shifted uneasily. "We ought to do something."

"Do what? We don't even know what it was they did!"

They watched intently. A long minute dragged by, then Stefan rolled out of the girls' toilets and joined Rich, trying to look nonchalant as he stuffed two empty pillowcases into his shirt. And waited.

In a few moments, the trio from Kittencurl came around the

curve of the lake. Jason could hear scraps of singing and chatter as they headed for the restrooms. Rich looked at Stefan and smirked as they moved back in the shadows.

"Whatever it is," Jason said, "I think we should warn them."

Trent started to shake his head, then muttered, "Too late anyway," as the three girls went into their half of the building.

A moment later, Ting screamed. Jennifer burst out of the building in long-legged strides, her blonde hair flying behind her, before she turned and stood, pointing wordlessly. Rich doubled over in laughter, leaning on Stefan.

Trent and Jason went to see just what it was. As they drew closer, they could hear . . . frogs.

Frogs croaking, ribbiting, and making whatever other noises they could. Ting stood in the open doorway to the bathroom, surrounded by green bodies of all sizes, hopping and croaking. Big frogs, little frogs. Ting seemed frozen, mouth half open. Bailey picked her way through, color blazing over her angry expression.

She pointed toward the doorway. "Out! Out! Everyone out!"

The frogs and toads began milling around, jostling each other. Ting looked at her and shook. "I . . . can't . . . move," she wailed.

Bailey put her hands on her hips. "Oh, really!" She took Ting by the wrist. "Follow me!"

She led the helpless girl out of the bathroom. There was a moment of silence as they emerged into the sunlight. Then, in a rippling ocean of green, the frogs and toads followed. Hop, splosh, hop, gr-beep, ribbit.

With a squeak of her own, Ting lunged away from Bailey and ran across the lane to where Jennifer stood. The pursuing frogs crowded in around Bailey. They ribbited hopefully. She stepped away.

Hop, hop, they followed. She moved again, trying not to step on anything.

The frog chorus eagerly hopped after.

Bailey threw her hands up. "Somebody do something!"

Stefan and Rich fell over laughing. Tomaz Crowfeather appeared on the pathway next to Jason and Trent. Trent could hardly stand up for laughing and hung onto a pine tree. The sapling bent and wobbled, waving its branches wildly.

"What's going on here?"

Everyone looked at Tomaz and shrugged.

He raised an eyebrow in gentle disbelief.

"Bailey is . . ." Rich caught his breath. "Frog herding." He doubled over in another fit of snickers.

"I am not!" Bailey tossed her head, ponytail bobbing. She marched off a few steps in a huff, following by a rippling, croaking, trail of green. The big ones hopped and plopped. With gleeful chirps, the little tree frogs pinged high out of the herd, soaring above the others. Jason watched them parade. Hop, plop, ping! Hop, plop, ping!

"Interesting." Tomaz crossed his arms across his chest, turquoises and silver glinting in the sun. "I think we need to talk, Bailey."

She opened her mouth to say something, but an immense toad plopped across her sneaker, puffed up, and beat her to it. "Rrrrrrribbit!"

Ting giggled and clung to Jennifer who laughed so hard a tear slid down her cheek.

"That . . . that's a lot of potential princes," Trent managed. He fell back into the pine tree in a shiver of branches and mirth. "You going to kiss all of them?"

"At least I won't draw flies!" She glared at them. "More than I can say about all of you, standing around with your mouths open!"

She stepped away. Hop, plop, ping! The frogs followed in adoration. Jason could not contain his laughter any longer. It bubbled out gleefully. Bailey looked at him, and then the others. Even Tomaz's mouth twitched although he tried to keep a careful lack of expression on his face.

"Am I amusing everyone?" Bailey looked around.

"Not quite," Rich snickered. "But if you wait a minute, I can get the rest of the camp here."

She snorted and flounced off then, down to the lakeside, her chorus line of frogs hopping and gurgling quickly after her. Every once in a while, she waved behind her, yelling, "Shoo!"

With a thoughtful look, Tomaz followed as well. They could hear his voice drifting back as he informed her that she had somehow summoned them, and only she could send them away. Bailey let out a groan, echoed in croaks loud and small from her adoring audience. When last seen before duty called them away, she was sitting on a boulder by the lake, frogs croaking in chorus to her, plopping in and out of the water, little tree frogs pinging high in the air to punctuate the deeper ribbits with cheerful chirps.

Snipe!

BAILEY'S amphibian audience still had everyone laughing at dinner. Having finally gotten rid of them, she took the joking with good humor, wearing a T-shirt she and Ting had decorated in Crafts Class which read DANCES WITH FROGS across the front.

"At least," Trent said to her when he caught his breath, "they didn't try to pull you back into the lake like Wanda did Jason."

To a chorus of "What?" Trent then had to tell Jason's story. Jason ignored him and picked on a meatloaf that, quite unlike FireAnn's usual fare, seemed rather tasteless and uninteresting. Jennifer, Ting, and Bailey all slid their food trays down to hear Trent, and Jon, Danno, and Henry swung around on their table benches to listen as well.

He made a well out of his mashed potatoes and gravy and hoped that would taste better. He really didn't want to think about the thing that had played with him in the deep Lake Wannameecha waters and whether he'd actually seen anything like what he thought he saw. Or if something about him or his hand, that cursed scar, had set it off. Was he now a doorway, drawing things through that should not be? And if he was . . . were they evil?

Trent drew oohs and aahs from his listeners as he spun the yarn out. Jason, catching a sentence every now and then despite trying not to listen, felt his ears grow warm and the back of his neck begin to itch. He squirmed on the cafeteria bench as Ting giggled at something, then scraped his fork over his plate loudly and rattled his cup. When he finally heard Bailey laugh, repeating "Wanda!" he exhaled, knowing the story was over. The fetish bag rested inside his shirt comfortingly, but he didn't like knowing that he would have to remove it again.

"That's a good one," Danno praised. "Tell it for the Talent Show!"

"Maybe." Trent grinned. "I have a certain roommate to live with, though!" They all laughed.

"I," announced Jon, "have a tale to tell at the campfire tonight." His tone drew Jason's attention. He gave up on his meatloaf and turned around.

Henry beamed in approval and pushed his glasses up his nose to their proper resting spot. Eagerly, he leaned forward on his elbows to listen, quite unaware of a puddle of gravy spreading around one of them.

Jonnard nudged a paper napkin across at Squibb before continuing, "It is the tale of the snipe bird, a rare bird which is most often seen at night, unlike other birds. Its feathers are coveted for charms and talismans. Shapechangers particularly value them." He smiled secretly.

"But a snipe hunt is a wild goose chase," Bailey said, looking at all of them. She wrinkled her nose, freckles dancing.

Jon continued smiling. "Precisely. However, the common snipe does exist, and I shall have a computer setup indicating that on its website."

Trent tilted his head. "I sense a plot."

"I should hope so." Jonnard pushed his tray away. "Shall we discuss it later? Much depends on secrecy. Tonight, before dinner."

They all nodded. It was time, it seemed, to get even with Rich and Stefan.

Ting took a bite of her oatmeal cookie before breaking it into crumbs and then showering them into Bailey's cupped hand.

Bailey looked about, then stuffed the crumbs into her pocket, which began to wiggle with a life of its own as Jason stared in fascination. As it jumped and moved, a long tufted tail snaked out and hung, twitching in satisfaction as its owner munched on cookie crumbs.

Jason grinned. "Your . . . erm . . . tail is showing."

Bailey blushed and swept the pack rat's tail back into her pocket. "She keeps doing that."

Ting considered her friend. "I should think she wouldn't like being pocketed up."

"Oh, Lacey sleeps most of the time. She only gets wiggly when she's hungry or at night." Bailey joggled her elbow into Ting. "That's when she makes all her noise!"

Ting rolled her eyes. "It's a good thing I'm a sound sleeper. I heard Jennifer complaining about all the scrabbling and squeaking earlier. Maybe we should let Lacey go free?"

As if knowing her name, the little kangaroo rat poked her head out, shell-like ears opening up attentively. Her dark eyes sparkled brightly and she seemed to show no fear, unlike the night when captured. The past few weeks had been good to her, and her coat glowed with health. She scrubbed at her whiskers busily, little paws shedding extra crumb bits like tiny dust motes.

"Lacey," said Bailey firmly.

The pack rat glanced up, then dove back into the shirt pocket. The tufted tail gave a defiant flick before disappearing after the rest of the creature. Ting laughed. Bailey squirmed a bit, then giggled. "Ticklish," she explained.

"I should think." Trent stood, empty tray in hand. "If Jon is going to try to set up anything in the computer room—" he gave a lopsided grin, "he'll need help! Henry is good with a PC, but he doesn't know half of what he thinks he does." He checked his watch. "I have just enough time before we're scheduled. I can set it up so all he has to do is push a button."

"Even that might be too much," Ting commented wryly as she trailed Bailey out of the cafeteria.

"You know," Bailey murmured. "When I talk to Mom tonight, I bet she'll have some ideas for our costumes. . . ."

Trent snorted at Ting's last words. He bolted out of the cafeteria ahead of Jason who looked after him, then shrugged. The two of them seemed to be going in opposite directions more and more these days, and he couldn't shake the uneasy feeling that something was wrong with Trent. It was nothing he could put his finger on, but just a nagging tug. If only he knew what it was he'd done, or hadn't done. He sighed and left the mess hall.

Dark clouds hung above the jagged peaks, but they seemed to be moving quickly, and the hot summer day was unaffected except for the humidity. Maybe rain at midnight or so, he thought. He rather liked storms, and lying in bed listening to one would be far better than lying in bed trying to forget another nightmare! Lightning and the boom of thunder would be welcome compared to the specter of a cold tomb and its occupant reaching for him. . . .

A shiver ran across the back of his neck.

"Are you feeling all right, Jason?" Dr. Patel asked kindly, behind him.

He jumped. She stood next to him and he had not even heard her approach. She put her hand upon his brow, a quick touch, before he moved away. "I'm fine."

"All right." She did not sound convinced and had a faint expression on her face that reminded him of his stepmother when she was about to lecture him about being careful.

"Really. I'm okay." He made a face. "Can't go out on the lake for a couple of days, but other than that, fine."

"Too bad. The lake looks pleasant in these hot days. But you don't look warm to me, Jason. You look rather chilled." Dr. Patel's brown eyes continued to watch him in concern.

He shifted. "You don't need to worry about me."

She smiled gently. "The Magickers are a big family. Like all families, we quarrel, even brawl a bit, but heaven help the outsider who tries to hurt one of us. In short, Jason, if you need us, we're here." She patted him on the shoulder and then moved off to her yoga class, sari wrapped about her slim figure.

He waited till she was out of sight before reading the schedule over again. Marked in bold handwriting next to the printout was his grounding from the lake for the next two days, and Trent's as well. It didn't seem fair somehow in the heavy summer heat that hung over the camp, yet he knew they'd probably earned it. But he hadn't told anyone what he thought he'd seen. Had he seen anything? Or had he just panicked in a brush snag? Or if he had seen something, what would happen to her . . . it? Would they rush out on the lake to net her? Even worse, with the mark of the wolfjackal on him, and not wearing his protection . . . had he drawn it somehow? Could he bring evil down on the camp simply by being here? He didn't quite know what to do or think. He had the uneasy feeling it was a secret he should keep, but he didn't know or understand why. He moved away from the schedule, sighing.

"That's a heavy sound."

Jason let out a squeak. He turned and looked up into Tomaz Crowfeather's weathered face. "Do you guys always sneak up on someone?"

"Us guys? Meaning Indians or counselors or . . ."

"Magickers," answered Jason.

Tomaz chuckled. "It is not hard to be silent when someone else is deep in thought. Care to walk with me? I have some tracking to do. I see your canoe time is canceled for a few days." He read over Jason's shoulder a moment.

"Sure." Jason didn't feel like he had a choice but to volunteer. Tonight was family calling night, and as he had no real burning desire to talk to Grandma McIntire, he had plenty of time. As Tomaz moved off, he fell into step. "What are we looking for?"

Crowfeather rubbed his heavy silver-and-turquoise bracelet. Then he answered slowly. "I am not quite sure, Jason. Let us hope I will know it when I see it." He paced slowly and deliberately and they walked in silence until they reached the edges of most of the cabin clusters. Once or twice he knelt to look at paw prints.

The third time, Jason fidgeted, then asked, "Wolfjackals?"

"No. See here?" Tomaz indicated the pad and toe imprints. "This is a lighter animal. Small pad. But, also larger toes. That is the sign of the coyote." He smiled faintly. "The yellow trickster has spent most of the last century spreading across the continent. Where we hunted the wolf, and drove him near to extinction, the little wolf sneaked in to take his place. The coyote is very smart, very quick." Tomaz straightened.

"If you know it's only coyotes, why do you patrol every day?"

"Because I don't know it's always coyotes." The Magicker faced into the wind and inhaled deeply as though he could catch scents carried on it beyond the norm. "The mana here is rich and heavy in spots. Other things could be carried in."

Jason repeated slowly, "Other things?"

Tomaz only said, "The world is full of many things, Jason, wonders that long ago took refuge in, for them, a safer place. Sometimes the tide carries them out, however." He spread his arms and chanted a few words, and stood, palms turned upward and cupped slightly as if he could catch the wind.

Jason stood quietly and just watched. For a moment, he wanted to tell Tomaz what he'd seen in the lake. But he hesitated. If only he could feel the Magick like that. If only he could inhale it and hold it deep inside, making it a part of himself. If only he could feel it in his bones. Did the bite keep him from that? Or the granite band in his crystal? Was he flawed too?

"Takes a long time to know yourself," Tomaz said quietly.

"Is that what we're doing here? Really?"

Tomaz studied him for a moment. Then he gave a slow nod. "Yes, mostly. We can use mana. We can bend it, even shape it, to our will. But if we do not know ourselves, do not know what we might be capable of, we do not know if we *should* do what we *can* do."

"Is the Dark Hand deadly?"

Tomaz scratched his brow. "Perhaps," he said quietly. "Based on what I have seen in my lifetime, yes, perhaps. One thing I know for sure, is that they must be treated seriously and cautiously. My view, however, is not popular."

Jason skirted a thick gorse bush as Tomaz strode the other way, his sharp gaze scanning the dirt and even the prickly bush leaves for bits of fur. "It's not?"

Tomaz shook his head. "There are many who say we are all Magickers. All one family. Even the black sheep. I say . . . they are not black sheep. They are sidewinders, snakes in the grass. Treacherous and deadly." He paused, and squatted next to a wild berry bush, its pickings lean, still greening in the summer sun. Instead of berries, he plucked a thick black tuft of hair off it. He rolled it in his fingers, then smelled it as Jason watched. Then Tomaz dropped it, stood, and dusted his hands off. "Bear," he said.

"Goes with berries, huh? They really have bears around here?"

"Yes. A young bear, from the print or two I've seen. Adolescent. But I've not seen any adult prints about, which is what I find baffling." Tomaz tugged on his vest. "A bear will stay with its mother, two, three years, even if another cub is born."

"What does that mean?"

"I am not sure . . . yet." Tomaz surveyed the edge of the wilderness fringe. "Tell me, Jason, can you feel it?"

He looked around. It was hot. He could feel the bright sun's rays streaming down, and a slight breeze off the lake fighting with them, but he didn't think that's what Crowfeather meant. He thought a moment, and then thought of the ley lines they'd been mapping. Like a glowing net over the grounds, they shimmered, but only in the computer simulation done of their positions. He shoved a hand in his pocket to curl his fingers around his crystal.

Without thought, he swung to his right, took a step or two forward, and put his free hand out, grasping at a ribbon of nothingness in the air. He felt . . . he felt a surge . . . like a quickening heartbeat, or the effort he put into a fifty-yard dash. His jaw dropped.

"There," said Tomaz. "You have it. Let it go, because you're not going to be using it."

Jason blinked once or twice, wondering how. Nothing worked until he held a mental image of simply relaxing his hand and dropping it, empty. The sudden, sharp moment faded. "That was . . . that was it, wasn't it?"

"A mana stream, and you went right to it. From the way you homed in on it, I doubt you even need dowsing rods to find them. Some people have that instinct."

"I did good!"

Tomaz grinned. "You did great. However . . . finding them is one thing. Using them, another."

"Why can't everyone be a Magicker, then? If they could only sense the mana? Like singing. Most of us can sing a little. Some of us can sing pretty well. And a few can sing well enough to break glass and stuff."

"It's far more complicated than that, and it's not an ability like singing. Truthfully, few of us have it. Think of it like the gene for pole vaulting. Most of us wouldn't even know we had it or try it out. But those of us who do, can vault so high . . . and maybe land safely, or maybe not. It's a rare few who can jump high enough to set records. Landing safely is still dangerous."

Jason thought of Henry Squibb, getting more and more nervous and clumsy and unsure of himself. Did he have the Talent to jump high and land safely? Would he be sent home like the campers last week, ten suddenly so homesick they left camp, each after drinking the feared Draft of Forgetfulness, and the others watching them go, knowing that the homesickness had been charmed on them. The only thing wrong with each of them was that they hadn't been enough of a Magicker. Could Henry survive much longer? He leaned more and more on Jonnard's power rather than his own. Jason tried not to sigh in worry.

Tomaz clapped Jason on the shoulder. "The senses are a wonderful thing, Jason, yet they can deceive you. I wish I could tell you to trust your heart, if your eyes and your mind worry about something. But I cannot. Sometimes the heart is the easiest to deceive, and that is why I fear the Dark Hand. Deception is their greatest ability." The sun glinted off the turquoise-and-silver inset watch he wore. Tomaz consulted it, and said, "If I don't get you back, I'll be grounded, too."

With that, they trotted back into Camp Ravenwyng.

They met behind the mess hall in the twilight. Neither of the girls was there.

"All right." Jonnard looked about. "Bailey and Ting can't sneak out after Lights Out, they've decided. Too risky. Jennifer is involved in some project with Eleanora, so she's in and out. She might catch them. So, it's up to you two while Henry, Danno and I run the Hunt." It's too bad we didn't know the girls weren't going to help sooner. We could have done this back at Skybolt."

He handed Jason a paper sack. Jason looked in it. Two large cans of shaving cream sat in it. Jonnard glanced at him. "Do I have to tell you what to do with that?"

"Nope!" Jason grinned and handed the bag to Trent, who looked inside, with Danno peering over his elbow.

"Good." Jon scrubbed a hand across his chin. "My mother thought I might sprout a beard this summer, and she likes to be prepared." He shrugged. "I didn't, and it would be a shame for those two cans to go to waste. Anyway, they took the bait. Rich and Stefan are meeting us at eleven thirty."

"If anyone can stay awake."

Jon looked at Trent sharply. "You can do anything if you prepare and plan for it. Jason?" He looked at Jason then.

"I'll be up."

"Good. We probably won't have much time out there. They're sharp, they'll guess they've been taken pretty quickly."

"Where is Henry, anyway?" Danno said.

"FireAnn kept him after herb and botany class. He was having some trouble identifying poison oak, kept trying to do it by touch. He'll catch up in a few."

"Gah." Danno shuddered, then began to rub and scratch at his hands in sympathy. "Henry always learns the hard way."

"Hopefully, after tonight, Rich and Stefan will learn not to mess with us." Trent stowed the paper bag under his elbow, and added, "I took a look at their cabin earlier. Even if they lock the door latch, they usually leave a window wide open. We'll get in, one way or another."

"All right. Good luck to everyone." Jonnard saluted them before moving off into the growing darkness.

"Good plan," said Danno.

"Yeah. The only thing that can go wrong is if Stefan bears out. Then, we've all got a problem." Trent scratched his nose. "Or maybe not. He can only chase one of us at a time!"

Jason grabbed Trent's sleeve. "Come on, bearer of great news. It'll be Lights Out soon enough."

Inside their cabin, they hunched over his flashlight and sketched out prime areas of attack. The beds and closet, of course, though Trent voiced a whispered opinion that Stefan was likely never to have used a closet in his life. Snide Rich was equally likely to have his things folded within an inch of their life and put neatly away.

"The object here," Jason mulled, "is to trash them without trashing them too much and getting in trouble with Rainwater."

"It's a challenge, but I think we're up to it." Trent stifled a yawn. "As long as we're awake."

"I'll be awake."

"Good. I'm gonna . . . lie down . . . for a minute or two." Trent crawled onto his bed and in seconds, the cabin filled with his soft snoring.

Jason crawled into his bed, cradling Trent's flashlight in his hands under the covers, reading one of his cabin mate's many *X-Men* comic books. Not the least bit sleepy, his duty was to watch the time for the appointed hour. He heard soft steps go past the cabin several times and then a heavier tread, which might be Hightower, Jefferson, or Crowfeather patrolling yet again. Finally, he heard an exclamation from Henry Squibb, high-pitched and excited, quickly smothered. He checked his watch and saw it was nearly time. He crawled out and woke Trent. They both hurried, putting their shoes on in the dark. Trent grabbed up the paper sack of shaving cream plus a few other goodies they'd found and waited by the shuttered front window, peeking through a slit in the slats.

Trent beckoned to him. "They're here."

Jason clicked off the flashlight, not wanting anything to give them away. He joined Trent and peered through the wooden slats. Even for Henry, the boy looked pale, and he paced nervously about in front of Skybolt. "I hope Jon knows what he's doing," he muttered. "I don't think Henry's up to this."

"Why?"

"I think he's scared, and not of Stefan and Rich. He wouldn't go at all, but he trusts Jon."

Before Trent could answer, Stef and Rich came up, and grabbed Henry by the elbow.

"We have to hurry. Someone's out patrolling. I heard them pass by the cabin."

"Move out, then," Jon ordered and Jason watched them go. He could barely see the group, pillowcases in hands, as they trotted off. Stefan took up the rear in the lumbering run he'd developed. He even *moved* like a bear most of the time.

Trent nodded, and yanked open the door. "They're gone, let's roll!"

They sprinted through the dark to the cabin occupied by Rich and Stefan. Later, Trent would claim he could find the cabin by the stench alone as he spun the yarn out. As they reached the steps though, it seemed no different than any of the other cabins although it seemed to be set apart from the rest, evergreens and bushes hugging it close. The door was latched firmly, but as Trent had predicted, the side window was wide open. He easily slipped the screen down and boosted himself through, then stuck his head and hand out for Jason.

"Hold your nose," he advised. "It reeks in here."

And it did, as Jason hung over the windowsill and then swung his legs over. It smelled strongly of old sneakers and something else, musky and animal. The next cabin inspection was only a few days away. Open windows or not, Jason did not see how Sousa or the others could not fail to notice it. Stefan-bear had a distinct odor that hung over nearly everything in the cabin.

Trent took the flashlight from him and aimed it at the bunks. Jason got out his crystal and concentrated until its golden lantern light flared. Trent tossed him a can, saying, "I'll get started on the bunks."

Jason played his crystal lantern over them. "Too messy . . . no way to short-sheet them."

"Ah, never fear, I have a plan." With a grin, Trent opened up the pillows and began to fill the cases with shaving cream. "Niiiice and fluffy."

Jason quickly began finding the worn sneakers scattered all over the cabin floor, filling them with quick squirts of shaving cream that seemed to explode into clouds. As a finishing touch, he tucked the scraggly laces into each billowy cloud. The two of them moved quickly through the cabin until first one, then the second can of shaving lather sputtered empty. Trent hummed off-key as he moved from window to storage cupboard. A can rattled as he shook it.

"I thought all the shaving cream was gone?" Jason peered at his silhouette.

"It is. This is silly string." And with a chuckle, he began to spray the plastic string through the air, enwebbing the door latch, the cupboard pulls, anywhere that had a knob or pull or latch. Satisfied, he stuffed the can inside his shirt. "I think our work here is done."

Jason lifted his crystal lantern high, spilling golden light throughout the entire cabin. The pranks were not obvious. Stefan and Rich could fall into any number of them, and even once they discovered that their cabin had been visited, there were secret, hidden traps of lather and other goodies which should befall them all night. He nodded in satisfaction. They slipped back out the window and fastened the screen in place when they heard heavy footsteps.

Backs to the cabin, they squatted down and held their

breath. Needles cracked and branches rattled, and then the figure, whoever it was, passed by. They waited long moments, till they gulped for air, then stood and sprinted back to Starwind. Once inside, they grabbed each other by the wrist and did a fierce little victory dance.

"That," Trent said when they finally stopped, "felt great."

"We got 'em good," Jason agreed. "Now," he added, pulling up a chair, "we listen."

"To what?" Trent dragged the other chair over and joined him at the window.

"To the noise of discovery, which ought to be any second. They've been out thirty minutes. I bet they've found out by now. . . ." He sat back in his chair and watched as Trent pulled over one of his favorite comic books and began to read by flashlight.

"Why don't you use your crystal? No batteries to worry about."

"Like Eleanora said, some people can't work with Fire that well. I must be one of 'em. I can hardly do that bit." Trent flipped a page. "Could be worse, I could be lighting up like Squibb does."

While he read, Jason watched the night activity. A possum sauntered past looking in the moonlight like an odd, hunched-over cat, with a ratlike tail trailing after it. Just a step or two behind came Hightower who paused to look at the tracks, then went on down the camp pathway toward the main buildings. Jon and Henry would be safe coming back for an hour or so, at least. An owl hooted as if to echo the lateness of the hour. Trent yawned as he turned a page.

Jason heard something. He put his eye to the shutters, watching. He saw Jon and Henry come stumbling back to their cabin. He put a hand out and shook Trent.

"Something's wrong."

"What? What is it?"

"I can't tell." He stood. It looked to him as though Squibb had been hurt, leaning on Jon as the tall boy helped him up the cabin steps. He could hear Henry's moaning voice. "Come on!" He wasn't going to stay there and guess, Lights Out or not.

Trent jumped to his feet to follow and they thundered across the wooden porches of both cabins. Inside, Jonnard had a switch on, and Henry sat on the floor, face in his hands, crying. Jon looked almost as distressed as Squibb, his face pale and his dark hair going in every direction.

"What happened?"

"He'll be all right," Jon said slowly. He sat down heavily on the desk chair, dropping the two pillowcases. "Did you get their cabin?"

"Yes, but—"

"He'll be all right!"

"No, I won't." Henry sniffled, looking up through his fingers. "It's gone, gone, all of it."

Jason stood, baffled. Trent stared. "What's gone?"

"He'll be all right." Jon sounded as if every word were an effort. "We took them everywhere. We had them looking in every prickly bush and disgusting hole around the lake." He took a deep breath.

Henry made a loud snuffling noise and dragged his sleeve across his face. "It's gone," he repeated, very muffled.

"Henry," said Jonnard. "Shut up and go to sleep, you'll be fine tomorrow."

Squibb shook his head mournfully.

"What's gone?" Trent shot looks from one to the other. "And where's Danno?"

"Danno didn't show up. We took Rich and Stefan out for snipes without him. Henry, it'll be all right."

"No, it won't." Henry stopped sniffling and instead sat on the cabin floor and began to shake. Pale and shivering, he looked absolutely miserable.

Jason squatted beside him. "Tell me what's wrong?"

Henry looked up into his face. "It's gone. My Magick. Look. . . ." And he pulled his crystal out of his pocket. The vibrant, sometimes fiery crystal had gone soot dark. It looked ab-

solutely lifeless. Henry poked a finger at it. "Blasted," he said.
"Like me." He sniffled again.

Jason touched the stone. Colder than ice. No matter what
Jonnard said, Henry was in trouble. Deep, deep trouble. . . .

"What's going on here?"

The boys all turned. Hightower stood in the doorway, waiting for an explanation. He did not look happy.

Shouts and yells of surprise and anger from several cabins
away did not lighten the solemn atmosphere, despite Stefan's
loud bellow cutting through the night. Rich shouted threats in
his high-pitched voice, although of what they could not tell.
Despite the commotion, Hightower's attention stayed fastened
on the boy in front of him.

Henry stood up, and held his crystal out on his palm, hand
wavering. "My . . . Magick . . ." he said, and looked at the Magicker hopelessly.

Hightower frowned heavily as he reached out and dropped
his hand on Henry's shoulder. "I'm sorry, son," he said. "There
isn't anything I can do."

Henry fainted.

You're Off the Island

ONE huge golden topaz, rough-shaped and unpolished, sitting on the corner of an old wooden filing cabinet like a crystal lantern, lit Gavan Rainwater's office. It looked like a fallen star, Jason thought, as he sat miserably next to Jon and Henry who could not stop sniffing. Trent stayed on his feet, one shoulder to the bookcase that overflowed with books and scraps of paper that looked very much like parchment, and even a few rolled up scrolls. Magickers stuffed the office until the only real room left was the chair behind the desk and that stayed empty for the moment as they waited for Rainwater.

Henry rubbed his nose dry, or attempted to. "I'm sorry," he said for the hundredth time. He shredded the damp tissue in his hand.

"You didn't do anything wrong," Jason told him, for at least the tenth time. Trent leaned forward and pounded on Squibb's shoulder.

Bailey and Ting shared a desk chair, leaning close together, their faces very pale. Lacey scrambled out of Bailey's pocket and down into the palm of her hand, where the pack rat sat very quietly, her tufted tail hanging out, a tiny spidery strand dangling from it. "It was just a snipe hunt," Bailey said quietly, to no one in particular.

Tomaz shifted at a sound in the hall, and opened the office door, holding it for Rainwater, who swept in with FireAnn at his heels, a goblet in her hand. Jason instantly recognized the tantalizingly sweet smell. Despite the wonderful aroma, every Magicker she passed seemed to shrink away from FireAnn and the goblet. Tomaz did not shrink back, but turned his face away. Gavan pulled his chair out and sat down, FireAnn at his elbow, his brow knotted. He looked as if he'd just been awakened, his hair slightly rumpled, his eyes not quite their usual brilliant blue. He leaned his cane against the desk.

"This is not good news."

"Gavan," began Eleanora, and then she stopped and tightened her mouth. Her dark hair had been pinned up for the night, in a mass of curls about her head, and she barely floated above the floor.

FireAnn shook her head at Eleanora. "It has to be done," the fiery-headed cook insisted.

Jason realized the Magickers had been arguing. They had that look as they traded glances. Maybe there was hope for Henry yet. . . .

"Well, Henry," Trent said loudly. "Looks like you've been voted off the island."

"No . . ." Henry whimpered slightly. He stared at his lifeless crystal.

Dr. Patel put a slim brown hand on Trent's shoulder and squeezed. Trent rolled his eyes but shut up as if she'd said something into his ear. Bailey and Ting shifted even closer together.

"This is not an easy thing to do, for any of us, Henry." Gavan nodded at FireAnn and took the goblet from her hands. He rolled the pewter chalice between his hands. "In the morning, you'll have good memories of camp. And a case of poison oak, I'm afraid, from tromping through all that brush. Dr. Patel will have called your parents, telling them she's sending you home early for better treatment, and she'll drive out with you."

Henry stared through his spectacles at the goblet. "But I

won't remember Magick," he said. "The . . . the binding . . . and . . . that."

"No. You won't."

A lone tear dropped from Henry's already red eyes, and slid over his cheek. He wrung his hands together and, then, slowly, nodded. Jonnard said, "I'll go with you in the morning, Henry, ride in the van with you."

Dr. Patel moved slightly, looking at Eleanora and Gavan. But it was Eleanora who said, "I think that would be nice of you, Jon. It would be good for Henry to have someone with him, and I think his parents would appreciate it, too."

Squibb scratched at one arm. He dug in his pocket to get out a small jar of ointment, and Tomaz leaned over and took it from him. "You're going to have to suffer through this one," he said quietly. He gave the jar to FireAnn who sighed as she tucked it away in her apron.

"Oh," said Henry. "I really have poison oak?"

"Afraid so. It'll be a mild but stubborn case. You'll be fine in a few days although nothing is quite as good as what FireAnn cooks up."

Henry pushed his round-lensed glasses back up his nose. "I'll do anything," he declared. "Don't make me go! Please?"

"We've no choice. We have to protect ourselves, Henry. Your . . . Talent . . . as a Magicker has been on the edge your whole time here. And now . . . this." Gavan picked up the dead crystal. "We've all seen it before, and it strikes fear in our hearts, because it could, possibly, happen to us as well. You've burned your power away and you're empty. It could come back, I've heard of a rare case or two where it did, but here and now . . . you've lost it, Henry. Without it, you're at risk here at camp, and there's little we can teach you. It becomes a matter of protecting you, and ourselves, against outsiders. The Draft of Forgetfulness is a kindness, really. You won't remember what you've lost. It's the best we can do." He extended the goblet to Henry. "Drink it all down."

Jason jumped to his feet. "No! Don't let them do it to you."

Tomaz put his hand around Jason's elbow. "Jason," he said, in warning.

"No, you can't do this. This is the best thing that's ever happened to him, to any of us. Don't take it away from him."

Gavan Rainwater said sadly, "We didn't take it away. He burned it out or lost it. All we can do is protect him, and the best way to do that is to return him to the ordinary world where he belongs."

Jason struggled. "But he doesn't belong there! Anyone can see that. You can, can't you?" He looked at Eleanora, then Anita Patel, then Jonnard. No one would meet his eyes. "Look, I'll protect him. I'll do whatever I have to do to keep him safe."

Bailey offered, "You didn't send me away when I goofed."

"This is different. This isn't to punish anyone, it's to protect them, and ourselves."

"I don't want to be protected like this."

"This is all my fault," Bailey blurted out.

Eleanora moved to the girls, murmuring, "It's no one's fault. It's the way things are."

"I dared them to get even with Rich and Stefan." Lacey raced up Bailey's arm and dove into her pocket headfirst, tucking her tail in after, quickly, as though sensing all the upset.

Eleanora gently brushed a loose strand of hair from Bailey's brow and tucked it behind her ear. "I think that was a given, regardless." She glanced at Gavan. "May I take the girls back, Gavan? I think they understand the seriousness of our situation here."

He scratched at his chin before agreeing, "Good idea."

Ting stood and pulled something from her pocket, a light pink stone wrapped in a bit of wire. It glowed faintly. She gave it to Henry, who stared at it a moment. "It's a good luck charm."

"A little late," commented Trent.

Henry curled his plump fist around it. He smiled nervously at Ting. "Thanks. I think I'm going to need a lot of luck." He watched as Eleanora led the two girls from the crowded office.

Jason shrugged against Tomaz. "Henry, don't let them do this to you."

Tomaz pulled Jason back against his chest and held him. "No, Jason. This is the best way."

"I did it to myself, I think." Henry shrugged. He put his charm into his pocket.

"If you do this to him . . . you could do it to any of us. To Jon or Trent, or . . . or me." His heart felt like it would explode in his chest.

Gavan Rainwater leveled his gaze on Jason's face as he answered, "Only if it were absolutely necessary. But, yes, if we had to, we would. Magick has dwindled through the centuries. We are nearly all that is left of it, and yet, even beyond our wish for self-preservation is the belief that we have Magick because we are destined to help with it. So saving ourselves is not as selfish as it appears. But it is necessary."

Jason thought of his own crystal, with the band of stone through it, edged by fool's gold. Was his already half dead? Was that why Gavan had not wished him to choose it? Would he be sitting at this desk tomorrow or the next day, with that goblet in front of him? "Why wait? Do it to me now!"

Henry reached for the goblet. He took a deep breath, then blurted out, "It's okay, Jason."

Jason let out a wrenching protest as Henry lifted the Draft and gulped it down, swallow after swallow, as tears streamed down his reddening face. Jon turned away and looked at the wall, as if it were too much to watch. Trent stared down at his sneakers.

Horrified, Jason could not look away as Henry set the goblet down. He belched, then colored brightly. Henry reached inside his pocket and pulled out three computer diskettes and gave them to Trent. "Better keep these. If I forget everything, they won't make any sense, anyway."

Trent pocketed the black squares. Henry had neat labels on them. The one in front read: Important! FireAnn's Herbs. Henry had put all his notes on disk.

Squibb scratched his other arm, tiny marks already beginning to welt. With a sigh, he glanced at the doctor. "Am I going to itch all night?"

She smiled softly. "I've something conventional that will help, although it's not near as good as FireAnn's ointment. You'll sleep soundly."

He nodded and stood, wobbly. He took a deep breath. "I wish I didn't have to forget you all."

"You won't, exactly. There will have been a camp. Canoeing. Lanyards. Baseball games. You'll have had a great summer." Gavan stood, as well. "You'll sleep in the infirmary tonight, and Jon will have your things all packed and ready to go in the morning."

Jon nodded.

"What about Danno? Won't he get to say good-bye?"

"Danno is sound asleep. I'll explain things to him tomorrow, as well as to the rest of the camp."

Henry nodded mournfully.

Gavan picked up his cane. "As for the rest of you, we are not done with tonight's activities. We will deal with all of you tomorrow."

Trent sighed and slipped out the office door. Tomaz squeezed the hard and callused hand he held on Jason's arm before letting him go. Whether it was meant to comfort or caution, he could not tell. Jason and Jonnard left together, paused in the doorway, and waved good-bye to Henry.

Henry brightened a bit behind his glasses. "Nice guys," he said to Dr. Patel. "Did we have fun together?" He smiled at her pleasantly before yawning hugely.

"Yes, Henry," she said softly. "You had a lot of fun with them."

Jason bolted from the office doorway. He did not stop running till he leaped up his cabin steps and threw himself through the door. Even at that, Trent had beaten him back. They did not speak to one another as they sank into bed and an uneasy sleep.

Jason woke early, but not early enough to see Henry leave. One of the buses was missing when he trotted up to the bathrooms, and he stood for a moment, looking at the small lot off the Gathering Hall. He remembered how they had all tumbled out of the buses that first night, tired but eager. The fear that had knotted in his chest last night would not go away. He could understand, for the first time, Trent's growing disenchantment. Although they were all here for the summer, the time was rapidly passing and could end abruptly for any of them. Maybe Trent was used to even harder knocks than Jason, for he seemed to have been expecting this all along.

One uneasy thought had been with him through his restless sleep. Up till now, he knew that he was accepted, mistakes and all. He had never asked why. He had never wondered what it was the Magickers wanted of him. Now, he did. It had become clear that something was wanted of each and every one of them, and it had gone unspoken. And, equally clear, if they could not deliver it, they would be shipped off and forgotten.

He shivered. He was never sure at home how long he'd be welcome, despite their cheer and smiles. He wasn't one of them, not really. Here he was one of them—or was he?

Unbearable

"HEEEEY, batta, batta!" yelled Bailey. She stared from the warped and weathered bench to the home plate where Ting tried to look mean and waved her bat in answer as she settled into a stance. On the pitcher's mound, Dr. Patel tried to look equally mean as she held the ball and read signals. It was the master Magickers against the new Magickers and the masters were ahead, 5 to 2.

Trent stretched his legs at second base, edging away, with a wide, knowing grin on his face. With another wave of her bat, Ting fidgeted in the batters' box again. Jason stood firmly on first, thigh smarting a bit where a wild pitch had winged him, before Sousa had pulled himself as pitcher and put himself in the outfield, sending Anita Patel in for him. The master Magickers all looked a bit overconfident as well as tired and dusty. Jonnard sat in the on-deck circle, waiting for his turn at bat.

Nearly four weeks of play on the baseball diamond had run the grass down to browning stubs. Dust flew into the air more often than baseballs, and the outfield fence had been moved several times, both closer to home plate and farther away. Today it sat a tad bit farther away, with Gavan roaming center field snagging any well hit ball that even looked like it might be a home run. Eleanora had been assigned to play first, but then everyone had protested as she levitated to catch balls slightly out of reach.

The counselors split down their ranks to play on one team or the other, so Jennifer made noises at him as she guarded first base. There was a whole raft of campers sitting in the main stands, cheering one side or the other. FireAnn had made cotton candy and everyone sat eating off their sticks, cotton spun in glorious colors that just also happened to color their tongues the same vibrant shades. With every cheer they made, a rainbow bloomed from their open mouths.

Dust rose as Jennifer shuffled her sneakers. Jason took a short lead off the base, just in case Ting got a good line on the ball. Dr. Patel wound up and pitched.

"Steeee—rike one!" bellowed Jefferson. He pounded his mitt with the baseball before throwing it back to the pitcher. Ting flipped her long dark hair over her shoulder and narrowed her eyes, staring Dr. Patel down.

It seemed to work because the next two pitches were balls. Ting dug in at the plate and look back at Jonnard for advice.

He gave her a signal that meant, swing away. So she swung at the next pitch and the ball popped up in a high, high arc that landed just out of reach of catcher Lucas as he came out of a crouch and ran for it. Two strikes. And then three balls.

Jason limbered up. If she hit it at all, on a full count, they were going to have to tag and run for it.

Dr. Patel touched the faint mark on her forehead as if for luck, wound up, and then pitched. Ting swung with all of her willow-slender strength, and the ball shot low and away from the bat. It sizzled between first and second base before hitting the ground and still moving like a cannonball, rolled to the back fence.

They were all a little slow to react, so Trent ended up on third base, Jason on second, and Ting on first. Bailey screamed and yelled at Ting, her tongue a brilliant cherry red. Rich and Stefan stood near third base, trying to distract Hightower and everyone looked at the scoreboard as Jonnard came to the plate. It was their last chance to score. Trent did a little warm-up dance on third base as if he might try to steal home.

Jonnard looked across the entire baseball field as if calculating his chances. He looked unruffled, as usual, and slightly cool, as usual. And his tongue was a normal pink as he stuck it out at Lucas who said something unheard to him in the batting box. Lucas grinned before settling into his catching stance.

The last batter of the last inning of the last game. The next two weeks after the Talent Show, the master Magickers had already told the campers, would be spent in intense courses on the crystals, and making individual plans for home study. Oh, the canoe races and relay races were yet to come and some Hoedown Barbecue or some such, but the end of their time drew near. And depending on the coming storm, they might be out of time altogether.

Jason looked at the mountains. It was a hot, crystal-clear day, not a cloud in sight. He had no idea what a mana storm would look like. Would it start like summer lightning, with nothing but heat shivering across the sky? Would it boil up in huge, dense white thunderhead clouds? Would it crawl out of the dusty lands and snake crawl through the camp like some growling beast?

Eleanora slapped Jason on the shoulder with her mitt. "Don't go anywhere!" she said, trying to sound gruff. He smothered his worries and concentrated on watching the pitcher and batter staring each other down.

Dr. Patel took a deep breath, wound up and threw hard, coming down off the pitcher's mound with the effort. Her slim strength snapped a fast ball at home plate. Jonnard stepped into his swing.

KER-ACK! The bat connected with the ball. It took off, rising, rising, arching over the infield, gaining altitude. Jason watched it go overhead. It flew against the blue sky, a white blur.

Bailey yelled, "It's going . . . going . . . it's GONE!" She spun around, ponytail flying like a pennant. "Home run!"

The ball sailed over the makeshift barrier in the outfield and thudded to earth somewhere out of sight. Jason crossed home with Ting panting right behind him, slapped hands with Trent who crossed ahead of him, but everyone charged the field to capture Jonnard as he circled the bases. Yelling in victory, they hoisted him up on a sea of shoulders and trotted around the baseball field chanting in mad confusion. They danced around the master Magickers who laughed and tried to pull Jon down from his victory perch and did not quite manage it.

They all ended up at the mess hall where FireAnn and her crew made more cotton candy and shaved ices, flavored with sugary, colorful syrups that turned tongues even more bizarre colors as they spooned the cold treat down. Danno and Jonnard cheerfully stuck their tongues out at each other, comparing the colorful stripes and blazes as they ate, and no one seemed to miss Henry.

When Gavan dropped an easy pop fly out behind second base, no one but Jason heckled him, saying that he'd pulled a Henry.

When Tomaz and Jennifer each ran for a slowing line drive and trapped Bailey between them in a sandwich, no one but Jason said, "That could only have happened to Squibb."

And when Bailey led her cheering section, there was no Henry to lead the other side, owlish face red with enthusiasm, hair sticking every which way out of his cap. No Henry to beg for an extra splosh of cherry syrup down his shaved ice, and no Henry to be squeaking back and forth on the mess hall bench, joking with Danno and teasing Jonnard.

"What's wrong?" asked Trent. He'd picked blue raspberry syrup and was working on getting his tongue a deep electric blue. He licked his spoon.

"I miss Henry."

Something went out in Trent's face. "So?" he shrugged and answered, looking down in his dish. He vigorously stirred his ice into a melting slush, picked up the bowl and drank it, his lips going blue as he did so.

"So . . . it could happen to any one of us."

"Yeah, but it didn't. And he asked for it, screwing around like that."

"We don't know what he was doing."

"Look, all they had to do was lead Rich and Stefan around in circles. I could have done it. There's no Magick in that. But he didn't, he screwed around with his crystal and he burned his nerves out. His own fault. It's been weeks, and if you went to see him, he wouldn't even hardly remember you. Yeah, I'm sorry, but . . . But I'm here right now, and so are you." Trent's expression stayed closed and he said nothing more. He got up and left without another word.

Jason looked over and saw Bailey watching them both. She slid her bowl down and scooted over on the bench. She fetched Lacey out of her pocket and held out a bit of cherry-flavored ice on her finger. The pack rat sniffed curiously before eating the fruity coldness. She shook her head several times, whiskers wiggling furiously.

Bailey giggled. "I don't think she likes the ice."

"Bet she's never had any before." Jason watched the pack rat scramble up her arm and dive into the pocket of safety. "She sure seems tame."

"Tomaz says I have animal sense." She let out a rich chuckle. "Better than no sense at all!" She looked down at her pocket, where the long tufted tail swung lazily, almost catlike through the air. She stroked the tuft affectionately. The tail stayed out, though it jumped and danced as if Bailey tickled its owner unbearably. The sight made Jason squirm. She looked at him. "What's wrong?"

"I'm . . . not sure. You ever feel disconnected from everything?"

"What do you mean?"

"I mean . . . no one seems to care about Henry. Or anyone else who's gone, you know?"

Bailey made a little face. "Well. I guess it's like . . . we're happy it wasn't us. And it's like . . . who wants to see Henry suffering cause he lost his Magick? It's not right, but it was a relief to see him go. He was so miserable!" She looked down, somewhat ashamed, and traced a finger on the tabletop. "No one really wants to think about something like that happening."

That didn't explain Trent's attitude, though. Not good enough. Jason sighed.

Bailey looked up. "You don't have to agree. I just don't think anyone wants to think about it. Maybe you're just a little braver than we are."

"Maybe." He didn't like the sound of it, knew it wasn't true.

"Give it a day or two. It's tough thinking about all this, all at once, you know? It's a big kettle of fish to catch."

He nodded. Bailey flashed him one of her big grins before getting up to leave. The little tufted tail hanging from her shirt pocket gave a wiggle like a good-bye wave. Jonnard was deep in conversation with Danno when he left as well. It was as though Henry had never existed.

The day dragged, in dusty shimmering heat waves off the campgrounds. Trent abandoned the craft project he and Jason had been working on, a pair of neat boxes with marquetry designs on the lids, leaving Jason to piece the inlay together. Instead, Trent started work on a silk flag design of some kind, sketching onto the fabric, and then brushing paint onto it quickly. Jason caught a brief glimpse of what looked to be a spread-eagled raven carrying a lightning bolt in its claws before Trent hid it away.

He stayed behind in Herb Class, volunteering to weed Fire-Ann's bountiful herb and vegetable garden while the others sprinted off to swimming. Trent stood on one foot and the other.

"I think . . ." Trent said slowly, "I'll go to the computer lab."

"Fine."

"There's work I can do there. The ley line map is almost finished. Some files should be backed up."

"We could get this done early and then go to the lab."

Trent scratched his chin. "I'd rather go alone, you know?"

"No. No, I don't know." Jason pulled out a weed and threw it across the garden. "What did I do?"

"Nothing."

"You won't even hardly talk to me anymore."

"I've got stuff on my mind."

"I can listen. Sometimes it helps to have someone listen."

Trent did not look at him. "Not this kind of stuff. Okay?"

"I can help."

His friend said harshly, "No, you can't, Jason. Just keep your nose out of this, all right? If I wanted your help, I'd ask for it!"

"I just wanted you to know I care."

"Jason, you can't solve everything, okay? There are lots of things you just can't help, and sometimes trying just gets in the way of everything."

"But—"

"No," said Trent firmly. "I don't want to hear it!" He stalked out of the garden, shoulders stiff.

Jason stabbed and dug at the weeds heatedly for long minutes. Bits of dandelion and errant grass and scrub brush came up in chunks. Dirt packed the nails of his hands and colored his knuckles as he used the hand tools to dig and turn the earth. By the time he finished, the garden had never been so well weeded. The earth looked wet and crumbly and rich, and his stepmom would have been proud of it . . . for the gardening. His hands, well, she would have handed him a scrub brush and told him to clean up!

He dusted himself off, swatting at the clods of dirt. The sun had begun to slant low in the sky, and dark purple shadows angled through the camp. Clouds rolled in, pushed by the wind, and the sky became dark. He'd missed Sousa's hike, but his legs nagged at him. He wanted to get out and run a bit, angry energy still boiling in him and aching for a workout. He put FireAnn's gardening tools in the old wooden bucket she kept for them, and left the fenced-in garden.

He stretched first, calf muscles loosening slowly after the hours squatting over weeds. Then he stretched his arms and torso before heading toward the hiking trails.

At one time, this camp had had horses, and the trails had been cut by hours of hooves moving over them as campers rode. Now, the dirt was pounded by sneakers and hiking boots. A quick jog would feel good, he thought, as he broke into a slow run.

He ran until the clouds mounding up over the mountain peaks looked black and angry as though they had inhaled his cast-off energy. He ran until he had to stop, bent over, and breathe deeply. He ran until he knew that his ankle was finally, completely healed, and only as slightly sore as the rest of his body from the exercise. But he couldn't quite outrun his thoughts.

Jason ran his hands through his hair, smelling the sweaty heat rolling off his body, then turned and looked back at the camp. Four more deep breaths, and he would head back. He looked skyward, wondering if it might rain before he got back.

He did a stretch again to keep his legs from tightening and launched into a slow trot. It seemed to be downhill going back, the sprawled-out vista of the camp and lake ahead of him, and he picked up speed easily. As the trail entered the main part of the camp and its dirt lanes, he could hear loud voices and the bleating cry of Stefan-bear.

Jason slowed, approaching the cabins through the evergreens. Stefan-bear sat on his rump, snuffling and bawling. A shredded shirt lay on his shoulders, and a pair of shoes had been kicked off to the side. It seemed that the bear side of Stefan had made a surprise visit. Gavan and Tomaz were arguing with Rich nose-to-nose, and a dozen or so campers stood around watching. What had happened, anyway?

Trent joggled his elbow as he took it all in. "Way to go, friend," he said. "Way to not be there when you're needed."

"What are you talking about?"

"That." Trent pointed. "But it doesn't matter now, does it?"

"I didn't do anything!"

"I guess that's the point, isn't it. You were all over me earlier with offers to help, but when you were needed, you were nowhere."

"What happened?"

"Someone spilled the beans on Stefan, looks like. And we're getting the blame. You disappeared conveniently." Trent wheeled around and walked away, leaving Jason sputtering for words. The evening lights came on with a sparkling golden blur, dazzling his eyes for a moment. When he stopped blinking, Gavan had Stefan-bear by the ear and Tomaz had Rich by the arm, leading both back to their cabin.

There was nothing for it now but to shower for dinner. The swimmers had finished showering, and it was foggy and steamy and empty when he went in. He scrubbed for a long time, working on his hands and looking at his scar. Would it ever fade away to nothingness? Maybe he could have it lasered off, like a tattoo or something. When he came out with clean skin, clean hair, and clean clothes, Ravenwyng seemed eerily quiet except for the noise of the mess hall, which blazed with laughter, clatters, clinks, an occasional cheer, and lots of chatter. Not really hungry, he headed for it anyway.

From the shadow, someone called his name.

He stopped in his tracks. Had he even heard anything? The skin on the back of his hand crawled. He stepped forward, aware of the trees and shadows and cloud darkened sky as deep as night.

"Jason."

He took a shaky breath. Man or woman, he could not quite tell. But not beast. Of that he was certain. He stood still. "Wh–what?" The wind shivered through his damp hair, chilling him. He rubbed his scar as if he could ease the sudden lancing of pain through his hand. Would it never heal? Could it heal?

"Help you need, help I would."

"Me? Why?" Jason listened, but he could hear nothing behind him. No steps or breathing. The voice was older, but he couldn't quite recognize it. He shifted as if to turn around.

"No, no. Better in the shadows to stay." The air smelled of crushed pine needles. "You worry about those sent away. It is good you do. There is much they don't tell you. Much that can go wrong."

"You know about Henry?"

"I know many things. Many answers. Ask yourself how, if the mana is everywhere, Henry could lose his powers? The others? Perhaps they have not told you everything, the way it is. Perhaps they are not telling themselves the truth."

Jason took a breath. He *had* wondered. "Who are you?"

"A friend. A helper. Someone who needs aid. We can help each other, perhaps."

"How?"

"From time to time, I might need you to answer a question. And I, of course, would answer any of yours. Lend you my knowledge, my training." Shadows billowed, dark and quiet, around Jason.

He might be a kid, but he knew nothing was as simple as that, as his left hand throbbed with urgent pain. He thought of the wolfjackal's low declaration, "You are mine." The shadows didn't hold that creature . . . but . . . something wasn't right. "What do you want from me?"

"A simple understanding. I can help you . . ." The voice trailed off.

A habit now, Jason put his hand into his shorts pocket and cupped the crystal. A wrongness shoved at him, from the outside, from the gloom enveloping him. "No," he answered.

"No? A generous offer I make. And you say no?"

"Why should I trust you? You're hidden."

The person behind him took a hissing breath. *"You're mine,"* it said. "And I will have what I want, one way or the other. Trust me, you will live to regret this."

A force like a shove hit him in the small of the back, sending him to his knees. And then his hand abruptly stopped its pinching hurt, and the trees rattled as if a furious wind raced through them, and he lost his appetite.

When he slipped into the mess hall, dinner was nearly over, but FireAnn brought the entrée tray back out and scooped up some lasagne for him personally. He picked at it, not saying much.

All he knew for certain was that his scar drew trouble. Evil. And he was a danger to just about anyone as long as he wore it. He sat miserably through dinner, and the song circle, and the bonfire, knowing that. Trent had not said another word to him, and perhaps that was even wise. He finally headed back to his cabin before it was over.

Duel

J ASON opened the cabin door, wondering what he'd done to
lose Trent's friendship. He didn't know where the old Trent
had gone, so he hadn't the slightest idea how to find him. He
only knew that he was missing. The old Trent he could have
talked to. Could have found some way to shake off what seemed
to be happening. Was it his fault? He didn't know. And there
was no way to get Trent to listen!

He had no need to even turn on a light. After all these
weeks, he knew the cabin by heart, and the mess he'd left behind and the mess Trent was likely to leave behind. He took off
his shoes and dropped them in his corner before heading to bed.
He'd peel down to his underwear, as he always did, just before
crawling inside the covers.

A feeling swept over him. The hairs at the back of his neck
prickled and his crescent scar grew chill. Had the whisperer followed him? He turned around slowly, thinking that he was not
alone in the cabin. Too far from the light switch, he pulled his
crystal out and focused the lantern light and held it up to see. A
tall, indistinct silhouette shape froze across the room. It became
clearer as his crystal gained strength.

His crystal flared with a white-blue light, picking Jonnard out of the shadows of the cabin. The tall boy made a face, a slight curve to his mouth, a bitter smile.

"What are you doing here?" Jason held his hand higher.

Jonnard held something in his hands, and he turned away slightly, letting it fall back to the tabletop. Trent's duffel of his prized possessions clattered to the surface.

"That's not yours."

"None of this," Jon replied smoothly, "is mine." He let papers cascade through his hands carelessly, as though not caring at all now that he had been found out.

"What are you doing?" Jason repeated. His voice caught slightly in his throat. He had no doubt that if Jon wanted to run over him to get out of the cabin, the bigger, older boy would. He wanted to know what to think, how to understand why Jon was in his place, looking through his and Trent's things.

"Getting caught, it seems. After all these weeks, I must have gotten careless. I was beginning to think there was no reason to be cautious. Certainly Eleanora's wards were nothing to fear."

"You're the thief."

"Oh, no. Bailey's pack rat is the only thief. I am merely a . . ." Jon paused, then smiled slightly. "A spy."

"Spy? What for?"

"Secrets, of course. Many, many secrets. Everyone has them. Don't you ever wonder?"

Jason watched him. "Sometimes." The uneasy feeling at the back of his neck shivered down his spine.

"I wonder all the time. Secrets can be so useful." Jonnard looked at him, his face even paler by the crystal lantern light. "Henry's secret was that he wasn't nearly as good at the computer as he said. He fumbled at that as he fumbled at most of his Magick. Talented, but undisciplined and untrained. Trent did most of the hard work for him, was always there with help and tips. Trent's secret . . ." Jon looked down at the table where the things he'd been looking through were spread around. "I'm not quite sure yet. His dad's a single parent who writes often. They seem to have a good bond, if a frugal life." He looked up.

"What about you, Jason? Have you secrets I haven't been able to find out? Oh, I don't mean your strange family with its stepmother and stepfather, and the fact you get very little mail other than cheerful postcards from them. Off traveling, are they? Freed of your burden for the summer? No . . . I mean the real secrets. The ones you have pinned away in darkness."

He felt something shrink inside him, knowing that the other had been through his letters, his notes, then told himself that Jonnard was just trying to psych him out. "Like you said, everyone has secrets."

"And do you keep them?"

"I won't keep this one. I don't know what you're doing, Jon, but it's creepy. And I think Gavan needs to be told."

"Oh, he'll learn soon enough." Jon tilted his head as though listening. "Storm's coming, can you feel it?"

"The mana storm?"

Jonnard arched an eyebrow. "No other storm would catch my attention." He lifted a hand. "Wild mana. There for the taking, bringing with it high winds and rain, lightning and thunder, as violent as it can be. Some storms are mild, some very powerful. I intend to drink deeply of the power, and it will be great. The storm grows every day. I don't think anyone in this camp can stand against it."

Jason listened. He heard nothing, and the heaviness settling over him could have come from anything that had happened in the past few days, but he wouldn't let Jon see it. He remarked instead on the other's lack of emotion. "Don't you even care?"

"No," answered Jonnard, slipping his hand into his pocket. "Not really. I won't be here." He brought out his crystal. "Shall we see just how good you are?" He held his crystal high and dark amber light blazed out like a sword, piercing the white cloud of illumination from the stone Jason held. It angled through; touching him, slicing like a knife with a pain that made him let out a high keening sound.

Jason stumbled back as it hit him. One breath, two, and then he realized he was under attack, as his own stone faltered, the light thinning and breaking up. It spun away, scattering about the cabin like a thousand tiny stars before winking out, one by one. He took his eyes off Jon and Focused on his crystal, pouring his thought into it. No time or breath to ask why. The life of his crystal depended on what he did, as Jonnard continued to attack.

The light of each crystal sharpened, Jason's flaring out until he was shielded by it. The amber sword cut at it, bounced off with a humming sizzle. Jon frowned. He took a step across the room, raising his crystal in his hand. As he moved, the crystal rang with a pure, clear note, and its light darkened. It thinned, widened, and began to descend on Jason. Wide and winged, like a great dark cloak, it hovered overhead. Then, slowly, both boys breathing hard, it began to envelop him.

Part of him wanted to scream at Jon. He stuffed that part away so that he could concentrate, or he would lose his crystal . . . and who knew what else. He furrowed his brow and thought as hard as he could into his precious stone. The bond between them warmed steadily, yet he could feel the cloak start to wrap its icy wings around him. It sucked at the light, absorbing it. Something in him began to realize that Jonnard knew exactly what he was doing, and had done it before.

Every muscle in him tightened. Where was Trent? Should he shout for anyone else? And even if he did, would they get here in time before Jonnard did . . . what?

Jason shuddered. He drew on everything he had inside him to keep his crystal light without firing up or going empty. The stone grew warm in his palm, faceted planes shimmering. Yet still Jonnard's dark cloak fell over him and began to wrap him tightly, its coldness sinking into his very bones. Jason reacted instinctively.

He dropped and rolled. As he did, he clenched his hand around his stone, cutting off all light, and the cabin went dark. The icy shroud disappeared. Jason rolled again, into the far corner, and lay in the shadows, clutching his crystal under him. He wasn't quite sure what had happened or had worked, but the attack stopped.

A long moment ticked by. Then Jonnard said carefully,

"Jason?" A board creaked as he took a step. "That was really very clever. Yes, I need to see you to target you. At least . . . now I do. When I get stronger, we shall see."

Jason held his breath. His crystal felt hot against his chest, and his marked hand twitched as if to toss it aside. He clenched his teeth, fighting himself, to stay down and quiet and unseen.

"A coward's way out. But clever, yes, I'll remember that. Is that your secret, Jason? You're a coward?"

Another board creaked, closer. He could almost feel the wood vibrating in his ear. Jason tried to decide what to do next. He was trapped, and they both knew it. The only thing he didn't know was what Jonnard intended to do with him.

He would have to try to make it to the door.

The screen door banged, loudly. Jason flinched and he could hear Jonnard jump, startled.

"All right, you two. It's payback time. It's time to get even for you narcing on Stefan." Rich's thin, unpleasant voice snaked through the air. Behind him on the porch, something heavy shuffled and lumbered up and let out a bleating whine. The smell of bear filled the cabin.

Jonnard let out a curse. Moonlight streamed through the opening door, outlining his tall body. He raised his crystal and then, in a blink, disappeared.

Jason stood slowly. The cabin door flung open and Rich turned on the light. "What are you two, mushrooms?" He stood in the threshold, hands on his hips, mouth curled unpleasantly. At his back, the bear that was also Stefan stood up and filled the entire doorway.

"You won't believe this but, number one, am I glad to see you! Number two, we didn't tell anyone about Stefan, and number three, I have to see Gavan." He uncovered his crystal and white-hot light shot out. Like a small star, it went nova in the cabin.

With a surprised yell, Rich and Stefan scrambled for their lives, rolling off the cabin porch in their haste. Jason watched the flare with eyes that immediately began watering. He shoved his crystal in his pocket, bolted out the doorway, did a leapfrog over Stefan-bear who was whining on all fours at the bottom of the porch steps. He hit the ground running and did not stop till he skidded into the bright lights of the Gathering Hall, the other two pounding on his heels and they all ran full tilt into Tomaz Crowfeather as he came around the corner.

Storm Warning

ALL three of them barreled into Tomaz. The Magicker rocked back on his heels with an *ooof* collaring Rich with one hand and Stefan with the other. No longer a bear, but a stocky boy again, Stefan rolled his head around and let out a low bearish grunt as though he might turn, and Tomaz said warningly, "None of that, now."

"Jon—in my cabin—spying," Jason blurted out.

"Now? It's late. Everyone's at the bonfire, and it's nearly Lights Out." Tomaz directed that last in a stern voice at the two he held in his grasp.

He had caught the sleeve of Jason's T-shirt, but he wriggled around and got loose, standing up as Tomaz added, "What's the story with you three?"

"He's a troublemaker," said Rich sulkily. Stefan only grunted unhappily.

"I told you—we didn't tell on Stefan." Jason cast his gaze on Tomaz. "I've got to see Rainwater. He's got to know what happened with Jonnard. Please."

Tomaz gave Rich and Stefan a little shake. "You boys will have to sort this out later. But it wasn't Jason who gave you away. Do you think I could track you all over camp for a week and not know?"

"Well." Stefan shuffled about. "Guess not."

"All right, then. Back to the cabin. I'll see you in the morning." He leveled a look into Stefan's face, and the other grunted and backed up, almost bearlike, before turning around and following Rich down the camp lane as Tomaz released him.

"Now . . . what's this about Jon?"

"I caught him in the cabin. He was going through everything. He said he was spying, had been, all along. And then he came at me with his crystal."

"Came at you? He attacked you?"

Jason nodded, still a little breathless.

"You find Rainwater, I'll check camp for Jonnard."

He bolted into the Gathering Hall corridor, uncaring of quiet or wards or anything else. The alarms went off with a howling screech as he skidded into Rainwater's office, startling Gavan. Amid bells and whistles, he skidded across the floor and thudded into the desk, panting, "Jonnard is spying . . . on everyone! I caught him, and he attacked me with the crystal, and he almost killed mine like he killed Henry's, and he said it was too late!"

Gavan narrowed his blue eyes and stilled the alarms with a wave of his hand. The office fell suddenly silent. "Explain yourself, and do it slower this time." He pointed at an empty chair.

Jason fell into it, and told the story again, this time from the beginning to the spy's vanishing end. As he told it, he realized what he had blurted out about Henry's crystal. Jon had been with Henry. He had no doubt and no proof that somehow what had happened to Henry had been something Jon had done . . . and Henry had not even been aware of it. Henry hadn't lost his power on his own . . . Jon had done it to him. How could they all have been so blind?

"Jonnard?" repeated Gavan again, tapping his cane on the floor. Disbelief filled his face. "Damn me for not catching it."

Tomaz came back in the doorway, a bit out of breath. He

tugged on his vest as if to compose himself. "He's gone, not a trace."

"But how—" Jason looked from one Magicker to the other. "How could he do that?"

"His crystal." Tomaz stared at Gavan.

"But . . . but . . . he walked inside it, like Bailey?"

"No, Jason, he knows how to use it to move." Gavan sat down again, heavily. "I'm a fool, Tomaz. He has to be one of the Dark Hand."

"No more a fool than I."

"But so young . . ."

"He's obviously been recruited, taught. Did we not recruit him ourselves? Dr. Patel brought him in. No doubt they placed him where she would run across him. They knew enough of us to infiltrate and spy effectively. I didn't catch him either, and who knows . . . there might be more here."

Gavan buried his face in his hands for a moment, then looked up. "We haven't long."

Infiltrated . . . Jason thought of the dark voice in his ear, the smooth coaxing promises. They'd reached for him, too! Caught by the shock of it, he stood speechless. He stared at the back of his hand. Had he any choice?

"All right, then." Gavan took a deep breath. "First things first. The Dark Hand knows we're here, can attack from inside as well as outside, whatever element of surprise we hoped to have is gone." He stood again, as if gathering his energy. "We need to find the Gate."

Tomaz gave a slight shake of his head. "Send them home."

The two stared into each other's faces. Gavan said slowly, "I refuse to give up like that."

"FireAnn has enough Draft for all."

Jason's eyes widened. Give them all the Draft of Forgetfulness and ship them home?

"Crowfeather, I can't bundle up thirty-some campers and send them home this early. The others who have gone were a big enough risk. This camp . . . this *school* has to stand. It has to, if we're to have any future. There is Haven beyond the Gate."

Tomaz hooked his thumbs in his concho belt.

"What kind of haven?" Jason asked, almost certain neither would answer him. He could feel the tension in the air. He understood then, that the Magickers were still fighting for survival, still unsure of what path to take. Older than him by far and yet, in some ways, no more the wiser.

"The Borderlands," said Tomaz shortly. "Think of them as pockets of free mana. They are next to us, but are not us. As the world changed, many things that were Magick fled there. For most, however, it was too late, and they died anyway, or so my people tell it. Coyote was once thought to be a Gatekeeper, and sometimes he is, but mostly he is a Trickster. He lives off the delusions of others."

"This is not a delusion."

"No, of course not." Tomaz answered Gavan. He set his jaw stubbornly.

Jason scratched his temple. Something nagged at him to be remembered. What would they have to do to be safe? Was Gavan going to try to hide all of them? What was it Bailey had said . . . hide in plain sight? He shifted his weight, tangled in his undone shoestring, and nearly fell over. Stooping over, he retied his shoe. The one lace, still frayed badly where the lake dweller had tugged and pulled at him, looked as if it could give at any time. Memory rushed in.

He blinked as the blood rushed to his head. "Excuse me . . . tell me about the Gates."

"The Borderland Gates? There is a long and dark history to them, Jason. I had planned to cover that in next summer's class, if not a bit sooner. The Iron Gate is the closest to us right now, and the easiest to traverse, named for the great Iron Mountain and its valley just beyond. The others . . . the Fire Gate and so on . . . well, some are even thought to be sheer mythology, and of course, it doesn't help that strange and odd things happen near the Gates, because of the mana that seeps through. Not to mention an occasional denizen the likes of which haven't been seen in modern man's world."

Jason waved his hands. "No, no. I mean the camp's gates,

front and back. Why can't we just shut the camp's gates against the wolfjackals and everything?"

"Most of the camp is not fenced, just staked out to show the boundaries," Tomaz began, "And with the mana sweeping in for them to use as they will, ordinary gates won't stop them—" Gavan stopped him sharply

"Wait a moment." Gavan stared at Jason. "Did you say, front and *back* gates?"

"Well, yeah. The ones under the sign at the front road coming in, and the old ones by the back of the lake."

"Ravenwyng has no back gate." Gavan reached out for Jason. "What did you see? Tell me."

"When Trent and I took the canoe way out that time we got grounded, we had a . . . a problem . . . I went overboard. We had to beach the canoe for me to climb back in. Anyway, I found the back gate there, just off the shore. There's a rough lane crossed by this huge, swinging gate. It's already open, though."

"That makes no never mind," said Tomaz. "What you saw may not be what actually *is*."

Gavan repeated firmly, "There is no back gate." He stared at Jason. "Could you find it again? Have you marked it in your mind?"

"I couldn't forget it."

"All right then. I'll get Eleanora, and we'll all take a look at it. Tomaz, get Lucas, Sousa, Hightower. Tell them about Jonnard and see if . . . well, see what you can do? He's probably covered his tracks, but you might be able to back trace him. Secure the camp against the storm if you can."

Tomaz nodded.

Eleanora was in the music room, practicing, stroking her fingers over her dulcimer and coaxing out beautiful strains of music. Gavan and Jason stood quietly in the doorway till she looked up, sighting them. She put her palm across the strings of the dulcimer to still it. She smiled faintly. "We each have our own way of dealing with things. I like my music."

"And it is no wonder, that." Gavan tried a smile. "I need a word with you, though I hate to interrupt."

A frown replaced the smile. "Sounds serious."

Gavan strode in, drawing Jason with him. In quick, terse words, he told her of Jonnard's betrayal and attack on Jason. Her face paled and her hands shook slightly as she slipped the instrument into its tapestry case. She reached for Jason's hands.

"Are you all right?"

He nodded.

"But that's not all," Gavan added, with a dramatic flourish of his cane. "He saw a Gate."

"Really?" Eleanora considered Jason. "Well, it's about time."

"About time?" Gavan's brows shot up, and he stared at Eleanora.

"Well, I should think it is, don't you?" She stood up and put her instrument away on a deep shelf. She looked over her shoulder at Gavan. "You didn't know?"

"Blast me for being blind," Gavan grumbled. "I was almost certain it was Bailey. Brash. Always rushing ahead to explore . . ."

Eleanora smiled faintly, and shook her head. "Bailey's power is with animal lore, that is plain."

"Know what?" Jason asked.

Gavan coughed. "Of course, there was a possibility . . . but with forty-nine of them to look over—"

Eleanora turned around with her hands on her hips. "The signs were all there. He was always about and around at night, restless, couldn't sleep. Looking for something, never quite sure what. It took me a while, too. He is very circumspect."

"Well." Gavan cleared his throat a bit. "I've been busy. There's no doubt we all recognized he is Talented. . . ."

Tomaz agreed. "I would have missed it, too, with the Council on my back. In fact, I did miss it . . . till now. Now it's as obvious as the nose on your face."

"Know what?" demanded Jason.

"That you are a Keeper of the Ways. In short, a Gatekeeper. I would bet my dulcimer on it." Eleanora tossed her head. "And I thought Gavan was keeping his eyes on you, because he knew that, too. I should have realized other things had you distracted,

Gavan." She took out her crystal and began polishing it in the deep folds of her brocade skirt.

The Magicker muttered something darkly. He leaned on his cane. "I don't intend to waste more of it. The Gate is at the far end of the lake."

"You've seen it?" Eleanora smiled sweetly at Jason.

He nodded.

"It's marked well in your mind?"

He nodded again.

"Then we won't be canoeing there." Eleanora took up Jason's hand again, and said briskly, "Hold onto him, Gavan." She raised her crystal in her free hand. "Picture it in your mind. Absolutely, firmly, no wavering. Focus on it!"

"What are we doing?"

"We have been practicing moving objects with the crystals. Now we are going to move ourselves," said Gavan flatly. He took up Jason's other hand. "Do as she tells you."

Eleanora held out her crystal to Jason. "Look in. This is a door, and it is opening. When you see, on the other side, that picture in your mind . . . just as sharp, just as clear . . . I want you to step through that door and go there. Don't worry about us, we'll follow."

"But . . . but it's your crystal."

"Yours isn't quite trained yet. Trust me, Jason." Eleanora leaned closer. "Think on it. Quickly now. Make it true and clear."

He looked into the pale rose quartz, thinking of the rugged shoreline, the split boulder just off the lake with the pine growing stubbornly out of it. He tried to think of the gate, too, but it would not stay in his mind. But the beach where he'd finally scrambled to safety, that he had. The gate would only be a few strides beyond that. The plane of her quartz began to open, like a door swinging inward, and beyond it, the vision of his thoughts lay. With a squeeze of their hands he stepped into the gemwork.

There was a moment of nothingness. It was dark and cold, and his whole body stopped as though he had sneezed violently.

Then he stepped onto firm ground, stumbled, and Gavan and Eleanora tumbled out of nowhere next to him. All three of them went sprawling.

"I shall have to teach him about landings," Gavan said dryly. He bounded to his feet, and helped Eleanora up.

Eleanora winked at Jason. "Just remember it's like parachuting," she said. "That first step is a long one!"

"You've parachuted?" Gavan considered Eleanora with an odd expression on his face. "Wonders of the modern age."

She did not answer but adjusted her skirt and blouse and bent to tighten the laces on her high-button shoes. When she straightened, she rose in the air her customary elevation of three or four inches as though nothing could be amiss.

Jason stood up. They faced the lake, with its deep waters like a mirror, reflecting the rain clouds mounding up over the hills, silver and black in the moonlight. He turned round. He could see the metal glint through the underbrush. "There," he said, and pointed.

They hurried to keep up as he went to it, his face all knotted in a frown because he *hadn't* been able to focus on it clearly and that worried him. Even as he approached it now, it seemed to have moved a bit from where he'd seen it originally . . . yet how could it? Rusting metal gateposts buried in the dirt, and fencing fading off into the heavy underbrush, and a huge swinging gate fastened back among the evergreens couldn't move on their own.

"Impressive." Gavan tapped his cane on the ground.

"It's rusting." In fact, the more Jason looked at it, the less sturdy it appeared.

The Magicker shook his head. "No, lad, not that. You landed us practically on top of it."

Eleanora put her hand on Jason's shoulder. "Gates, you see, shift in time and place. That's why we can't hope to find them without help or Talent." Her ruffled blouse moved restlessly in the strong, cooling wind off the lake.

"It *did* move, then."

"No doubt."

Gavan reached out with his cane, probing. "And it is on Ravenwyng property, or within a jump of it." He smiled thinly. "I think even Tomaz would agree we ought to be able to get the Border to take the camp in." He tucked his cane under his elbow. "All right, everyone through for a quick look-see, and I'll leave word what we're trying to do with the camp, and then we go batten the hatches."

The moon was engulfed by clouds. A dark shadow fell across them, as the wind howled up, cold and harsh. Eleanora turned as a wailing howl broke the air, followed by another and another.

"Too late!" she cried.

Harsh clouds hid the sky and the moon's light boiled in shades of black and gray. Lightning split the clouds as the wolfjackal pack touched down in triumph. Ivory fangs flashed, and pewter claws raked the ground. Dull thunder rolled behind them. The very air seemed to shiver and dance as they materialized out of the nowhere to the now.

Eleanora drew her crystal, and Gavan brought his cane up to face the pack. "Stay behind us, Jason."

He drew his own stone and cupped it. Uneasily, he waited for its welcoming glow, worried that the battle with Jon had harmed it. The unpolished edges jabbed him as he held it tightly. The wolfjackals paced and stirred around behind their leader, just as the clouds in the sky seemed to rise and fall and boil behind one immense thunderhead as it grew over the mountains. The beasts snarled and snapped at the darkening air, their eyes flashing with an eerie green glow.

"Now we both know where the Gate is," Gavan said grimly.

"They would have found it anyway."

"Yes . . . eventually. No time to set up wards."

Eleanora did not look at Gavan but kept her gaze leveled on the wolfjackals as they stopped, then circled and fanned out into an attacking stance. Ivory fangs gleamed in the scant moonlight left. He counted a pack of seven, larger than before, and the wolfjackal in front loomed the size of a small pony. "They're bigger," he stammered, surprised.

"Feeding on the mana storm." Gavan braced himself. He focused his wolfhead cane so that the immense crystal held in the wolf's jaws aimed less than a few feet away. "That's far enough," he called out.

The wolfjackal pack slowed to a stop, and the others began to pace back and forth behind the leader, who seemed momentarily content.

"A Gate," growled the wolfjackal leader. "We but seek to pass. We have that right."

"Not here and not now."

"Our rights!" The pack leader threw his head up, letting out a baleful howl.

"You have none."

"The Gate is as much ours as yours." The packleader snarled and snapped at thin air.

"I deny it to you. Later, perhaps, when I've talked with the Hand."

The wolfjackal grinned, his tongue lolling out of his sharp jaws. "Sooner!" he promised, his thick tail low and moving from side to side, but it was not a canine wag. Every move the dun-and-silver beast made was one of menace. Jason found he was holding his breath, and tried to relax enough to get some air.

A bolt of pale green light shot from the cane Gavan gripped tightly in his hand. It struck the ground in front of the pack, sending up a puff of scorched dirt. The wolfjackal jumped back with a startled yelp. He reared back against his followers, then shook himself indignantly. His ruff bristled up, and he lowered his head as he paced forward. "You shall pay for that."

"Here they come," Gavan warned needlessly, and the three of them braced themselves.

With a snap and snarl, the pack launched itself. Jason froze. His marked hand twitched so hard, he could barely grip his crystal. His breath caught in his chest as he tried to bring up a shield of light from his stone, but all he could manage was a pale, quivering glow.

Gavan abandoned the crystal embedded in his cane, and

drew forth one hanging from a thick-linked gold chain about his neck, drawing it out of his collar. Instead, he used the cane like a wooden sword, parrying, thrusting, and sweeping. The wolfjackals yelped as he rapped sharply at their heads and limbs. Froth flew from their snapping jaws as they bit at the cane and caught only air.

The pack leader crouched and lunged at Gavan. Rainwater parried with the cane, catching his jaws, but unable to stop the body from ramming him. Both fell and tumbled. The wolfjackal ended up on top, jaws spread wide as Gavan shoved the cane crosswise into them. The wood clattered against ivory fangs.

Eleanora let out a small sound, as three battered at her shield, and she retreated a step, coming up against Jason. "Run," she said. "We're outnumbered!"

"I can't leave you."

Gavan gave a loud grunt and yell and shoved the wolfjackal back onto his haunches as he scrambled up, panting. "I think retreat is advisable."

"Where?" Jason backed up, as the pack re-formed and began to slink close, their hot breath filling the air.

He pointed toward the open Gate. Jason turned to lead the way. Something hot and heavy hit him full tilt, sending him rolling through the gateposts. It snarled and snapped as he threw his hands up to protect his face, and the crystal flared weakly. He shoved the beast away and clambered to his knees, but the wolfjackal jumped again, jaws snapping. Jason fell back.

His head snapped against metal with a stinging, slashing jolt. He cried out as pain lashed through his scalp, red hot and pounding. Dazed as the beast drove at his chest, teeth gleaming, he rolled over and managed to stagger up. He clung to the gatepost, evergreen branches whipping around his body. Sickened to the pit of his stomach by the sudden pain, Jason fell against the Gate. Hot blood poured from his scalp, into his eyes and, over the metal framework. The Gate moved as he clung to it, swinging inward. Double vision wavered in front of him. Jason groaned as the Gate dragged him through the dirt, a vast great

Iron Gate of intricate scrollwork and heaviness that he clung to desperately, his hands and face slick with blood.

As he hung on it, stomach heaving with the pain shouting through his head, the Gate shut with a heavy clang, all of them on the outside.

Eleanora and Gavan swung around. "Oh, no!" she cried in dismay.

"We'll make a stand here," Gavan said grimly. He swung out and slashed the wolfjackal away from Jason's ankles. "Hang on to me, lad!" He reached out, and slipped an arm under Jason's shoulders.

"We can't hold out here, Gavan."

"I won't lead them back to camp. Not yet." Holding Jason on his feet, he parried, then slashed at a wolfjackal slinking close.

"I know where. Wolfjackals won't dare to follow."

"Oh . . . no . . . Eleanora . . ."

His words did not slow her. She linked elbows with Jason and cupped her crystal close, crying out a single word: "Auntie!"

Before the word faded, Jason felt his guts wrenched yet again and they were snatched into chill darkness, then dumped unceremoniously in a patch of clover in front of a small, thatched cottage.

Jason blinked.

Aunt Freyah came out, brandishing a broom in her hand. Then she stopped. "My, my. A visit is always welcome, I say. Can't look a gift horse in the mouth! Up with you before those foul beasts track you in!" With that, she swept them to their feet and into her home.

30

Always Eat Dessert First

S HOOING them inside to a sunny and cheerful parlor with huge overstuffed chairs covered in bright fabric with immense sunflowers on it, Freyah sat down and watched them sharply. "Unexpected, but always welcome," she said and beckoned for them to sit.

"A warning. This is a Haven only so long as no unpleasantness enters. Whether in Evil as those who chased you to my Border, or in your thoughts and hearts." Freyah folded her hands.

"Aunt Freyah, you know we'd never—" Eleanora looked appalled.

"I find it is always better if a guest knows what to expect."

Gavan plopped Jason down in a chair, before turning away a bit, whispering, "She is a true Magicker. She pulls all this out of herself. Enjoy it . . . as she grows older, she is losing the strength to do much else. We'll try not to upset her if we can." He turned his back completely and walked away a pace or two.

She watched Gavan sharply. "How much trouble are you in?"

"No one said anything about trouble."

Freyah raised her eyebrow. "I doubt you are here to ask me about firing the greenware in the kiln. All that wonderful artwork is finished, is it not? And with a pack on your heels, there is always trouble."

Eleanora bobbed up and down a moment as though having trouble holding her height. Jason watched her until he grew a little queasy, and his stomach complained. Gavan took out a handkerchief and pressed it to the side of his head, which throbbed horribly, although it no longer felt as if hot blood oozed through his hair. He wiped the blood off deftly before pocketing the handkerchief.

Freyah's sharp black-eyed gaze was on him instantly. "What's wrong?"

All he could think of was Gavan's warning not to upset her. "Well, I . . . I haven't eaten . . ." He faltered. He couldn't remember since when. Or where, for that matter. Well, he could remember where he was when he usually ate, but not where this was. They'd gone from stormy night to sunny day. *When* were they, and *where*? It was confusing to think, so he stopped. He caught sight of himself at a mirror's edge across the room and saw that his wound did not show, although he looked rather pale.

She rocked back in her chair, color flooding her already apple-bright cheeks. "Not eaten! Honestly, you two, what sort of heathens are you?" Without waiting for a response from either Gavan or Eleanora, she fished out a huge wicker picnic basket from behind her chair. Nearly the size of a clothes hamper, its woven sides glistened a pine yellow. "The stomach is directly responsible for the well-being of the rest of the body. Particularly at his age. Eat now, talk later."

She flipped open the hamper top, and wonderful aromas filled the air. His knees went weak. He could smell freshly baked turkey. Cherries. Chocolate fudge.

Gavan made an impatient movement with one hand, but Eleanora gave him a look that could have dropped a wolfjackal in its tracks.

Freyah put a napkin over his knee, snapped her fingers, and

a dining tray came scampering over on aluminum legs to stand by Jason, supports quivering.

Freyah looked at the serving tray. "George," she said firmly. "Do stop that."

The tray bobbed in a quick curtsy and froze into position as Jason stared in amazement. Freyah sighed as she reached into her picnic hamper. "He loves company," she said apologetically. "The more food I can heap on him, the prouder he is. Never dropped a crumb, he has! Just like his sainted father whom I finally retired into a picture frame." Freyah glanced across the room at a picture with an ornately braided metal frame, a fond expression crossing her face.

Gavan drummed his long fingers. Turned away from Freyah, he studied the other end of the room. Jason peeked but could not see what Gavan was eyeing.

Eleanora found a height she liked and stuck to it, the hem of her skirt shimmering about her ankles. She smoothed her outfit down over her knees as if she'd meant to come to tea and not retreat from a full-blown attack. "Aunt Freyah. Would it be a bother if we ate as well? I know I haven't seen a meal in quite a while, and I'm almost certain Gavan here—"

"Can do very well for himself, thank you!" Gavan interjected.

". . . is famished as well," finished up Eleanora smoothly. She smiled brightly at Freyah.

"Well." Freyah's chin dimpled as she looked into the basket. "Well, well. I hadn't really planned for more than the lad here. . . ."

"You planned for him?" Gavan found something interesting on Aunt Freyah's face to stare at.

"I, well. Hrmmmm." The rounded woman stirred uncomfortably on her plush armchair. "That is to say." But she didn't say it. Instead, "I sensed a Gatekeeper had begun to test his skills."

Eleanora shot Gavan a look as she leaned forward and hugged Freyah. "Now, Auntie. I've seen you pull all sorts of wonders out of that basket before. You could easily feed four, no doubt. We won't impose, but if you've anything extra at all, I know we could use a bite or two. Before we talk about things necessary and a bit odd."

Jason found himself looking down at a small tag affixed to the side of the reed hamper basket where it nudged his knee. It read "Feeds 5–6." He blinked. The serving tray in front of him gave itself an impatient shrug.

Freyah took a deep breath. "Well, then. Let's see what I can muster up! Eat dessert first, I always say! The rest of the meal may be uncertain at best." And with that, she dug her dimpled hands into the picnic basket's interior and began to pull out china dishes covered with food. An ivory china plate with crimped edges came out, filled with fresh baked cherry tarts. Then an etched crystal dish piled with chocolate fudge cupcakes, their icing creamy and swirled into little peaks. Both Jason and George fairly shook with delight as she set them down on George's tray.

"Help yourself. Milk over here." She pointed, and the little sideboard behind them bloomed with four chilled glasses of frothy milk.

Eleanora sighed wistfully, her hands empty, as she settled into a chair. She stared wistfully at the pastries. "Aunt Freyah."

Jason grabbed a cupcake and devoured it in two gulps. Never had anything more wonderfully chocolate melted on his tongue. He washed it down with half a glass of milk before sitting back happily, eyeing the plates. Another cupcake or a tart? The throbbing in his head had nearly disappeared.

"Both," Aunt Freyah said to him, smiling as if she could read his thoughts.

"Good idea." Gavan filled his own hands with both, his golden-brown hair falling over his brilliant blue eyes, heedless of the mournful look Eleanora gave him.

Eleanora sighed. "Aunt Freyah."

"Now, eat your fill, but don't eat too many. Vegetables and main course to come, you know!" Singing happily to herself, a wordless and nearly tuneless tune, Freyah sat back with a tart in her fingers and nibbled delicately at the edges.

"Aunt Freyah," said Eleanora yet again.

Freyah blinked. "What, child? What, and what again? Spit it out!" She wrinkled her nose. "Oh, you can't. You haven't eaten a thing. But I thought you said you were hungry."

"Vegetables and main course to follow . . . which would be what?" Eleanora asked primly.

"Oh." Her aunt leaned forward to rummage around in the picnic basket, saying, "You would ask before he's quite ready, and you know it makes him ticklish." A faint giggle from the depths echoed her statement before she looked up in triumph. "Aha. Carrot and raisin salad and turkey sandwiches on squaw bread. Not ready yet, though."

Jason managed to gobble his cherry tart a little slower than his cupcake. The cherry was both tart and sweet, juicy in its filling and the crust buttery light. He chewed, his whole mouth delighted by the flavor, and his stomach growing happier by the swallow. He looked up to see Gavan licking the top frosting off his cupcake, before popping the cake part in, a pleased grin on his face.

Eleanora crossed her arms. "Well, really." She looked pointedly away from all three of them as they ate.

"What's wrong?" Jason peered at Eleanora.

Gavan speared another cherry tart with his long fingers. He ate half before saying to Jason. "You know. Diet. Girlish figure, all that."

"I know?" Jason began to repeat, puzzled. Then, "Oh." He grew quiet. He looked at the back of Eleanora's head in sympathy.

Freyah snorted. "She wouldn't have to worry about her weight IF she ever walked with her feet on the ground instead of in the clouds. Got some decent exercise."

"I don't have to. I choose to. It's important I carry myself well, or else everyone else towers over me."

Taking her linen napkin off her lap, a shower of chocolate crumbs falling to the floor and then mysteriously disappearing, Freyah dabbed the corners of her mouth. "Of course, I made them nonfattening, but if she wants to be a martyr—"

"Oh!" Eleanora's head swung around like a shot. "Auntie! Bless you!" Eleanora dove onto the plates, her quick, neat little hands easily outsprinting Gavan for the last cherry tart and cupcake.

"Indeed? Bless me? Now, there's a thought!" Freyah sat back, patting her silver curls into place about her face, with an enormously pleased expression. A tinkle of china came from inside the basket, ringing like a bell, and she leaned forward to peer inside. "Second course!"

With that, she pulled out saucers heaping with carrot, raisin, and pineapple chunk salad, followed by a simply enormous platter of turkey sandwiches. Gleaming silverware shot out of the wicker picnic basket like a fountain. George leaned sharply right and left to catch all of it on his tray top, the utensils clattering noisily into place.

Freyah and Jason clapped. "Well done, George!"

The tray quivered with pride.

"Graceful and strong," Eleanora cooed and patted one of George's few open spots. The tray sidled a little closer to her in the gap between Jason and her chair, whereupon she took advantage of the shorter reach to snag a sandwich plate and balanced it on her knee.

Jason grinned as Gavan frowned, then took a slightly smaller sandwich, its multigrained bread and thick crust nearly overwhelmed by thick slices of turkey, lettuce, and a cranberry sauce filling. He managed it in three bites. Jason took his time with his, savoring every juicy and tasty bite of the turkey, slices of white and dark meat neatly layered, and coated with a tangy white mayo. Every mouthful tasted like the best, warmest memories he had ever had of Thanksgiving. When he finally sat back, it was with a very full and happy stomach.

Freyah gathered up all the empty plates and put them back in the wicker picnic basket which immediately began a crunching and crackling sound. She smiled fondly. "His favorite part," she said. "He does love to eat the china." The basket churned and bobbed as it consumed the remnants of their lunch. She closed the lid, patting it. A muffled burp ensued.

Jason smothered a laugh.

Eleanora dabbed her napkin at the corners of her mouth, her eyes sparkling as she smiled at Jason. Freyah, however, smoothed her face into seriousness. She pinned her sharp gaze on Gavan. "Now, then. Trouble. Explain it."

"We didn't say there was trouble . . ." Eleanora protested faintly.

"No, no," Gavan added. "Nothing about trouble, at all."

Freyah stared.

"That is to say," Gavan continued. "Not that each of us doesn't face adversity in some small way, every day." He brushed a lingering tart crumb off his cloak, avoiding her un-blinking dark eyes.

One eyebrow rose, punctuating the black stare which threatened to become a cold glare.

Gavan cleared his throat. "That is."

"Nothing important, Aunt Freyah, really," supplied Elea-nora. Gavan shot her a grateful look as Freyah now began to stare at Eleanora.

The room chilled. Jason shivered slightly, drawing his legs up to curl into his armchair. George darted to the side and came back with an afghan curled on his tray. Jason took it, and tucked it about him. "If no one wants to tell her, I will."

All three Magickers looked at him.

"Someone with spunk," Aunt Freyah remarked.

He shook his head. "No," he said slowly. "I think it is mine to tell because I was the one who did it." He put his hand to the side of his neck and rubbed it slowly, still feeling a sharp pain ebbing away. Eleanora's mouth curved sympathetically as she watched him. Gavan muttered something in a low voice, as he wrapped his cloak about himself, sinking into his chair, long legs jutting out. He did not, however, move to stop Jason from speaking.

"I found the Gate."

"Excellent. However that does not explain the three of you being dumped on my doorstep, does it?" Freyah looked to Gavan sharply, her silvery curls bobbing. "Pleasantries aside, I warned you. I told you there would be trouble if you pursued this course. You stubbornly did as you wished."

"There is a massive mana storm sweeping our way."

Her eyes snapped. "Again. Do you presume me to be an old fool or just old? Of course, I know a storm is headed our way."

"I intended to use it, if I could, to bring the camp inside the Gates. Barring that, to open up Iron Mountain Academy again, if I can free it."

Freyah sat back in her chair, and Eleanora stared at Gavan, openmouthed. Her hand went up to wipe away a crumb from lips parted in surprise.

"A bold move."

"We need our children, our future. We need to educate and protect them. How many of us died because we had no warning and no shelter when . . ." Gavan paused. "Well, the past is history. Let the lad continue."

"I found the Iron Gate. Accidentally. It's at the far end of the lake, and I thought it was just, you know, the back gate to camp."

She beamed at him. "Smart lad. And, while coincidence is rampant, I don't think that was any accident. You were meant to find it! Still . . . that is not the problem?"

"The Gate is closed."

"Oh, dear. My, my. That is a pretty kettle of fish."

Jason wondered for a moment if Aunt Freyah had ever talked at any length with Bailey, or vice versa. She took a napkin and pressed it exactly upon the scalp wound hidden in his sandy hair, and took the napkin away to examine it. Old and fresh blood stained the crisp white linen. She frowned at Jason. "Closed with blood?"

Gavan pursed his lips and looked nonchalantly at the ceiling. "Aye. Likely it was. The lad *is* wounded."

"And you let him sit there, in pain?"

"It doesn't hurt so awfully. It's the camp that's important," Jason said faintly.

Freyah stood up. She flipped the lip down on the picnic hamper and shoved it back behind her chair again. There was a faint crash inside as if someone had dropped something breakable.

"No help for it, then. If the Gate is closed, it's closed."

Eleanora folded her hands on her lap. "None? Are you sure?"

"I am certain, and none." She unclipped a brooch watch from her vest and looked at it. "My advice is to hurry home, and make whatever plans you can to ride it out. I'll notify the Council, but I think we'll all be nailing our windows shut." She refastened the watch. "It will be a rough one."

Gavan nodded. He extended one hand to Eleanora, and the other one to Jason. "My thanks, then, Aunt Freyah, for the refuge." He lifted his cane to focus on his wolfhead crystal, and Jason noticed the teeth marks and notches in the wood.

Freyah reached for both shoulders and drew him close in a big hug. She whispered in his ear, "Only you can undo what has been done," before letting him go. She kissed his temple lightly, and the pain and throbbing of his wound dropped away immediately. Jason blinked.

He had scarcely a moment to wonder when the door in the crystal opened and he fell through, and they landed at Lake Wannameecha Gathering Hall.

31

Wild Magick

J ASON managed to stay on his feet. Sandwiched between Gavan who smelled faintly of chocolate and vanilla, and Eleanora who smelled of roses, the three of them alit in the courtyard of Ravenwyng. The faint coppery smell of blood still clung to him, though the wound seemed to have closed. It was his hand that hurt now. Fretting, Jason rubbed the back of his left hand.

Tomaz stood, his arm outstretched, sending a raven into flight from his fist. He turned and looked, his arm still in the air, the raven an ebony blur. Jefferson was there, watching, his muscular arms crossed over his chest. And FireAnn and Sousa came running from the mess hall across the way, her face pale with alarm and fiery red hair wild about her face. His cornet rattled from its chain on his belt.

The storm began to pelt rain, hard and heavy, on all of them. The raven circled once overhead and disappeared into the swirling clouds, with a loud cry.

"It has started," Tomaz said heavily to Gavan.

"So I can see. We've a day or two, no more. The rain has begun moving in, and it will only worsen." Gavan appeared to make a decision. "Tomaz, you and Jefferson, come with me. We've been outrunning wolfjackals at Iron Gate."

Tomaz's face reflected his surprise. "You've found it? Good. We need the hope."

"Not unless we can get the Gate open. Eleanora . . ." Gavan took her by the elbow, steadying her. Winds buffeted at her and she bounced slightly in the air away from them, unsteadily, like a ship that had lost its rudder in a heavy sea. "Send the children home."

"All right. What will we tell the parents?"

"Tell them . . . tell them . . ." Gavan looked around the grounds. Evergreens had begun to creak and bend, their branches brushing the ground. The lake itself rippled in high, icy waves as the light wires overhead danced furiously in the wind. "Tell them the camp is old and the electric system went out in the rainstorm. It will take several weeks to make repairs and update the camp, and by then summer will be over."

She said softly, "If this storm hits us as hard as I think it's going to, we'll lose Ravenwyng."

"Then it won't be a lie, will it?"

"No. It won't." She leaned on FireAnn. "Let's make the camp announcement. I'll have to talk to them, make sure that . . . that they understand." The two women helped each other cross the courtyard, the screaming wind pulling and tearing at them. Eleanora gave up her levitation, dropping to the ground as if it could anchor her.

Gavan dropped his hand on Jason's shoulder. "Thank you, lad, for all you've done." He leaned over, looking into Jason's face. "You're a Magicker, lad. Never let that go. No matter what happens here, I'll be back for you someday. Understand that?"

"You will?"

"It's a promise," Rainwater said. "You are one of us. If not me, then Tomaz, or Eleanora, or whoever can come, will come."

Jason felt a tightness in his chest. He nodded.

Gavan straightened. He shook his wolfhead cane at Sousa and Hightower. "Drive them out, as soon as everyone is ready.

Take their crystals, mark them . . . make sure they've had the Draft."

"Gavan!" It was one thing to leave, another to have to drink the Draft.

He dropped his hand on Jason's shoulder again. "It's all we can do, lad, for now. The promise is not broken, only dimmed. Have faith in me, for now!" He turned on his heel, beckoning to Tomaz and Jefferson and in a blink, was gone.

He looked at Sousa. The Magicker looked back with gentle dark eyes. "It wasn't meant," he said, "to end this way."

Jason nodded. That barely helped. To have come so far and lose it all hurt.

Sousa added, "Better go pack." Before he stopped speaking, Eleanora made the same announcement over the loudspeakers. Jason headed to his cabin. The cabin across from Starwind stood, its shutters closed, and the screen door battened shut. He stared at it a moment, thinking of both Henry and Jonnard, before going inside. He did pack. He set aside his backpack, leaving some critical things until last. Trent came in.

They looked at one another. Trent went silently to his side and began to pack, thunking his things into his bag as though punching his fist into a mitt.

Finally, Jason said, "I have a plan."

Trent looked up. "You think you can fix this?"

"I don't know. What I do know is that I don't want to drink that stuff and go home. I don't want to lose this summer. I don't want to lose my friends. I don't want to lose anything that's happened."

"They're not just taking us home . . . they're taking everything away?" Trent's expression changed. "What are you going to do?"

"Stay and fight. Or shield. But I intend to stay."

Trent considered him for a long moment. Then he went to the small closet in the cabin that held their few cleaning supplies. He brought out the broom and his knife, and sat down.

"What are you doing?"

"You'll see." The bright red Swiss army knife flew as if it had wings. In moments, Trent had whittled off the broom head and instead had a wicked, wooden point on it. Then he reached into his duffel and brought out his painted silk banner. He fastened it to the other end of the broomstick. The white silk background brought out the vivid black raven, its wings outspread, and the gold paint used for the lightning bolt it carried glittered with flecks of mica. "This is a lance. And I'm ready."

"That's awesome."

Trent rested it on its point, and leaned back to look at it. "It is, isn't it?" His face stretched in a grin. "I don't intend to go easy."

They marched out of the cabin, down to the Hall, where Bailey and Ting had already climbed into a bus, and looked out at them with worried faces. Bailey hung out the window.

"Jason, you're hurt!"

He touched his scalp with gentle fingers and winced. "Yeah."

"Aren't you coming?" Ting watched both of them.

He shook his head. "Come out, I want to talk to you." They climbed past the hustle and bustle of campers loading their things on the bus.

Bailey held her pack rat in her hand. As she stepped down, she smoothed her thumb over the little creature's silky head. "I don't know whether to keep her or leave her. I think if I left her . . . she might . . . well . . . something awful might . . ."

Trent stroked his hand down Lacey's back. Her tufted tail twitched in happiness. "She's not a wild animal anymore, Bailey. You might as well take her. Like a . . . a hamster or something."

She smiled at Trent. "That's what I was thinking!"

"I only hope her mother does not mind," Ting said. "I don't want her at my house." She eyed the pack rat a little suspiciously.

"Can you believe it?" Bailey added excitedly. "We live across the bay from each other. It's not such a horribly long drive. We can visit."

"If you remember," said Jason quietly.

"Why would we forget?"

He just watched her face.

The two girls looked at him. "Oh, no." Bailey frowned. "They wouldn't do that to us. We've got our crystals."

"They're taking them back."

Ting gasped at Jason.

"Not because they want to. But they're not prepared to send us home this way, and it'll save a lot of questions."

Ting flung her arms about Bailey's neck, almost catapulting Lacey into the air. "I don't want to forget!"

"Forget, or stay and stand."

"We can't do that!"

Trent nodded at her. "Oh, yes, we can." He leaned on his lance. "Jason has a plan."

Biting her lip, Ting said, "They'll secure all the cottages and cabins."

"We meet," Jason said firmly, "at Dead Man's Cabin. Immediately. Get your bag and leave."

The two girls nodded as they scrambled back onto the bus. Jason and Trent watched for a moment. They turned around and ran into Rich and Stefan, who'd obviously heard every word they'd exchanged.

Stefan rubbed at his stub nose. "That junk you said true? No crystal and the drink and stuff."

"Yup."

He moved his stocky body from side to side. "What happens to me then?"

"I don't know."

"I," said Rich edgily, "am probably allergic to that berry junk in the Draft."

"I can't go back like this," Stefan said. "I'll keep changing, probably. They'll put me in a circus or something. They haven't shown me enough to control it." He'd gone pale.

Jason hefted his backpack over his shoulder. "Then you heard the rest . . . Dead Man's Cabin. And I'll show you what we can do. They need us, but they don't want to ask us." Jason saw Sousa approaching, backed up, and ducked around the back of the bus, Trent at his heels.

Lightning split the sky. In an eerie flash of green and silver, Gavan and Tomaz and Jefferson came down from the sky with a boom of thunder, their hair standing on end, crystals flashing in their hands. For a moment the three stood in a blaze of shimmering color, then everything stilled.

Gavan said to the others, "The Dark Hand is closing. If I had any doubt, Tomaz, that they unleashed this, I've no doubt now."

Tomaz nodded slowly.

"Retreat?"

"We can't until everyone is safely out. We'll make a stand here, and we will let them know that this battle has just begun. Iron Gate is reflecting the mana back, and they'll feed on it if we let them. I don't intend to let them." The trio went around the corner, and Jason and Trent skittered off, out of sight.

Halfway to Dead Man's Cabin, they ran into Danno trudging up the path, his haversack on his back. He looked at them. "Where are you two going?" The wind nearly tore the words away before he could be heard.

"We're not leaving." Trent waved his lance and banner defiantly.

"Man, don't be stupid. We've gotta go. This is like a hurricane coming down on us." He stared from one to the other. "You're serious?"

"I can show you how to make the crystal shield you and two or three others. If even a handful of us stay to help like that . . . we can shield the other Magickers while they strike. There's going to be a fight, Danno. Mano a mano, I think. We can help even if we're not trained. If we go, to protect us, they're going to take our crystals and make us drink."

"Like Henry."

"That's right."

Danno shook his head vigorously. "No way am I going out like that! I'd rather be dragged out. Poor Squibb didn't know me. Didn't know anyone but Jon." He shuddered. He fell in behind them. They made their way through the groves and underbrush to the cabin. Already abandoned, its door had not been lashed shut against the storm. They ducked inside.

"Go look for the girls," Jason told Danno. As the other went out, he took Trent by the elbow. "Okay. Now, once we get everyone set up as shields, then you and I are going to find the Gate. We're going to get it open."

"You can do that?"

"I don't know. I know I have to try."

Trent licked dry lips. "Okay. You're sure?"

"If I can get that Gate open, the storm should drain off through it. The Borderlands live off mana washes. Right now the Iron Gate is like a wall . . . the mana is coming in to pound on us and it'll just bounce off that wall and pound us some more."

"Sounds dangerous."

"Chicken?"

"Nah, but frankly, I think your plan needs some work."

"Think about it, then."

Trent nodded. "I intend to!"

Danno came in with the girls and Rich and Stefan. They dropped their bags in the corner.

"There's seven of us. I think we can make a difference, and this is how." He pulled out his crystal and lit it, then formed the shield which he had accidentally formed against Jonnard's attack. He strengthened it, extending it as he concentrated, until he had both girls behind it.

"Hit 'em, Stefan."

"Me?" The stocky boy's face reddened. "C'mon."

"Just do it."

He rocked from side to side. "Lissen. I play pranks now and then, but I never clocked a girl in the face."

Rich said calmly, "This is just for demonstration purposes. It's okay, big guy."

Stefan rubbed his nose vigorously. "Well. Okay." He lumbered over and swung halfheartedly at Bailey. He wouldn't have hit her anyway, her reflexes were too good for that, but before she could even dodge away, he bounced back with a yelp, thudding to his tailbone on the cabin floor.

He grunted. "Ow." He rubbed his face again.

Rich nodded to Jason. "That'll work. Show me?" He tugged on Stefan's ear. "Get up, you aren't hurt!"

"Just my dignity." Stefan grunted again as he shuffled to his feet.

Danno grinned. He danced on the balls of his feet. "Try again? On me?"

Jason put his shield down and said, "Everyone get their crystals out and let's do this." Trent moved to Ting, helping her Focus.

Stefan scrubbed at an itchy ear. He rolled his eyes. "Buses are all gone."

"Can't hear 'em?"

"Nope. Last one pulled out about ten minutes ago. Haven't heard one since."

The rain beat down. "We have a day, maybe two."

Rich gave Stefan an uneasy look. "I don't know if we can keep him quiet that long . . . especially if he gets hungry. . . ."

"We have to try. I want to show you all what we're doing and then, we can practice."

After what seemed hours, Ting and Stefan could manage a shield over themselves and two other people. Danno wavered, sometimes himself and two, sometimes himself and three. Bailey could shield herself and four, and Rich a surprising six people in total. Trent had been with Jason, moving back and forth, testing the crystals once they got everyone Focused.

They went to sleep, after pooling their resources and making sure Stefan ate well. Lacey even stayed quiet through the night, as if tired by all the Magick being wielded around her. They woke to a gray, misty morning, with rain glistening blackly on the ground.

Trent and Danno made a run to the mess hall and brought back leftovers from a refrigerator.

"Where is everyone?"

Trent shook his head. "In the Gathering Hall, I guess. Making a fortress out of it. Warding it, maybe?" He held out a bulging bag. "This ought to hold us for a day."

Stefan reached out and hugged the bag to himself, grunting.

"Or not." Trent looked at him thoughtfully.

They all did eat, although Stefan grudgingly passed out helpings of this and that from his grocery sack.

They practiced all day, in shifts, until Jason knew that they would be a help to the Magickers and not a burden. It was Trent, though, who said, "We have to hit the computer room."

"Why? That could get us busted."

"They called all the relatives, Jason, told them we were being sent home. We have to let them know something."

Ting made a small sound. Bailey hugged her. "A quick call each," she pleaded.

Finally, he nodded.

Perhaps it was the tone in their voices. Perhaps it was the hidden knowledge that loving parents and children share. Not one parent said no, although several said, "Do you want us there?" without even knowing what the problem was.

Bailey's mom, sounding ever so much like Bailey, choked a little when she said, "Good-bye, hon . . . and be careful." It was heard throughout the room despite the tight hold Bailey had on the receiver. She took a deep breath as she hung up. "Jason. How are we going to get home if everything goes wrong?"

He hesitated a moment then said, "I'll show you."

And back at Dead Man's Cabin, he showed them how to open a door in their crystals and walk through. None of them dared to try it, knowing that the working of such Magick would alert Gavan and the others. Trent clutched his crystal tightly. Stefan told them when all the buses returned. They ate whatever was left for dinner and fell into fitful sleep, dreaming of tombs and howling storms.

If that first morning was eerie, the second morning was worse. The sun struggled to pierce the storm clouds that turned day into night. The strings of lights thrashed back and forth, and those on the outbuildings glared dimly, as the wind tugged and roared about them.

They were down to juice drinks and polished them off quickly. Stefan licked his mouth and drank the one remaining carton. No one begrudged him seconds. Ting looked at him in sympathy. "Not only is he a growing boy, but he's got to eat for a growing bear, too."

Stefan sighed sadly and nodded.

Jason gazed up from the cabin doorway. "It's dark and quiet. I'd say the attack is about to begin. Let's go set ourselves up." Before he could say anything else, a tremendous ker-ack and BOOM split the skies. The lights went out all over the camp.

Tomaz sensed them first or perhaps he caught wind of Stefan. He turned on the heel of his cowboy boot and then frowned heavily as he caught sight of the group.

"We had just come to the conclusion that a few of you had slipped away. We all mistakenly thought you were on another bus."

"We came to stay."

Gavan shook his head. "We cannot let you do this."

"We are all Magickers." Jason nodded to Stefan who already had his crystal curled in his big hand.

Without a word, Stefan slipped in behind him, and set his shield up over himself, Tomaz, and Hightower. Both Magickers raised eyebrows in surprise.

Each of them did the same, except for Jason and Trent. Trent shadowed Jason as he raised his shield over Gavan and Eleanora. The two of them would likely take the brunt of the attack, so they had agreed to swap shielding. When one tired, the other would take over.

Gavan considered Jason, his lips pursed in thought. "This is something you want to do?"

"This is something we have to do."

The Magicker nodded. The dark skies reflected in his eyes, making the blue irises almost black. "I cannot tell you if we'll see the Dark Hand themselves or not. They may stay behind the storm and the wolfjackals. But whether we see them or not, they'll throw everything they can at us, to break us here, and drain the mana. So if you see the line breaking, lad, take the others and flee. Promise me that?"

"Bailey has those orders," Jason said calmly. "I've shown them how to walk through their crystals."

"And you can do it?"

He nodded solemnly.

"All right." Gavan turned about, settling himself. He put his face into the wind, as the first drops of rain began to fall. "Here it comes."

If he lived to be a hundred, he would never be able to tell the wonder and horror of the storm that came sweeping down to attack them. Cloud creatures of twisted form and might rose to pound at them, swirling around into motes of sizzling energy. Rain that poured for hours and lightning that crashed around them till the very earth crackled with its discharge. Wolfjackals that came and went in howling packs, circling and attacking only to be driven away gnashing their ivory fangs.

He thought he saw forms striding through the clouds now and then. Once, he glimpsed the pale angry face of Jonnard staring at him, but of that he could not be sure. He was too busy to be frightened.

And no matter what they faced, they turned the enemy back. Again and again, until Eleanora sat in weariness, one hand bracing her wrist to hold her crystal up. Until Stefan lost his shield entirely and sat snuffling and bawling, bearlike, at failing them. Rich took over, shielding all of that group, his face dead white under his coppery head of hair. All he said was, "You done good, bro."

And they fought like that with no end in sight.

Until, hours later, when Gavan looked into the sky grimly through weary eyes and said, "Now comes the worst of it."

"It's now or never," Jason said to Trent, and signaled with a jerk of his chin. Rain fell and evaporated in sizzling drops as it spattered across the lines of Magick and wild mana and energy. The air shivered electric blue and stank of ozone and spent spells. Lake Wannameecha moved in obsidian black waves, reflecting the storm boiling over it.

They fell back from the battle line and ducked into the Gathering Hall. Jason shrugged out of his backpack and dumped its contents out quickly. Firecrackers, duct tape, and other odds and ends slid onto the varnished floor.

Trent said dryly, "Everything but garlic." He leaned over, then poked a finger at curling white cloves lying amidst the other junk. A pungent aroma drifted up. "Never mind, I stand corrected."

"You never know," Jason said. He tucked some unpeeled cloves into his pocket, and the Chinese firecrackers into his shirt. Matches went in the other pocket. The box of kitchen matches had come from FireAnn's apron and, before that, apparently an English pub. He stood up.

"What's the plan again?"

"We crystal to the Gate. The wolfjackals, some of them, will be on us almost instantly. I'm fairly sure they'll sense us right away. You'll have to hold them off while I get the Gate open." He didn't mention what he thought he would have to do to open that Gate, what Aunt Freyah had hinted to him. They had tried nearly every other way, and nothing had worked. But the Gate had to be opened. Left shut, it was damming up the mana and the storm, and the camp lay helpless in a hurricane of uncontrollable, raging Magick. Open, the mana would sweep through, into a world that not only could absorb it, but most likely needed it. Once past, the Gate's boundaries could be extended to embrace the camp. Jason had been over and over and over it in his mind. He couldn't see any other way. He left his backpack on the floor. He wanted to travel light in case he had to sprint. He touched his crystal in his pocket for the third time, just to make sure he had it. "Ready?"

Trent took a deep breath. He shook his head. "No."

"What did we forget?"

"I'm not going," Trent said.

"What—" Jason stopped in his tracks. "I can't do this without you!"

"You're going to have to."

He could not believe his ears. "You're with me. You helped

me plan this. You *know* what I have to do. Look, I'm scared, too, but we've got to try this."

Trent shifted his lance in his hands. "It's not that. I'm not a Magicker. I have no Talent. I can't help you."

Jason stared, thinking he hadn't heard right, but his friend's face was serious. "You . . ."

"I'm a poser. I've been faking it. And, lately, I've been wondering when it was going to catch up with me. Well, it just did. Maybe that's why the other failures got sent home, because when you need to count on somebody, when you need them the most, you've got to know what they're made of." Trent looked up. "I'm not made of Magick, Jason. I wish to God I was, but I'm not. You know I'm telling the truth. I kept backing out on you, because I didn't want anyone to know. I didn't want anyone to catch me."

"I . . . I don't believe that."

"Have you ever seen me light my crystal?"

"Well . . . no."

"Because I can't." Trent inhaled deeply. "Ever seen me move anything through thin air? Did you see me put a shield up? No, you haven't, because I can't. You were busy with the others. I was, too. No one ever noticed I never did it myself. Henry Squibb had more Magick in his little finger than I've got in my whole body. I've been ducking out on stuff for weeks, wondering when someone was going to notice, especially you. You, with all your Talent." He smiled sadly.

Despair sank into Jason. "Come anyway. You can . . . you can use the lance. You don't have to have Magick to fight the wolfjackals."

"You don't need to be worried about protecting me. You need to be doing what you have to do. And let me do what I can."

"Which is . . . what?"

"I can get the backup generator hooked up, pump some electricity into this place. I am pretty sure, with the computers up, I can put on a sound and light show that will knock 'em off their feet. Remember, I've been in the computer lab for weeks. Gavan is pretty savvy, but even so . . . this is my magic. I can use it. They depend on other means. I may even have a few moves in me that would halt a Magicker in his tracks."

They looked into each other's faces.

Jason hardly knew what to say. "Sure?"

Trent nodded solemnly. "Pretty sure."

"I can't do this alone."

"Sure you can. All you need to do is swing that Gate open. We're doing the tough stuff here. Give me those firecrackers."

Jason took the long string of small crackers out of his shirt. He could smell their sulfur and gunpowder as he handed them over.

"No sense lighting these all at once. Three or four at a pop," Trent said, as he took them. "That should give the wolfjackals something to think about, while I get to the generators." He gave a shaky smile as he opened his prized knife and began to cut the firecracker string up and shove the small strands inside his shirt, the lance curled inside his elbow.

"Trent—"

His friend frowned. "What are you waiting for? It's now or never!" He laid the lance on the table and fished around till he grabbed the roll of duct tape. He took his Swiss army knife and fastened it to the end of his lance, wrapping duct tape about it tightly, then handed the lance to Jason, silk flag rippling with the abrupt movement. The raven painted on it seemed to snap at the air.

"What's this for?"

"That's a sharp knife. That's a long pole." Trent shrugged. "It's the only thing I can give you to defend yourself, okay? You do it quickly, and you get out. That's your only chance. You hesitate, Jason, and they'll pull you down." He took Jason by the shoulders. "Go! We can't make a stand out there much longer. I'm no Magicker, but I know everyone is dog tired."

He ducked his head and ran back into the storm, leaving Jason quite alone in the huge Hall. With a sigh, he reached for his crystal again and pictured Iron Gate.

Endgame

H E fell to his knees in front of the rusting gate. Jason held his hand up, setting crystal lantern light to play over its surface, and he saw the true Gate embedded around it, iron and implacable. He stood and ran his hands over it, one at a time, shifting Trent's lance back and forth. With every touch, the true Gate emerged until it was the only vision filling his sight and senses. It towered over him, and he could see the granite it had been set into. The evergreens that crowded about it were not the evergreens that grew at Camp Ravenwyng.

He pulled at it. He found the great locks that bound it shut, but they had no keyhole, and thus needed no key. He shined his crystal light onto the locks and chanted for it to open, but nothing happened.

He could feel the mana storm rolling toward him like a great tidal wave. The barricade of the lower campgrounds would not contain it much longer. Like an inexorable force, it would roll through, smashing him into the Gate's bars and battering him to pulp if he stayed. And then it would recoil with even greater force back onto the camp. Below, near the lake, he could see the lightning stabs of the fierce battle continuing. Suddenly, white light flared up. Like a beacon, it speared the mana clouds, and he saw the darkness recede abruptly, boiling around in turmoil. The light flashed off. Then on. Trent was at work. There would be sound, too, but he could not hear it.

His left hand prickled as he ran it over the lock again. His scar gave an icy, stabbing throb. They had come, sensing him. He knew it before their lupine howls cut through the sounds of the storm and Magick battle. Jason turned slowly, knowing that he had drawn them.

Five wolfjackals raced across the broken country, whipping their furred bodies through underbrush and pine branches, heedless of pain and obstruction. Jaws agape, tails like stiff banners, bodies of black and silver and dun and charcoal. Their eyes glowed reflected green and red in the night as they howled and bore down on him.

He froze.

If he'd had Trent with him, he'd have some hope.

Or anyone.

But he stood alone at the locked Gate without a clue what to do. He held his crystal with both hands, one fighting the other to throw it, to hold it. His left hand would betray his right, if it could. His hands shook. Jason clenched his jaw. He set his back to the bars.

The wolfjackals came to a halt one long jump from him, milling around, their jaws drooling, their glowing eyes slitted. They snapped and mauled at one another almost playfully, ears pricked in eagerness. They panted and eyed their leader.

The pack leader stepped forward. "It is time," it said, shuddering even as the words were forced from its throat. Its voice was hoarse and torn. What pain the language must have cost it! "I make my claim." It gave an immense convulsion on that last word, then shook itself vigorously. Hot spit flew from its jaws.

The pack behind it howled in triumph. Their eerie voices echoed off the mountains and perhaps, even the gate. They circled and paced, back and forth, forth and back. Fangs and talonlike nails flashed. He had nowhere to run.

Below, white light flared again, and he could hear a trumpet blast of sound, Sousa, amplified vastly, like Jericho from long ago, with Trent's help. Was it working? Would they stand at the camp while he fell here? Not if he could help it. He lifted the lance.

"Come get me, then."

The pack leader snarled and tensed. Muscles rippled through his furred haunches. Jason took a deep breath. He might be able to Focus and get out, but not in time.

Magicker.

Jason could hear the soft sighing, creaking word. It came from the back of his head, but he could not sense anyone there. And, if anyone was behind him, he was in more trouble than he knew, his back unprotected!

A lesser wolfjackal from the back lunged at him, hurling past the pack leader, snapping. It yelped in dismay as Jason parried with his lance, and the Swiss knife cut surprisingly deep. The beast swerved away, jowl gashed open and flapping as it tossed its head from the stinging pain. Pink foam flew from its jaws. It pawed at its face, yelping, and rubbed its wounds against the ground.

He bumped up against the Gate, recovering his balance. He gripped the lance tightly.

Magicker.

Again, that breathless, low groaning voice.

Something was calling . . . him.

Jason chanced it. He half turned and glanced, looking, despite the danger. That flinch drew the pack leader in a massive leap. Its body struck hard, hot breath in his face, and bore him down. The lance went skidding away. Jason buried his hands in the creature's ruff, holding its head back, fighting to keep the jaws from his face. It was heavier. He could not throw it off. It snapped and thrashed, coming closer and closer. In moments the others would be tearing at his feet and legs.

The mana storm hit with a boom directly overhead, and hail peppered down. He could feel the Magick turn upside down and inside out. His senses whirled.

The wolfjackal thrashed in his hold, shaking his crystal

loose. It dropped and rolled. Jason gritted his teeth. He tore the fetish bag from his throat, Tomaz's charm, and shoved his fist down into the beast's mouth, as he had once before. His scar ripped open anew as it caught on the gleaming canines. He screamed with the pain, clawing at the inside of the wolfjackal's throat.

The beast spit him aside and rolled back on its haunches, howling in its own pain, pawing at its jaws. It choked and howled and pawed madly at its muzzle. Jason scrambled to his feet, gathering the crystal, blood flowing everywhere. He got the lance, leaning heavily on it, dizzy from wrenching pain. The wolfjackal choked and spit again in an attempt to expel the fetish, then gathered itself, drooling in foamy spittles of blood. The mana storm hammered at him. Wind and rain nearly flattened him. It took the breath from his lungs. His skin stung like fire from pelting hail.

He leaned against the Iron Gate, weary and hurting. He could not stand against it. It would bring him down and leave him at the mercy of the howling beasts in front of him. He faltered and put his hand back to the Gate, trying to stay on his feet, as the wolfjackals growled and tensed to rush him.

His hand shook. Blood poured out of the gash, splashing across the metal, his crystal, the ground. As he staggered back, the Gate swung open a crack. It groaned as it did so, the metal thrilling with sound.

His body went cold. He looked into a tomb carved out of cold, gray stone. He knew this place from his worst dreams. Jason wanted to slam the Gate shut, but his body was wedged in the opening.

It was worse—and bigger—than his dreams. He could feel the icy cold of the stone. He could see the body lying on the coffin clearly. It was not dead, only nearly so, rather like a vampire at his rest. Jason slipped a hand inside his shirt, feeling the garlic cloves. He could not look away from the tall, elegant man who lay there. Fine purple veins ran just under the marblelike skin, and dark chestnut hair curled about his head. He wore clothing from long ago, but nothing seemed diminished by time.

Jason tore his gaze away. At the far end of the tomb lay another Iron Gate, also closed. He knew what he had to do.

He had to walk past the tomb between the narrow stone walls, and open the other Gate. It would be barely wide enough for him. He might even have to brush the raised coffin with its human adornment to do it.

He could not breathe. The iciness of the cave sank into his own bones, and he shook.

"I opened one Gate! Isn't it enough?"

Silence answered him. Jason gripped his crystal tightly. He Focused on it, and a golden lantern light filtered from between his fingers. It shone across the tomb floor, and pooled at the base of the faraway Gate.

He took a step forward, feeling the storm raging at his back, the dim howl of wolfjackals now in his ears, pushing the first Gate open so that he could get through entirely. It gave reluctantly, with a rusting squeal that shot and echoed through the stone chambers of the tomb.

Jason licked lips gone dry as sandpaper. His heartbeat sounded louder than his footsteps as he neared the coffin. He felt as though he were caught between two worlds, the muffled battle of one he could hear, and the other not, though his body anticipated . . . something.

Another step. He held his lance tightly, and his crystal even tighter. It kept a lot of lantern light hidden, but he could not chance dropping it again. Something snarled and tore at the back cuff of his jeans. He shook it loose.

Another step, and he stood at the foot end of the coffin. He turned sideways to sidle past. The back of his shoulders scrapped the gritty wall, and he held his breath.

Now he was nearing the head of the coffin . . . and its occupant. One last squeeze and he could bolt through to the second Iron Gate. Jason's lungs ached.

The . . . figure turned its head. One marble-white hand rose in the air, reaching for him. "Come to me," it said, in a thin voice that pierced the rising noise of the mana storm leaking in behind Jason.

"You are marked for me. Let me teach you the truth of Magick."

He wanted the truth. He always wanted the truth. But what was it? Once he thought this entombed figure was his father. Now he knew better, but what he saw and listened to was still not true. The only truth he could think of, here and now, was that he would die if he could not breathe, and he could not breathe in this tomb. His friends would die if he could not get the inner Gate opened. Beyond that, nothing he knew was true anymore.

The eyelids slowly began to open. Jason knew one more thing, and that was that he did not want to see what was in those eyes. He threw himself sideways, away from the hand, the face, the coffin, and fell onto the floor. He crawled to the Gate and put his still bleeding hand upon it. With a great roar in his ears, the second Iron Gate swung inward, and all . . . everything . . . disappeared. Jason looked down into a valley of lively green, and he lay stomach down on a road leading to it.

Suddenly— Silence. The storm gathered up and rushed past him, pushing him across the threshold, as it poured into the open valley. The wolfjackals were carried past, borne by a great tide of mana which they could not resist, and he alone was left to stand, anchored by the Gate he held onto.

He looked at his hand. The bleeding slowed, then clotted. He touched his head, wincing slightly at the tenderness. What one blooding had done, another had undone. He shuddered at the idea.

His crystal grew warm.

Faintly, he could hear . . . shouts of triumph and joy from the world beyond. The old world. His world. The sun rose somewhere, for the sky went to a thin gray-purple, and light flooded him.

Jason turned slowly to see the world he had opened the Gates to.

He stared across the vista. He stood in a pass between two rolling hills of verdant green, grasses lush from rain and sun. He didn't think civilization had ever reached into this place. A rough lane ran down the hills and into a valley, and a great, dark gray mountain towered above the scene. A waterfall pierced its side, waters tumbling down in a crystalline spray from impossible heights and foaming into a pool of darkest blue. Along the foot of the mountain, a sharp-featured rock of dark red and orange curled about half the pool, sprawling upon the landscape.

If he ran downhill, he might be at that pool in just minutes, he thought, touching that rock that looked as though molten fire itself might have poured from the iron mountain and then cooled just enough to stop at the water's edge. He paused, lance in hand, a faint breeze rippling Trent's pennant. He had no idea what lay at his back, other than his real world. He didn't want to look back to find out. He'd been there. What tugged at him now lay ahead of him, unfolding. He took a step forward.

Even as he did, he felt the real world at his back move, almost as if he wore it like a vast pair of wings or a cloak. Unseen, it billowed around him. The wind picked up, snapping the pennant flag on his lance as he leaned against it, steadying himself. And down below, a ripple ran through the dark orange-red rock. As he fastened his whole attention upon it, it moved.

An immense wedge-shaped head lifted to stare at him, and he saw then, as it stirred, its serpentine body as it pushed a paw forward and flexed long talons. The sharpness of the rock had been spines and fins that moved now, as it shook itself awake. The dragon opened eyes of orange-and-amber fire to watch him. He was too far away to see the details of its scaly form, but not too far to see the ebony sharpness of the claws it stretched out and raked into the ground. The dragon yawned, showing catlike sharp white teeth. After a very long moment, the wind carried the scent of sulfur breath to him. He wondered if he could feel the heat of its immense body if he got closer. If the eyes were cat-shaped. If it could or would speak . . .

He took another slow step toward the dragon form. He

gripped the lance in his hands, though it would be a poor weapon against such a beast. Jason paused.

The wingspan at his back yanked sharply at him, dragging him onto his heels. From far away, scarcely more than a whisper, he could hear Gavan Rainwater's voice.

"Not now, Jason. Do not take that journey now. Next time. . . ."

Jason inhaled. He swung about sharply and just before plunging through the great Iron Gate posts, he stabbed Trent's lance into the ground. And it was marked, not only for him, but for anyone who looked for it now. The pennant snapped about as he did so.

Even Trent, who could not see the Magick, would be able to find this Gate one day. He was the Gatekeeper and had made it so, until he came back to change it.

And he would return.

Stepping past the flag, he strode across the threshold and back into his own world.